A More Perfect Union

A Novel by
Paul Shemella

Copyright © 2020 Paul Shemella
All rights reserved
First Edition

PAGE PUBLISHING, INC.
Conneaut Lake, PA

First originally published by Page Publishing 2020

ISBN 978-1-64628-295-1 (pbk)
ISBN 978-1-64628-297-5 (hc)
ISBN 978-1-64628-296-8 (digital)

Printed in the United States of America

For Eva

Chapter 1

The Hero

Gabriele Barnes thought she'd paid her dues. She was wrong. She sat with her husband, Carl, on the starboard side of the Boeing 757 as it followed the Potomac current. As the plane made its final approach to Reagan National Airport, the couple felt as though they were in a time tunnel. Gabriele, sitting on the aisle, caught a fleeting glimpse of Georgetown University to the left. With a flash of nostalgia, she thought fondly of her years there studying German literature. Carl looked to the right and savored the memory of meeting his wife on a Rosslyn sidewalk. *Has it only been one year?* Shifting from one reverie to another, Carl raised his gaze and refocused. Almost level with the descending plane was the condominium, its picture window reflecting the monuments and memorials. He had held that view for five years.

The five most exciting years of his life.

"How does it feel to be coming home, Carl?"

"Bittersweet, Gaby," he said with a half-smile. "Bittersweet."

"I think I know how you feel, dear. Good memories and bad for me too." The plane's engine whined with a sudden increase in power as Gabriele winced. She held a breath of stale air and, with effort, rested her blond head on Carl's shoulder.

Carl had never really considered Washington home. Until he met Gabriele, his only pleasures had been found outside the capital—birds in the tidewater and risky combat operations further afield. Washington itself resided in his memory as a long series of traffic jams, cookie-cutter offices, soulless bureaucrats, and decision-makers not burdened with the inconvenience of moral standards. His real home had been in Boston, but only his undying allegiance to the Red Sox still connected him to the place. Somewhere in the world, he had even managed to lose his New England accent.

Born in Germany, Gabriele had been reborn in Washington. Twice. The first time had been after running away from a bad marriage. Literally running. She had known what she was running from, but not what she was running *to*. Washington had been her haven but also her prison. Gabriele had buried herself in the liberal arts, hiding from the unpredictable cruelty of passion. Her second renaissance had been years later on that sidewalk in Rosslyn. Carl had returned to her more than a purse; he had given her back the ability to risk loving someone. She was truly happy for the first time in her adult life.

The plane lumbered over the Fourteenth Street Bridge as the pilot adjusted for a strong crosswind. Gabriele closed her eyes and mumbled something about salvation. She dug her nails into Carl's flesh as they bounced onto the runway and roared to a stop. To Carl, the former warrior, it was a textbook landing; to his wife, the former teacher and aerospace skeptic, it was a near-death experience.

"I guess I'll never get used to that," said Gabriele, exhaling.

"It's a good thing I have a high threshold for pain," replied Carl, smiling while inspecting the cuts on his forearm.

"Carl! I'm so sorry… I drew blood!" She reached into her pocket and extracted a tissue as the plane taxied to the terminal.

"Don't worry, Gaby… All my good scars are covered most of the time. I need some that everyone can see."

"I can't wait to uncover the other ones." She grinned.

"I like the sound of that," said Carl with a broad smile. He also liked the sound of her voice. American language, but with no dropped endings, fewer contractions, and tongue-behind-the-teeth *t*'s. English the way it *should* be spoken, yet somehow exotic. It was one of the first things that had attracted him to Gabriele. He kissed her forehead and, clasping her hand, turned toward the window. Outside, August pressed down on the capital, trapping big-city residue close to the tarmac. Bad memories were already seeping into his consciousness.

Without another word between them, Carl and Gabriele watched most of the other passengers stand up, waiting in awkward positions for everyone ahead of them to file out of the plane. Gabriele gave Carl a mock frown and pointed surreptitiously to a pair of huge polyester buttocks competing for her personal space. She slid over onto his lap while they waited, making the best of an uncomfortable situation they could not change. *Make lemonade.* That was just one of the things she had taught her perfectionist husband.

Carl had been somewhat receptive to learning patience. Before Gabriele, he had practiced it at the superhuman level. But that was in the field. Carl had developed the ability to sit in the mud of the jungle without moving for days, watching and waiting for the enemy. It was a matter of survival. In his off-duty time, he watched and waited for birds to come into the view field of his binoculars. He could sit for hours just to glimpse a rare species. In spite of this—perhaps because of it—he had never been a patient member of society. From Gabriele, he had learned the art of dealing with ordinary people.

After spending his whole adult life learning to hunt and kill other men—and doing just that—Carl had dreaded living an ordinary life. Gabriele's love had given him the confidence to abandon his warrior existence and take his chances with the real world. But circumstances had forced him back into the jungle—to eliminate the threat from the cartel that still had his name and address. And to make sure they didn't go after Gabriele. Having protected himself and his wife once and for all, Carl now spent his days as a laid-back fishing guide on a small island in Southwest Florida. Short on stress and far from the cartel, he dealt with ordinary people every day, patiently teaching them to relax and just have fun.

Soon enough, Carl and Gabriele made it out of the plane and through baggage claim. They rented a car and found themselves sitting in traffic between the Potomac and the Pentagon. The building reeked from a history of bad decisions. Carl, having come very close to being killed by one of those decisions, began getting impatient again. The air conditioner strained under the weight of humid air and little forward motion. Horns blared. A volley of airplanes, coming at them on final approach, added to the din. *Washington, Jefferson, and Lincoln*, he thought, *would have been appalled.*

Suddenly, he was driving close to the speed limit. A new feeling of freedom seized him. His fatigue evaporated in a flush of anticipation. Looking at his stunning wife with one eye, he almost missed the turn into the concrete suburb he knew so well. Approaching the corner where he and Gabriele had met, Carl gestured with his left hand.

"This is the famous site where Gabriele Bach, the renowned teacher and scholar, was mugged by a drug-crazed youth exactly one year ago."

She jumped in to say, "And where Carl Malinowski, fearsome warrior and amateur naturalist, came to her rescue." She smiled at him and continued, "And I am very glad you changed your name, Carl… Can you imagine me as Gabriele Malinowski?"

"I should have taken *your* name to protect myself," he joked. Then he changed his tone completely. "But when we spread Billy Joe's ashes on the Gulf, I thought taking his name would be a fitting way to honor him… And at that point, I still didn't know if you'd ever forgive me."

"I knew I would, Carl… I just needed a push."

"You got a big one."

"Yes… The assassination attempt was a surprise…," she said, laconically. "But I learned a lot…about you, about love, and most of all, about myself." Looking right at him, Gabriele spoke from her heart. "You had better take care of yourself, my love. It would be impossible for me to live without you."

The hotel was just down the street. Carl registered them while Gabriele contacted the bellhop and looked for a place to freshen up. Carl parked the car and met her at the elevator less than five minutes later. She winked.

"Going up?"

"Ah, yes…anywhere you want to take me."

"I really need a shower," she said with another wink. "You look like you could use one as well."

They both looked at the floor indicator and then at each other.

"I like this hotel," said Carl, laughing, "but they have the slowest damn elevators!"

Later—much later—they lay next to each other. Resting. Motionless. Separate beings again. After a while, Gabriele reached out and drew him closer. In a hoarse voice, she bared her soul once more. "When I make love to you, Carl, I cannot tell where you end and I begin." She stretched lazily and recovered her normal voice. "This is one of those times I do not want to let go of you…in case I wake up tomorrow and find today was just a dream."

"The dream lasts all night and all day tomorrow, Gaby." He laid her head on his chest and stroked her fine hair. He could sense the darkness creeping up on them through the window. He felt safer in the dark. Baggage from his past.

"I wasn't thinking about tomorrow just yet," said Gabriele thoughtfully. "No matter what happens, I will always love you."

She fell asleep to the steady rhythm of his heart, undisturbed by her old life lurking in the glare of the city outside.

***

The man sitting by himself looked like a cowboy. It wasn't just the boots and jeans that distinguished him. He rode the Metro as if it were a horse. Back straight, knees up, eyes front, hands resting on the large backpack in his lap. Expressionless, but pleasant enough. The Marlboro Man without a cigarette. Cracked bronze skin marked him as an outdoorsman, probably much younger than he looked. He sat stoically in the relative cool of the train car, wearing a polo shirt instead of his habitual leather jacket and red bandanna. He didn't have a hat, but his bristled brown hair ached for one. Another citizen from the interior, visiting his tax money at work. The man looked like he'd have preferred to be out on the plains in the dust and sun.

Rather than riding the Blue Line.

As the train slowed, he stood up and shouldered his backpack. No one noticed the man straining to lift the pack over his head. Exiting the car, he walked underneath the security camera on the tunnel wall and rode the escalator to street level. The heat almost knocked him down. He stood at the mouth of the Smithsonian Metro station and shifted his load. Steeling himself to the elements, the man teetered imperceptibly before continuing. Then he walked slowly along the grassy National Mall past the Castle, looking like he belonged someplace else. But every tourist in Washington looked like he belonged someplace else.

The cowboy fit right in.

He was a strong man for his 160 pounds. That was one reason they had chosen him. Only five-nine without a hat, he would not be noticed in the crowd. More importantly, he had demonstrated courage before. They trusted him to carry the message into the belly of the beast. They would have to settle for the belly. The building on the hill in front of him was the beast's heart. They had wanted to deliver the message there, but reconnaissance had revealed too much security. The Holocaust Museum had been the alternate site, but that had also appeared too difficult to penetrate. Bastards had surely lobbied the criminals on the Hill for more cops. *Too bad*, thought the cowboy. Jew lovers crying over something that never even happened. The Air and Space Museum would have to do. There would be Jews there too. They were everywhere.

The man began sweating like he had never sweated before. Not on the range. Not on night maneuvers. He was sure it was the heat, but he knew it was more than that. The pack was heavier than it had seemed during his training, but it was even more than that. He told himself there was no shame in being nervous. He was carrying the message deeper into the beast than ever before. The people who had hijacked his government would hear this protest loud and clear. Mud people back where they belong. A white Christian nation. Back to the founders. Before the Fourteenth Amendment. He'd argued for the Lincoln Memorial, but the group had decided to leave that one for the next time. Ah, Lincoln. That was where the country had started to go downhill. *I'll be back, Abraham… Name like that, you must have been Jewish.*

After struggling for another few yards, the man's clothes were soaked. Paranoia waited at the edge of his awareness. He could *feel* the traitors staring at him from all directions. Trying to remain inconspicuous, he stopped and carefully took off the pack. He sat in the shade of a tree. Despite the fear of discovery, he sat for a long time.

***

Carl and Gabriele got off the Blue Line at the Smithsonian stop and ascended into the humid oven. Carl had never adapted to DC weather. The steamy heat of the South American jungle had not bothered him as much. South Florida in summer was even hotter, but his life there was defined by water. He fished in it, swam in it, waded in it, and walked next to it. Sometimes, he and Gabriele even made love in it. Away from calm salt water, heat and humidity were almost unbearable.

"Let's get inside, Gaby, before we melt!"

"Where do you want to start, dear?"

"I'd like to go first to the Air and Space Museum," replied Carl. "Then we can go over to the National Gallery so you can see pictures of all those dead guys."

"Very funny, Carl… I predict that someday you'll appreciate Rembrandt and his contemporaries. Maybe it just takes time."

"I promise to try again," said Carl with a boyish smile. "But only after I get my fill of airplanes and spacecraft."

Gabriele laughed. "Blast off!"

They crossed Twelfth Street and headed along Jefferson Drive past the Castle. They failed to notice the man with the backpack sitting under a tree, not twenty yards from where they walked. Carl *did* notice a small excavation, surrounded by construction barricades, farther out on the lawn. He wondered what was going in the hole, hoping it wouldn't be another monument. Washington already had enough monuments. And where were all the heroes these days anyway? *At the Vietnam Memorial*, he answered to himself. That had been the turning point.

When a country loses its innocence, the next thing it loses is its heroes.

They entered the Air and Space Museum at the Jefferson Drive entrance. As Gabriele surveyed the array of airplanes and space vehicles standing and hanging around them, Carl went to the wall and read the plaque he knew would be there.

Dedicated to all those who have given their lives in the exploration of air and space.
1 July 1976

"Here, too," he said aloud to the stone. Out of respect, he stood there for a few seconds of silence. Then he heard Gabriele's enthusiasm fill the large hall.

"Carl…isn't it wonderful!"

"I thought you didn't like machines with wings on them," he called as he went to her.

"No, dear, no! I love the *idea* of flight… That's why I like birds so much. I simply do not want to get *into* one of those machines. It's more claustrophobia than fear of flying." She gazed at the ceiling, imagination in gear. "Oh, to be free as a bird!"

"This is a great way to sum up the idea of flight," lectured Carl. "Here you have the Wright Brothers' flying machine right next to John Glenn's space capsule. Fifty-nine years, but only twenty feet apart!" Carl was talking animatedly, gesturing with his big hands. His Sicilian mother would have been proud.

"I think I could fly in space," said Gabriele in a dreamy tone. "But not in this." She pointed to *Friendship 7*. "Something like a Zeppelin, possibly… The higher I went, the better I would feel."

"I can tell you as a parachutist that higher is better," replied Carl. "It feels more like flying than falling." He regretted once again that he'd deceived her for so long. "But I'm out of that business."

"Thank God!"

They walked across the hall to get a closer look at the strange aircraft hanging over the information counter. "Over here is *Voyager*," explained Carl. "A man and a woman flew around the world in this thing without stopping for gas."

"How big is the cockpit, Carl?"

"Let's see," he said, surveying the airframe. "About seven by three."

"Feet?"

"Yeah…feet. After all the gas tanks, they didn't have much room left. Dick Rutan is about my size; fortunately, Jeana Yaeger is a very petite woman."

"How long a trip?"

"Nine days."

"That is truly my idea of hell, dear. I hope they liked each other."

***

The man stood up again and slowly shouldered his pack. The shade had done the trick; his shirt was still wet, but no wetter than those of other tourists shuffling in and out of the museum. From the grassy field, he walked to the Jefferson Drive entrance. During the reconnaissance, he had come through these doors wearing an empty backpack. The guard had simply smiled at him. No metal detector. No search. Just a nod to one citizen from somewhere else. This time, he avoided eye contact with the guard. He avoided eye contact with everyone.

It was an effort to walk slowly. Slowly enough not to draw the attention of the guard, or anyone else. Even in the air-conditioned building, everyone was moving slowly. A habit of summer. The man carried his pack to the theater entrance where dozens of people sat waiting. Laying the pack on a seat in the middle of a row, he sat down next to it. He wanted to blend in with the others. Looking around, he could not distinguish between real Americans and foreigners in this kill zone. That was the problem, wasn't it? *Yahweh* had chosen him to purify America. There were a few pure whites in this part of the museum, and he wished he could warn them. But they would go to heaven—that is, the ones who were not Jews. The darker faces would not see *Yahweh*.

They would just die.

The man prayed for success. He did not fear for his life; he feared only failure. To become a martyr in this holy war would be a fitting way to die. But he had convinced himself that there weren't enough patriots like him to carry the flag. Living to fight another day would help the cause. He'd be a hero either way—but first, he had to deliver the message. Never before had his group gotten so close to the heart of the beast. Tim McVeigh had dealt the tyrannical government a blow, but the Murrah Building had been too far away. Nobody in Washington cared what happened in Oklahoma City. Nobody in Washington cared what happened anywhere outside the beltway. The heartland was about to speak.

It was too late to stop him.

***

Carl led Gabriele past the theater, catching bits of *Star Wars* playing on a television screen in the hall. There were at least one hundred people standing around or sitting in front of the tube, killing time. Comfortably numb.

"Here it is!" said Carl, walking up to the black and white V2 rocket now towering over them. "The first ballistic missile. Fine German engineering, Gaby."

"We did a better job with automobiles, I'm afraid."

"A mass terror weapon," Carl continued. "But its German designers helped us win the Cold War."

"And Dr. von Braun and his colleagues got us to the moon as well," responded Gabriele. "Technology is not the problem, Carl. Politicians are. Those who decide how to *use* all these great machines."

"Government…a nasty business," said Carl. "I'm glad I don't have to deal with it anymore."

As he spoke, Carl took his eyes off Gabriele and looked into the distance. Just a feeling. A sense that something was out of place. He flipped the warrior switch, still fixed in the back of his military mind, scanning the hall for anomalies. He quickly locked onto a weather-beaten face. A man sitting a bit too upright next to a rather large backpack, and studying the crowd around him.

What's wrong with this picture?

Carl looked back at Gabriele. "Gaby…let's go over to the moon lander, okay?" Carl's voice wavered slightly as adrenaline pumped into his bloodstream.

"Sure, *Liebling*," said Gabriele, unaware of his growing apprehension. "After that, I want to go upstairs to see World War I planes."

Taking her hand, Carl started toward the Lunar Excursion Module. Surreptitiously, he glanced over his shoulder. Just as he did, the man inserted his hand under the top flap of the pack and quickly withdrew it. Carl would have missed it but for his training. The man stood up and began to walk away, leaving the pack on the seat. Heading straight for the exit, he quickened his pace.

Holy shit!

Carl sprang into action. He dropped Gabriele's hand and grabbed her attention. "Gaby…listen to me!" His eyes spoke to her from a place she could not identify. She swallowed hard and froze.

"Run to the cafeteria…now!" Before she could protest, he sprinted off in the other direction. On instinct alone, he ran toward the vacant seat. In less than a second, Carl had made the decision to go after the pack and not the man. He knew what it was. He knew that if he went for the man instead, hundreds of people would die! What he saw when he opened the pack vindicated that decision.

Inside the canvas bag was the largest pipe bomb Carl had ever seen. Running his hands along the surface, he came upon a small cylinder sticking out of the lead casing. He recognized it immediately as a military clock-firing device. There was no way to determine what the setting was, but that was not the worst thing. Staring up at him like a cobra was the same anti-removal device he had used in the Navy. He couldn't just pull out the firing device and call the bomb squad. If he tried to do that, he and a lot of others would die horribly.

I hope to God Gaby's out of range!

For all he knew, the pipe bomb could go off any second. He had to get the thing out of the museum…and fast!

By this time, Carl's actions had caused a stir in the hall. A ripple of utterances emanated from where he stood in an expanding wave. Gabriele had not run very far toward the cafeteria before she stopped and turned to watch Carl fumbling with the pack. She had no idea what it was, but she knew something was terribly wrong. Her anxiety grew into sheer terror as Carl picked up the pack and lugged it toward the exit.

Away from her!

Gabriele stood frozen to the floor, paralyzed with fear. As Carl disappeared through the door, she began to follow. Tentatively at first, she plunged into the crowd that separated her from her husband. Gabriele's terror was reflected in the faces in front of her.

Blocking her way!

Abandoning all caution, she tore relentlessly through the crowd toward the exit. The heavy door did not slow her down.

***

The fleeing man had the discipline not to run. He walked across Independence Avenue and down Sixth Street, past the NASA building. Still a tourist. He even stopped momentarily to look at the Capitol—and to glance behind him to see if anyone was in pursuit. Seeing no one, he resumed his getaway walk.

The dirty gray pickup truck was waiting for him on the other side of the building as planned. He strode to the passenger side and got in. As the rumpled-looking driver pulled away from the curb, he glanced at his partner for some indication of success. Receiving nothing, he turned his attention back to the road and entered the tunnel that would lead them to the highway.

Back to America.

"Message delivered," said the cowboy, staring straight ahead. "Let's go home."

***

Carl struggled frantically to get the bomb away from the crowd. He carried the pack into the open as if it were a baby. A very heavy baby. *Too heavy to carry in front!*

He stopped and hurriedly donned the pack. *Big-time shrapnel... people everywhere...fuck!* Carl ran as fast as he could with fifty pounds on his back. The pipe bomb bounced up and down inside the pack. He scanned the field, thinking as fast as he ran. Fewer people than inside the museum, but if the bomb went off here, many of them would die.

Running out of time…shit!

Carl suddenly remembered the excavation pit he and Gabriele had passed on their walk from the Metro stop. It took him almost three minutes to get there. Three minutes, plus the time it had taken him to figure out what to do. *There it is!* He crashed through the wooden barricade with the last of his strength.

"Run!" shouted Carl to the smattering of tourists in front of him. "It's a bomb!" Those close enough to hear him started running away as fast as they could, repeating his warning as they fled. Staggering with exhaustion but sensing victory, Carl slipped off the backpack, lowered it gently to the ground, and spun around. He lifted the pack and held it over the excavation pit.

Then he dropped it.

The bomb detonated just after he let go of it. The blast launched Carl Barnes back across the field in the direction he had come. His body landed with a sickening thud almost twenty yards from the hole that had contained the explosion. Gabriele, running as though her life depended on it, was the first one to reach him.

Or what was left of him.

Chapter 2

The Widow

The crowd gathered around Gabriele. An older black woman sat down on the grass and held her tightly as Gabriele cried convulsively and gasped for breath. Bits of sound—echoes of tragedy—came to her as the reality began to sink in.

"He saved the lives of a hundred people… Who *is* this man?" Anonymous voices from the fringe. "What gives a man the courage to sacrifice his own life for others? What kind of animal could have put a bomb in a *museum*?"

Had she been able to answer, Gabriele would have told them that her husband had stood for justice, that he had always lived according to a moral code. Later, when the numbness had worn off just a little, she would think that it had perhaps been Carl's destiny to die for others. She would also think it was her destiny to suffer. But at that moment, all Gabriele could do was hang on to her sanity as chaos catapulted her toward the edge of hysteria. She held the black woman as she had once held her own mother, waiting for someone to put the pieces of her world back together.

"Please come with me now, miss." The police officer helped her up and walked her gently away from the scene. "You knew the victim?" The word *victim* penetrated her torment like the nails that riddled Carl's body.

"My husband…," was all she could manage to say.

"I'm sorry," said the cop. After a brief hesitation, he proceeded. "We need to ask you some questions."

Gabriele did not acknowledge but continued walking. She could have been shuffling toward her own death. All that kept her going was the remote feeling this might actually be a nightmare from which she would awaken. Next to Carl. The feeling receded completely as she walked. Slowly, her hopelessness was replaced by an even stronger feeling. Rage. It was rage that kept her on her feet, and she somehow realized that rage would keep her alive—long enough to find out who had killed her husband and why.

A few minutes later, she was sitting inside…somewhere. "If you're ready, ma'am, this won't take long. We need some information, then you'll be given whatever you need.

I need my husband, and you cannot give him back to me.

"Okay," she said meekly. She did not look at the person sitting across from her. She knew it was a man only from the sound of his voice.

"What is your name, and what was your husband's name?"

Gabriele was stunned by his use of the past tense. "My husband's name is Carl Barnes… Mine is Gabriele."

"Mrs. Barnes…can you tell us what you saw?" There were several uniforms standing and sitting at the periphery of her vision. Flash cameras were popping off like lightning as responsible officials documented evidence at the far end of the gallery.

"We were standing in front of the V2 rocket," said Gabriele hoarsely. She cleared her throat and went on. "Carl saw something to his left, over by the television. There were a lot of people…waiting." Gabriele took a delayed breath and tried to continue. "They were waiting to die!" She broke down again.

A female police officer took her into the restroom. Gabriele washed her face then promptly wept again. She rinsed the tears again but could not stop them. After a few minutes, the police officer led her back to the circle of interviewers.

"What happened then, Mrs. Barnes?"

"My husband told me to run in the other direction… He ran into the crowd. I started to run to the cafeteria, but I could not. Carl was in danger! I turned around and watched him." Gabriele had settled into an emotionless monotone. A voice coming from her head, temporarily bypassing her broken heart.

"What was your husband doing?"

"He ran to one of the seats and picked up a backpack. He seemed to be looking for something inside the bag. I just froze. I could not run away, and I could not run toward him. I simply watched as he… fiddled with it."

"Did you notice anyone else, ma'am?"

Gabriele took a few deep breaths and blew her nose. "There was a man walking quickly away from the seats. Everyone else was frozen like me. We all knew something was terribly wrong, but we didn't know what to do."

"What did the man look like?"

"I only saw his back, but I would recognize him if I saw it again," said Gabriele more animatedly.

"Why? Was there anything distinctive about him?"

"Both his arms were covered with tattoos," said Gabriele with a degree of confidence that raised eyebrows among the notetakers.

"That helps us a lot, Mrs. Barnes… Thank you." The cop smiled with gratitude, and Gabriele finally looked at him. Exhausted, she was back in the dark refuge of her grief. Rage still boiled in her head. Then she was bludgeoned one more time.

"This is Officer Mackenzie of the District Police. She will find you a place to stay and arrange for you to take your husband's body home."

***

Susan Mackenzie drove Gabriele back to the Key Bridge Marriott and walked her to the room. The second-honeymoon suite.

Gabriele pleaded, "Officer, please stay for a while… I need someone to be with me right now."

"Of course, dear. Please call me Susan. I'll stay with you as long as you need me…even after the casualty affairs people help you with the arrangements for going home."

"Thank you so much… I must make a phone call. Then I think I will need to talk. I want to tell you about Carl."

Gabriele picked up the receiver and dialed information. "Yes, Operator, can you tell me the area code for Wyoming?" After dialing another number, she spoke again. "I don't know exactly…near Laramie… Thank you." Gabriele dialed information for the Laramie area.

Another minute went by. Gabriele's tears had not stopped. "Yes, can you give me the number for a Jerry Tompkins? I think the first name is listed as 'Jerold,' with a *J*." She took another tissue off the table.

"No… I do not know the town. I just know it is extremely small…west of the city, maybe an hour or so. I've never been there."

Susan Mackenzie watched Gabriele from the end of the bed. As a police officer, she had seen a lot of unpleasant things; this was, by far, the most unpleasant. A woman who had just lost everything… calling for help…not even knowing if she could get it. *The only thing she has right now is* me.

The operator came back on the line. "I have a Jerold A. Tompkins in Lone Mountain."

"That's it," said a relieved Gabriele. "Thank you… Can you connect me?"

Susan came to the chair in front of the phone and took Gabriele's hand.

"Tompkins," answered a strong voice.

"Jerry…this is Gabriele." She forced herself to breathe and just blurted it out. "Carl is dead." Then she broke down again.

Jerry Tompkins, a warrior's warrior, absorbed the news like a bullet tearing through his gut. In shock, but still on his feet, he kept going. "How…and when?" he asked grimly.

Gabriele composed herself. "A bomb in the museum…this afternoon…in Washington… You have to help me, Jerry. I don't know what to do!"

"Gaby…listen to me! Where are you now?"

"At the Marriott… Yes, Key Bridge."

Jerry knew it well. The Marriott had been where he and Carl had planned the Putumayo mission. Their last mission. "Stay where you are, Gaby... I can be there by midnight. Is someone with you now?"

"Yes."

"Ask her to stay with you until I get there. Call the police. Whoever did this could be after you too."

"The woman is *from* the police, Jerry. I'll be okay... But hurry!"

Jerry put down the phone and turned on the television. CNN's special report was still being aired, but the information was sketchy. There was no indication the cartel was involved, and it appeared as though the single victim (as yet unidentified) had been killed while trying to carry a bomb away from the crowd. Jerry's leader and mentor. His best friend. Jerry fought the tears, but they came anyway. It was time to cry. In private.

He and Carl had always operated at the edge of death. They had almost *expected* it then. But *now*? They had left the jungle work to younger men. To men who still had something to prove. But Jerry had worried that the cartel might find them. It was easy to believe the bombing was revenge for Colombia. There had to be an explanation with some meaning. He had not been prepared to lose Carl to a random act of violence.

Gabriele hung up the phone and turned to Susan. "Carl's best friend will be here tonight. Can you wait with me?"

"Of course, I'll stay," said Susan softly.

A battle raged inside Gabriele as she started to pace the room. A battle between the inner strength she had accumulated over a lifetime and the paralyzing weakness of the moment. She did not know which condition would prevail in the end, but she fought as if it still mattered.

"I can't believe this has happened!" she wailed. "I just cannot understand it, Susan... Why Carl...and why me?"

"Do you believe in God, Gaby?" Without waiting for an answer, Susan got off the bed, stepped into the bathroom, and turned on the faucet. The police officer was barely thirty but sounded to Gabriele like a peer. Empathetic. Educated. Someone to listen. A friend.

"Here, take this." Susan handed Gabriele a steaming hot towel.

"Yes… I mean in an abstract sort of way," replied Gabriele, slowly rubbing the terrycloth over her face. "But I never got to know him personally."

"Now's a good time. You need something stronger than any of us, Gaby. I can't explain why this happened, but the fact is that it did. There is a plan. We just don't know what it is."

"I wasn't ready… I'll never be ready," said Gabriele evenly. "If this was God's plan, then he must have some punishment in mind. I am not a vengeful person, Susan, but it makes me feel better to think about punishment."

"That's our job, Gaby…not yours. At least to apprehend… Then we have to let the courts mete out punishment."

"I had something more certain—and more severe—in mind."

"If it makes you feel better, then focus on that. But there's no way to act on it. You should save your imagination for remembering Carl."

With Susan Mackenzie listening intently, Gabriele began talking about her husband. She started with their storybook romance and—without the slightest hesitation—explained how Carl had run missions for the CIA until quitting that life to be with her. The man from Wyoming, she told Susan, had been Carl's second-in-command. Gabriele even told Susan about her own narrow escape from a cartel assassin, bent on taking revenge for Carl's operations. She talked until the sleeping pill delivered her temporarily from the grief she could not suppress.

Susan waited until Gabriele was asleep before going into the bathroom to make a phone call.

"FBI Headquarters, Counterterrorism Office. Can we help you?"

"Yes," said Susan in a low voice. "This is Officer Susan Mackenzie of the District Police. I would like to speak with Gerhard Beck."

"Special Agent Beck is not here, but I can have him call you. What do you need from us?"

"I am with the woman who lost her husband in this morning's bombing. I happen to know that Special Agent Beck will want to talk to her as soon as possible. I'm at the Key Bridge Marriott, room 1414." She dictated the telephone number. "Please tell him what this is about, and have him call me after seven, tonight."

"I'll have him call you. Did you say your name was Mackenzie?" Beck's secretary recognized the name, but not the voice.

"That's right… Thank you."

Susan settled into a chair across from the bed and read a magazine. She knew that Gerhard Beck would be inundated with work in the wake of what looked like a terrorist attack on federal property. She also knew he would take the time to call her. Their marriage had foundered, but mutual respect was still strong. It was certainly stronger than the bureaucratic walls separating two law enforcement agencies with overlapping responsibilities. They had been married long enough for Susan to know more than she should about Gerhard's work. She had heard enough to know that Gabriele Barnes was precisely the person Special Agent Beck needed. Susan was happy for Gerhard; she felt even more sorry for Gabriele.

Gerhard called exactly at seven. Susan picked up the phone just as it started to ring. Gabriele didn't even stir.

"Susan, it's me. What have you got?"

"Gerhard," she began in a low voice, walking into the second room of the hotel suite. "I've been talking to the woman who lost her husband in the bombing. I'm with her now. I think she can help you with your most important project. The victim's best friend is coming in from Wyoming tonight. He's a former Navy SEAL. Can you come up here late…say, after midnight? I recommend you talk to both of them."

"I'll be there, Susan. The traffic between Quantico and DC at that hour is light. I'm up to my ass in alligators, but I trust your judgment." She noticed a short pause. "How are you?"

"Fine, Gerhard… But I actually miss you."

"I hate to admit it, but I miss you too. I hope we can stay friends."

"Count on it," said Susan firmly. She had never regretted her decision to leave, but a surprising nostalgia found its way into her core.

Susan called room service and ordered a thermos of coffee, to be placed in the hallway. Gabriele continued sleeping, while Susan retrieved the tray and poured herself a cup. Mind in overdrive, she waited for the man from Wyoming.

***

The knock Susan expected came just before midnight. When she opened the door, she was staring right into the heaving chest of Jerry Tompkins.

"The elevator was broken… I ran up the stairs," huffed the big man.

"I'm Officer Susan Mackenzie," said the woman, still in uniform. "You must be Mr. Tompkins." *Thirteen floors…with a suitcase!*

"Yes, I am," said Jerry, looking across at Gabriele on the bed. "Jerry Tompkins." He extended an enormous hand. "Nice to meet you… How's Gaby?"

"I drugged her… She needed it… She's in bad shape, Jerry. You probably know more than I do how much she lost today."

"I do."

The big man was stoic, but Susan could tell he'd been crying. She was amazed at his size—at least six-three, she thought. At five-three, she felt like a child. "Please come in. I think it's time to wake Gaby."

Susan went to the bed and shook it gently. Nothing. She shook harder. Gabriele sat up so fast Susan had to lean back to avoid knocking heads. "Carl! Where is Carl?" Gabriele cried out. Susan and Jerry watched as reality came back to crush her again.

"Jerry…you're here," she sighed tearfully. "Thank God."

"Gaby. I got here as soon as I could." The big man sat down next to the woman he had met only once and hugged her like he'd known her forever. Gabriele sobbed into his massive shoulder, while Susan got another hot towel.

"Jerry…I need a lot of help to get through this. I don't know whom else to turn to. Susan has been so kind, but I cannot ask her to stay on."

"Oh, yes, you can!" said the policewoman. "I'm not due at work until tomorrow afternoon. After that, I'll be on call…for as long as you need me."

Gabriele smiled for the first time since the explosion. "Thank you. I will never forget what you've already done for me. I needed a friend."

"I won't insult you by saying it's part of my job, Gaby. It's the right thing to do." Susan looked at Jerry. "There's only one piece of business left for tonight… And then I'll leave you guys alone."

"What's that?" asked Jerry. "I think we should let Gaby rest, don't you?"

"There's a man coming here in a few minutes… He's from the FBI. He works counterterrorism for the bureau, and he wants to ask Gaby some questions."

Jerry's sense that he should protect Gabriele gave in to his understanding of the intelligence process. He knew that the sooner an investigator can get good information about an incident, the sooner he can compare and combine it with all the other pieces of information he has. The result, he knew from long experience, was "actionable" intelligence. Whatever the emotional cost to Gabriele now, the interview would be worth it in the long run.

"Okay," said the big man. He directed his intensity at Gabriele. "Is that all right with you?"

Gabriele looked at him and then at Susan. In a burst of new strength, she found her rational voice again. "I will do anything to help them find whoever did this to Carl."

"Good," said Susan. "I know this man… He's tough on criminals but very good with people." She gave them both a knowing smile. "And I'll boot him out of here when you've had enough."

Jerry Tompkins had attended Gabriele's wedding but had not gotten to know her. It occurred to him just how few people he *had* gotten to know outside a small brotherhood of warriors, now long in his past. He had always been on a team. Now there was no team. He had envied Carl for having found real happiness with a loving woman. Isolated on the high plains, he had not found anyone to fill the void. For the first time in his life, Jerry Tompkins did not have a cause—or a person—to live for…or to die for.

"Thanks, Susan. Like Gaby, I'll do whatever I can to help find the killer." He wanted to add that he would be happy to administer justice without the assistance of the government.

Jerry understood how much Gabriele would need his strength, but he wasn't sure he could give her the comfort she deserved. He was glad Susan had been there for her and happy that she wanted to stay involved. But something about Susan bothered Jerry. It took him a few minutes to figure it out. She was professional and friendly, with an energy-packed body and short chestnut hair. Cute. What bothered him about Susan, he realized, was his own reaction to her. He had taken his mind off Carl and Gabriele in order to *notice* her. On this day of mourning, thought Jerry, that was a sin of the highest order.

Twenty minutes later, there was a knock on the door. Susan opened it and ushered a tall middle-aged man into the room. Jerry's first impression was that the man looked like an FBI agent. On second glance, he thought the man would look quite comfortable in a general's uniform. His graying blond hair was freshly cut, and Jerry noted that, under the dark suit, the man carried an athletic build. He was breathing hard but trying to hide it. The lawman reached for Jerry's hand and shook it firmly.

"Gerhard Beck."

"Jerry Tompkins…did you have to take the stairs?"

"I did. It wasn't fun." Under any other circumstances, both men would have laughed. Instead, they turned grimly to Susan.

Gabriele, still wearing the summer dress she had put on that morning, waited for Beck by the couch on the other side of the suite. "Gerhard," said Susan slowly, "this is Gabriele Barnes… Gaby, this is Gerhard Beck from the FBI."

As a European, Gabriele offered her hand first. Beck seemed to understand the protocol. "Mrs. Barnes…I am terribly sorry to bother you now, in your grief. I cannot begin to express my sympathy. I will make this as painless as possible."

"Mr. Beck…I lost everything today. As for the timing, I will never stop grieving. All I ask is that you discover who did this. I do not care if it is painful for me." Gabriele had fallen back on rage as a source of strength. It felt good, she thought. Like a drug.

"Mrs. Barnes, I can assure you that we will do absolutely everything we can. That's why I'm here."

"Please call me Gaby."

"All right… But I'd rather call you Gabriele. That was my mother's name."

"Are you German, Mr. Beck?"

"My name is Gerhard…and yes, I'm second generation. Would you feel more comfortable speaking German?"

"I have been here so long," said Gabriele without hesitation, "that I actually prefer English. But I appreciate the offer." She sat down on the couch. "What do you want to ask me that the police have not already asked me?"

Special Agent Beck took Gabriele through the same battery of questions she had answered that afternoon. He also asked her about her childhood in Germany, her family, her American journey, and her teaching. Gabriele was beyond exhaustion. She failed to realize how much she was telling a total stranger about her personal life. All her analytical powers, painstakingly developed through the interpretation of language and literature, did not prompt her to wonder why Beck wanted to know all these things. She was on automatic. Careful thought was a luxury she could not afford at the moment. Analysis was out of the question.

After only thirty minutes by Susan's watch, Gerhard was finished. Jerry took Gabriele a glass of water, while Susan led the FBI man to the door. "You were right," Beck told her softly. "I would like to attend the funeral. Can you arrange that?"

"Sure, Gerhard… I can do that. Call me tomorrow?"

"Okay. You haven't moved, have you?"

"Nope. I look forward to following up."

Gerhard Beck closed the door and raced down the stairs with a new sense of optimism. He had found the right couple. Now he would need to convince them.

He was confident he could.

Chapter 3

The Recruit

Gabriele drew heavily on her third cigarette of the day. The Florida sun was still rising over the mangrove forest behind Captiva. Carl's mangrove forest. Carl's Captiva. Gabriele's hell. She pulled smoke into her breast slowly and deliberately, as if she thought it could heal her broken soul. As if it would penetrate the veil of her flickering spirit. She sat alone, looking at the Gulf of Mexico through the window.

"Soon you'll be back in the water, dear."

And she wept again, knowing that she would join him when the pain became too much for her to bear.

Gabriele had known sadness in her life—even grief—but nothing had prepared her for this. She had lost the only human being who'd ever made her feel truly alive. It had been nothing less than the sudden, graphic obliteration of her future. The explosion that had taken Carl from her side had torn every dream from her head. She didn't know how she'd survived the last five days; she didn't know how she would last until the end of this one. She had no idea where she would go—everywhere reminded her of Carl. She understood, maybe too well, that she would never be able to outrun this nightmare. A nightmare worse than the death of her parents. More devastating than the loss of her son.

Gabriele doused her cigarette in a cup of cold coffee and stood to face the day. Dropping her silk kimono (a gift from Carl), she bent carefully to gather the jeans and T-shirt thrown on the floor the night before. Her face was swollen with sorrow. Her brain throbbed from the alcohol ingested to induce sleep. Jerry would come by at nine thirty; she still had time for another walk on the beach. Her last walk before returning Carl to the Gulf he loved so much. As she stepped out the door and onto the sand, she felt closer to him. The beach was all she had left.

Something Nietzsche had written came to her as she looked at the horizon.

When you stare into the abyss, sometimes the abyss stares back.

The abyss was staring back. It seemed to beckon her.

The images of events since the explosion returned to her as she walked. It was all a blur, not only from the speed at which things had transpired, but also from the shock of Carl's violent death. Her life was like a pair of fine binoculars, abruptly dropped to the floor. Everything was out of focus. The golden sunlight of Captiva was now flat, the colors gone. Waves lapped at her feet, washing a million shells farther onto the sand. She felt them digging into her flesh, but she could not see them. She could only see herself kneeling next to Carl's dismembered body, as strangers came running to her from all directions.

***

Jerry Tompkins pulled his rental car into the driveway of the beach house at exactly nine thirty. Gabriele was dressed in black and waiting in the window. She moved to the door, and he walked mechanically up the steps to escort her. Jerry's movements were slowed by the heat and also by his attire. He had not worn a civilian suit since Billy Joe's funeral the year before. Aside from making him uncomfortable, the suit reminded him he was no longer in the Navy. This was going to be a long day.

"It's time, Gaby." He said it as softly as he could.

Gabriele looked at him through her veil but said nothing. She took his outstretched hand and followed him to the car. Once inside, staring straight ahead, she took his hand again.

"I need you to help me get through this, Jerry. I do not want to embarrass Carl. Please make sure everything goes well." She continued staring at the road as Jerry left the driveway.

"That's always been my job, Gaby... Making sure things go well. I won't let you down."

"Thank you, Jerry, for all you have done for me." She turned to him and lifted the veil. "I have seen why Carl worshipped you."

"You have that backwards, Gaby... I worshipped *him*. There was never a better human being in this world. I wish I had a dollar for every time he saved my life."

"And he told me about all the times you saved his."

"Except this time."

They said nothing else during the ten-minute ride from Captiva, over the low bridge, to Sanibel Island. The Catholic Church was situated in the center of the island, a mile from the Gulf and a mile from the bay separating the barrier islands from mainland Florida. Jerry turned off the main road and parked; then escorted Gabriele into the church.

As they walked down the aisle, he saw that General Stewart had made it to the service after all. The African-American general, now retired and soon to be ordained as a Baptist minister, had been on a wilderness retreat when Jerry had first called with the news. It had taken some time for the church to get him the word. Late and devastated, the man had driven all night from North Carolina. As Jerry deposited Gabriele in her seat, he also noticed Jose, standing next to Stewart. He didn't say a word to either man. He knew what they felt: a mixture of sadness and rage. Feelings he knew would not be dampened by words or hymns.

Eternal Father, strong to save
Whose arm hath bound the restless wave.

Jerry fought the emotion that overwhelmed him whenever he tried to sing the Navy Hymn. He wore his game face, his jungle face. He would not let anyone see how weak he had become. Furtively, he looked around the church. There were about fifty people, most of whom he didn't recognize. Carl had not been in the islands long, but Jerry could see that he'd made many friends. Scanning further, he saw Susan Mackenzie, wearing black but somehow shining through it. She was standing next to Gerhard Beck, singing,

Who bids the mighty ocean deep
Its own appointed limits keep.

Jerry shifted his eyes back to the altar and focused on the silver box of ashes they would soon pour into the Gulf of Mexico. He had been through the same ritual less than a year ago with Billy Joe's ashes. But Billy Joe had died in combat; Carl had been killed. Jerry thought about the difference. Billy Joe had been fatally wounded while shooting Colombian criminals trying to kill his teammates; Carl had been blown up by an American criminal trying to kill innocent civilians. Jerry decided there was no difference. Carl had died in combat. It made the big man feel better to know that.

Oh, hear us when we cry to thee
For those in peril on the sea.

Gabriele cried. Jerry took her hand again while his own tears finally came. He just let them come, and he was surprised at how they made him feel better—even in public. It was expected. No shame in that. He knew that Carl would have cried for him. Jerry had seen him cry for Billy Joe. He remembered that now. Gabriele looked at him and, for a moment, forgot her own grief. She felt comfortable with Jerry. She hoped he would stay long enough to help her process all this. To keep her from dishonoring Carl by giving up on life. Gabriele didn't need a man; she needed a male friend.

They were outside again, headed for the dock. Jerry drove the lead car, with Gabriele, Jose, and General Stewart. Gabriele held the silver box on her lap. Carl's closest friends had wanted to reserve the second ceremony for their band of brothers. Bonds stronger than love had brought them here. The laying of ashes on the water was, to them, the final demonstration of devotion. Gabriele was grateful to be honored with their kinship. These men were the friends who would sustain her. If she could be sustained at all.

They walked along the floating planks toward Carl's pride and joy. His charter boat—a twenty-six-foot Mako, with a Bimini Top for shade and two large outboard engines for power—had been more than just a tool of his new profession; it had been a symbol of his transition from warrior to husband. Gabriele stepped aboard as a widow, straight into the brotherhood. As they gathered around the console, *Madrugada* rocked silently back and forth. Jerry started the engines, while Jose and General Stewart tossed the mooring lines on the dock. With Gabriele sitting next to him on the bench seat, Jerry eased the charter boat into the bay.

"This was his office," said Gabriele as the mangrove forest floated slowly past them.

"My kind of office!" Stewart was the first to smile. The other men, out of habit, followed his lead. Gabriele remained stone-faced as Jerry pushed the throttles gradually up to speed. In a few seconds, they were racing across the bay toward the entrance to Redfish Pass. Gabriele had removed her hat. They had all replaced their dress shoes with sneakers. The other guests would have to wait for them at the restaurant.

Jerry cut the engines back as they bounced through the low surf at the outer edge of the pass, continuing to judge the waves as he shouted to Stewart behind him. "I think once we're outside, I'll be able to cut the engines and drift while you give the blessing, General."

"My name is Reggie," boomed the general, looking back and forth between Jerry and Jose. "I know it's a tough habit to break, but you guys need to stop treating me like a general… Got that?"

"Yes, Sir!" they answered together.

Gabriele allowed herself to smile.

Reginald Stewart had earned the right to be there. Jerry and Jose owed him their lives. He was on the team.

"There you go again… Hey, I'm proud of my twenty-eight years in the Army—especially being your commander—but it's time to move on."

"*Estamos de acuerdo,*" said Jose to all of them. "We got it."

The paramedic had come running to Captiva the moment Jerry called him. He had been invaluable to the big man (as he had been for fifteen years) in preparing for this day. Jose had not brought his jokes to Florida; he was still stunned. Like Jerry, he wore a game face. It was the worried look he had always worn in the field. Only this time, there was nothing left to worry about. No gunfire. No crosswind landing under a half-deflated canopy. No wounded frogmen to patch up. Jose's nostalgia had gone up in smoke with his team leader. Carlos, the warrior. Carl, the friend. Perhaps the humor would come back, he thought. Maybe after the ashes were in the water.

Jerry pushed the throttles up to full bore, as everyone hung on for the three-mile ride to the site. Gabriele had wanted to place Carl's ashes closer to the beach and to her. But the authorities had told her it had to be three miles. And so it would be. She could see that far—even during a storm.

Ten minutes later, *Madrugada* drifted peacefully in the smooth water. Reginald Stewart squinted into the sun and began the final act in Carl Barnes's extraordinary life.

"Almighty Father, whose way is in the sea…whose paths are in the great waters…whose command is over all…and whose love never fails. You have taken Carl's soul from us. We give you his body and ask you to nurture it as you care for all things you have created. Carl always believed that you reveal yourself in nature. The sea was his confessional, the forest his cathedral. He worshipped you every moment of his life. Protect Gabriele, Lord, and give her the strength to rebuild her life on this Earth. Take care of Carl until we are all accorded the honor of joining him in heaven. In Jesus's name, we pray. Amen."

Gabriele opened the silver box and poured her husband's ashes into the clear salt water. She watched through silent tears as they descended to the bottom of the Gulf. One last free fall. Back into the womb. Jerry took the wreath of flowers and laid it gently on the water. No one spoke for several minutes. One by one, they looked up…and then at each other. They came together at the bow of the boat and held the preacher's black hands in theirs. Stewart spoke to them in a different tone.

"That's all we can do for Carl, my friends. We have placed him in the loving arms of the Lord. Grieve as you must… But get on with your lives. He would want all of you—especially you, Gaby—to pick up the pieces and make the most of every day." Still looking at Gabriele, Stewart continued. "God has spared each one of you for a purpose. It's up to you to figure out what that purpose is. Carl always tried to plan as though he would live forever, but to live as though he would die tomorrow. I think that sums it up pretty well. Carl was a true warrior." Stewart lingered over the thought and then continued. "An ordinary man takes everything in life as either a blessing or a curse. A warrior takes everything as a challenge. You all need to be warriors in your own ways. Remember that not every day is good… but that there is some good in every day. Find the good."

There was absolutely nothing else to say. Jerry fired up the engines and took them back to the island. Stewart's words echoed inside their heads, mixing with private thoughts and open feelings. Each of them had come close to death in the last year and survived. As the preacher had said, each of them now had a renewed purpose for living. Designated by God. Jose figured he would find out sooner or later. Jerry waited for a sign. Gabriele already knew.

***

After the last of the guests had left the restaurant, Jerry drove Gabriele back to the beach house. Gerhard Beck and Susan Mackenzie, as agreed, followed them. Once inside, with the Gulf of Mexico visible through the window, the four sat around a small dinner table. Jerry fidgeted, thinking he knew what was coming. Susan stared out across the beach, knowing. Gabriele fixed her ice-blue eyes on Gerhard, smoking anxiously as she waited for him to present the proposal.

"Gabriele." The FBI man hesitated long enough to draw a furtive deep breath. "You told me last week that you want me to do everything I can to find out who murdered your husband. I have something in mind…a way for you to help me. I must warn you, though, that if you accept my proposal, you will be in great danger."

She cut him off. "I have been in great danger before, Mr. Beck. What do you have in mind?"

"Please call me Gerhard." Softening his commanding features for a few seconds, he tried to get her to relax. He failed. The tension was about to increase. "I'd better start by showing you this."

He placed a newspaper clipping from the pile of papers in front of him and placed it before her. Gabriele crushed out her cigarette and read.

Group Claims Responsibility for Museum Bomb

Washington. A terrorist group calling itself DEFCON One has taken responsibility for the pipe bomb that exploded in the nation's capital last week. The bomb, which is estimated to have contained more than twenty pounds of plastic explosive, had been left in the Air and Space Museum by a lone male suspect. Had it not been for the heroism of the one man killed in the blast, the bombing would certainly have resulted in the death and maiming of hundreds.

Killed in the incident was Carl Barnes, a fishing guide from Florida. Mr. Barnes had been visiting the museum with his wife when he discovered the bomb lying on a seat in front of the Langley Theater. Mr. Barnes, who apparently had some military experience, carried the bomb outside onto the mall and attempted to deposit it in an excavation hole to shield others from the explosion. The bomb went off before Mr. Barnes could let go of it.

The following communiqué was transmitted over shortwave radio five days after the blast: "We, the patriots of DEFCON One, in order to form a more perfect union, do solemnly swear to uphold and defend the organic Constitution of the United States against all enemies, foreign and domestic. With the support of all real Americans, we will bring down the Zionist-occupied government and build a new nation—armed and ready, white and Christian, sovereign and free."

DEFCON One is thought to have been responsible for a series of lower-profile bombings around the country over the last year. The group has eluded federal authorities as its terror campaign gathers momentum. The Washington bombing, though unsuccessful as an act of mass terror, represents a new phase in DEFCON One's war against the American government. A spokesman for the FBI told the *Post* this morning that no stone will be left unturned in the search for those responsible for these attacks.

Gabriele was unable to cry. The newspaper account summoned her rage to the surface once again. Anger was a painkiller to which she was rapidly becoming addicted. She read again the last sentence of the article and lingered over the thought. In the moment before Gabriele cast her eyes back to Gerhard Beck, she promised herself two things: first, she would not allow herself to cry again until Beck found Carl's murderers; second, she would do whatever he asked her to do.

But she had one question: "These people describe themselves as patriots, Mr. Beck. How can that be?"

The FBI man looked at everyone in turn. "These people are not patriots. They are white nationalists. A patriot is proud of his country *because* of what it does. A nationalist is proud of his country *in spite* of what it does."

Beck tried to remove the anguish from his voice. "I've been looking for someone to help us penetrate DEFCON One." He let the idea settle in her mind before continuing. "In other words, I need someone to go under cover… But we haven't found anyone within the bureau or in the local area who might have a reasonable chance to do it successfully…until now."

"And you think I can do that?"

"Actually, I've been looking for two people…a married couple."

Gabriele's tone suddenly shifted. "But I am no longer married… My husband is dead."

Beck looked at Jerry Tompkins before responding. "We could arrange to have you marry again, just for the operation. Then you and your husband would attempt to join the organization."

Gabriele sat up straighter in her chair. "And whom do you have in mind to be my husband?"

"I thought Jerry might be willing to do it."

The big man's eyes caught fire, but Gabriele was the first to react. "You want me to marry Jerry...then go out and find my husband's killers?"

"Yes...in simple terms. That would be the plan." Gerhard was now looking right at Jerry. "Jerry would make the perfect agent for us, but—in our judgment—he could not succeed alone. These people are pretty smart. They would be too suspicious of a single man with Jerry's experience suddenly trying to get into their inner circle. Also—and this is key—we know that the individual who leads the group brings only couples into his ranch compound. That's where the real decisions are made. We think they might accept another couple—that is, a couple that sends them the right signals. We need a man and his woman to go in there and look these animals in the eyes, listen to them, and then get out."

Jerry burst in before Gabriele could respond. "Yes, Gerhard, of course, I'm willing to do it." The man his teammates called Butkus sat forward in his chair and clenched his enormous fists. "*More* than willing."

"I thought so," said Beck with a grin. "We checked out your background—as much as we could get access to—and you are exactly what we need." He glanced at Susan, nodding imperceptibly.

"But why recruit Gabriele?" asked Jerry. "We could just find a law enforcement officer to 'marry' me," he continued, using air quotes. "I'm not sure we should expose Gaby to the danger." Jerry had to force himself not to look at Susan.

"We could do it that way," said Beck thoughtfully. "Until I met Gabriele, I thought law enforcement would be our only option. I've been on this case for more than a year, Jerry. Trust me...you are the perfect agent for us, but not without Gabriele. You would need her to pull it off. That's why we're here."

"You think Gabriele has something unique to offer?"

"Yes, I do," responded Beck firmly. "As I hope to show you, this group needs your skills, but they suspect anyone who's ever worked for the federal government."

Jerry nodded vigorously. "I get that, Gerhard. Terrorism is hard work…even harder than counterterrorism. The men probably do the dirty work, while the women sustain them." He ducked a frown from Susan and kept going. "But what does Gaby bring to the table that another woman would not?"

"Motivation, for starters," said the lawman, looking at the widow. "If she goes in with you…and you get involved with real terrorists…it will be extremely risky. Whoever you go in with would need an unshakable reason for doing it."

"Okay," said Jerry, "but a professional police officer also has a reason to assume that risk… It would be her job."

Gerhard replied quickly, perhaps a little too quickly. "The real reason Gabriele could do a better job than a cop is because she's not a cop." Slowing down, Beck went on. "The target organization has a very keen sense of security—paranoia, in fact. A civilian would have no bad habits to give herself away…right, Susan?"

Susan Mackenzie, a veteran of almost ten years on the DC police force, nodded to her ex-husband and then to Jerry. "He's right, you guys. Law enforcement habits would make it tough for a policewoman. Shooting, for instance, is a reflexive act for a trained person. Jerry has an *excuse* to be able to shoot like the Sundance Kid… But I would not. This outfit shoots a lot…even the women. They would pick that up."

Jerry started to answer, but Susan wasn't finished. "If it were *me* in there with you, it would be difficult to explain where I learned to draw quickly and double-tap a silhouette." She looked at the former warrior and raised a finger as if to shoot him. "Am I right?"

"Sure," said Jerry defensively, "but I could just say I trained my wife to shoot like me… I spent a lot of my Navy time training people to shoot like me."

The FBI man looked at Jerry but spoke to Gabriele. "That's very true... But I want to make sure that, whoever your wife is, they will accept her. I want them to *want* her."

"What else does my undercover wife need?"

"This group appears to be run by educated people," replied Gerhard in a scholarly tone. "They borrow from Nazi and revolutionary rhetoric. Gabriele's cultural and academic background could be the crucial factor in getting you into their decision circle. Frankly, I'm more interested in someone who can talk than someone who can shoot."

"It will still be a big risk for someone who isn't trained," insisted Jerry. "Have you ever tried sending in one of your own agents?"

"Yes, we have," said Beck evenly. "We got a man into their public umbrella group earlier this year."

"What happened after that?"

"He disappeared."

Gerhard's eyes found Gabriele's. She showed no reaction. This was the moment of truth. The truth hadn't seemed to shake her. He didn't know whether to feel triumph or guilt. Looking at the beautiful woman he was asking to risk everything, Gerhard Beck felt a little of both.

"And just who *are* these people?" asked the man from Lone Mountain.

"We suspect," ventured Gerhard, "that DEFCON One is a small covert cell within a larger, overt organization."

"And what organization is that?"

"The Militia of Wyoming."

Jerry had never heard of the militia and found himself embarrassed. More testimony to the fact that his years away from the Cowboy State had left him out of touch. "I did not know about that... Where is their base of operations?"

"Mineral King," replied Beck.

"In the middle of nowhere... That makes sense." Jerry still felt clueless.

Gabriele, who had not said a word for almost ten minutes, got up and walked to the window. Looking at the spot where she and

Jerry had just parted with the last thing she cared about on earth, a strong voice came from her pounding heart.

"Mr. Beck. I have heard quite enough reasoning. What we need now is information. I believe that God has given me a new purpose in life now that my husband is gone. It is my destiny to exact retribution for his death. Consider me recruited."

Gabriele did not turn around. Without taking her eyes off the Gulf, she fumbled for another cigarette. With secret enthusiasm as well as fear, she stood there awaiting further instructions. Waiting for Special Agent Beck to build her a new life.

Chapter 4

The Plan

Gabriele's new life would have to wait, Gerhard Beck had told her. The FBI man would return to Washington and present the plan to his superiors. Even the FBI's fastest decision-making process would take at least three weeks. That would give Beck time to prepare a comprehensive set of briefings for the launch. Shakespeare was wrong, Beck had always said; all's well that *starts* well.

Susan Mackenzie stayed in Captiva for the ensuing weeks. She had worried that the wait would erode Gabriele's enthusiasm for the operation. If anything, it had strengthened her resolve. After some frantic politicking by Gerhard, Susan had been seconded to the FBI for a period of one year. Her first, and only, assignment was to support Gabriele Barnes, prospective confidential informant for the bureau—operationally, logistically, and psychologically. In between long walks on the beach, Susan had fleshed out the mission requirements, helped with moving arrangements, and boosted Gabriele's confidence. She and Gabriele had become close friends.

Jerry had gone back to Wyoming to tend the ranch for a couple of weeks. The wait had also given him time to think, riding and driving around his nine hundred acres. Beck's concept was unlike anything he'd ever been involved in. He was about to go undercover in his own country. He knew how to execute a plan, and he knew how to defend himself. Beyond that, he would be out of his league, improvising all the way. But the operation was his duty—to himself and to Carl. Beck had said that Gabriele would be the key to their success. Jerry would make sure she survived—even if it cost him his own life.

But there had been a lot to do first. In his former life, Jerry had been focused on foreign threats to American security, spending a lot of time outside the country. He had not thought much about domestic terrorism; that was the FBI's responsibility. Now he *was* the FBI, and he had a lot of catching up to do. By the time he drove into Gabriele's driveway, Jerry had learned a lot about the right-wing fringe in America. But not enough. Gerhard would tell them what the government knew—but that would not be enough either. Jerry's mission would require him to find out what the government did *not* know and to get it straight from the horse's mouth.

***

The four of them sat, as before, around the small table by the window. The curtains were drawn, keeping the September sun at bay. The curtains also prevented Gabriele from searching the Gulf with her memory. She and Jerry had a lot to absorb in the next eight hours, and they would need to concentrate. Retribution, she was about to find out, required a lot more than motivation. Bitter memories would have to be overlaid with names, dates, events, and procedures. Susan sat between her and Jerry, ready to add her own perspective. Gerhard punched a laptop keyboard and put his first briefing slide on the projector screen.

The slide read "*Operation Lariat.*"

"I like the sound of that!" exclaimed Jerry as he felt the excitement of going back in the field. *God help me, I love this shit.*

"This is the situation," began the FBI man. "In the last year—in fact, beginning on July 4 of last year—there have been five bombings on federal property. The Air and Space Museum is the first, and the only, incident for which the terrorist group DEFCON One has taken responsibility. We believe the group is responsible for other bombings, but this one may be a preview of things to come."

"What kind of people would do this?" interrupted Gabriele.

Beck nodded grimly. "We have no concrete evidence regarding who these people are, but we have some clues." Gerhard looked at them with a professional mask that reminded Jerry of the way Carl had often looked at him before a mission. "All the successful bombings have something in common. That something is the State of Wyoming." Beck hesitated just long enough to take a breath. "And that's where you'll be going to live your undercover lives."

"Where in Wyoming, Gerhard?" asked Jerry.

"You get to live on your ranch, cowboy." Beck smiled for half a second then recovered his joyless tone. "At least for a while."

Jerry looked at his new teammate and future wife. "I have a big place, Gaby. Three bedrooms, three baths, comfortable places to sit privately, and lots of grazing land."

"I am sure it will be fine," she replied. "I would like to rent this place out furnished while I'm gone," said Gabriele, gesturing to the four walls. "In case I come back," she continued. "Do you have enough furniture for me?"

"Absolutely. There's a guest room all prepared, and the floor plan is split. We can live separate lives inside the house."

"I hope you have room for me to visit," added Susan carefully.

"I do," said Jerry, smiling. "I do."

"*We* do," said Gabriele, turning to her new friend. "We want to see you as often as Mr. Beck authorizes you to come."

Gerhard Beck looked at his newest subordinate more warmly than his professional position required. "I really wish you'd call me Gerhard, Gabriele."

She paused before responding. "Okay, Gerhard…you *are* older than I am," she acknowledged, bowing to German custom. Gerhard smiled, but Gabriele did not.

Gerhard resumed his briefing. "These are the bombings we think can be attributed to DEFCON One… Only the last one has been claimed."

Jerry studied the list.

07/04/98	Office of the US Forest Service, Sundance, WY
10/21/98	Office of the Bureau of Land Management, Buffalo, WY
04/19/99	Office of the US Forest Service, Big Piney, WY
06/07/99	Office of the Bureau of Land Management, Mills, WY
07/22/99	National Air and Space Museum, Washington, DC

"Is there a pattern here other than federal property?" asked Jerry.

Susan put down her pen. "Looks like they took the winter off, Gerhard."

"Nice symmetry," said Gabriele. "Until they hit Washington, they had two of each type of federal office."

"Yes," said Beck, responding to all three. He turned and pointed to a map posted on the wall to their left. Each bombing location was circled in red. "As you can see, the targets were scattered all over the state…until they went to Washington." He nodded at Gabriele and then went on. "We think the first four bombings were just a warm up. They clearly intended to make a big splash in the capital."

"And Carl prevented them from doing that," said Gabriele in her best professional tone. "If he were still alive, DEFCON One would probably be after him now…just like the cartel was." She stared at the far wall, lost in thought.

Beck tried to connect with her on a personal level one more time. "What your husband did, Gabriele, was the most heroic act I have witnessed in a full career with the FBI. Together, we will find out who tried to murder hundreds of innocent people, all of whom owe their lives to Carl. Then we will see to it that the killers are punished to the maximum extent of the law."

Gabriele's eyes filled with tears. "What is the connection between Wyoming and the Washington bombing?"

"I was coming to that," said Gerhard, suddenly impressed with Gabriele's analytical ability. "We found some dirt on the floor of the museum in what we think were the footsteps of the bomber—your testimony was critical here. We sent the dirt to our crime lab and found it matched the brick-red soil of an area in Wyoming known as the Red Desert. This is a unique basin in the south-central part of the state, nestled between two mountain ranges. The Red Desert gets only about nine inches of rain a year. It's a forbidding place with no trees and no fences—in fact, it is the largest unfenced expanse of land in the lower forty-eight. The soil has a geologic composition that is unmistakable. The bomber had that soil on his boots."

Jerry jumped in. "I know that part of the state... You're right. It's harsh and completely uninhabited. A great place to train. I'd say it's about three hours from my spread." Visibly excited, he added, "You said these guys operate out of Mineral King."

"That's right," said Beck. "Right on the edge of the Red Desert."

Gerhard looked at each of them in turn before continuing. "The Militia of Wyoming has taken an ominously low profile since it was founded in 1994. Its leadership discourages lawlessness while preparing its members for what they say is the coming revolution. If we are guessing correctly, it's a brilliant strategy. The terrorist core of the organization provokes the government into overreacting. The rest of the organization, wittingly or unwittingly, protects the identity of the core. A militia of law-abiding citizens is the perfect cover for DEFCON One."

"I'm surprised I haven't heard of this militia, Gerhard... It's pretty near my ranch, at least by Wyoming standards."

"The Militia of Wyoming, sometimes known as MOW, has not gained the public attention that its sister organizations in Montana and Michigan have," lectured Beck. "Its membership is limited, and those inside are encouraged to keep quiet. DEFCON One leaders, masquerading as MOW leaders, don't want any scrutiny from the federal government. We know they are extremely serious about security."

"Tell me about your undercover agent who disappeared," said Jerry. "We'll need to know everything you know about what happened." Jerry shot a glance at both women. Susan was listening to him intently; Gabriele was too busy taking notes to look up.

"His name was Seth Goldman," Beck began. "We got him a false identity and sent him into Mineral King as a gas station attendant."

"As I remember," said Jerry, "there's not much in that town *except* a gas station."

"That's right. They don't even have a stoplight. Mineral King is an old mining town, killed by the steep fall in uranium prices after Three Mile Island. The only place the militia has room to meet is an old run-down theater. After we got Seth into position at the gas station, it was easy for him to get to militia meetings. What we didn't realize was that all newcomers are automatically suspected of being federal agents."

Jerry nodded while Gabriele continued scribbling notes. "Did you learn anything at all from Goldman?"

"From what Seth could tell us through dead-drop communications, we know there's an inner circle that keeps a different routine than the rest of the members. We assume they ran Seth through their investigative mill, and it is likely they interrogated him until his cover story just didn't hold up. All of a sudden, he was gone. We have not found him…or his body."

"And you think Gaby and I can pass their tests better than Goldman could." It was a statement.

"Yes, we do," said Gerhard.

"That's good enough for me." It was Gabriele, momentarily putting down her pen. "Before you continue, though, please explain to me what a dead drop is."

Beck almost smiled with the pleasure he felt. *Brainy as well as beautiful.* Gabriele, he could see, was channeling her rage into an intense concentration. This would be the key to her survival. Gerhard felt even more pleasure when he thought of Gabriele's survival. He was too busy to analyze why.

"A dead drop is the remote transmission of a message inside a concealment device. The agent leaves the device at a prearranged location, and the recipient picks it up later. The system works both ways. It's a proven technique. The biggest danger is that the agent might be followed and the recipient ambushed."

"I guess I'll have to learn not to be followed," replied Gabriele.

"I can help you with that," said Jerry confidently. "We have a lot of training to do in the next few months."

Beck took a deep breath. *So far, so good.* "That's probably a good place to leave this for now. Let's take a thirty-minute break."

***

After stretching their legs on the beach, they convened again to finish the morning session. Beck put the first slide on the screen.

"These are the unsolved murders in Wyoming we suspect can be attributed to DEFCON One."

"Other than Goldman," added Susan.

"Other than Goldman," repeated Gerhard. They read the projected words.

9/11/97	Japanese tourist	State Route 28, Farson
5/1/98	Ethnic Indian	State Route 487, Medicine Bow
7/4/98	Black Trona miner	State Route 372, Seedskadee

"Pretty easy to see the pattern here," observed Jerry. "I was still in Virginia Beach at the time of the second killing, but Medicine Bow is not far from my ranch."

"You're not a suspect," quipped Gerhard, "but someone is definitely targeting minorities."

"What does the name DEFCON One mean?" asked Gabriele. "What does it have to do with these killings?" She looked up from her notebook. "And bombings?"

"DEFCON One," replied Beck, "has a double meaning… At least we think it does. Jerry will recognize it as a national security acronym. It is the 'Defense Condition' utilized to signal that war is imminent." Gabriele could see Jerry nodding vigorously in her peripheral vision. "The second meaning—and, again, this is a guess—would come from the group's strongly expressed defense of the US Constitution."

"Do you mean to tell me that a group whose members bomb innocent human beings is worried about the integrity of the Constitution?" Gabriele again felt rage escaping from the iron grip of her concentration. "You'll have to explain that one to me." Her voice trailed off.

"The Constitution they defend is not the same as the Constitution you and I know," explained Beck. "They want to take this country back to the beginning, to erase all the social progress we've made—and to the time when, with no standing army, most male citizens were obliged to belong to an organized militia."

Susan continued the lecture. "The heartland is full of men and women who see government tyranny in everything Washington does. These people often see themselves as patriots the way Sam Adams did. Add fundamentalist religious beliefs and unlimited gun ownership…it's a dangerous brew."

Trying to understand, Gabriele pressed. "But how did the Constitution become a symbol to the militia—and how were some of its members radicalized to the point of mass murder?"

"That's two questions," Susan began. "I'll take them one at a time… First, ask any militia member today why he or she hates the government, and you'll hear 'Because I love the Constitution.'"

"I still don't get it."

"The individuals who flock to the movement feel estranged from the political process. They believe the government takes away their rights, infringes on their religious beliefs, and destroys their way of life. These are people who respond to what they describe as a 'higher calling.' Rather than obey the laws, they resist them as a matter of principle…even to the death."

"Even to the death of others?"

"Yes… To many of them, this is a holy war. No compromise is possible. It's a battle for American values that some of them have chosen to fight with bombs and bullets instead of words. You've seen in the Middle East what a holy war can do."

"They are no different than the extremists who ruined Europe and killed most of my relatives," said Gabriele firmly. "What about question number two?"

"Ah, yes… The militia movement started bringing a collection of extremist elements together in 1994…in response to the sieges at

Ruby Ridge and Waco, as well as to the momentum toward sensible gun control, accelerated by passage of the 'Brady Bill' in 1993."

"I read about all those things, but I never paid much attention." Gabriele felt a wave of guilt as she realized that—along with most ordinary citizens—she had simply assumed the government would take care of these problems. "How did this happen…right under our noses?"

"The nationwide militia movement is an underground that is actually aboveground," replied Susan. "It starts just outside the American right wing. There are militia members in every state, but they tend to cluster in rural areas. Family farmers and ranchers, Gaby. You wouldn't see them in Captiva."

"I had never even heard of the right-wing militia until right after Oklahoma City… Then they just disappeared!"

"They didn't really disappear, Gaby. Individual militias still meet regularly. They go shooting all the time. They go to gun shows, where a wide variety of weapons can be bought without any background checks. They have their own echo chamber on shortwave and AM radio. They are starting to use the internet more, especially the so-called dark web. They're here… We just don't notice."

"Until they attack ordinary Americans."

"That's right, Gaby. This is why we need to crush the movement. It will only get worse if we don't. You and Jerry are about to perform a great service for your country." She smiled at the big man.

"But how do people get involved with militias in the first place?" asked Gabriele, fascinated and horrified at the same time.

"The militia movement has been described as a funnel moving through space. At the front end, it catches people who feel strongly about one of the core issues, say gun control. Sucked farther into the funnel, you find people who have developed an anti-government ideology. Still further in are the conspiracy theorists. These are citizens who see the federal government behind everything they can't explain…from UFOs to black helicopters in the night. Some of them believe there's a plan to use the National Guard to establish martial law."

"I wish the government was that organized!" exclaimed Jerry.

"The narrowest part of the funnel draws in the hard core," continued Susan. "The moving funnel imparts momentum to the process. If you get involved because you don't like what the government did to the Branch Davidians, the echo chamber gives you all kinds of other reasons to hate federal authority. The militia is a good example of what group behavior can do… Irrational thinking breeds more irrational thinking. The farther into the funnel you go, the harder it is to get out."

Jerry realized he was already at the open end of the funnel. He admitted to himself that his conservative views—and his love of guns—might have prompted him to join the movement. Just for the sense of belonging he no longer had (members of his own tribe were scattered around the country, or dead). Now he was going to allow himself and Gabriele to be sucked into the narrow end of the funnel. Then they would have to climb out again. Against the wind.

Gerhard put the next slide on the screen. "With your permission, Susan?" His ex-wife smiled, and he nodded. "Great discussion," said Beck.

"Yoshihiro Genda," announced Gerhard, as a picture of the murdered Japanese man lit up the room. "Someone followed him along the highway and waited until he stopped…probably to go to the bathroom. It appears he was headed to Flaming Gorge for a photo shoot. He never made it. Two pistol shots delivered from close range. The local authorities found film in his camera. When they developed it, they found pictures of the Wind River Mountains. I've seen the pictures. Genda was a very talented photographer."

"But the wrong race," added Susan.

"And the local police never found the killer?" asked Gabriele.

"No. They didn't even find the body until three weeks after the murder. It was buried in a shallow grave about two hundred meters from the road. Actually, the cops didn't find it…the Coyotes did."

"What did the killers do with his car?" asked Jerry.

"No one knows… They probably just drove it into the reservoir." Beck straightened just a bit. "It seems to us that the local police didn't try too hard to find out what happened. This is consistent with a militia philosophy that emphasizes loyalty only to local authorities.

They *hate* national authorities, especially the FBI." Beck hesitated again. "We can assume these people took particular pleasure in killing Seth Goldman."

"What was Goldman's cover name?" asked Jerry. "If the leaders bring it up, I'd like to know who they're talking about."

"Matt Snell," replied Beck. Seth was a New York Jets fan as a kid. Snell, a black running back, was his boyhood hero. Maybe they figured that out."

"And you think Gaby and I can pass muster with these killers?"

"Yes…for all the reasons we've already discussed…but also for one more." Beck locked eyes with Jerry. "'Colombia gate.' When you tell them about what the government did to you, they'll have no trouble believing it."

Jerry glanced at Gabriele and found her lost in thought. "The reason the Colombia story will work, Gerhard, is because it's true. The CIA really *did* try and sacrifice us!"

"A rogue operation if ever there was one, Jerry… But it will make a terrific hook for the Militia of Wyoming." Everyone except Gabriele nodded in agreement.

"Next victim," said Beck, as the image of a South Asian man wearing a turban came onto the screen. "This is—was—Karan Singh."

Jerry broke in. "When you said they'd killed an Indian, I thought you meant a Native American… Wyoming is full of them. I remember hearing about the murder, but I didn't realize the victim was a foreigner."

Beck glared at him. "He wasn't a foreigner, Jerry. Mr. Singh, an American citizen, owned a construction company. He was driving from Cheyenne to a road repair site near Casper."

"I didn't mean that the way it sounded," said a flustered Jerry Tompkins. "Sorry."

Gabriele looked right through him. "Let me remind you, Jerry, this is a country of immigrants. I am, myself, an immigrant." Tempted to give Jerry a lecture, she let her frown complete the thought. At the same time, Gabriele knew that Jerry was far more prepared than she was to blend in. She would have to change her vocabulary, replacing the word "immigrant" with "lousy foreigner." She would have to learn to blame them for everything from crime to racial pollution. Gabriele would not be blamed for anything. As long as she sympathized with Nazis old and new, the militia would celebrate her foreign birth.

"Same MO," said Beck, turning back to the screen. "Someone followed Singh along the road until he stopped for some reason. It was dark. We think the assailant might have been wearing night vision goggles because the victim never turned around."

"Makes sense," said Jerry, nodding.

"The killer shot him in the back twice with a pistol. Local authorities found his sport utility vehicle a week later, parked well off the road, way back in a canyon. Singh's body was inside the car. A bumper sticker was taped to his forehead."

"What was on the bumper sticker?" asked Gabriele.

"A Christian fish."

"We're dealing with some very sick people here," said Susan with disgust.

"Nothing would surprise me," said Jerry.

Gerhard, who had been looking at the screen, faced the table again. "Maybe this one will, Jerry." Another slide materialized. "This is Luther Malone. He worked at the Trona mines, west of Green River."

"What's Trona?" asked Gabriele.

"It's an obscure but important mineral," replied Gerhard. "It's used in hundreds of everyday products from glass to baking soda. I know that because I looked it up... I had the same question."

Jerry went to the map on the wall. "What do you think he was doing up by the Wildlife Refuge?"

"Probably looking for some shade," responded Beck. "It was very hot at the time of the murder."

"How did they kill him?" asked the big man.

"Shot twice in the chest...broad daylight."

"That *is* surprising," conceded Jerry. "Someone likes to take chances."

"Next to the road?" asked Gabriele.

"Yes. Malone was buried just off the road…shallow grave in the marsh."

"Where did you find the car?" Jerry was still at the map.

"In the weeds…about two miles down the road."

"Any help from the local cops?"

"None, Jerry. Absolutely none. As you well know, there aren't many African Americans in Wyoming…and even fewer in that area. Malone stood out like a sore thumb. He was well-known within mining ranks, but the sheriff didn't even interview his coworkers."

Beck suddenly changed his tone. "Let's take an hour for lunch, folks."

They ate in silence on the patio. In the intensity of the briefing, Gabriele had laid aside her grief. It came back to her now with even greater force. As she looked longingly at the Gulf, she remembered a quote attributed to Frank Lloyd Wright.

There is relief for anguish in action.

***

After lunch, they sat around the briefing table again. Gerhard put the first slide on the screen. Gabriele picked up her pen.

"This is James Thorne…better known as Red. He commands the Militia of Wyoming. We think he also commands DEFCON One."

Jerry stared at the picture of an overweight man with a long red beard. "He looks like Jerry Garcia! Doesn't look very tough to me."

"According to Seth Goldman," continued Beck, "Thorne's an intimidating presence. We don't know too much about him, but we do know that he grew up in Hoback Junction, at the north end of the Bridger-Teton National Forest. He is fifty years old. He has a master's degree from the University of Wyoming and began a career as a professor. He was seeking a PhD at the time… That was in the seventies."

"What was his field?" asked Gabriele.

"History," replied Beck. "He quit before he got the degree. We don't know why."

"It's an easy thing to do," quipped Gabriele. "I had a love-hate relationship with the classroom myself."

Beck went on. "We also know that Thorne worked as a local hunting and fishing guide. We think that, through exposure to rich eastern elites, he came to believe that urbanites have lost touch with what made this country great. He tells the militia that the only way to make America great again is to fight."

"He calls for revolution?" asked Gabriele. "Can't you just arrest him?"

"It's not that simple," said Gerhard. "He stops short of calling on his followers to *initiate* revolution. He urges them to be ready to fight the government when our agents come to get their guns. It's a defensive message… Can't pick him up for that."

"And you want us to record him saying what's *really* on his mind," added Jerry.

"Yes…that's the minimum objective."

"And the maximum objective is to find out where he is planning to strike next," added Gabriele.

"Exactly," said Beck, looking directly at Gabriele. "You should have been an FBI agent." She did not smile. Neither did Beck. "You tell us when to come in… Then you and Jerry go home."

"What if we can't get you a message…and things go south?" asked Jerry, the tactician.

"Then you'll have to escape and evade," said Beck evenly. "The closest Susan and I can station ourselves will be in Cheyenne."

Gabriele knew nothing about escape and evasion, but she did not like the sound of the words. She thought that Jerry must be good at it, but all his experience had been in the jungle. Gabriele knew how to run, but she didn't think she could run halfway across Wyoming.

***

Beck had saved religion for last. After a short break, they were all sitting at rapt attention.

"Thorne and his people are believers in 'Christian Identity,'" began Gerhard.

"You mean they're fundamentalists?" asked Jerry.

"Yeah," interjected Susan sarcastically. "If you think Christian fundamentals are ignorance and hatred. The Identity Christians believe that white Aryans are the true Jews…God's chosen people. They believe that those who are *called* Jews are the offspring of the devil. Some of them even think that blacks and other minorities are in a different species. That's what I call fundamentalists from hell."

"You mean they actually believe that crap?" Jerry thundered.

"They quote scripture to prove it, Jerry. It's real to them. Like gun culture and freedom from big government, Christian Identity is a pillar of the militia belief system. They say they're working *Yahweh's* will."

"*Yahweh?*"

"The original Hebrew name for God…the God of Abraham, Isaac, and Jacob. Identity 'clergy' refer to their flocks as 'Christian Israelites.'"

"Now there's an oxymoron!" observed Gabriele. "How can such self-proclaimed Semites be so anti-Semitic?"

"Even if a person with right-wing views doesn't buy all of it," added Beck, taking the lead again, "the notion that America is a divinely inspired nation that should belong only to white Christians is a principle that unites them in a holy quest."

"Another Crusades," sighed Gabriele. "That's all we need. A thousand years from now, students will be shaking their heads…just like they do now."

"Lots to study," said Jerry, glancing at Gabriele. "We need to talk the talk, and it won't come naturally."

Everyone nodded as Beck put another slide on the screen. It showed a weathered face under a cowboy hat. Gabriele had a strange feeling she'd seen the man before.

"This is Thorne's number two. His name is Will Jeffers. Seth told us he almost never speaks but that when he does, he preaches. He's a deeply religious man, a zealot. Guess what religion."

"Identity," said Gabriele.

"Yes, and he sees Thorne as a prophet. He is, according to Goldman, completely devoted to the man. Will—I think that's short for Wilson—seems to be the manager of Thorne's ranch."

"He looks the part," said Jerry.

"Jeffers and his wife live in a compound made up of trailers… We know that others live there. They all have wives. We think that is a prerequisite for living in the Thorne compound. We don't know why."

"You've said that a lot," Jerry pointed out.

"Yes, I have. After the mission is over, I won't have to."

"After the mission is over, Gerhard, I want to be sure that Gaby and I are protected from any kind of retaliation." The big man looked at Gabriele, who was nodding.

"We'll put both of you in the witness protection program."

"You mean we'll have to *testify* against Thorne and his henchmen?" asked Gabriele apprehensively.

"We think you will," replied Beck. "If you do, it is my responsibility to shield you from any harm. We do that all the time… We're good at it."

"I hope you do a better job than those bastards at CIA," said Jerry acidly. "What else did Goldman tell you?"

"Not much, actually… But he did report on other couples who appear to live at the ranch. One of the men was described as looking like you, Jerry. Another is apparently short, skinny, and sloppy-looking. These guys all bring their wives to militia meetings…although Goldman told us he had never seen Mrs. Jeffers." Beck drew a long breath. "Once you're in the militia, you can find out much more about all these people."

"And get invited to live at the ranch," said Gabriele, finishing Beck's thought.

"Precisely. That's what we want you to do…if you can. Then we can learn what these God-fearing Americans are up to."

As the others watched, Gabriele got out of her seat and disappeared into the kitchen. Quickly reappearing, she stood in the doorway. Drawing on a cigarette, she threw a cold stare across the room.

"If they killed my husband, they're going to fear a lot more than God."

Chapter 5

The Cowboy

At the end of the day, Gerhard returned to Washington. Susan spent the night in Gabriele's house, while Jerry slept in the back of his truck. Morning found the women packing Gabriele's things. Jerry drove to a pay phone and called a number in Virginia Beach.

"Rios."

"Jose…it's me, Jerry."

"Butkus! Where *are* you, man?"

"Back in Florida… But I'm on my way back to Wyoming. Before I go, I need to know if you can take a leave of absence."

"When?"

"Not for a while…maybe in a few months. Can you get away for six months?"

The paramedic hesitated, but only for a few seconds. "Yeah, I think so, man… What's goin' down?"

"Can't tell you now, amigo. Let's just say I might need your tactical skills. I may also need your medical skills."

"Sounds like old times, Butkus." Jose felt the call of the field. It was a great feeling.

"It's more than that, Bosco. I'm about to put Gaby in deep shit. I want to be able to call on you when I need backup. Can you be ready to come to Wyoming on short notice?"

Jose Rios had spent most of his adult life backing up Jerry. "Sure, man... I can do that." No more questions asked. His fiancée would have to adjust.

"Thanks, brother. I'll get in touch again as soon as I get settled out there."

Jerry drove back to Gabriele's beach house to borrow the bathroom. "I'll be set to go as soon as I get cleaned up."

"Gaby won't be ready for another two hours... No need to hurry."

A few minutes later, Gabriele called to him, and Jerry opened the door. He looked even bigger without a shirt. "Susan told me to start acting the part now. She said we need to give each other pet names for added authenticity." Gabriele smiled. "So, here goes... Where are we getting married, big guy?"

For a long second, Jerry felt as though he and Gabriele were *already* married. He leaned out of the bathroom grinning. "I know a little chapel in Lone Mountain, sugar... You'll just love it."

Gabriele frowned. "Can you call me *Schatze* instead?" A harmless appellation, she was sure. "That's the German word for *treasure*, a common term of endearment."

Jerry made a valiant attempt to pronounce the word, but he couldn't get it quite right. Gabriele was used to Americans not getting German pronunciation quite right. "Why don't you just call me *Schatz*? One syllable is enough... And it's more familiar."

"I love it when you call me big guy, *Schatz*... But I think we can do better. Beck said the leader of this outfit is enamored with all things German. Is there a German equivalent?"

Gabriele thought for a few seconds before responding. "The word *Wunderknabe* comes to mind... That means something like 'impressive young man.'"

"That doesn't sound very intimate to me." Jerry laughed.

Gabriele thought again. "Okay... I will call you *Junge*." She gave him a mischievous grin. "That translates as 'kiddo,' but you look young enough to wear the name. It's a term of endearment featured in one of my favorite Hans Fallada novels."

"I like it too," replied Jerry. "*Junge* it is, then."

She closed the door and left him alone.

An hour later, Jerry was carrying heavy bags out to the truck. When all of Gabriele's things were stored for the long ride west, Jerry stood in the kitchen facing her and Susan. Gabriele took out a pack of cigarettes and started to light up.

"*Schatz*," he began, "I have to tell you that I can't live with a smoker. Even though our relationship will be platonic, it would be best if you quit." He almost winced as he braced for her response. Susan turned and walked into the other room.

"You're right, *Junge*. I have the feeling this escape and evasion thing is going to require me to get back in shape. I should not be smoking anyway. I just needed something to keep me sane."

"That's *my* job now," said Jerry without emotion. "And I can definitely get you back in shape."

Gabriele walked to the trash basket and tossed in her Marlboros. Then she dunked the lighter in the garbage with a bit more flair. She was smiling as she looked back at him. "There... Any further requests?"

"None, *Schatz*... I'm good. You and I are going to make a great team."

***

Jerry left the house and sat in his green Dodge RAM, waiting for his new teammate. Now that he had a mission, he was anxious to get started (his life had been one long series of missions). While he waited, Gabriele walked to the window one last time and looked out at the Gulf. She wanted to strengthen the image she would cling to when the going got rough. She wanted to tell Carl what she was about to do, but she feared he would disapprove. She wanted to live, but only to come back and tell Carl that his death had been avenged. Only then could she live—and die—in peace.

Jerry watched her lock the door and walk slowly to the truck. She was beautiful, he thought again, but so very sad. A woman grieving. Someone with the courage, but not the skill, to make *Operation Lariat* work. Jerry promised himself that, whatever else happened, he would make sure she came back. He had a lot of confidence in his ability to improvise. He hoped Gabriele also had a good feel for improvisation. She was going to need it.

"Ready to go?" asked Jerry cheerfully, as he reached across the seat to open the door from inside the cab. Privately, he didn't think it was possible that Gabriele would ever be ready for what lay ahead. Too many things in her life had suddenly changed. Over and above the loss of Carl, she had rented out the house, sold Carl's boat, and given the cat to neighbors. She was about to leave the island she loved. He decided it was a *good* thing she didn't really understand yet what she was about to do.

"Ready, Jerry." She glanced back at the beach house. "That is, as ready as I shall ever be… Do you like my hat?"

As he had instructed her, she wore a baseball cap…of sorts. He had forgotten to mention that *Tommy Hilfiger* was off-limits.

"That hat will be fine for the trip, but I have to get you another one for militia meetings." He laughed. "If you wear that one into a Wyoming bar, you might as well wear a shirt that says, 'I'm a tourist from the East.'"

"Oh!" She said it as though someone had just pinched her on the back pocket of her very acceptable blue jeans. She plopped herself in the passenger's seat, feigning hurt feelings, and closed the door. "I could not have known, you understand. There is a lot to learn, I see."

"And the designer sunglasses," said Jerry with a smile. "I'll buy you a pair of Oakleys."

"I'm sure they will look fine," said Gabriele, returning the smile. "I can drive when you get tired, okay?"

"Thanks, Gaby… Next stop, Tallahassee."

They proceeded into the sun, already hot over the southland, then turned north, bound for a different universe.

"September is so hot in Florida." Gabriele sighed. "I look forward to being cooler."

"Careful what you wish for… Where I live, it can snow during any month of the year. I'll buy you a warm coat when we get there."

"Thanks, *Junge*… Will that be before or after the wedding?"

"Before, *Schatz*, before we tie the knot." Jerry looked straight ahead, into the future, trying to imagine what it would be like.

Gabriele noticed his discomfort. Talking to his profile, she attempted to put him at ease. "I cannot think of anyone else I would rather be married to under these circumstances, Jerry."

Gabriele was surprised by her own reaction to the statement. The act of putting Jerry at ease had also put her at ease. She regarded the man she barely knew with an affection she did not completely understand. Perhaps, she thought, it's because he was so close to Carl.

"We do make a good team," said Jerry, his eyes still fixed on the road. "I'm going to make you a cowgirl, and you're going to be the militia's rookie of the year."

"I will be the best cowgirl in Wyoming, Jerry… Promise. When I was a little girl, I dreamed of being—"

"A cowgirl?" interrupted Jerry.

"An actress!" They both laughed easily, blowing away the lingering tension. "But you'll have to explain to me what a rookie is."

"A baseball reference."

Gabriele sighed. "Carl was a fanatic baseball fan… I never knew what he was talking about."

"Just one more thing to learn."

"And when you were young, what did *you* dream of becoming, Jerry?"

"A football star." He said it with a straight face.

"I guess I'm in for a rougher ride than I thought!" She was laughing again.

"I'll do my best to teach you the vocabulary, Gaby. The first word you'll need to learn is *Broncos*. Where we're going, football is a religion."

"Then pray for me."

***

A harvest moon hung just above the horizon as the people of Paso Robles slept.

Most of them.

Eduardo Cruz parked his Chevy pickup truck in front of the Safeway, turned off the engine, and looked around. There was no one in the parking lot, and the street was empty. Of the twenty-four hours the store sold groceries each day, he thought, the hour between four and five in the morning must be the slowest. He had sometimes wondered who in his right mind would shop at that hour. Now, he walked out of the moonlight and into the store. It was virtually empty, but Cruz was nervous. He needed a reason to be there. A reason he could explain to someone…just in case. He selected a cart, quickly placed some vegetables into it, and made his way to the dairy case.

While Cruz feigned shopping, another figure stepped from behind an oak tree adjacent to the parking lot. Confident no one could see him, the man looked at his watch and stood in the morning chill for another minute. If anyone *had* been observing, they would have seen a large white man with broad shoulders and blond hair. Another working stiff on his way to the vineyards. Or maybe a cattle ranch. Some kind of hard work. He wore the uniform worn by most young men without education in the dusty hills of central California—jeans, work boots, and an un-tucked flannel shirt. The shirt was bulky enough to conceal a Beretta nine-millimeter pistol wedged between his belt and the small of his back. He squinted at the moon then looked at his watch again. Slowly and inconspicuously, he moved to the door and into the store. Passing a bank of shopping carts, he strode directly to the dairy case.

Shifting his eyes to either side, Cruz waited. The man was late. Only a few minutes late…but late. He felt as though there were a hundred people watching him. Every doubt came rushing back into his head as he tried to remain calm. It had been two months since the first mysterious phone call. Three days since he had called the man back. Three days to wonder if he had made the right decision. He knew this was a serious offer because the man had done his homework. *How did he find out my mother is dying?* Cruz hadn't trusted the guy, but he had been desperate enough to agree on the deal. The money had overridden every other consideration. The money was why he was standing in front of the dairy case at four in the morning, waiting for a lunatic who knew everything about him. Eduardo put down the sour cream and slowly turned around.

Just in time to protect himself!

Cruz cringed as the larger man crushed him with a bear hug, lifting him off his feet. Circling once, the man put him down and backed off to arm's length.

"Teddy! You kept your word. Soon we'll both be rich!" The man released him and stood there waiting for his old friend to say something.

"It's been a long time, Roy," said Cruz, still shaken.

"It's great to see you, amigo." Roy Murdock glanced behind him to see that nobody had wandered within range of their voices. "I have great news… The buyer is lined up. All you have to do is deliver the goods. How does it look for this weekend?"

"Good, Roy… It looks good. My unit has a drill. We'll be firing AT-4s. I think I can lose some." Cruz lowered his gaze to Murdock's boots.

"The more rockets you lose, the more money we make," said Murdock. "Let's go see the rally point."

"Follow me, Roy." Cruz spoke in a monotone, suggesting his heart was not fully involved in stealing shoulder-fired rockets from the California National Guard. He had disliked Roy Murdock in high school and found he disliked him even more fifteen years later. Other than his *Anglo* mother, no one had called him Teddy since their football days. Glory days, to be sure. Before they'd had to deal with the real world. There had been rumors that Roy, after getting out of high school, had started dealing drugs. It wasn't exactly a surprise to Eduardo; Murdock had always lived in the shadows—even as a kid. Though poor, Cruz had, so far, managed to deal with his problems legally.

That was about to change.

"You don't sound all that thrilled about this," said Murdock, following Cruz out of the store. Just outside, he grabbed his accomplice by the elbow and spun him around. Roy Murdock looked into the young man's half-Hispanic face and asked the only question on his mind.

"Can I count on you?"

"Yes, Roy... You can count on me," replied Cruz in the lowest tone he could find. "But I don't have to *like* it."

"You'll like the money, Teddy. I know how much you love your mother."

"She's the only reason I'm here."

Cruz got into his truck and waited for Murdock to start his own car. Seeing the lights come on across the empty parking lot, he drove to the main road toward Highway 101. He sped up the on-ramp with Murdock's Jeep Cherokee right behind him. Eduardo Cruz relaxed for the first time since leaving his run-down house outside Paso Robles. The forty-minute drive enabled him to think again, to think about what he was doing, to ask himself if what he was doing would be worth the risk of going to jail for a long time. He thought about his mother, his wife, and his young son.

Por cierto, he said to himself. *It is worth the risk.*

Cruz drove into the blackness toward the spot where he knew the sun would rise in a little more than an hour. Just before the 41 junction, he turned left onto a two-lane asphalt road. The sign said "Parkfield," but he wasn't going that far. Precisely two miles past the turn, he made another left and followed a dirt track about four hundred meters into the brush. A low wall of rotting wood came into his headlights. He stopped and got out, momentarily alone in the wild silence.

Not for long.

Roy Murdock skidded to a stop just behind Cruz. He stepped into the predawn glow, wielding a flashlight. He pointed it at Eduardo's face and saw fear. That was good. Fear would motivate the man to go through with the heist. *Yeah... Fear is good*, thought Roy as he pulled the Beretta from under his shirt.

Cruz almost choked. "What's *that* for?"

"Just in case," said Murdock. "You never know when some fucking cop might blunder into one of our meetings." He pulled back the slide and let it slam home with a metallic thud. "I hate cops."

"Roy!" stammered Cruz, breathing again. "No cop has ever been here. This is my personal spot...a *sitio* where no one can hurt me."

"Good," said Murdock. "We'll do the transfer right here... Sunday at midnight. Got it?"

"Got it... But that means I will have to keep the stuff in my truck for *eight hours!*"

Roy Murdock was losing his patience. "Just drive around, Teddy... Or you can come up here and wait for me. I'm not moving till eleven."

"Okay... How much will the buyer pay us for each rocket, Roy?"

"Ten thousand," said Murdock evenly. "We split it down the middle, just like I promised. Anything else?"

"No...nothing else. See you Sunday night, with as many rockets as I can get away with."

Cruz fought to keep his facade of control. Focusing on the risks he would take just to get the weapons, he had not considered the possibility he would be double-crossed. He did not consider it now. He didn't like Murdock, but he trusted him to come through. Just like the old days...on the football field. He was a halfback again, running for daylight behind the decisive block. Eduardo was running for the biggest score of his life, and he needed a decisive block. The even split was generous of Roy, but it made sense.

Without me, there will be no rockets.

"Bring a lot of cash, Roy."

***

Gabriele had never seen anyone eat two complete meals at Cracker Barrel. "Where do you put it?" she asked him, shaking her head. "I hope you don't want me to cook in those quantities!"

"I don't expect you to cook for me at all, *Schatz*. We can share the house without making you a housewife."

"Oh! I appreciate your strict adherence to our arrangement, *Junge*, but I genuinely *like* cooking. I'm just afraid you will not care for it."

"You cook German stuff?"

"French, mostly... I do a lot of interesting things with chicken." Gabriele was beginning to enjoy herself. "I bet I can make you a *gourmet*."

"As long as I can eat a lot."

"That would make you a *gourmand*."

"Can I be both?"

"I suppose you can... I promise not to tell our militia friends."

After lunch, they drove the rest of the way to Tallahassee and checked into a Holiday Inn Gabriele had found in the AAA book. It was quiet (her number one requirement), and it had two beds. The dinner was fit for neither *gourmet* nor *gourmand*, and they agreed that Jimmy Buffet had been right. The next morning, Jerry was up at dawn and out the door for a conditioning run. Gabriele was still asleep when he got back. Trying not to wake her, Jerry rested on a stoop in front of the room, doing push-ups, cooling off, and getting hungry. When she came to the door, it was almost eight o'clock.

"I think we found another point of contention," said a groggy Gabriele. "You are just like Carl...up and out at the most barbaric hour. You guys never stop moving!"

"Old habits, Gaby. There's not enough time in the day to do everything I want to do. Carl was right... Live as though you'll die tomorrow."

"I'm afraid I might die *today* unless I get a cup of coffee!"

Thirty minutes later, Gabriele was watching the big man devour a large stack of pancakes. Nursing a cup of bad coffee, she silently considered how lucky she was not to be grieving alone. She had almost nothing in common with Jerry, but she felt safe with him—a strong man with a lot of the right kind of experience. She would play his wife with an acting ability she knew lurked within her. Gerhard Beck had summed it up well.

The way you relate to each other must be completely natural. Learn everything about your spouse and be ready to improvise.

Gabriele, a seasoned academic, continued to ask questions. "So what do you do besides eat and watch football, Jerry?"

"I raise cows," replied Jerry, munching on a piece of sausage. "It doesn't pay very well, but it's in my blood...and fun." He sat forward and swallowed. "Not as much fun as the Navy, though."

"You were Carl's number two."

"Yeah... We made a great team. There will never be a better one." He drained his orange juice and abruptly stood up, taking the receipt off the table.

"Can we continue this in the truck?" he asked nervously.

"After you," said Gabriele, gesturing. "I'm now *your* number two."

He sat down again and looked her in the eye. "You might have that backwards, *Schatz*. According to Beck, you're the key to this whole thing."

"I don't believe that," replied Gabriele. "Beck was just trying to talk me into doing it. I have no experience. I don't even know how to defend myself."

"I can help you with that," said Jerry cheerfully. He stood up again and went to pay the bill.

They walked out into the Florida heat, got back in the truck, and roared onto the interstate. Having interrupted an important conversation, Jerry didn't know how to restart it.

"Mind if I play the radio?"

"I was about to ask *you*," she said with a hint of apprehension.

The first day, they had not been in the mood for music of any kind. Music had somehow seemed inappropriate so soon after the FBI briefing. The prohibition on using the radio had not been announced; it had simply happened. Jerry understood that their success—and, ultimately, their survival—would depend on their ability to read the other's intent. Action without deliberation. Simply knowing what your teammate would do in a given situation. Pickup basketball. Jerry thought they were off to a good start.

"How 'bout some good ol' country, Gaby?" He snapped his head around to catch her reaction.

"You must be joking."

"Hey," came the reply. "If you're gonna learn to be a cowgirl, how ya gonna do that without bein' country?"

"Of course, *Junge*... I should have anticipated this." She sat back and listened to a combination of songs and lectures on country music. The songs came from artists with names like Jo Dee Messina, Shania Twain, George Strait, and Willie Nelson. Interesting names, she thought, as the new sounds penetrated her East Coast urbanity. The lectures came from her cowboy driver.

"Where we're going, Gaby, you'll have to be able to talk about these things. Country music used to be called Country and Western. Somewhere along the way, the Western part was dropped, but folks in Wyoming still consider it their music."

I'm a little way from Little Rock
But a long way from over you.

As she listened, Gabriele began to soften her criticism. True, it was not Mozart. These compositions would not be performed all over the world two hundred years from now. But there was something about country music that suddenly appealed to her. Was it the raw emotion? Was it the melodies that reached into her soul as she surrendered to the corny lyrics? She found herself enjoying music she had instinctively hated.

"Are all the songs about drinking and cheating?"

"You mean drinkin' and cheatin'," said Jerry, laughing. "Country has come a long way from when I was growing up. Just like other music, it's mostly about love."

"With only occasional drinkin' and cheatin'," she mimicked.

"It happens," said the driver.

"I guess I won't hear an oboe for a long time," mused Gabriele to herself. The radio kept playing, and she began to interpret every song personally.

Here I am
On the road again.

It seemed to Gabriele that she had been on the road all her life. Fleeing an abusive husband and the land of her upbringing, she had started a new life in Washington. Another episode had come along after her chance meeting with Carl. A life almost snuffed out—on the road—by a Colombian assassin. Soon after that, she and Carl had sought refuge in a remote backwater in Florida. Now she was on the road with a man she didn't know to a place where evil lurked. At the end of this road lay vengeance—and, quite possibly, her own death.

There I go
Turn the page.

By the time they got to Shreveport, they no longer felt like strangers. Jerry and Gabriele had been thrown together by circumstances rather than chemistry, but a team was forming and a friendship growing. During the briefing, Jerry had asked Gerhard Beck why he and Gabriele would have to actually marry. Gaby had suggested they just get a fake marriage certificate (a snap for the FBI). Gerhard had told them that only a Christian wedding, conducted in public, would create the credibility they needed. He expected militia members to interview the witnesses. Posing as husband and wife had seemed difficult to them at first, but now it promised to be the easiest part of the mission.

Exhausted by the long drive, Jerry and his fiancée checked into a nondescript motel and got cleaned up for another dinner date. Over piles of meat loaf, they continued their research. Gabriele wanted to know more about the man she had just seen half naked in their very small room.

"Have you ever been married?"

Jerry finished chewing and put down his fork. "Yes, I was… But it didn't work out."

"Neither did my first one, Jerry."

"You were married before Carl?"

"Does that surprise you?" She raised her very blond eyebrows. "I *am* forty-one, you know."

"You look thirty…if I may say so."

"You *may*," replied Gabriele. "You can tell me that every day if you want."

"We're the same age."

"You look thirty yourself, big guy." Gabriele wasn't attempting to flatter him; Jerry Tompkins still looked like the young lifeguard he had once been. Where Carl's face had been angular and rugged, Jerry's cheeks were baby's-bottom smooth.

"I wish I looked older, *Schatz*." He paused. "That way, other men would take me more seriously."

"Good god, Jerry! How could you think they *don't*?" Gabriele was floored by his humility. She thought it must be false. "You have been in combat, right?"

"Yes."

"I could not help but see the nasty scar on your thigh."

"Courtesy of the Revolutionary Armed Forces of Colombia," he announced with what sounded like pride.

"You have killed other men?"

Jerry looked around the near-empty restaurant. A habit.

"Yes."

"And you still think you're not taken seriously?"

"Gaby...I don't wear my combat record on my sleeve. I've always been taught that men are judged by what they do...not by what they say."

"Then you have solved your own problem, have you not?"

"My fieldwork was appreciated by the team, but that team is no more. Beyond that operational family, I've never been able to talk about what I've done. I shouldn't talk about it now."

"You're not in the Navy anymore," replied Gabriele, still astonished by Jerry's lingering sense of duty. "I think I have a pretty good idea of what you did. Carl told me some stories he said were classified."

Jerry grimaced. "Okay... But not here. I'll tell you everything that has ever happened to me...except for the really embarrassing stuff. Everyone has things they never want to share. I got plenty of those."

"So do I," said Gabriele sincerely. "We have plenty of time to talk... How much farther is Wyoming, anyway?" She speared a piece of iceberg lettuce and dipped it in what the waitress had identified as Italian dressing.

"We could do it in two days, but we're not in that much of a hurry. I want to stop in Oklahoma City long enough to show you something."

"This country is just too big," said Gabriele with a hint of frustration in her voice. "I mean, we're not even going across the whole thing. If we had started in Germany, we would be in Spain by now."

"You're right, Gaby, but it'll be worth the drive…you'll see."

"Perhaps we could see some things on the way back—assuming we make it through this alive."

"I'm going to make sure you come out of this alive, Gaby." Jerry drew a deep breath and continued. "With any luck, I'll survive myself to drive you home."

"I just want Carl's killers to pay."

"They will, Gaby. Trust me. But first we're going to have to explore the operational area thoroughly. This thing will play out over half of Wyoming. It's a big stage. I hope you're ready for more long drives after we finally get there. Long drives are a fact of life out on the plains."

Gabriele nodded grimly.

"My life is full of facts, Jerry. Facts are all that's left when dreams are taken away."

Chapter 6

The Heist

Staff Sergeant Eduardo Cruz drove his pickup truck through the main gate of Camp Roberts and followed the red arrows toward the Ammunition Supply Point. Passing the base chapel, he said a quick prayer.

Maria, por favor...ayudame.

Cruz did not worry about going to jail; he worried about going to hell. Although the penalty for failure would be high, he had a good plan and a healthy measure of confidence. As the ordnance sergeant, his job was to break out the tools needed for weapons practice during drill weekends. His infantry platoon had been scheduled to shoot anti-tank rockets for some time, and National Guard units had few opportunities. Cruz had been told to take all the AT-4s out of the magazine for Sunday's evolution. It was the end of the fiscal year, and his commander wanted to expend everything they had left. That was great news for part-time soldiers whose antidote to boredom was firing modern bazookas at authentic-looking tanks. The order to fire everything was even better news for Sergeant Cruz.

Cruz parked his Chevy behind a building near the ASP. Looking around, he congratulated himself for finding the perfect spot. Out of sight, in the trees, no one around. He checked to make sure the canvas *tonneau* cover was stretched tight over the bed of the truck and walked ten minutes to the guard shack. He signed for the keys to a weapons carrier and drove to the magazine. The chill of the morning was disappearing quickly as the California sun climbed above the barbed wire fence. Cruz backed the olive-drab vehicle up to bunker no. 7 and got out to open the heavy metal door. He surveyed the area anxiously and, again, found no one. He relaxed a bit and thought about his mother.

This is for you, Mom.

The boxes were heavier than he remembered. The breakout was normally managed with two soldiers, but today the platoon was shorthanded. Cruz's first sergeant had thanked him for handling the rockets himself. Eduardo had said he was just trying to be a team player. Staff Sergeant Cruz was a highly trusted member of the unit, and he knew it. He hated to use that trust against his fellow soldiers… But they would never know. They would continue to rely on him. He would continue to work in the vineyard. He would do his weekend drills with the unit, occasionally assisting the community with firefighting or flood relief. He would still be a hometown hero. His family would survive. That was what counted. Eduardo Cruz suppressed the guilt that hammered at his whole body and carried the first box out the door.

Over the next hour, Cruz loaded a total of thirty-five AT-4s into the truck. Using a pair of bolt cutters, he severed the metal bands binding each box before stacking them in the bed. Pacing to burn off still more anxiety, he inspected the parking area before closing the now-empty magazine. He drove out of the ASP, stopped, and got out to lock the gate. Returning to the vehicle, he proceeded to the other end of the base, glancing back obsessively to make sure the $10,000 rockets were still there. He turned off at the sign for the anti-tank range. His platoon would be waiting for him. It was ten o'clock. He was ready.

The range consisted of a firing line in front of a wide field of armored rubble. A civilian would have had trouble discerning what the rusty metal objects were, but soldiers had no difficulty imagining a formation of tanks, heading into battle. Against *them*. Cruz and his men would stop the tanks dead in their tracks. That was the scenario… And they believed it. Soldiers believed a lot of things, thought Cruz as he parked the weapons carrier behind the bleachers. Soldiers were *trained* to believe.

Tanks coming over the ridge.
That's all the rockets we have.

Now wearing his helmet, Staff Sergeant Cruz gave them all a briefing on how to fire the AT-4. He then stood on the firing line and sent a rocket downrange. The fiery tail behind him served to warn them: tanks are toast downrange, but soldiers are toast behind the shooter. They broke into pairs, while Cruz started walking back to the weapons carrier.

"Hey, Eduardo!" someone called out. "Let me give you a hand with those." The man started walking toward the truck.

"I'm okay," replied Cruz. "You guys talk through the procedures while I bring your weapons." Eduardo opened one of the boxes and lifted a rocket, cradling it like a baby. "One at a time!" he shouted across the gravel parking lot. "I want to control the pace of firing. Slow and steady... Too much help and I lose it."

"Okay," came the response from the firing line.

The lieutenant, standing in the bleachers, nodded approval. He stepped down and approached Cruz. "How many rockets do we have?"

"Twenty-five, sir... That's it for the year."

The lieutenant took a quick look at the boxes piled in the bed of the weapons carrier. Eduardo held his breath and prayed the boss wouldn't count them. "Good, Sergeant. Let's get started."

The firing went smoothly. Staff Sergeant Cruz was all efficiency, handing the weapons to each firing pair one at a time. He used each firing to teach the rest of the unit the finer points of taking out a tank with one shot. He also kept everyone away from the truck. As he placed the twenty-fifth empty box on top of the ten full ones, he paused to take a few furtive deep breaths. It was only a little after 1300. The workday was scheduled to last until 1600. His cleanup routine would take about two hours. He did not need a bunch of idle soldiers hanging around the magazine area while he disposed of the boxes. He needed for them to be engaged in something else, preferably far away from the ASP.

"Sir," he began, standing far enough in front of the truck to prevent the lieutenant from inspecting his cargo again. "That's it for ordnance today… I recommend you take the platoon on a rucksack march while I get rid of these boxes." He motioned to the hills. "It is still a beautiful day!"

The lieutenant thought a minute and decided that a five-mile hike with combat-loaded packs would be a good way to finish the day. His men were full of adrenaline from the shoot and would appreciate a chance to burn it off. "Okay," he said. "Good shoot today, Sergeant. You've earned yourself an early knockoff."

The lieutenant's smile told Cruz that everything was falling into place.

"Thank you, Sir… See you next month." Staff Sergeant Cruz saluted smartly, got into the weapons carrier, and drove it across the post to the Chevy parked under the trees.

It took him only ten minutes to make the switch. He broke the ten rockets out of their crates and placed them quickly under the Chevy's *tonneau* cover. After placing all the boxes back in the weapons carrier, Cruz drove to the ASP. *The point of no return*, he thought. *From now on, I am a criminal.* At the disposal area, he counted the boxes again, just to make sure. Then he recorded the expenditure of thirty-five AT-4s and turned in the military truck. It was an effort for him not to run, but he resisted the urge. *All will be fine*, he told himself. There was no way anyone could possibly know. The main gate was unmanned. He would merely have to drive away.

***

The Murrah Federal Building had stood in the center of Oklahoma City. Now there was an empty field where government employees no longer worked and their children no longer played. The single worst act of terrorism in American history had been perpetrated, not by an Arab fanatic, but by an average young native from the heartland.

The speculation had been otherwise at first. And with good reason. The United States, having been largely immune from the international terrorism of the seventies and eighties, was now at the top of multiple foreign terrorist target lists. Some called it the downside of being the world's only superpower. Others explained it as a consequence of high technology and globalization. Still others blamed America's unflagging support for Israel. It was, in fact, all those things and more. The World Trade Center bombing of 1993 by Muslim extremists had brought a new feeling of vulnerability.

Not even during the Civil War, where battlefields were mostly well-defined, had US society at large been subjected to the specter of random violence. Terrorist battlefields were, by definition, *unde*fined. Every citizen was a potential victim. But domestic terrorism had never been considered a serious threat. The American system of openness and freedom of expression had not been thought to lend itself to shocking political violence—that is, until Timothy McVeigh had demonstrated his freedom of expression using five thousand pounds of fertilizer mixed with fuel oil.

Jerry and Gabriele stood at the chain-link fence surrounding the site where a monument would soon rise. Even though it had been four years, the fence was still adorned with flowers and words from loved ones. As she read about the project, Gabriele thought about the chairs that would represent each victim. One hundred and sixty-eight chairs, sitting empty atop a stone pedestal, would provide the same number of martyred souls with a physical connection to the site. She silently thanked them for giving their lives, however unknowingly, to make America wake up to the reality of homegrown terrorism. Perhaps, she thought, there was a place in heaven reserved for people who gave their lives for others. If there was, she knew that Carl would be there. Gabriele walked away from Jerry so he wouldn't see her tears.

She looked up and noticed a large tree standing alone in the field. The old American elm had somehow survived the blast and now served as inspiration for people mourning those who did not. She and Jerry walked over and found a plaque at the base of the tree.

The spirit of this city and this nation will not be defeated; our deeply rooted faith sustains us.

Gabriele looked at the sky for a full minute. Then she lowered her gaze to the man beside her.

"Thank you for bringing me here, Jerry."

"We'll come back when the memorial is finished, Gabriele. It is our duty to remember."

It was the first time Jerry had called her Gabriele.

***

With Oklahoma City behind them, Jerry began to sense home. It seemed to Gabriele that his disposition improved with declining population. He had finally yielded the wheel to her and found that she could handle a large truck with ease. It was nice for Jerry to just relax and watch the cornfields race by, thinking all the time about the plan. They would get married and settle into his ranch house, then he would teach Gabriele the things she needed to know. Shooting, self-defense, and clandestine communications topped the list. They would also need to drive all the roads, devising an escape and evasion plan. He would have to train his new wife to act like a local, if only to exude enthusiasm for the cause. Jerry couldn't imagine Gabriele as a cowgirl, but he was prepared to be surprised yet again.

By late afternoon, with Jerry back behind the wheel, they were sailing through eastern Colorado. Gabriele was amazed at how all the Plains states looked alike. Without the road signs, it would have been impossible to tell the difference.

"When are we going to see the Rockies?" she asked. Gabriele had seen pictures, but after twenty years in the United States, she had never made it to the continental divide.

"They're just on the other side of Denver, *Schatz*. We won't see them until tomorrow morning. Once we get to Denver, we're only three hours from Cheyenne. Then the fun begins."

A hundred miles east of Denver, a relatively clean-looking motel came into view. The road had punished them for the fourth day in a row, and this was the only place they had seen for a long time.

"This looks like our best bet," said Jerry cheerfully.

"You mean our *only* bet, *Junge*."

"Yeah... But all we need is a hot shower and two somewhat comfortable beds," said the big man. "Maybe they even have a gourmet restaurant," he teased.

"Right... I haven't been to one of those since we met. What will it be tonight? Rubber chicken? Burned hamburger?"

They laughed, but then Jerry dampened the mood. "You'll have to learn to eat crappy food, *Schatz*, especially if we're accepted into Thorne's compound. I'll try and make it up to you after this is over."

Gabriele spoke to his profile. "When do you think that will be?"

"I wish I could tell you." He turned to look straight at her. "Remember the moving funnel? Once we get sucked down deeper, it might be a long climb out."

"I'm scared, Jerry."

"That's a *good* thing... Being scared makes you careful... And being careful increases your odds of survival."

"Are you not ever scared?"

"Yes... In fact, I'm scared right now." Jerry slowed the truck and veered onto the exit ramp. "But *courage* is the key, Gaby...doing what needs to be done—in spite of being scared." Jerry started to pull into the motel's parking lot. "I learned that from Carl."

"That's good enough for me," said Gabriele. "Just teach me the skills I will need to get things done, and I will do whatever it takes."

She hesitated then continued less confidently. "What does it feel like to kill someone?"

Jerry answered carefully. "I'll teach you to do that, Gaby, but if I do my job, you'll only need that skill as a last resort...self-defense if I can't be there. Killing is sometimes part of the mission. You just do it...and try not to think about it."

"Okay... I am ready to learn."

"Roger that," said the big man, pulling into the parking lot. "We start the day after tomorrow."

***

As they approached the Rockies the next morning, Gabriele was disappointed. The high mountains, already dusted with snow, were farther from the city than she had imagined. And the peaks were partially obscured by an orange haze, hanging over Denver. She could remember visits to the Bavarian Alps as a child. Granite spires towering over villages, reaching into blue sky. Progress, she thought, certainly has its drawbacks.

"This is not what I expected," said Gabriele. "Perhaps something…cleaner."

"Denver is a huge city now," responded Jerry. "When I was a kid, the sky was always clear. Wait till we get west of Cheyenne, Gaby. Fewer mountains, but no pollution." A big smile lit up his face as he lapsed into local dialect. "Hell, there ain't enough people livin' there ta do the pollutin'!"

It was true. Jerry was happy to be from a state with more senators than congressmen. The cattle easily outnumbered the people. So did the prairie dogs and the antelope. He was proud of his turf and couldn't wait to show it to Gabriele. Three hours later, they crossed the border.

Gabriele glanced at Jerry as if to make sure he was still there. Somewhere out there, she mused, is the man who ruined my life. Her focus shifted back to the boat off Captiva.

You all need to be warriors in your own ways.

When she'd listened to Reggie Stewart that day, she had not understood the reality of her commitment. Now she did. The challenge of her life—her life's very purpose, she now thought—lay ahead. Thanks to fate (she wasn't completely sure about God's role in all this), Jerry would be by her side. Two warriors seeking justice. Retribution. Everything made sense. The first period of waiting was almost over.

"I want to go straight to the ranch," said Jerry as they sped past Cheyenne. "We'll come back here once you get comfortable at home, okay?"

"Sounds good to me," replied Gabriele. "It looks like Cheyenne will not require too much time. It's so small, and there is no urban sprawl, just nothing."

"Wait till you see Lone Mountain, *Schatz*. Population: 168. And that's a metropolis compared to some other towns in the area. I've seen larger settlements in the Amazon jungle."

"I find this fascinating, Jerry," responded Gabriele, gesturing at the window. "I mean, look at the landscape. So brown and so… empty," she said with a childlike sense of curiosity. "I have never seen anything like it. No wonder Germans want to see the American West. There is nothing remotely like this in Europe…no pun intended."

Wyoming spread before them, seemingly to infinity. Grassland and rock, rock and grassland. Undulating, then flat, then undulating again. Miles of nothing. Miles from nowhere. An oil refinery, its towers peeking over a low ridge, the illusion of a cargo ship plying the sea of sage. A gas station on the interstate, abandoned. Farther ahead, a green sign announcing the iconic town of Laramie. No mountains at first, but slowly rising terrain far off in the clear sky. The Snowy Range emerging to the left, then a single snowcapped peak growing right in front of their eyes, still way in the distance. There was something mysterious about it, mused Gabriele. Like it didn't quite belong there. She imagined that the Creator had finished the Rocky Mountains and, having some material left over, had simply tossed it over his shoulder to this spot. If so, she thought, this accidental monument must be one of his proudest accomplishments.

"That's home, Gaby," said Jerry, pointing ahead. "Definitely a different planet than Captiva. It's your home too now. You'll have to act like you love it."

"No need to act on that one!" she burst out.

Unlike most people, Gabriele became more serious with excitement. Instead of laughing, she turned to Jerry and asked him the most important question on her mind. "How's my audition going so far?"

"You have natural acting ability, Gaby. After this is over, you'll probably end up onstage somewhere."

"And where will *you* end up, Jerry?"

The question caught him off guard. "The ranch, *Schatz*. I want to die in Lone Mountain."

As they made the final push toward the ranch, Gabriele could see why. Jerry's spread was at the base of the mountain that had stirred her imagination from so far away. The sun had already dropped behind the summit, but she could see black-and-white images that promised color with the morning light. Raising a long cloud of dust, Jerry applied more speed as he approached the house.

"I smell the barn…literally!" shouted the big man.

Gabriele had not seen Jerry so animated since the day she'd married Carl. In the wake of the tragedy, she had watched him carry an enormous weight on his shoulders. That weight seemed to be lifting, at least for now. She felt her own load lighten a bit and enjoyed the moment. They both needed moments of bliss to propel them forward…into a violent world of unknown dimensions.

Without the benefit of a familiar fragrance, Gabriele's first glimpse of the compound came a few seconds later…six buildings, clustered together in a grove of trees. There was a big brick house, a guesthouse for Jerry's ranch hands, a long wooden barn, a garage for farm vehicles, a large aluminum shed, and a smaller shed made of wood. Jerry stopped and looked at Gabriele in the waning light.

"Welcome to my home, Gaby. It looks like Jack and Diane are out…probably at a meeting in town. You'll get to greet everyone in the morning, including the dog and all my cows."

"Jerry…it's beautiful!" Gabriele stepped onto the gravel drive and shot another look at the mountain. "You can be forgiven for wanting to die here."

"I'd like that to be a long time from now, Gaby." Jerry's mood turned serious. "We'll get each other through this…I promise you." He motioned to the door, but Gabriele stopped short of the threshold.

"After you, cowboy."

***

Eduardo Cruz, citizen-soldier, merged onto Highway 101 going south. It was only four o'clock. Eight hours until the meeting with Murdock. He had already rejected the option of staying on post. It was too early to wait at the rendezvous. It would be foolish to go home. He decided to drive up and down the highway until it got dark. Only on the road, in the company of other vehicles driving the speed limit, did Cruz feel safe.

He became more and more paranoid as he killed time. Even though the rockets were wrapped in gray army blankets, he feared they might slide into the wall of the bed and explode. He worried about the consequences of getting into an accident, but he tried not to drive *too* carefully, thinking that might attract attention. He also worried about his Hispanic face being pulled over for a green card check. That would be the ultimate insult, he thought.

My father's name has been here longer than any Anglo *name!*

The flash of outrage actually served to soothe him. But not for long. He spent the next three hours looking in the rearview mirror.

At seven, the sun was finally on the horizon, and Cruz made for the rendezvous site. He turned onto Highway 46 east into the parched hills, following the route his father had taken them twenty years before. An hour of careful driving later, he was sitting in his truck behind the duck blind at the end of a dirt road. He stared into the blackness all around him. No cars. He listened for animals. Nothing. Only dead wildflowers covered the San Andreas Fault for the night. It was the most remote place he'd ever been. For the first time since he had become a criminal, Eduardo Cruz relaxed.

He fell asleep in the stillness. Just for a few minutes. He woke with a start and continued looking for the headlights he thought might come early. The lights did not come until a little before midnight. It had to be Murdock. There had been no other cars for a long time. As the headlights came closer, Cruz got out of his truck and walked to the edge of low the wooden wall. Soon he would have his fifty thousand dollars. Enough to solve all his problems. He decided his criminality had been worth it. But he was still overwhelmed with guilt. On the way home, he would stop at the San Miguel Mission and beg forgiveness.

Maria, lo siento mucho.

The headlights went out. As if synchronized, the moon drifted into a bank of clouds. Cruz could hear the sound of an engine, but he could not see the approaching vehicle. *It* must *be Murdock!* Paranoia returned. If it wasn't Murdock, then it would be the police. Cruz realized he was trapped at the end of a one-lane, dead-end road. The rationale for choosing the rendezvous site had backfired miserably. The car kept coming. He had no gun and nowhere to run. He knew Murdock did not know the road well enough to drive it without headlights. He thought he was dead.

The vehicle stopped a few yards in front of him. Cruz stopped breathing. Roy Murdock, wearing night vision goggles, got out and closed the door. Without saying a word to Cruz, he walked around and opened the rear hatch of his Jeep Cherokee.

"That you, Roy?" Cruz whispered as loudly as he dared.

"Yes, Teddy, it's me," replied Murdock in a normal tone. "You got the stuff?"

"I have them," whispered Cruz. "Ten of them."

"You don't have to whisper, dude," cracked Murdock without taking off the goggles. "There's no one within twenty miles of this place." He wore a cocky grin, but Cruz could not see it. "Let's see the loot."

"Let's see the money first, Roy."

Murdock laughed. "Oh, yeah," he responded slowly. "The money." He tore off the goggles and produced a red-lensed flashlight. Reaching into the back of his vehicle, Roy withdrew a metal box. In the dim light, he opened it to reveal a pile of cash bigger than anything Eduardo's imagination could have conjured. He held the box at arm's length. "Fifty grand…your half…just like we agreed. "Now let's see the AT-4s." Murdock laid the box back in the bed.

Cruz led Murdock back to his Chevy and ripped off the *tonneau* cover. Roy picked up one of the rockets and pretended to sight it in. "Oh, baby… What I could do with one of these!"

"You're selling them," Cruz reminded him. "Who's buying… *Narcotraficantes*?

"Yeah, if ya wanna know. It's those Mexican dudes."

"They are very bad people," said Cruz firmly. "Let's get this over with."

Murdock laid the flashlight on the ground, and the two men transferred all ten rockets to the Cherokee in less than five minutes.

For Cruz, the mission was almost over; for Murdock, it was just beginning. Equal risk, transferred along with the weapons.

When the last rocket was loaded and covered, Cruz walked to the front of the Cherokee for his payment. "Okay, Roy... I've done my part. Give me the money and go do whatever you have to do."

"Here," said Murdock, handing him the metal box. "This'll get your mother all fixed up...with maybe some left over for you."

"Don't call me again, Roy."

"Don't you worry about that, Teddy," said Murdock with a smirk Cruz could only hear. He picked up the flashlight, turned it off, and put his night vision goggles back on.

Eduardo walked quickly to the Chevy and opened the driver's door. He leaned in and placed the box on the passenger seat. He wanted to be back in the safety of the open road. The cars, like birds in a flock, would hide and protect him.

Roy Murdock pulled the nine millimeter out of his belt and sank into a combat stance. Cruz stood erect, preparing to sit down in his truck. Murdock fired two slugs into his back. It was such a simple kill, thought Murdock dispassionately. A quiet kill. Only the soft thuds of silenced rounds leaving the barrel—and the even duller thud of a body slumping to the earth.

"You never were much of a halfback, Teddy." Murdock walked over to make sure Eduardo Cruz was dead. He was. Rolling the body over with his boot, Murdock reached into the cab and retrieved the box of counterfeit bills. Except for Murdock's footprints and tire tracks, there was no evidence that anyone besides Cruz had been there. The authorities would think it was a drug deal. All those Mexicans were dealing drugs.

The killer looked out at the cold night and then back at the bleeding carcass. Vulture food. *Fucking spic!*

Roy Murdock drove the Cherokee back to Highway 46 and followed the road east to Interstate 5. Feeling the high of a close kill and the satisfaction of a job well done, he settled in for the duration.

It was a long way to Wyoming.

Chapter 7

The Homestead

So gorgeous was the dawn that Gabriele, who never got up early on purpose, stood outside listening to the day begin. It was chilly, and she wrapped herself more tightly in the blanket from her bed. As the sun winked at her from the east, she turned to behold its light, cast on the mountain behind. God's wonderful mistake. She could not begin to describe the orange and yellow hues emerging from the snow-streaked slopes. Looking across the field, she was startled by a pair of antelope staring at her. At the other end of the pasture (if that was the correct word), she saw scores of cattle grazing. Jerry's cattle. The scene was beyond bucolic. There was magic here that would take her some time to define. That, she noted with real pleasure, was the purpose of this day.

Gabriele threw off her blanket and walked toward the fence. The illusion of being in a zoo prompted her to try to touch the antelope. When they ran, she was not disappointed. There were many more, farther out in the field, along with deer and other wild animals she did not recognize. She lowered her eyes and examined the grass. The soft light gave it a yellow-green tint she had never seen before. Almost the color of a Vireo's breast feathers. It was as if the sun had penetrated the brown blades at just the right angle to expose a hint of green underneath, waiting for a far-off spring.

A golden eagle glided over her head. She had never seen the golden but recognized it right away because Carl had shown her bald eagles in Virginia. Her sudden sadness was diminished by the belief that Carl might be with her now. Gabriele now saw the eagle as a reincarnation. She was tuned into nature. It was the only way she knew how to pray, to listen to the heartbeat of the earth and *feel* its splendor. Yes, she thought with overwhelming joy. *Carl is here!*

"Gaby! What are you doing out here in the cold this time of day?" It was Jerry, still in his robe, walking from the porch, calling to her. "I thought you were a late sleeper," he said in a normal tone as he joined her.

"That was before you brought me here, Jerry. This is one of the most beautiful spots I have ever seen…and certainly the quietest." She looked at him apologetically. "I have to admit that my expectations were quite low."

"I'm glad you like it… How 'bout some breakfast?"

"Some dark coffee would be lovely."

"I have an expresso machine, *Schatz*. One cup of European coffee coming up."

Jerry went back into the house, while Gabriele lingered another minute. She wanted to record the scene and save it for a time she knew was coming. A time when should would need to call on something bigger than herself. Bigger than herself, plus Jerry. Gabriele wanted this moment in her memory for when the demons came. Whatever happened, she would be protected by the magic of a Lone Mountain morning.

After a huge breakfast of pancakes and eggs, cooked by Jerry, Gabriele was ready to get started. She had turned the page; now she would have to begin reading it. The first order of business was a tour of the ranch. She went up to the bedroom, got her notepad, and met him in the driveway. Before they could begin, a young man in work clothes came out of the caretaker's house, followed by a black-and-white Border Collie.

"Mornin', boss… Time for me to meet your lady!"

Carefully, Jerry placed his oversize hand on Gabriele's shoulder. "Meet my fiancée, Jack… Gaby, this is Jack Ellis." Jack, who was young enough to be Gabriele's son, extended his hand and smiled up at her.

"Pleased to meet ya, ma'am."

"Call me Gabriele," she said warmly. "Like the tennis player."

"What tennis player?"

"Never mind, Jack… How 'bout just Gaby?" She was attempting to change her manner of speaking, just a little. She wanted to be a bit more colloquial. A bit less foreign.

"Sure…and congratulations! Jerry's told me and Diane a lot about you."

"Oh, he *has*, has he?" Gabriele had not been part of a family since her early teenage years. Suddenly, she remembered how it felt.

"This here's Trampas," said Jack, bending down to scratch the dog behind the ears. "He belongs to the boss, but Diane and I keep him busy."

Gabriele reached for Trampas's head and delivered a good introductory scratch. "I guess he works here too," she offered.

"You should *see* him work, Gaby… We couldn't run this place without him."

Jack motioned to a small group of large black cows, separated from the rest of the herd. "Got to feed the bulls, Jerry. Diane'll be back from the store in a little bit. She'll catch up with Gaby then… See if she needs some help gettin' ready for the weddin' or anything… See you folks later." Jack got on a small tractor and drove off toward the hay enclosure, Trampas bounding along behind.

"A very nice young man," confided Gabriele when they were alone.

"Jack will be my best man, Gaby. Susan will attend you, right?"

"Yes," replied Gabriele tentatively. "I need a maid of honor, and she is very anxious to visit us."

"We'll explain that your parents have passed away and that Susan is your best friend from Washington." Jerry smiled. "She doesn't look like a cop."

"Can she stay for a few days?"

"Absolutely!" said Jerry, trying unsuccessfully to temper his enthusiasm.

"She likes you, *Junge*." Gabriele watched Jerry's eyes as they widened slightly.

"What makes you think that, *Schatz*?"

"She *told* me, dummy!" Gabriele was laughing and enjoying the moment.

"That right?" he asked with a broad smile that gave him away again.

"Let me put it another way, Jerry… She *really* likes you. Except for that crew cut!"

Jerry rubbed his head self-consciously. "It's comfortable…and more acceptable to the militia people."

Gabriele gave him a mischievous look. "And I think you like *her*… Am I right?"

"She's a nice girl, Gaby… But I'm marrying *you*." He thought for a second, and added, "Although Susan should visit us about once a month, don't you think?"

"That sounds about right…until, that is, we are lucky enough to move in with Thorne's gang."

"We'll need to make them feel lucky to have us, and we will." Jerry and Gabriele nodded up and down to each other and changed the subject.

The tour began. "Here we have the famous 'Jumping Frog Ranch,'" Jerry announced with flair. "You missed the sign on the way in last night. It's a cigar-smoking frog under a parachute."

"A nice touch, if I may say so," said Gabriele playfully. "Did you buy this place a year ago when you got back?"

"No, not at all. I couldn't have afforded it. This spread is almost nine hundred acres. A conservative estimate puts the value at around $900,000. Then there's the stock and the machinery. Hell, you're looking at $1.5 million here, maybe more. If my uncle hadn't left it to me, I'd be doing what Jack and Diane are doing."

"I didn't know I was marrying a rich guy, Jerry."

"You're not," he said dismissively. "Just 'cause this place is worth that much doesn't mean I could ever sell it. Who's got that kind of cash, anyway?" Jerry let her digest that fact. "Not Jack Ellis. He's got a good deal, though. He and his wife run the place for me. I pay 'em a salary, and they get to raise cows without going into debt. Problem is, when I give them that salary, there isn't much left over. Ranching is a brutal way to make a living."

"So you're land-rich and cash-poor," she responded quickly. "That puts you in the same league as most of the aristocracy in Europe. You're a gentleman farmer."

"I hope you like being 'Mrs. Jumping Frog Ranch,' Gaby."

"I always wanted a title." She laughed.

Jerry took Gabriele's arm and guided her to a maze of split-rail fencing and chicken wire. Crude wooden structures covered some of the dark soil. Other enclosures contained giant rolls of hay. Muddy tire tracks led them into the largest of the pens. "This is where we gather the cows to load them," said Jerry, gesturing. "We move 'em up that ramp and into the trailer."

"How many to a trailer?" asked Gabriele, taking notes.

"Usually, we get ten or eleven… Depends on how big they are." He stopped to think a second then began again. "Most of 'em weigh between 1,100 and 1,200 pounds when we ship 'em."

"Do you have to push them into the trailer?" asked Gabriele with growing fascination. "That could be a real fiasco."

"No…mostly they go on their own. The cows don't know where they're going. They're not very smart, ya know."

"Where do you take them, Jerry?"

He hesitated, not wanting to offend her. "To a broker, *Schatz*. Then they're sold again and turned into steaks."

Gabriele did not normally feel stupid, but the reality of slaughtering cute, innocent cows had somehow escaped her analytical grasp. "Oh," she said. "I knew that."

"It's a terrible thing, Gaby, but man has got to eat. I don't do the killing myself… Please don't look down on me for it."

"I don't… Really, I don't, Jerry. I just wish they were not so adorable. How do you keep from getting to know them personally?"

"First of all," he instructed, "there's a whole lot of 'em. That's why they call it a herd and not a family. We usually keep 'em until they're around three years old, but we don't name them. They get a number, tagged on the ear."

"And a brand?"

"Yeah, the Jumping Frog brand." Jerry scanned his realm and then focused on Gabriele. "They have a nice life while they're here."

"I can see that," said Gabriele, looking up at the slopes of Lone Mountain. The Quaking Asps and Cottonwoods laid a carpet of brilliant orange up the small valleys at the base of the peak. "That's quite a mountain you have there."

"If I were an Indian, I'd worship it." He paused then quickly added, "I mean a Native American, of course."

Gabriele smiled at his political correctness. "You have my permission to worship it anyway," she replied thoughtfully. "God has made it worthy."

"You have a way with words, *Schatz*."

"You have a way with cows, *Junge*, at least for the first three years."

***

Jerry walked Gabriele through the rest of the compound, explaining how the ranch was managed. Back at the house, she found herself out of breath again.

"How high are we, Jerry?"

"Jeez... I forgot to tell you about the altitude!" Sheepishly, he continued. "It's about a mile and a half... You'll feel it for a few days, and then everything will be normal. I forgot to say anything because I'm so used to it."

Gabriele took an exaggerated deep breath. "Thanks for the tour, Jerry... I look forward to breathing normally again." She took off the designer sunglasses he had yet to replace. "What's next?"

"We drive around the mountain."

They took the smaller four-wheel drive pickup and followed a dirt road all the way around Lone Mountain. A creek, struggling in the same direction they traveled, revealed a rainbow of colored grasses. It was not the moonscape they had seen from the interstate; there was great beauty in the desolation before them. And no people. Gabriele was amazed they could still pick up a radio station. Again, the song was about her.

She needs wide-open spaces
Room to make a big mistake.

She needs new faces
She knows the high stakes.

They came to the end of the dusty track and drove back toward the ranch on a state road. Being from a small country with many rivers and then the East Coast, Gabriele had never seen a road with absolutely no bends in it. More seafaring than driving.

Thirty minutes later, they cruised into Jerry's hometown. Lone Mountain reminded Gabriele of the small farming villages she had visited as a child in the German countryside. Only smaller. The first thing she saw past the Welcome sign was the chapel.

"That's it," said Jerry. "I called the preacher this morning to reserve it for next Saturday."

"There does not appear to be a rush," said Gabriele with a surging sadness. She had been married for the second time in a cathedral the size of the *Münster* of Ulm. Now she would go through the motions of getting married in the smallest church she had seen since the farmers' chapels of her youth.

There was one main street, with a general store, several warehouses, an old wooden barn, and a library. Gabriele estimated the library to be just large enough for her own book collection back in Florida. A few modest houses lined the end of the street, one of which sported a large sign: "Walter Johnson, Sheriff." The Medicine Bow River separated the main part of town from its only hotel. Coming off the one-lane bridge, Gabriele saw another sign: "Food, Bar, Rooms." It was a tired wood frame structure with a shriveled garden in front. She guessed the garden looked better in the spring.

Driving back over the bridge, Jerry stopped at the general store. "Come on in, *Schatz*. This is pretty interesting."

It was more than interesting, she thought, looking over the varnished wooden shelves lining three of the store's walls. Not efficient, but somehow effective. The store looked like the living room of a country house.

"*Sehr gemütlich!*" said Gabriele, feeling the warmth of a small town. "Very cozy!" She smiled warmly at Jerry. "When are we going to see the preacher?"

"We won't see him until the day he marries us, Gaby. He lives down the road."

"How *far* down the road?"

"Only about seventy-five miles."

Gabriele raised both of her perfect blond eyebrows.

"That's not very far by Wyoming standards," explained Jerry. "Everybody here drives a long way to get anywhere. He knows what to do when he gets here."

"I guess he does," said Gabriele, wondering just how she would get through the ceremony. Her life was upside down.

A long way from over you. Turn the page. Room to make a big mistake.

Gabriele fretted about her situation for a while, then she accepted that it was all part of the mission. What irked her, she supposed, was that Jerry seemed to be enjoying this part of the mission more than she was. *The mission always comes first.* It had been his mantra. She decided to enjoy this scene in their play.

Neither of them expected to enjoy what they hoped would come later.

***

Susan Mackenzie walked into Gerhard Beck's office at FBI Headquarters. It was exactly the same as the last time she had visited. Papers and books everywhere. Like a small bomb had recently exploded. Three coffee cups, only one of which contained hot coffee. An old couch made of fake leather on which he slept a couple of nights a week. One straight-backed chair for visitors. Pictures, plaques, and certificates all over the walls. Susan's last name was the only thing that had changed.

Beck put down the phone and looked up from his notes. "Hi! Cup of coffee?"

"No, thanks, Gerhard… I'm back to one a day. What's up?"

"I wanted to go over our end of *Lariat*."

Susan sat down in the visitor's chair. "I got a call from Gabriele this morning… They're at the ranch."

"How's she doing? I'm worried about her."

"She says everything is okay. The altitude took some getting used to, but she is comfortable. They seem to be on track."

"When are you going out?" asked Beck.

"On my way," replied Susan. "They're getting married day after tomorrow. I'm going to attend Gabriele."

"Good," said Gerhard, businesslike. She hated him businesslike.

"Do you have anything specific you want me to pass on to either of them?"

"Just give them the plan for meeting with us in Cheyenne."

"Okay, Gerhard. I'll go through the whole thing with them. I would like to move out there soon so we can start rehearsing the SOPs… That okay?"

Beck looked at the ceiling. That was the only part of the office without distractions. He rubbed his close-cropped hair and looked back at his ex-wife. It was hard to imagine her as a colleague, but he was glad he'd brought her into this. Susan was the key to his control of the operation. Getting her out to Cheyenne was the next step. "You can move out there after they've made first contact with the militia." Continuing without a smile, he asked, "Any potential problems so far?"

Susan hesitated momentarily. "Jerry didn't mention this, but he has a caretaker couple working the ranch for him. They live on the premises."

Beck sat up straight, and Susan braced for impact. "God*dammit*, Susan! What the hell did he withhold *that* for?"

"I guess he thought it was a detail that would give you second thoughts about the plan."

"He's right about that!" thundered Beck. "I had reservations about that guy right from the start," he stammered. "He's a cowboy!"

Susan mustered a kindly smile. "Of course he's a cowboy, Gerhard. He's from Wyoming."

"You know what I mean!" Beck shouted back. "If this thing fails, it will be because of that egotistical muscle man."

"Gerhard, dear, you're being way too hard on Jerry. He has a personal stake in the success of this operation…just like Gabriele and the rest of us. He brings skills you could never find anywhere else, and he cares about Gabriele. He's got the perfect profile for Thorne and his gang, and he's proven himself under the pressure of combat. Did you know he was wounded in Colombia?"

"Yeah, I saw it in the investigation report. He's got courage, Susan... That's not in doubt. I'm really worried he'll get Gabriele killed."

"Oh, I see," she shot back. "This is a *rivalry* we have here!"

"What are you saying, Susan? You think I'm being too protective of Gabriele?"

"I think you have the hots for Gabriele."

"Horseshit! I just want her to be alive at the end of this thing. I feel responsible for her. Christ... I *am* responsible for her!"

"I think you should just let Jerry take care of her. He won't touch her, if that's what you're worried about. I know women. Gaby's too devastated to get involved with him." She wanted to add that Gabriele was too devastated to get involved with Gerhard either, but she didn't. "Okay?"

"Okay, you're right. I've got enough to worry about."

Susan nodded, businesslike. "I'll be staying at the ranch for a few days after the wedding. That'll be the best time to go through our dead drop and personal meeting procedures. We have to assume that they'll be followed after they make contact with the militia, so we'll have to recon all the sites now."

"Absolutely," responded Gerhard. "Get the clandestine infrastructure laid out, go through the SOPs, then brief me when you get back."

"I'll also be able to give you an assessment of whether or not the caretaker couple will be a security problem, okay?" She softened her tone. "And I'll make sure that Gaby's doing well."

"Good... You think I like putting her in this position? It might be the only chance we have to infiltrate this group and bust them. Otherwise, I wouldn't be taking advantage of a grieving widow."

"I know, Gerhard. But try not to worry. We have the right team out there... And that includes me. Gaby trusts me, and I trust Jerry."

Sergeant Mackenzie stood up, leaned across the desk, and kissed Special Agent Beck on the forehead. "Relax, dear... Everything will work out."

She walked out of Beck's office and drove to the airport.

***

Shortly after 3:00 a.m., a Jeep Cherokee cruised past Memorial Stadium. There were two men in the vehicle, both wearing camouflage uniforms, or what *looked* like camouflage uniforms. These days, as the men had observed, if you wanted to look like a soldier, all you needed to do was buy a forest- or desert-patterned set of fatigues and put on a pair of hiking boots. Stores selling these, as well as uniform accessories (and weapons), had proliferated in recent years. Uniforms, thought the bigger of the two men, are not what they used to be.

The Cherokee pulled into the parking lot near the softball field and stopped. While the driver waited, the bigger man shouldered his military ALICE pack and walked slowly across the field to the trees lining the fence. It was a cyclone fence with barbed wire coiled at the top, tracing the perimeter of the installation. The barbed wire was loose and broken in several places, and the cyclone lattice was full of corrosion. The man had heard the Wyoming National Guard used a lot of taxpayer money—his money—but he knew from his reconnaissance that Detachment One of the 155th Engineers did not use it for fence repair. Neither had they spent it on a surveillance camera for the back lot where the unit's trucks were parked. Perimeter security, he thought with a smile, is not what it used to be.

Our militia is much better than their militia.

The soldierly man put down his bulging pack and started cutting the cyclone fence mesh with a pair of heavy bolt cutters. The trees shielded him from the road. Dragging the pack, he peeled the bottom of the fence away and crawled under. Once inside the parking lot, he put on the pack and stood behind a large truck, looking for movement. There was none. National Guard units were not at the top of anyone's target list. This operation, he told himself, would be like taking candy from a baby.

The smaller man watched through binoculars as his partner went under the fence and picked his way through the truck farm. As soon as the intruder got to the side of the main building, the driver put the Cherokee in gear and turned the corner. They had rehearsed the mission profile many times. He knew it would be exactly two minutes until the pack had been laid next to the brick wall, and the attacker had slid under the fence again.

The driver scanned both sides of the road as he coasted to the pickup point. Still nothing. Laramie, being a college town, did not get quiet until after midnight. But then it got real quiet. And 3:00 a.m. was near the end of the midnight watch when attention spans lagged. The getaway car glided by without stopping as the man came from under a tree, opened the door, and jumped in. The driver accelerated and found the interstate just as the bomb detonated.

The explosion rocked half of Laramie. It was heard by a state trooper five miles down the road toward Rawlins. But the Cherokee did not travel that far. The vehicle left I-80 and sped toward the Snowy Range without lights. The driver wore night vision goggles, illuminating the gravel road as he put distance between the bombers and their victims. The police quickly set up two checkpoints, east and west of the scene, but the Cherokee would not rejoin the interstate for a long time. There had been no witnesses. No one would be able to identify the getaway vehicle. Nobody was even sure there *had* been a getaway vehicle.

The police disestablished the roadblocks at daybreak and concentrated on forensic evidence that might lead them to the perpetrators. They discovered that the explosive used had been C-4 plastic, a very difficult material to obtain. By the end of the morning, they had learned from the Defense Department that no C-4 had been reported missing at any military installation in the last year. An all-points bulletin was issued for…who or what? The motive was also a mystery that could only be solved by a claim of responsibility that had not been forthcoming. Multiple law enforcement agencies were quickly at a dead end.

The brick building lay in ruins. First responders had arrived at the scene within minutes to search for and rescue victims. Miraculously, according to the commander of the unit, only one solider had been killed, an active-duty buck sergeant assigned to perform administration for the reservists. The others, sleeping at the facility, had been saved from fatal wounds by an interior wall and several heavy safes. Despite disappointing casualty figures, the attackers believed they had successfully delivered their intended message.

It had been a very productive morning for DEFCON One.

Chapter 8

The Bride

Gabriele wore last year's wedding dress, unwrapped carefully and cried over privately the day before. Jerry had found an old suit that still fit. Susan, after fixing a flower to Jerry's lapel, had driven them to the church. Jack Ellis stood at Jerry's side in a pressed pair of blue jeans and a clean flannel shirt. In the back of the church, which was only twenty-five feet from where Sam Iverson did the honors, sat Sheriff Johnson, Diane Ellis, and the proprietor of the general store, Ernie Sylvester. Ernie's wife was taking pictures with her new point-and-shoot camera. There was no organ, so they played the appropriate music on a boom box behind the sheriff.

The tears in the bride's eyes were genuine. The congregation, such as it was, believed the tears came because Gabriele was happy to be marrying such a good man. In fact, she cried for the missing life she had hoped to share with Carl. The ceremony began, and as rehearsed, Jack produced the diamond Jerry had entrusted to him.

With this ring, I thee wed.

For Jerry, this statement marked the official beginning of *Operation Lariat*. He kissed Gabriele for what he knew would be the only time in his life. The bride kissed him back as authentically as she could. She had always wondered if actresses were able to feel the kisses they delivered on-screen. She found the answer to that was a resounding yes. Gabriele had no romantic feelings at all for Jerry, but those in the church would have been surprised to hear it. As the couple left the tiny chapel, they were pelted with birdseed (Gabriele had insisted on seed instead of rice). Staying as much as possible with tradition, Gabriele turned and handed her bouquet to Susan, the only single woman present. The police officer blushed as Jerry watched. Then they all drove across the bridge to the wedding reception.

They dined in the town's only hotel, which had been contracted to serve an authentic Wyoming meal. This was for the benefit of the women from the East, but it was also because the hotel had nothing else to serve. As she stared at the plate in front of her, Gabriele thought the meal might be part of her training. Slicing into the chicken-fried steak smothered in a white sauce, she tried to make her criticism sound funny.

"Jerry," she deadpanned, "this is the worst schnitzel I have ever eaten."

"It's not a schnitzel, *Schatz*," responded Jerry without missing a beat. "If Wyoming were a separate country—which lots of people out here think it is—then chicken-fried steak would be the national dish."

The wedding party—all nine of them—laughed heartily. Eight of them were amused by the notion that anyone would be incapable of enjoying a good chicken-fried steak; the ninth laughed at herself, pleasantly surprised that she really liked these Wyoming people.

"It *looks* like a schnitzel," she continued with more confidence. "And this white stuff looks like *bèchamel* sauce…only with sawdust mixed into it." After the second round of laughter, Gabriele realized she had a talent for entertaining people. She also realized that this translated into a talent for fooling them, whether a tearful wedding or a chicken-fried steak.

"Actually, this is the best meal I've eaten since I got to Wyoming… Jerry's been doing all the cooking, you see." As they all laughed again, Gabriele found that she enjoyed being funny in front of a crowd. Like some of her other recent self-discoveries, it felt good.

Susan spent the night in the hotel and thought about Jerry. Jack and Diane stayed in their cottage and did not disturb the newlyweds. Jerry and Gabriele were left to enjoy each other on their wedding night, alone in the big farmhouse. The happy couple enjoyed each other, but not in the way everyone imagined.

Jerry spread a map of Wyoming on the dining-room table and went through the most likely spots they would select to perform clandestine communications with Susan. They drank beer and talked some more about ranching. With more candor than ever, they also talked about themselves. Jerry learned, with the help of the beer, that Gabriele had gone through a terrifying first marriage. She had fallen in love with the wrong man, who had beaten her and left her pregnant. She even told him about the desperate abortion and her lingering guilt.

Gabriele learned a lot about Jerry that she hadn't heard on the drive up from Florida. She found out that his marriage had suffered and died from a lack of intimacy in the face of a Navy career that had always come first. He had been surprised, he had told her, that the marriage lasted as long as it did. She found Jerry's story strikingly similar to Carl's. Seeing the bigger picture, she suddenly became more serious.

"Jerry...are you afraid of dying?"

"Not really," said the big man. "I know it's coming...someday... maybe sooner than I want." He took a deep breath and locked eyes with Gabriele. "I'm more concerned with the way I'll handle it... I mean, people die the way they've lived. I've seen it with my own eyes. Those who live bravely die bravely. Cowards die like cowards."

"You have certainly lived bravely, Jerry. I am sure that wherever—and however—it happens, your death will be a brave one."

Gabriele averted her eyes and said the first thing that came to mind. "I have always lived curiously, so I suppose I'll die wondering what there is to learn about the experience."

There was nothing left to say. They would never talk about the prospect of death again. As the evening came to an end, Gabriele found herself liking Jerry more than she had imagined she ever could. Her comfort was reinforced by the large collection of books surrounding them. She had been furtively checking the titles all evening, not asking, but wondering how a warrior-cowboy had ended up with the classics. There were complete sets of Jack London, Mark Twain, John Steinbeck, and Ernest Hemingway, along with a few American authors Gabriele had never heard of. Astonishingly, Jerry also kept books of English poetry. She assumed the books had been given to him along with the house.

"You have a great book collection here, Jerry."

"I have lots of time to read them...especially in the winter."

Gabriele was momentarily taken aback. "And how many of them have you read?"

"All of them," said the cowboy. "I majored in American literature."

"You have a degree?" asked Gabriele as diplomatically as she could.

"Not quite... I was going to night school in Norfolk for years, but I was too busy working for Carl to finish the program."

"I see," said Gabriele, not quite convinced. She got up and went to one of the bookshelves. "Where did you go to night school?" There was no skepticism in her tone.

"Old Dominion."

"They used to beat the daylights out of us in basketball," responded Gabriele.

Jerry's eyes widened perceptibly. "You played basketball?"

"Point guard," said Gabriele, beaming. "The older I get, the better I was."

Jerry's laughter put her back at ease. Leaning against a row of William Faulkner volumes, she studied him more intently. Gabriele's hasty assumptions were evaporating before her eyes.

An interesting man, to be sure. "Good night, *Junge*."

"Good night, *Schatz*." He hesitated and then smiled warmly. "And congratulations...to both of us."

The bride went upstairs to her own bedroom. That was the deal.

***

The next morning, Susan returned from the hotel, and the three of them got into Jerry's truck for the long drive through south-central Wyoming. They planned to come back to the ranch that night. Jerry had told Jack Ellis they would be coming in late, explaining that he would be giving Gaby and her best friend a tour of the area. When Jack had asked him about the honeymoon, Jerry had given him a manly grin, explaining that he and Gaby had spent a romantic vacation recently at her beach house in Captiva. That was the end of speculation that the newlyweds had not had a proper honeymoon. Jack would tell everyone else in town.

Jerry drove them out to the interstate and headed west at the posted seventy-five miles per hour. He was feeling very good, with Susan next to him and Gabriele at the far end of the bench seat. He glanced at the two women talking excitedly to each other—one, a partner; the other, perhaps more than that.

He was lucky to be paired with Gabriele, for whom he was developing great respect. Under different circumstances, he could have easily fallen in love with her. She was, he had discovered, more than a beautiful woman with a lot of courage. She was more intelligent than he was. She soft-pedaled her intellect, he suspected, to make him feel more comfortable with her. Gabriele had a way of making Jerry feel good in a nonsexual way.

Susan, on the other hand, reminded Jerry that he needed a woman. She did not flirt openly with him but drove him crazy nonetheless. Jerry had always had a crush on Dorothy Hamel, and Susan was her double. He thought that Susan could probably skate like Dorothy Hamel if she put her mind to it. Right from the beginning, Jerry had decided that Susan Mackenzie was the woman for him. Given the tactical situation, however, he didn't know if he could ever make it happen.

West, down the straight pavement they went, until turning north. Jerry drove an undulating road through some of the most desolate country either of the women had ever seen. Antelope watched them from both sides. A moonscape upon which the sleek animals looked strangely out of place yet somehow belonged. Twice, the trio passed small ponds that concentrated ducks and other wildlife in marshy oases. Then moonscape again, with barren hills rising in the distance. Gabriele wondered how anything could live on the alkali-stained dirt, dotted with sage and stretching to the horizon. She had read about the wild horses out there, and she hoped to actually see one. Instead, she saw the earth begin to wrinkle. Rocks protruded from the tops of steep ridges like giant teeth, set in reddish gums.

They had been driving for two and a half hours when they passed the sign for Mineral King. Uncharacteristically, no one spoke; they all knew what it meant. The headquarters of the Militia of Wyoming was only twenty-three miles away. It was time to start looking for a good spot along the road for future dead drops.

They found it at Split Rock, ten miles farther on. As he pulled into the parking lot, Jerry explained that Split Rock is a national historic site, commemorating the pioneers who trekked west in wagon trains during the nineteenth century. Both women were amazed by the enormous rock formations, now looming in front of them. The rocks framed a notch in the soaring landscape. Through this notch had passed some of the toughest people in history.

Susan, aware that Jerry had more experience than she did, looked around the parking lot for a suitable dead-drop site. Gabriele, hands on hips, beheld the rocks rising from the shallow basin of the Sweetwater River.

If the pioneers could do this, I can do whatever I have to do.

She felt him next to her. "Why Wyoming, Jerry? I mean, why did they come through *here*? It looks so inhospitable!"

"Three reasons." He raised a large finger to count them. "One, they needed good water every day. They got it from the river down there," he explained, pointing to the valley below. "It's not too much, but it flows all year—and it flows west to east. That's hard to find on the plains." He continued counting. "Two, they needed a dependable supply of grass for the horses. As you can see, there's enough of that along the river too." Jerry handed the binoculars to Gabriele. "Third, they needed a passable grade though the Rockies. That can only be found, it turns out, at South Pass, about sixty miles that way." He pointed straight west.

"How did they know where they were going?"

"They used scouts—mountain men—who rode ahead and found the three things wagon trains needed. After the first few years, there was a trail the wagons could follow. The ruts are still visible in some places." The big man drew a deep breath. "It sounds like a great job…to be a scout. If I'd been here back then, that's what I would have done for a living."

"You would have been great at it," affirmed Gabriele. The sun, unhindered by clouds, glinted off her new

Susan came back from the restroom and motioned them into the truck. They sat as before but didn't drive anywhere. "Okay, folks, this is the primary."

"Dead drop?" asked Gabriele. Jerry nodded, enjoying Susan's first attempt at clandestine communications. Not judging her. He was simply anxious to see how well Gerhard Beck had trained his newest employee.

It wasn't really that hard. You just needed a spot to locate a concealment device—with a note or a tape recording inside—and another spot for placing the load signal. He looked around the parking lot and realized they were absolutely alone. He checked the road and again saw no one. This, he confirmed, would be a good spot for communicating with Susan.

Susan continued. "This is where we leave messages for each other after you guys get into Thorne's compound."

"*If* we get into Thorne's compound," Gabriele interrupted.

"Yes, but let's assume you do. The bigger assumption is that you will have the opportunity to visit this site in time to get information to me, or from me."

"We'll all have to be patient," Jerry put in. "Gaby and I will improvise as best we can…even if we have to escape and evade." He smiled at Susan. "Tell Gerhard he did a good job making you into a spy."

"I'll tell him you said that, Jerry." Susan waited a few seconds then added, "I'll also tell him that he got the right husband for Gabriele."

Her manner was so professional it was personal. He could feel her trying to impress him with her skill. She was succeeding. He thought at that moment that he and Susan might actually have a future someday.

"This is a concealment device," Susan went on. She held one of those fiberglass rocks homeowners sometimes use to hide spare keys.

It was about the size of her small fist. "You put the note or cassette tape in here and carry the rock out to the farthest history sign from the restroom."

Susan led them to the posted narrative, describing the lives of pioneers on the Oregon Trail. She squatted down and furtively laid the fake rock behind the wooden post holding up the sign. It blended perfectly with the soil.

"Any questions?" she asked, looking up at Jerry and Gabriele.

Gabriele had many questions but blurted out the most important. "What if a child—or a dog—finds the rock and breaks it open before we can get to it?"

"That's why we encode the note," replied Susan. "I'll cover our encryption system back at the ranch. It'll be impossible for anyone without the codebook to know what we say." Then she said grimly, "Now a cassette tape would be another story altogether."

"It's a good spot," Jerry offered. "Where are you going to put the load signal?" He had explained to Gabriele earlier that the load signal was something visible during normal activities. The signal would indicate that a concealment device was in its place and contained a message to be serviced. Without the load signal, there would be no reason to risk retrieving the device.

"In the restroom," responded Susan. "I'll smear lipstick in the corner of the mirror."

"Which restroom?"

"Female. You'll have to send Gaby to this site...or just wait until you can check it yourself. There don't seem to be many women—or men—around here." It was true. They still hadn't seen anyone else. Not even a car going by.

"Which corner?" asked Jerry. "And how are you going to make sure the signal we see is not from the last time the site was used?"

Susan looked up at him, trying not to appear as though she hadn't thought of that. But she hadn't. "Southeast corner. Imagine a map of the US... I'll mark Florida. Erase it with a tissue when you leave the site. That way, I'll know you picked up my message next time I check."

Gabriele was nodding up and down, feeling the thrill of communicating back and forth without anyone knowing. This seemed so easy...just common sense, really. But then she remembered Jerry's warning about not being followed. In its practical application, she realized, clandestine communication would not be as easy as it looked.

Jerry was more impressed with Susan's ability to think on her feet than with the repetition of rehearsed procedures. Her inexperience, he decided, would not be a problem. "Good plan, Susan... But I'm not going to carry a lipstick around, and Gaby might not be able to either."

"Use soap," she said quickly. "If there's no soap, use mud."

"Okay, that's a plan. But you know what they say about plans."

"What *do* they say?" Gabriele blurted out, fearing the answer.

"No plan survives first contact with the enemy."

Gabriele frowned. "Very reassuring. So *then* what do we do?"

"We go to the secondary dead-drop site." He shifted his attention to Susan. "Where do you propose to put the alternate?"

"I think we should try a place called Red Canyon," Susan responded. "From my map study, that looks like a good choice."

They got back in the truck and headed west. Mineral King came into view on the left side of the road through the blowing dust.

"Do you think we should stop and look around?" asked Gabriele. "I mean, we need to know the town well, do we not?"

"I think that would be a bad idea," said Jerry. "First of all, Susan can't be seen at all. If they recognize her as the woman with us today, she'll be joining Seth Goldman...wherever he is."

"Thanks for the heads-up, Jerry," Susan chimed in with a tinge of annoyance. "You're right, though, in this kind of town everybody knows everybody...who should be here and who should not."

"Second of all," Jerry continued, "Once we get to know these fine people, I want to pretend I've never been to Mineral King. I don't need to know anything beforehand that I can't learn from just driving by."

Gabriele did not understand Susan and Jerry's reasoning until she got her first look at Mineral King. At that moment, she saw how easily Susan could be recognized after one visit to the town's only café. There was almost nothing else there! You couldn't even call it a town. But there *were* signs that Mineral King had once thrived. Living quarters for the miners, boarded up. A brand-new elementary school, unused. A bowling alley, crumbling. A second café, shuttered. A dilapidated movie theater, not advertising movies. The ninety-eight residents lived rough in run-down houses and trailers. The town had dried up along with the demand for uranium.

Mineral King was, in a word, depressing.

"A great place to start a revolution," announced Jerry. "Let's go inspect the Red Canyon site."

They drove on toward Lander, turning left in the direction of South Pass. The site appeared well before the pass. They stopped the truck and found themselves alone again. Susan went through the procedure, identifying locations for the concealment device and load signal. She explained that they would have to use something other than a rock; in case the primary site was compromised, the bad guys would not know what to look for (assuming they found the secondary). Susan produced a plastic dog turd, opening it to show them the compartment. She walked to the dirt trail running parallel to the road and placed the device in the grass just beyond the path. She took a Coke can from her bag and demonstrated the load signal they would use: a common can of Coke, placed at the base of the sign describing Red Canyon to the few tourists that visited.

"If you bring binoculars, you can pretend to be looking at the large herds of elk that usually graze the opposite slope," added Jerry, helpfully. "This site will work, Susan… Thanks for doing your homework."

Gabriele's curiosity still haunted her. "What if the secondary site is compromised?"

"Then we improvise," said Jerry in a military tone.

"Escape and evasion, right?"

"We have a lot of work to do, Gaby."

"Where to, now?" asked Susan, sensing Gabriele's need to change the subject.

"Back to the ranch," replied Jerry. "It'll take us at least three hours." He grinned at both women. "So, we'll have to stop for chow on the way. Otherwise, I would fix you my famous meat loaf for dinner!"

The women looked at each other and just laughed.

***

The next morning, they were back on the road, this time driving east.

"Laramie has the only four-year college in the state," Jerry announced as they got off the interstate. There were some trees, but from a distance, the educational hub looked like most other Wyoming settlements. No urban sprawl. Just barren high plains, surrounding a town of Western legend.

Jerry drove through the town and then straight to the university. Gabriele was surprised again. The University of Wyoming campus was beautiful. Also a breath of intellectual fresh air. They stopped in front of the Coe Library, under a blazing willow tree.

"Come on in and check this out," said Jerry, stepping onto the curb. "Gaby, you may want to come here once in a while to read or do research. They have lots of stuff you can't find anywhere else in the area—even German-language magazines." They walked inside and passed a sign announcing "Gay Awareness Week," another indication of just how different Laramie was from the rest of Wyoming. Gabriele spent a few minutes going through the stacks. This would be her refuge, she decided.

They cannot touch me here.

Back in the truck, the trio rode past the bombed out National Guard armory down the street from the stadium. "Nice job," said Jerry, the tactician.

"Had to be the militia," responded Susan.

"We'll find out," said Gabriele with foreboding.

The ride to Cheyenne was more of the same. The road went up for a while and then down to a lower plain. The long snow fences continued to remind Gabriele that winter was on the way. Winter was always on the way in Wyoming.

"Most folks upstate consider Cheyenne a part of Colorado," lectured Jerry. "I don't care… I like it. Imagine a capital city of only fifty thousand people!"

"More of a capital *town*," added Susan.

It was a *nice* town, they all agreed. Gabriele noticed that the buildings—though unspectacular—were almost all made of brick and stone. A city built to last. She hoped Cheyenne would never develop the urban problems of coastal cities. She found herself liking it just the way it was—small, clean, and manageable.

"This is the O'Mahoney Federal Center," said Susan. "That building is where Gerhard and I will set up." She did not point, but she didn't need to. They stood in front of an eight-story structure, dominating the neighborhood south of the Capitol. It looked just like a federal building, thought Gabriele. Like the Murrah Building, pictures of which she remembered from news accounts. She decided that the government must use the same architect for all its outside-the-beltway buildings.

"We have arranged to borrow some office space from the ATF," Susan continued. "I'll take an apartment nearby. Gerhard will visit as much as he can. We'll be monitoring the militia and providing you with whatever you need to know."

"And backup," added Jerry emphatically.

"The best we can," said Susan weakly. They all recognized there was not much the bureau could do for them once Jerry and Gabriele were inside the Thorne compound.

"That will have to do," said Jerry a little more optimistically.

By now, all their objectives had been met—except one. Gabriele needed some new outfits, and Jerry knew just the place. They walked into a large wooden store specializing in all the articles of clothing she had never dreamed of wearing. There were Western shirts, cowboy hats, leather jackets with frill, and belt buckles as big as teacup saucers. Gabriele walked out of the place wearing a $300 pair of buff Tony Lamas. The boots made her look even taller, especially next to

Susan. Still sporting Jerry's gift of Oakley sunglasses—for the first time—she felt ready for *Operation Lariat*.

Gabriele looked like a cowgirl on a mission—exactly what she was. She hoped the militia would assume that her mission was the same as their mission. Jerry was more proud of his wife than ever, but he tried not to show it. Susan, fearing conflicts of interest and emotions, concealed her growing infatuation with Jerry. Under a facade of confidence, Gabriele was terrified. She had paid attention to the preacher.

Till death do us part.

Chapter 9

The Prophet

A man the size of a small grizzly crouched over the rickety podium. He leaned into the microphone and spoke again with a voice that shook the flimsy walls.

"So, what it boils down to, my friends, is this: We are embarked on a crusade, a struggle with the twin forces of government tyranny and genetic pollution. These challenges not only threaten our nation, but they are—right now—ruining our very lives. As white god-fearing Christians, we must heed the call of the growing militia movement. As a nationwide citizen army of freedom fighters emerges, we have to prepare ourselves to fight the evildoers wherever we find them. In order to do that, we must have our guns…and the courage to use them."

The bearlike man hesitated long enough to dramatize the bottom line. Then he looked straight at the back row. "When they come for us in the middle of the night, we—the patriots of the Militia of Wyoming—*will* be ready!"

The applause came even before he finished.

Following the example of three camouflage-clad figures in the front row, the crowd of men and women rose to their feet inside the old movie theater. Cries of "Right on" and "You betcha" could be heard above the din as the speaker stroked his flaming red beard… waiting. This is the best part, he thought.

I have *them.*

"Any questions?"

A dozen hands sprang into the air. "Yes, down there on the left," said the speaker, pointing.

"Mr. Thorne." A clean-cut man of medium height came to attention. "If we are an army, as you say, then why don't we have uniforms?" The man grabbed a handful of his flannel shirt to gain everyone's attention. "I mean, if we're soldiers, then we ought to dress the part...like those guys down in front."

Red Thorne nodded as if to agree, then he gestured at the front row. "These men are in camouflage because they like it...not because we make them wear it. I'm glad you brought this up, though, 'cause I don't want t'be misunderstood." He spoke an educated English, softened with a genuine country lilt.

"The reason we don't have uniforms is that we're not a *conventional* army. We are a guerrilla force. The Army of the United States—supported by troops from the United Nations—plans to enslave us!" A meaty finger rose and fell to the rhythm of the warning. "That army is the enemy of every red-blooded, white-skinned, loyal American. We are part of a great militia, made up of local citizens—armed to the teeth and dedicated to protecting our families and our society. The last time a militia saved this nation, they fought against the British Army. Our ancestors came from behind rocks and trees, wearing rags. And they harassed those Redcoats until the bastards finally went home. Thanks to our guerrilla militia, many of those guys never made it home at all!"

"Damn right!" shouted someone from the back.

"Guerrilla fighters must be like fish, swimming in the sea of the people," Thorne continued. "Uniforms would just make it that much easier for the federals to identify us. Think of our militia as a friendly neighborhood watch—with a pit bull in the yard. No better friend, no worse enemy."

A hundred heads nodded up and down. There was a palpable electricity in the air. A sense of anticipation. A feeling of belonging. The collective belief in a just cause. Confusion, so prevalent in America at the end of the twentieth century, had given way—at that moment—to a comfortable clarity. For the people in the theater, the issue was simple: us versus them. The huge man behind the podium radiated satisfaction as he saw his message resonate.

"Hey, Red!" one of the men in camouflage called to the stage. "Tell 'em these ain't uniforms at all. Cammies make us invisible in the forest, and they got more pockets than a pair o' jeans! We don't wear 'em in public, but we're gonna wear 'em when the war starts. Tell 'em that, Red."

"You just did, Jake," said Thorne, frowning a bit.

Jim Bridger Thorne scanned the audience for a woman to call on. Any woman. There were about thirty of them scattered around the room, all sitting with their men. He wanted to get them actively involved in the rally. He wanted them to become more like his wife, Jane. Married, yet independent. Soldiers too, teaching their children what to believe. Red Thorne would be their cheerleader; Jane Markham—plain to the point of invisibility—would be their inspiration. Staying with Wyoming history, Thorne had taken to calling his wife Calamity Jane. Most of his followers thought the nickname was a joke; some of those closest to him knew differently.

A female hand went up in the middle of the theater. The woman sat forward in her seat but didn't stand. She and her husband did not look out of place in the crowd. Neither would they have looked out of place in a country church.

"Sir, I'm trying to homeschool my kids. The government tells me I should send them to public school so they can learn about how bad white Americans are. I have four young ones, and I want to teach them the truth." The woman's husband nodded, looking around the room at the other people nodding their heads.

"I mean, one day, it's evolution, and the next day, it's how we killed off the Indians. I'm sick of havin' to tell my kids to accept creation and be proud of their heritage!"

Perfect, said Thorne to himself. *A candidate for Jane's circle.*

"*Yahweh* is almighty!" he thundered. "The Lord made us, and he will destroy the godless system that plagues us. He will free us from government tyranny, but in the meantime, your militia leaders are lobbying politicians in Cheyenne to allow more homeschooling. We need more mothers willing to educate their children with the truth. The federal government is out to get us. Armed defiance is the only way to stop them. For now, we must make our own classrooms at home—even if they *force* us to send our children to public school. Over time, this country will have a society where church and state work *together* to protect us all from evil."

Someone shouted from the aisle. "Why should we obey their godless laws, anyway?"

Thorne grinned at the man with whom he had planted the question beforehand. "Because if you openly break the tyrant's laws, you'll end up in the tyrant's jail. If that happens, you won't be ready when we need you. Keep a low profile. Buy guns and ammo while you still can. Attend our meetings and shoot whenever you get the chance. The *Brady Bill*, enacted just six years ago, was the first step toward civilian disarmament. Just look at what the government did in Waco. The day of reckoning is coming soon!"

Men and women shouted their approval as Thorne's words rattled around the old theater. Somewhere in the back, Jerry and Gabriele came to their feet again, clapping vigorously. Gabriele had struggled into the tightest pair of jeans she could find. She was wearing her new Western shirt, with a green John Deere hat. Jerry was decked out in his ranch attire. He felt more at home than he should have. If Gabriele was nervous, she didn't show it. Jerry thought she looked better than ever.

They studied the others in the room. Jerry was focused on the men, thinking about how he would bond with them. They were ranchers, farmers, firefighters, and mechanics. Even businessmen. He felt he understood them. He was, in fact, one of them. Gabriele concentrated on the women. She wondered why they were there at all. It must be more, she thought, than just having militia children and homeschooling them to hate the government. As far as Gabriele Tompkins was concerned, America was fine the way it was. More freedom than the rest of the world put together. The freedom, even, to preach revolution! She groped for some way to connect with the other wives.

As the sounds of followership (or was it cult behavior?) subsided, Thorne leaned into the microphone one more time. "This meeting is adjourned, folks. We've got some literature for you in the lobby, and we have a training schedule posted. We'll be shootin' at the end of the month. You can sign up for the best times now. I'll be takin' the men out to the north range, and Jane'll take the women south. Thorne smiled down on his adoring wife, stick-thin but packed with energy. "I know a lot of you are driving a long way to get here, and believe me, we appreciate it." He raised his meaty fist in affirmation. "See you folks outside!"

The lobby of the theater was full of tables, some displaying weapons, others laden with books and papers. Draped from the ceiling on the back wall was an American flag. It was upside down. A large Nazi swastika hung next to it. One sign summed up the speech they had just heard:

It's 1999. Do You Know Where Your Rights Are?

There was a pile of bumper stickers for sale. The usual.

Gun Control Is Hitting the Target with Every Shot
***Vegetarian*: Old Indian Word for "Poor Hunter"**
This Property Insured by Smith and Wesson
Buy More Guns

Jerry took Gabriele by the hand and led her to the books. Without speaking, they perused the collection. Jerry picked up a copy of *The Turner Diaries*, a novel about the coming race war in America, written long before the militia movement. Timothy McVeigh had taken a copy with him to Oklahoma City. Gabriele leafed through a copy of *The Anarchist Cookbook*, trying not to show the fear she felt in her stomach.

Bomb making for public consumption?

She asked herself what kind of country would allow such a thing. Her answer was easy enough—a country with too much freedom. She held in her own hands the recipe for the bomb that had taken Carl's life and ruined hers.

"The internet is making this stuff even more available to the average angry citizen," said Jerry, looking over her shoulder. It was almost a whisper. "And look at all these weapons…"

It was quite a collection. The militia owned more guns—and more *types* of guns—than Jerry had ever seen in private hands. There were American AR15s, Austrian Glock pistols, M9 Berettas, Chinese AK-47s, and a large assortment of hunting rifles, as well as the ancillary gear to go with all of it. He didn't take time to handle the weapons; he could fondle them later. At the moment, Jerry was more interested in meeting Jim Bridger Thorne.

"Let's slide over toward the door, Gaby… Time to meet *da man*."

Gabriele looked up from her reading and quickly composed herself. "Okay, let's do it."

Without attracting any more attention than they already had, Jerry and Gabriele picked their way through the crowd. As they moved toward Thorne and his wife, every man in the room stopped what he was doing to look at Gabriele. Jerry stood out as much as she did—not with the women, but with the men. He was getting used to it. Men looking at *him* to see if they had a chance with her. They didn't. He was confident he could protect her. From anything.

"Mr. Thorne," Jerry began, sticking out his hand. "I'm Jerry Tompkins… I'd like you to meet my wife, Gabriele." Jerry glanced at Gabriele lovingly.

Thorne shook Jerry's hand and nodded at Gabriele. "Nice to meet you both… This is my wife, Jane." Jerry could not remember the last time he had looked up at another man. *He's fat, though… Probably can't run at all.*

Jane Thorne took Gabriele's hand and smiled at Jerry. "You have a very beautiful girl here… Keep a close eye on her."

"I always do, ma'am… I always do."

"Please, Jerry, call me Jane." She looked up at her husband. "And call him Red…'cause everyone else does!"

"This must be your first militia meeting," said Thorne. "I don't think we've seen you before."

Jane looked at Gabriele. "That's right… I would have remembered that."

"Yeah," responded Jerry cautiously. "Gaby and I just came back to the state…to my ranch over in Lone Mountain." He paused, searching for something to add. "It's great to be back in Wyoming. Don't know why I ever left!"

"Why *did* you leave?" asked Jane without taking her eyes off Gabriele.

"My husband was in the Navy," said Gabriele, following the script.

Both Jane and her husband raised their eyebrows in unison. "Workin' for the New World Order, huh?" asked Red. It was not a question.

"I don't know anything about a New World Order, Red. I was a SEAL for twenty years. I did what I was told. But I just listened to your speech, and I agree with everything you said."

Thorne tried to disguise his surprise, but he could not. "Well, the Lord must be our personnel officer as well as our general! Would you like to join us? The militia needs people who know how to shoot."

"Yes, we would!" It was an energized Gabriele. "Jerry and I are tired of seeing this country ruined by the government. We want to help bring back the freedom they're taking away from us day by day."

"Amen," said Thorne. Looking at Jerry, he asked the question they knew would come. "Do I hear a foreign accent in your wife's voice?"

"Yes, Mr. Thorne—I mean, Red. She was born and raised in Germany, but I can assure you, she's a loyal American…a patriot."

"I can see that." Thorne grinned at his wife. "What we need around here is another good role model for the women…an Aryan goddess like Gabriele."

"I am hardly a goddess—"

"Oh, yes, you are," said Jane, cutting her off. "We have quite a few women in this group, but none of them are like you. They concentrate on their children—not that there's anything wrong with that—but most of them have nothing important to say. Do you have children, Gaby?"

"No!" she blurted out. "Jerry and I like each other too much!"

"That's good!" Thorne laughed. "Very good!"

Suddenly, Red Thorne was as serious as they had seen him on the stage. "No *Mutterkreuz* for you, eh, Gaby?"

Jerry shot his wife a blank, almost-panicked look. She kept her eyes on Thorne and fabricated a quick response.

"My grandmother had ten children, Red. Hitler himself gave her the award. I think that lets me off the hook."

"I guess it does!" said Thorne, obviously impressed. "Jane's not a mother either. Let's us concentrate on the mission."

"Us, too, Red," said Jerry quickly. "When's the next meeting? Gaby and I don't want to miss it… Right, *Schatz*?"

Gabriele nodded on cue. Red appreciated the German nickname. Jane ran a hand through her close-cropped brown hair and kept staring at Gabriele.

"We have rangework in two weeks. That's the 30th and 31st of October. Can you make that?"

"Absolutely. I'll arrange to have the hands take care of the ranch. Is there a place here where we can stay overnight? I'd hate to drive all the way back and forth twice."

Thorne grinned. "We have one run-down motel in town. The militia has given the owner enough money to fix up a couple of the rooms. That's where most of our long-distance members stay… those who don't have RVs. I can tell them to save you a room."

"Thanks, Red… Gaby and I would be much obliged."

"See you then, folks. Jane and I look forward to watching you shoot."

As they walked back to Jerry's truck, Gabriele wondered how on earth she'd be able to develop acceptable shooting skills in such a short time. Jerry was thinking about how they would script the scene in a motel room he was certain would be bugged. Once they were driving away, Jerry let out a long sigh of relief.

"A great first contact, Gaby… You were just perfect."

Gabriele reached for his shoulder with a hand still trembling. "Thanks, *Junge*… I find that I'm good on my feet, but Jerry," she sighed, "I don't know anything at all about guns."

"I have two weeks to turn you into a soldier," said Jerry evenly. "That should be enough."

"A soldier is the last thing I ever wanted to be."

"You have no choice, *Schatz*." A quick glance told him how worried she was. "This is war."

***

Jerry drove his bride back to Lone Mountain over empty roads. Even in the dark, it seemed to Gabriele that half the wildlife in Wyoming found its way into her field of vision. She couldn't tell which predators waited behind the luminous eyes beyond the pavement or which of those eyes belonged to prey. Darkness had taken away the landscape, leaving only wildness. Out there, she reminded herself, survival depended upon guile and luck. The same rules now applied to her. She had felt like prey in the presence of Thorne's evil.

Gabriele tore her attention away from the void. Jerry was lost in his own thoughts. She assumed it was "tactical stuff," as he had put it. Not wanting to discuss either tactics or her own fears, she pretended to sleep. There would be plenty of time tomorrow to learn about weapons and shooting, but Gabriele didn't have anyone at the moment with whom to share the terror in her soul. It was almost midnight by the time they got to the ranch.

They slept late the next morning, and after another of Jerry's pancake breakfasts, Gabriele went for a strenuous walk. Walking had become her greatest pleasure. In addition to the solitude, she needed the exercise. Jerry briefed Jack Ellis on the ranch chores and then got on the phone.

"Rios."

"Bosco, Butkus... How's the paramedic business?"

"Same as always, man... Long periods of boredom interrupted by sheer terror. Just like the old days, huh? I love it."

"I wanted to give you an update," said the big man. "We made our first contact with the target audience. Now that we've taken that step, I'd like to explain to you face-to-face what the hell we're doing."

"I'll just come out there," responded Jose. "You have room at the ranch?"

"Can't do that, Bosco… I don't want Gaby to know that you and I have a back channel, okay?"

"Got it, man."

"Can you meet me at Warren Air Force Base in Cheyenne?"

"Sure, I can," said Jose with enthusiasm. "I could use a vacation, and the Air Force always comes through." Laughing, he continued, "I joined the wrong service, you know… Should have gone into Para Rescue."

"You wouldn't have looked good in light blue, amigo… Can you be there on Wednesday at 1500?"

"Where on the base?"

"I'll take a room at the visitors' quarters. Find the number at the billeting desk and just knock. You can sleep there after I leave. I'll tell Gaby I'm going to the commissary… We need some groceries anyway. She won't know, and I don't want to worry her," Jerry rationalized. "She'll be fine at the university library. I can give you about an hour."

"That's probably enough to get me started, Jerry. Then I can see some of Wyoming. It's one place in this country I've never been."

"That's my recommendation anyway, brother. It would help all of us if you could do a thorough recon of the op area. You'll just need to stay away from Lone Mountain and one other place. I'll fill you in when I see you."

"Got it, man… See you then." Jose hesitated before adding, "Be careful, Butkus… The team is down to you and me now."

"Roger that, Bosco… You and me."

Jerry put down the phone and walked outside with a pair of binoculars. He found her on the creek road, power walking past his cows at the far end of the ranch. He stretched his legs and shoulders before going inside. Laying the binoculars on the table, he pulled a sweatshirt over his head and bolted out the door on a dead run. Trampas fell in behind him as he steadily ate up the distance.

Jerry Tompkins was a product of the toughest military training in the world. He was as strong as Dick Butkus in his prime, but he could run much faster. Except for wild horses, the high plains did not normally see such a combination of strength and speed. Jerry put on a show. *Perhaps she's watching me.*

She was. Walking fast on the windward side of the road, Gabriele was on her way back to the ranch when she saw him. She was waving. Like a truck in the dust, Jerry carried a cloud behind him. It looked to her like an approaching storm.

Then he was with her. "Mornin', *Schatz*." He was out of breath but able to talk. Gabriele kept walking, with Jerry and Trampas by her side. A seemingly carefree threesome. A family.

"Wanna run back?"

"Not at your pace, *Junge*."

"Your pace is mine," he countered, grinning. "Actually," he continued, "it would do you good to run."

"Escape and evasion?"

"Yeah, you never know when you'll be in a footrace with an opponent. It pays to be the winner."

"I cannot outrun a bullet, Jerry. As I understand these people, bullets are the fundamental means of communication." Gabriele broke into a slow run.

"They can't hit what they can't see. If we have to run, it'll most likely be dark."

"Running from Mineral King…to where?"

"To the road, Gaby."

"Will they not just chase us in a car?"

"We use the road to navigate, but we don't set foot on it. The road is the only thing out there that tells us where we are."

"Okay, big guy, you win." She sighed, picking up the pace. "Last one home does the dishes!"

Jerry was surprised again. Her body suggested an athletic youth, but he had not expected her to *still* be an athlete. Most women Gabriele's age were overweight and underpowered. She was a graceful machine.

After deliberately losing the race, Jerry washed dishes and cleaned the kitchen. They showered and were ready to go in less than an hour. It was just nine o'clock, she noted, as they jumped in the truck. Her unexpected energy in the wake of a bad night's sleep was liberating. Jerry had been right again.

Gabriele remembered the pioneers. *Toughness is an attitude.*

***

They drove across the interstate, back into the void. The widely scattered towns seemed like afterthoughts, not quite belonging to the terrain. As they sailed over the sagebrush sea of Jerry's imagination, the area reconnaissance continued.

"Medicine Bow," lectured Jerry, "is one of the most famous towns in the West."

"You have my full attention." Gabriele actually had a pad of paper in her lap.

"In the late 1800s, a man from the eastern establishment got off a train and stepped into the wilderness. That was Medicine Bow." Jerry looked out at the moonscape. "There was nothing here back then."

"Excuse me, *Junge*," Gabriele put in soberly. "There is nothing here *now*." The town was still over the horizon, but there was not yet any evidence to suggest civilization had arrived.

"I meant that there was no railroad beyond Medicine Bow."

"Go on," she said, taking notes.

"That man was Owen Wister, *Schatz*. He wrote a novel called *The Virginian*."

"Was that not a television show?" asked Gabriele. "I learned a lot of English from watching TV Westerns when I first got to this country."

"Yes, it was made into a series…great show."

"I do not remember anything about it except that the man was very handsome."

"Yeah, Gaby. He was the hero who got the girl…a schoolteacher, by the way." He shifted uncomfortably in his seat. "The kind of hero we don't see much anymore."

"Tell me about this Virginian… Is he *your* hero?"

"Yes," said Jerry with more emotion than usual. "He symbolizes everything an American is supposed to stand for. I have the book at home… I'll lend it to you."

"I would like to read it," said Gabriele thoughtfully. "Perhaps the story will allow me to understand *you* better."

"It will," replied Jerry. "You might as well read Mark Twain and Wallace Stegner while you're at it."

"Mark Twain?"

"Yeah, the book is called *Roughing It*. Twain came through Wyoming in the 1860s and made some interesting observations."

"Wallace Stegner?"

"The best twentieth-century writer, in my view, for describing the settlement of the American West." Gabriele copied the names in her notebook.

As they cruised into Medicine Bow, Gabriele was disappointed. There was only one real building in town, a hotel, three stories high, made of granite. The sign said the Virginian Hotel. A museum stood, rotting, next to the railroad tracks. Boarded-up stores, testaments to rural poverty, dotted the main dirt road. Medicine Bow, she thought, had probably looked a lot better in Wister's time.

"Jerry," she began, "this place is a dump."

"That's right, Gaby. This town is so focused on its past they haven't figured out that it has no future. The hotel will still be here when archaeologists dig for it, but there will be no evidence there was ever a town around it.

He parked the truck in the nearly empty lot, and they climbed out into the dust. "Come on in." He motioned her toward the stone monument.

As they entered the historic hotel, Gabriele was transported back more than a hundred years (not very long by European standards, she noted). Some of the interior reminded her of a modern truck stop, but the rest was a living snapshot of the old West. The obligatory animal heads looked down from every wall. The walls that still had enough space held black-and-white photographs of Medicine Bow in the old days, confirming that the town had indeed looked better then.

"This is the primary rendezvous site," whispered Jerry, bending to her ear. "If we get separated, this will be your destination. Get a room and avoid being seen. If I get here first, I'll do the same."

Jerry led her to a cozy bar. More animal heads. Men smoking. Television tuned to the Broncos pre-game.

"Football," she said.

"Quick," responded Jerry. "Who's the quarterback for the Broncos?"

"Number seven...John Elway."

"Very good, *Schatz*. You've been studying!" Jerry beamed. "If you have to come here, it'll be because we're separated and on the run. Under no circumstances can you go back to the ranch, okay?"

"Got it, Jerry... Let's get out of here."

They drove to the nearby town of Hanna so Jerry could show her the abandoned coal mine. It was a series of scars in the earth. Gabriele hated the very idea. Even *desolate* earth, she believed, should not be treated this way.

"This is the secondary rendezvous site, Gaby." They both looked around, memorizing the ghostly scene. "We shouldn't need to meet here, but if we do, there's enough cover and concealment to survive for a day or so."

Gabriele couldn't imagine herself evading across such a barren wasteland. "Assuming I survive to make it this far," she mused. "Teach me how to do that, Jerry."

"That's my job," said the big man. "Before we go into Thorne's compound, we're going to bury provisions here and along the route from Mineral King. These caches will sustain us in the worst-case scenario. I'll go through all of it, *Schatz*. When I'm done, you'll know how to knock a man down and steal his car."

Jerry paused as her eyebrows went up. "Survival is a series of problems to be solved, Gaby. You solve them one at a time until there are no more problems. Only then can you relax."

The drive back to Lone Mountain was by a different route. More sprawling wilderness, racing by her window. It was clear to Gabriele that she was going to need her new mental toughness. Powerless to explain it, she was actually looking forward to becoming a warrior.

Chapter 10

The Range

Five minutes after Jerry checked into his room at Warren, there was a soft knock on the door. He wasn't surprised that Jose had beaten him to the visitors' quarters and observed his arrival from across the courtyard. That's what he had been trained to do. Jerry unlocked the door and swung it open.

"Bosco!"

"Butkus!"

After a back-slapping bear hug, they got right down to business. There wasn't much time.

"Gaby and I are trying to infiltrate the terrorist organization that placed the bomb in DC that killed Carl. The group is based here in Wyoming," Jerry began. "We're working undercover for the FBI."

"Holy *shit*, man... Is Gabriele okay with that?"

Jerry gave his friend a broad grin. "She's a natural, and she's committed."

"You should tell her you're talkin' to *me*, man. She has a right to know."

Jerry considered his teammate's recommendation. He had argued with himself about this many times. If he told her, she would worry. If he didn't, she would find out eventually, and he might lose her trust. Now that he had brought Gabriele this far, perhaps it was time.

"You're right, Jose... I need to tell her. She's in this up to her neck, and she doesn't even know how bad it could get."

"That's the right call, man."

"But I'm not going to tell my contacts at the FBI about you," added Jerry. "The responsible agent is not totally convinced about *me*. His female colleague—our only link to the bureau once we go inside—she's another story that I don't have time to go into right now."

Jose Rios was the ultimate jack-of-all-trades. A one-man wrecking crew, ready to go anywhere and, if necessary, give his life for Jerry. They both knew this without saying it. The Latino was a former medic and fearless jungle warrior who could think or fight his way out of any situation. Jerry was *hoping* the FBI would be there for him and Gabriele; he had total confidence that Jose *would* be there. Anytime, anyplace.

"The Militia of Wyoming is an aboveboard organization with the usual anti-government rhetoric and a sharp focus on guns," explained Jerry. "Gaby and I have joined the group."

"And what does the militia say about your naval service?"

"I told them about the CIA trying to kill us… That seemed to help them overlook my government stink."

"Yeah, man… That would do it for me!"

"The FBI likes my combat record, and so does the militia," Jerry continued. "But our controllers think Gabriele is the key to getting us into the fold, that her German background will give the militia something ideological to admire."

"Makes sense," said Jose, nodding.

"And you should have seen her improvise at our first meeting with the militia leadership! She made up some bullshit story—on the spot—about her grandmother having met Hitler personally. It was impressive."

"The militia likes the Nazi thing, huh?"

"Boy, do they ever! They're not exactly history buffs, though. They never listen to anyone outside their own echo chamber."

"What's the plan?"

"I teach Gaby how to shoot. After she gets that down, we'll be working on escape and evasion. Then we just keep teasing the leadership at militia meetings until they bring us into their version of Club Med."

"You mean Club Dead, man."

"Yeah," said Jerry. "They're dead. They just don't know it yet."

He drew a long breath and switched gears. "Jose, I think you've figured out that the Militia of Wyoming—as an organization—did not bomb the National Air and Space Museum."

"Yeah, they're probably way too big…and too public. No operational security."

"The FBI thinks that the militia leadership operates a tight-knit terrorist organization, embedded in the larger group. The limited intelligence they've been able to gather points to a ranch outside the town of Mineral King. Our controllers want me and Gaby to get ourselves invited to live at the ranch and to report what we find out. There are a handful of other militia members out there, probably doing the dirty work. The FBI believes they operate covertly as a group calling itself DEFCON One."

"Great name," Jose put in.

"Yeah, this is the group that took responsibility for the DC bombing. And we think they have also conducted bombings of government targets in Wyoming. The ranch is isolated—within an area that's already one of the most remote in the whole country. The militia they use as a cover meets at the old theater in Mineral King. It's a great setup. You need to go out there and look at these places, but you can't let anyone observe you."

"You mean that I can't let anyone see my Colombian face, right?"

"That's right," said Jerry. "It would be like *me* showing up at a birthday party in Medellín."

"*Por cierto, amigo*… I got this."

"Also go to Lone Mountain… But the same thing applies. You'll have to be invisible to everyone in Wyoming until I call on you to come out of the shadows." Then he added, "Remember, Bosco, these people play jungle rules."

"I know the game, Jerry… But you and I need a way to communicate."

"Yes, we do. Gaby and I are using coded dead drops to communicate with our controllers. I'm planning to meet with you clandestinely at least once more as the operation develops. After that, you'll have to place all of us under surveillance—good guys and bad guys."

"I'm at your service, Butkus. It's great to be back in the field!"

With the aid of a road map, Jerry spent the next forty-five minutes filling Jose in on as many details as he could. At the one-hour mark, he got up and bear-hugged his friend again.

Leaving his room key on the dresser, Jerry left to pick up Gabriele at the library in Laramie.

***

Jerry spent the next two weeks teaching Gabriele to shoot like him. They worked all day, every day. He found her to be an eager student with a surprising aptitude for putting bullets into targets. That she could be taught to shoot at all was a great relief to him… But he had not been prepared for the complete transformation of a pacifist academic. Gabriele was quickly becoming a credible gun nut, with tight shot groups and a mastery of the technical details. Even her speech was evolving into something more acceptable to the militia faithful. Red and Jane Thorne, he was sure, were going to like what Gaby brought to the firing range.

On the day before they were to leave for Mineral King, Jerry took her to his personal range one more time. He had all his weapons laid out on two tables, one for rifles and one for pistols. He handed her large olive drab green cans of assorted ammunition and watched as she prepared to fire each gun. Jerry spotted her rounds, ready to offer adjustment tips and keeping score. Gabriele didn't need much advice. When she was in the groove, he took his eyes away from the spotting scope and admired her, crouching like a lioness, golden hair blowing in the wind. Jerry had never before felt pride in something he did not own. If those men in the militia have any testosterone at all, he said to himself, Gaby'll have 'em eating out of her hand.

Gabriele stopped shooting and brought the last of Jerry's weapons back to the table. "I like the AR15 best of all, Jerry. It's light enough to shoulder easily, and it doesn't kick too much." She brushed a strand of blond hair away from her eyes.

"What's your favorite pistol?"

"Your cannon is a bit too big for my hand. I actually prefer the Walther PPK."

Jerry laughed. "That .380 round isn't big enough to kill someone with a single shot, ya know."

"I know," she responded quickly, "but it fits underneath a belt in the small of my back… Or I can wear it in an ankle holster." Gabriele did not smile. "I like the feel of a concealed pistol against my body."

"If you have to use the PPK, double-tap the guy's center of mass and run like hell!"

"I can do that, big guy… Just make sure you're somewhere nearby."

Jerry walked over and patted her on the shoulder. "Great job, *Schatz*… You're ready to show off to the militia… But first we need to clean all these weapons!"

Gabriele reached out and gave Jerry a friendly hug. With a serious look, she said, "Thank you, Jerry, for getting me ready to do my duty. I won't let you down."

"No… I don't think you will."

***

It was still dark when Jerry's truck bounced along the dirt driveway, outbound. They had packed enough food and clothing for the weekend. Jerry took his SIG Sauer P226, but he'd left the other weapons at the ranch. The miniature tape recorder—the evidence-gathering machine he could fit inside his boot—remained locked up at home, along with his guns. Another step closer… But Jerry did not want to appear too eager. He would let himself and Gabriele be drawn into the funnel gradually, like most people. They had only one shot at it, and they could not afford to miss.

The drive to Mineral King would take three hours. Not many vehicles. No real speed limits. Only one traffic light at Rawlins, a

Wyoming metropolis of ten thousand. They did make an unplanned stop…for an antelope, merging without warning at almost the same speed as Jerry's truck. Completely alone, they glided over the moonscape, trying not to think about the worst-case scenario. Gabriele was the first to break the silence.

"Where's Susan today, Jerry?"

He pretended he had not been thinking about Susan. "Oh, I don't know… Let's see." He paused for effect. "She's moving into the apartment in Cheyenne this week, isn't she?"

"That was the plan."

"I want to debrief her at the ranch right after we get back."

"Yes," replied Gabriele. "I think we should… There's a slight chance that Thorne will invite us in sooner than we expect. I don't want Susan to be left in the dark."

Gabriele looked at Jerry's profile as he piloted his truck to their fate. "And I think you *need* to see her, Jerry." Carefully, she continued. "I just want you to know that I am ready to give you some time—just with Susan."

Jerry gave her a broad smile. "That would be great, Gaby. You know more about me than I thought."

"I'm a woman, Jerry. I see things that you might not."

"Human intuition is a skill set I just never developed, Gaby… You'll have to use it to protect me when we start living with the enemy."

"Gotcha covered, *Junge*."

Jerry hesitated and stroked his chin. "You okay with our script for the room tonight, *Schatz*?"

"I'm confident we can put on a good show… I studied my lines."

"Good… We'll need to assume that Thorne has the room bugged." Jerry took his eyes off the road and fixed them on his wife. "I won't touch you, Gaby, but the people listening must be convinced we're having rough sex… Sorry to put you in that position."

"So to speak," responded Gabriele seriously.

Jerry replied just as seriously. "Actually, I hope the room *is* bugged. That way, we'll be able to generate some early credibility. It'll be worth the discomfort."

Gabriele changed the subject. "I finished *The Virginian*... It *is* a great book."

"Now you can see why I've read it four times."

"I certainly learned a lot about *you*... But I also picked up a lot of historical context on Wyoming," she replied. Gabriele had discovered something else, something she did not want to discuss with Jerry. She'd found that she had a lot in common with the hero's wife, an independent-minded young woman from New England, out of place in the West but thriving. Beautiful, to be sure, but with a toughness developed through hardship. The parallels were striking, almost scary.

They tried to pass the remainder of the trip with small talk. But soon all conversation yielded to the silent visualization of what would happen in Mineral King. After a while, Jerry turned on the radio. They listened to right-wing talk shows until the town suddenly came into view. Perfect, thought Gabriele, as they rolled into the potholed parking lot.

"Showtime, *Schatz*," announced Jerry as they got out of the truck and stepped into enemy territory.

***

Jerry took in the rugged outback beyond Mineral King. Nothing between them and the white rocks of the Wind River Range on the western horizon. It was soothing to him.

"This is not the end of the earth, Gaby... But you can *see* it from here!"

He took her hand firmly as they walked into the building. Gabriele wore the John Deere cap, with a ponytail threaded through the backstrap. She had replaced her Tony Lamas with a pair of jungle boots Jerry had bought her at the base. He had helped her break them in with conditioning hikes on Lone Mountain. Gabriele was getting into the best shape of her life. Baggy pants and a large flannel shirt could not hide the evidence. She glided confidently into the crowded theater. Jerry held the door as the other men held their breath.

Red Thorne extended his hand to Jerry. "Welcome back, soldier." The bearded face turned to Gabriele Tompkins. "Good to see both of you!"

"It's good to be back, Red," said Gabriele. "Jerry and I can't wait to shoot."

"First we'll have a meeting," said Thorne. "Then we'll shoot." Looking over his shoulder at Jane, he joked, "Hey, Calamity, you didn't find any government officials to shoot at, did ya?"

"No, Red, I didn't," said Jane loudly. "I looked all over this part of the state... Couldn't find any." A small group had gathered around them, and everyone laughed. Gabriele laughed right along with them.

"I have a good imagination," she said, suddenly serious. "I will apply it to the targets."

"Bring any of your own weapons, Jerry?"

"Naw, Red, just the SIG. No room in the truck for the whole collection, but from what we saw last time, it looks like you folks got plenty o' bullet launchers."

Jerry surveyed the crowd and found a pair of eyes fixed on him. It was almost like looking in the mirror. The man was nearly as tall he was, blond, and obviously well-built. Jerry also noticed the man's eyes. They were the coldest eyes he had seen since the Putumayo mission. The men belonging to those eyes had never used them again. This man, cold eyes and all, would be Jerry's teammate, possibly his friend.

Red Thorne stepped between the two men and made the introduction. "Jerry, this is Roy Murdock. He's one of our best shooters. Runs the range most of the time. I want you to help him today and tomorrow."

Jerry stuck out his hand. "Pleased to meet you, Roy... You could be my brother!"

"I was thinking the same thing," said Murdock, softening at Jerry's greeting. "Red tells me you were a SEAL." Murdock's eyes quickly cooled again.

"Yeah... Now I got a ranch down in Lone Mountain." Jerry placed his hand on Gaby's shoulder. "This is my wife, Gabriele."

Roy Murdock had been looking at Jerry's wife ever since she'd walked into the theater. He switched to charm mode as he turned to Gabriele. "Hello, Gabriele... Hey, there's nothing finer than a beautiful woman who can shoot. Glad to have you here."

"Are you married, Roy?"

"Yeah... My wife will be over when the kids have finished their lessons."

"I look forward to meeting her," said Gabriele pointedly.

Thorne called the meeting to order. There were close to one hundred of his followers assembled. "Okay, folks... This is the last range time we're gonna get before the snow comes, so let's make the best of it. Roy's got some help today from our newest member." The bearded man pointed at Jerry and Gabriele. "This is Jerry Tompkins and his wife, Gaby. Jerry'll be helping Roy run the men's range. Gaby gets an A for just showin' up!"

All the men laughed. The women did not. Without smiling, Gabriele took off her baseball hat and held it up to the throng. She was very conscious of the looks she was getting. Lust from the men; ice from the women. She was used to it. She put her arm around Jerry and looked at the floor.

Thorne continued to whip up the crowd. He loved it. "We come together today to share the gift of firearms. *Yahweh* has given us freedom, and he has given us weapons to defend it. Shoot well so you and your families can sleep well... And when the time comes to fight tyranny, you will be ready. Remember Lexington and Concord!"

Applause, and some cheering, erupted in the crowd. *This is how that bastard must feel when he gives the State of the Union.*

The militia leader's voice had been transformed. It was joyful. It was rhythmic. It overflowed with authority. It was scary. The people were in his spell. Gabriele thought of Adolf Hitler, mesmerizing ordinary Germans, inducing many of them to commit mass murder. Jerry was still thinking about Roy Murdock.

After the speech, Murdock found him again. "Red told me to give you a ride to the range. Your wife will go with Jane and the women." Jerry nodded and followed. He caught Gabriele's eye on the way out and noted she was talking animatedly to Jane and three other wives. *So far, so good*, he thought as he climbed into Roy's SUV. Jerry looked behind him and saw that the Cherokee's back seats had been folded down, supporting an array of guns and ammunition. As they pulled onto a dirt road heading south, dozens of other vehicles turned into their dusty wake. It looked like a funeral procession. In truth, Jerry was looking forward to shooting. It relaxed him. It was also a good way to avoid talking.

"Red wanted you to help me run things today," said Roy. He turned to Jerry. "I don't need the help…just so you know."

"I'll try and stay out of your way… Is Red coming out?"

"No," replied Murdock. "He and Will are working the ranch today."

"Who's Will?"

"Will is Red's right-hand man. Didn't you meet him at the last meeting?"

"Is he the guy with all the arm tattoos?"

"That's him."

Jerry had seen the man in the crowd but had not been introduced. In fact, he felt that the stranger had been trying to avoid him. Now Goldman's reporting made sense. Will Jeffers, the monastic religious zealot, lurking in the background. *History is riddled with religious zealots*, thought Jerry.

Like bullet holes in a paper silhouette.

Jerry said nothing more about Will Jeffers. He wanted to strike up something close to a friendship with Roy, but he couldn't pass up the opportunity to take him down a peg. Right off the bat.

"So, Roy, you're not from around here, are you?"

"What makes you think that?"

"Er…just the way you talk, I guess."

Murdock fidgeted just a little then responded, "I grew up in California, but I've been with the militia for five years."

"Where do you live?"

A momentary hesitation. "Sadie and me, and the kids, live at Thorne's place."

Bingo!

"Sounds like Red has more help with *his* ranch than I have with mine."

"It works out okay for all of us," said Roy absently. Jerry got the impression the man realized he'd said too much. Jerry warned himself not to ask too many questions too soon. For different reasons, each man was happy to see the parking area.

Murdock stopped the Cherokee in another cloud of dust and got out.

The shooting range was five miles into the barren hills, nestled in a canyon, dotted sparsely with cottonwoods. The ravine provided about two hundred yards of shooting lanes and roughly a quarter mile of lateral maneuver space. The colors of the creek had so far ignored the threat of winter; the canyon still had an oasis feel to it. Out of sight and out of earshot.

Butch Cassidy, mused Jerry, would have liked this place. It was even possible that he and the Kid had taken refuge here.

Men of all shapes and sizes climbed out of the other trucks and began arranging their own weapons. Beards and smooth faces (but mostly beards) earnestly anticipating the practice of a sacred ritual. Wyoming men from diverse backgrounds, brought together by the dual belief systems of freedom and firearms.

"Listen up, people," began the range master. "Jerry here is gonna help me today and tomorrow. Everybody got a rifle? I got two AKs here if you wanna try 'em."

Roy Murdock proceeded to run the range—with very little help from Jerry—for the rest of the day. Jerry understood why Murdock was snubbing him. The man felt threatened. Jerry *wanted* him to feel threatened. From his low-profile position, he watched the man he assumed to be one of Thorne's killers. Jerry was impressed with the guy's bearing, his command of the situation, and the way he instructed the others. What Jerry found most useful was the way Murdock focused so completely on the task at hand that he seemed to lose the big picture.

He sacrifices strategy for tactics!

***

At the end of the day, the vehicles convoyed back to town and all the men pitched in to clean weapons. Later, Jerry found Gabriele in the bar with Jane and a few of the other women. Roy and most of the men sat down on the other side of the room, so Jerry sat with them. In their separate groups, Jerry and his wife spent the next two hours eating hamburgers, drinking beer, and ranting about everything from the tyrannical government to a decaying American society. The two reconnected in the parking lot and drove a short distance to the motel.

Gabriele introduced the next scene in their play the moment Jerry opened the door to the room.

"What a great day, Jerry! I spent all morning thinking about how good it would feel to shoot federals instead of paper targets! I spent the afternoon handling hot gun barrels, thinking about getting my hands on *your* barrel... I need the big gun, and I need it now!"

"How do you want it?"

"Use your imagination, *Junge*... Just make sure you're on full automatic."

"Think we can both fit into that shower?"

"Last one in has to soap down the other!"

"That'll be after I slam you standing up."

"Gimme that zipper... I don't think I can *wait* to get in the shower!"

"Jane was right... You're an Aryan goddess, my Nazi *Schatz*."

"I like the Aryan part better than the goddess part."

"I prefer the goddess part." Jerry paused. "Yeah, that's what I mean!"

As they had rehearsed, she was silent for a long minute.

"Fill me up, big guy!"

Somewhere at the Thorne ranch, Red and Jane would be having fun listening to their newest recruits. Jerry turned on the shower, interrupting the broadcast. The militia leaders had heard enough to believe that Jerry and Gabriele Tompkins were not FBI agents coming to roll up DEFCON One.

After taking turns in the shower, Jerry signaled to Gabriele to meet him outside. Once in Jerry's truck, they were able to talk freely.

Jerry turned on the cabin light and gave her a sympathetic look. "Sorry you had to go through that, Gaby. Pretty embarrassing… But I'm sure it'll pay off."

"It wasn't so bad, Jerry. All for the cause, you know." Gabriele was indeed embarrassed, but not in the way Jerry thought. She had been surprised to find their play within a play rather exciting. She looked away and changed the subject.

"How was *your* day?"

"Murdock still hates my guts, but I think we can work together. I'm in a pretty good position… How about you?"

"I have to say that it went very well with the women. I must thank you again, Jerry, for getting me ready to do rangework. I think they all expected me to be shy with a gun. I wasn't. None of the others had tighter shot groups than I did. Jane even asked me to run the range in the afternoon. I did better than I thought I would."

Jerry beamed with pride. "Beck was right, Gaby… You're the key to getting us invited to live at the ranch… By the way, I found out today that Roy and his family live out there. I'm not sure who else, but with luck, we'll soon find out."

"Would that be good luck or bad luck?"

"Good question, Gaby." Jerry looked at his watch to remind her that they needed to get back inside. "I think it depends on what they ask me to do in order to prove myself."

"You mean they'll give you a loyalty test?"

"Yeah, I just hope they don't order me to kill someone."

Gabriele was shocked. She had not considered murder as a possibility. Apparently, Gerhard Beck hadn't either. "Oh!" was all she could manage to say.

Jerry placed his hand on her shoulder. "If they do something like that, it will be *me* they test, not you. If that happens, I'll need all the good luck I can get."

"I'm scared, Jerry."

"Remember what courage is, Gaby. Now that we're in this, I have to do everything I can to gain their full trust. Try not to worry about me... You just keep kissing Jane's ass. And watch her... I think she likes you a little too much, if you know what I mean."

"I know what you mean... I felt it too."

Jerry carried a sleeping bag into the room and spent the night on the floor. Gabriele was comfortable in the queen bed but hardly slept at all. The next day was almost a replay of the first. Murdock gave Jerry more responsibility for the range, clearly on orders from Thorne. Jerry could see that Roy was watching him, evaluating him. Fair enough. Playing the rookie, he did his best, seeming to enjoy every aspect of supervising other men practicing to kill real people. Jerry blocked out the vision of government officials in a gunfight with these men. *Susan?* He concentrated on the shooting itself, just like he had as a chief petty officer all those years ago. He passed the day in a state of near bliss. By the time they had finished, he sensed that Roy had warmed to him, however slightly. On the way back to the Cherokee, Jerry decided to show Roy just how committed he was.

"I didn't see a .50-caliber sniper rifle out there, Roy. You need one?"

Murdock looked at him with a sudden excitement Jerry had not seen before. "Can you get us one?"

"Sure... I have one at home. You want it?"

"What kind is it?"

"It's a McMillan M88," said Jerry. "We used them in the Navy. One day I just took two of 'em, and no one said shit to me. I even have a box of ammo for it."

"Jerry, that's great! I'll tell Red and Will... They'll be grateful."

"I'll bring it to the next meeting, okay?"

"Okay, man, and thanks for the help out here."

Jerry would never be able to tell Gerhard or Susan what he was about to do. Giving suspected terrorists a sabotage weapon would be *way* out of bounds. He didn't care. It was his ass on the line, not theirs... And he needed the *bona fides*.

Jerry and Gabriele linked up at the theater, said goodbye to the others, and pulled out of the parking lot.

"Why do you always park backwards?" she asked. "Just curious."

Jerry smiled at his wife and pupil. "Tactical parking, *Schatz*. In case we have to leave in a hurry, I don't want to have to stop and shift gears."

Gabriele acknowledged what should have been obvious to her. "Escape and evasion, of course. Let's go home."

Chapter 11

The Promise

Susan Mackenzie made the two-hour trip from Cheyenne to Lone Mountain in just over four hours. A foot of snow had been cleared from the roadbed, but the relentless wind had blown most of it back. Visibility was near zero in places, and the temperature was not much higher. Susan approached the base of the mountain just in time to negotiate Jerry's driveway in the daylight. She pulled into the compound as a worried Gabriele was reaching for the phone.

"Come in, come in," said Jerry, quickly closing the door. "You must be freezing!"

"The winters out here are worse than I thought," announced Susan, glad to be safe, soon to be warm. "That windchill goes right through this jacket!" Jerry shook her hand and took the jacket. Gabriele gave Susan a long hug and showed her to a soft chair in front of the roaring fire.

The table had been set for a long time, so they sat down right away to one of the tastiest meals Jerry could remember. They had agreed to avoid all talk of the operation until after dinner. For more than an hour, it was just three friends and lots of laughing. Leaving the dishes on the table, they gathered in the living room for the meeting.

"Hot chocolate or whiskey?" asked Jerry with one last smile.

They all opted for whiskey.

"Okay, you two," began Susan. "Let's start from the beginning."

Jerry and Gabriele took turns narrating the events of the preceding three weeks. Susan took notes, stopping them frequently to ask detailed questions. She also asked for their opinions and assessments. By the end of the evening, everything had been said. Everything, that is, except the plan to meet with Gerhard Beck.

"When do we see Beck?" asked Jerry, looking at his watch. It was almost midnight.

"I would like to make it soon," replied Susan.

"Where?" asked Gabriele. "I assume we can't just walk into the federal building in Cheyenne."

"We should do it at Warren," said Jerry emphatically.

"Warren?" Susan was not familiar with the Defense Department's vast network of bases. Jerry's meeting with Jose had gone well, and he didn't see any reason not to use the venue again.

"It's an Air Force base outside of Cheyenne, Susan... Gaby and I use it for shopping sometimes. Military retirement privileges, and all that."

Susan nodded in agreement. "Okay... Warren it is."

"You and Gerhard could get access through Air Force headquarters in the Pentagon. It should be easy to come up with a cover story... Tell them you need help from the security police on one of your cases. Something like that."

"Good idea, Jerry."

"You can meet with Gaby and me at the visitors' quarters. The bad guys won't be able to see or hear us."

Susan's face betrayed a frightened look. She was impressed by the way Jerry and Gabriele had bonded so quickly. Anyone watching them would think they were really married (technically, she remembered, they *were* married). As a professional, she was encouraged; as a woman, she was scared. She did not believe that Gabriele had slept with him, but if she hadn't, her new friend was a very good actress. The pair was under tremendous pressure. If Gabriele fell in love with Jerry, it would be Susan's own fault.

The policewoman looked back at Jerry. "I'll get Gerhard to start lining up a visit. Let's try for next Monday... That okay?"

Jerry nodded his agreement as Gabriele stood. "Good night," she said, starting up the stairs. "I'll do the dishes in the morning, Jerry. See you then."

A few minutes later, Gabriele was in bed, and Susan was alone with Jerry by the glowing embers of the fire. "Do you think we'll keep her awake?"

"No way," responded Jerry. "She sleeps very soundly."

"You're her husband... You should know." Susan's voice was trembling.

Her comment was lost in Jerry's gratitude. "I've been wanting to say how much I appreciate your bringing me into this."

"It was my pleasure," she answered uneasily. "Gerhard needed you guys... But I feel terrible about getting Gaby involved. I don't think she realizes how easily she can be killed."

"Yes, she does... Believe me, she does."

"You think she'll be all right?"

"Trust me, Susan... She'll be all right. It's been one surprise after another," he continued. "She can act, she can think on her feet... She can even shoot. Gaby's perfect for the role."

"Can you protect her?"

"We can protect each other."

"I see," said Susan grimly. "Then I don't need to feel so bad about starting all this."

This time, Jerry noticed her discomfort. He didn't have time to beat around the bush. The amusement of idle flirtation, the thrill ride of turning lust into love, had been overtaken by events. He looked straight into Susan's large brown eyes.

"I'm not in love with her."

"Did I say you were?" She eyed him nervously.

"I just wanted you to know that."

"Why?"

"Because I'm in love with *you*."

Susan was taken aback with the sudden admission. *Wow!*

Jerry stood up, and she hurried into his outstretched arms. "I love you too, Jerry... I've been dreaming about you ever since the night of the Washington bombing."

"That makes two of us."

He held Susan's head to his chest and stroked her soft hair. "I wish the circumstances were different, but I know we can work it out."

"Does Gaby know how you feel about me?" asked Susan apprehensively.

"No… But I don't think she would mind," replied Jerry. "She knows how *you* feel about *me*."

"She told you!"

"Not as bluntly as you think… But, yes, she told me."

"Loose lips sink ships… Isn't that what they say in the Navy?"

"Yes, they do… But, believe me, Gaby can keep a secret." Jerry smiled at Susan again and continued to praise his undercover partner. "And she is really good under pressure… I was amazed at her act around the militia leadership."

Now reassured, Susan was elated to hear that Jerry and Gabriele were good enough together to actually survive the operation. "Do you think there's any hope for *us* after this is over?"

She looked up at him with tears running down her cheeks. Jerry wiped them away with the cuff of his shirt. He held her by the shoulders at arm's length. "I will be here when we're finished, Susan. If you still want me then, I'll explain it to the good people of Lone Mountain."

"I want you *now*."

Jerry struggled in silence for a moment, balancing all his personal and professional instincts.

"That wouldn't be right, honey."

"I know it wouldn't," she replied. "Maybe we can find another time and place."

"We will," said Jerry firmly. "Believe me, we will." He drew her to him again. She could feel his heart beating fast and knew it was because of her. Susan Mackenzie had been lonely a lot longer than six months. She had never met anyone like Jerry. She had never been so happy. She had never been so worried.

"Tell me you'll survive this, Jerry…I need to hear it."

"I'll make it through this…I promise." He looked into her eyes so deeply Susan could actually *feel* his fear. She could also sense that fear would not defeat him.

"You're afraid… How do you deal with that?"

"Fear is a warrior's friend, Susan. It keeps you focused… But you have to consume it before it consumes *you*. I'm not ashamed to be afraid… Don't you be."

Susan buried her head deeper in his chest. "I'm only afraid for you, dear." Her voice was stronger, and she loved him even more.

They went to bed in separate rooms, each dreaming of another time and place.

***

Jerry flashed his identification card and drove Gabriele through the main gate of Warren Air Force Base. She had been there before to buy groceries and, of course, her jungle boots, but this trip would be different. She felt a sense of wariness as they turned onto Old Glory Road, just short of the commissary. This visit was not personal; they had a job to do. She put on her game face and prepared for the meeting with Gerhard Beck.

They cruised through officer housing, where Gabriele was amazed at the quiet neighborhood of enormous brick structures. "Do *all* military officers live like this?" she asked.

"It depends on the base, Gaby. Warren happens to have all these huge houses from another time…when we were taming the frontier. The officers stationed here are luckier than most…although the guys who grew up in Florida might argue with me on that." He chuckled as Gabriele nodded. "Even after Carl got commissioned," Jerry continued, "he never lived in a house like that."

Susan and Gerhard had taken a room at the visitors' quarters. Jerry had agreed to come to them. He and Gabriele stood in front of a numbered door. Without knocking, Jerry opened the door and stepped into a medium-sized suite. Gabriele followed him to find Gerhard and Susan getting up from their comfortable chairs. Two empty reading chairs were positioned on the near side of a small table in the middle of the living room. After shaking hands all around, Jerry and Gabriele sat down to conduct business.

"How are you both?" asked Beck, looking at Gabriele.

"As Susan has undoubtedly told you, everything is on track." It was Jerry, but Gerhard didn't notice. He was still looking at Gabriele.

"The operation is proceeding better than we expected," reported Gabriele in a professional tone.

Beck nodded at Gabriele and focused his tired gray eyes on Jerry for the first time. "I appreciate your taking Gabriele under your wing. This is a cold business."

"She's doing very well," responded the warrior. "In fact, I'm not sure who's under whose wing." He glanced at Gabriele. "As you predicted, Gerhard, she is more trusted by the militia leadership than I am. We make a great team, and I'm getting more confident about the outcome."

"Have you been followed yet?"

"Not that we know of… But we're checking all the time."

"Meeting us on the base was a super idea, Jerry." It was Susan, flushing ever so slightly in the presence of the big man, the man who loved her. "It would be very hard for them to follow you here."

"We hope," continued Jerry, "that, if they *are* watching, they'll think we just went to the base for groceries…and maybe a workout. The gym here is better than the one I have at home."

Gerhard looked at Gabriele again. "This brute doesn't have you lifting weights, does he?"

"Yes, he does, and it feels great! I'm in the best shape of my life."

"I can see that," said Gerhard a little too directly.

And he could. She looked better than he remembered. And he remembered her every day.

They went through everything Jerry and Gabriele had done since their last meeting with Beck. Following the update, a discussion of all possible outcomes ensued ("the good, the bad, and the ugly"). By the time they were finished, it was dark outside, and everyone was hungry. The new plan called for Jerry and Gabriele to drive back to Lone Mountain that evening.

But first they had to eat.   —

"Can I take you all to the Officer's Club?" asked Gerhard.

"Not me," replied Jerry. "I wasn't an officer… How 'bout I take Susan to the NCO Club and you take Gaby to the O'Club?"

Gerhard Beck still had not figured out a few things. He wasn't aware that his ex-wife wanted to be alone with Jerry. Neither did he understand that Jerry had no interest in Gabriele beyond *Operation Lariat*. (She was off-limits, even if he hadn't been in love with Susan.) Last of all, Beck had failed to recognize that his own attraction to Gabriele was unlikely to be reciprocated. He dared to think that she would be able to love him someday. He was willing to wait for that day, and he wanted to tell her. Gabriele smiled at him for the first time. He took it as a sign she was willing to listen.

"It would be my pleasure," said Beck.

***

Jerry Tompkins had learned through long experience not to set patterns. It was one of the most useful habits he had ever developed. Setting a pattern was an invitation to ambush. This time would be different. He assumed the militia would not try to kill them…at least not yet. Red Thorne would have them followed. Jerry was not trying to *avoid* being followed; he was trying to detect it. The pattern—now set deliberately—was to leave the base the same way they had come in.

"Okay, Gaby… If you see someone just sitting there with nothing to do, sing out. I'll watch our six in the mirror."

"Gotcha covered, big guy." She scanned the area with Carl's Zeiss binoculars as they began to merge onto the highway. There was no one broken down, waiting for them to pass. In the darkness and the wind, there was nothing at all. Just as she was about to give Jerry the all clear, Gabriele noticed a nondescript gray sedan parked on the other side of the road, facing the base. At least it *looked* gray to her in the artificial light of the junction. Before Jerry reached highway speed, she saw the sedan move toward the on-ramp across from gate 2.

"We got company, Jerry…I think."

"Where?"

"Coming onto the highway now…way behind… There he is!" Gabriele's voice revealed a level of excitement that was not lost on Jerry.

"The guy came from the opposite side of 25," she reported. "My best guess is that he was watching the gate from there with binoculars."

"Or a spotting scope," said Jerry. "Keep an eye on him."

"What are you going to do?" Gabriele kept her eyes on the sedan. "I'm not completely sure he's after us."

"Just watch him, *Schatz*. I'm not completely sure what I'm going to do yet. The tough part will be to confirm the tail without letting him know that *we* know."

The snow had been plowed from the road, but it didn't matter. A forty-mile-an-hour wind blew it across the plains and over the snow fences, turning a clear night into a blizzard. Gabriele, on her knees and facing backwards on the seat, could keep the sedan in sight only part of the time. But the headlights she had memorized continued to flash into her field of vision through the flickering blackness.

Jerry pulled his truck onto the shoulder of the interstate just west of Laramie and stopped. The few vehicles on the road were moving slowly, and the sedan was easy to monitor as it went by them.

"He's stopping," said Gabriele. "I can see his brake lights."

"I'm gonna raise the hood and check the engine," responded Jerry. "Let me know what he does."

Jerry stepped into the freezing wind and pretended to be a mechanic. Gabriele kept her binoculars on the target, ascertaining after several minutes that the driver was alone. Jerry came back inside the cab and sat next to her.

"It's one man," she said without taking her eyes off the sedan. "Still there… What now?"

"Now we just get back on the interstate, Gaby. If he's actually following us, we'll know right away."

"How will you know for sure?"

"I'm going the other way," answered the big man. "I think we need a new fan belt. I know an all-night gas station in Laramie. If he turns around and follows us, that'll be confirmation."

Jerry merged back onto the interstate and took the next exit to double back. The sedan followed them all the way to the station, lurking in the distance as Jerry bought a new fan belt and pretended to install it.

"It appears as though Mr. Thorne is concerned about us after all," said Gabriele, finally taking the binoculars from her eyes. "And thanks for the lesson, *Junge*."

"Simple stuff, *Schatz*, but it's a good example of why we need to be ready to improvise."

It was quite late by now, and they were both tired. But the pressure was off for the moment. They had learned what they needed to know.

"It's good to find out the militia's tailing us, Gaby." He glanced at her on the other end of the bench seat. "And bad."

"I know," she said with a gulp. "They want to know who we really are." She felt the grip of fear closing around her throat. "It's happening, Jerry... Tell me we'll be all right."

Jerry locked eyes with his wife. "We'll be all right, *Schatz*."

Now was the time to tell her about Jose. He fixed his stare back on the interstate. "We have a secret weapon to protect us."

"We do?" she asked with genuine surprise. "And what is that?"

"Jose Rios," said the man behind the wheel. "He'll be watching the militia as they watch us."

Gabriele's surprise quickly turned to anger. "Why did you not tell me this before? Have you told Gerhard and Susan? I thought we promised to avoid keeping secrets from each other!"

"I didn't want to alarm you," said Jerry calmly. Even as he said it, though, he realized that not telling her about the back channel had been a mistake. "At this point, I know you better—and I know you can handle it. I wasn't sure about that before."

"What about Gerhard and Susan?"

"I don't want them to know... It will only complicate things. They might even shut down the operation." He took a deep breath.

"And once we go into the belly of this beast," he continued, "they won't be able to help us anyway. They're too far away and can't react in time." He turned again to a still-unsettled Gabriele.

"Jose can."

"How can he do that?"

"He's saved my life before… He will not let us die in there. Let's just say that Jose has all the right skills…and he knows how to improvise."

Gabriele again summoned her trust in Jerry, built up over the preceding months. He and Jose had been a combat team for a long time. Carl's team.

She suddenly felt safer.

"Okay… But no more secrets!" said Gabriele firmly. "And I will not tell the FBI."

"Deal," said Jerry in a humble tone.

Gabriele put away the binoculars and thought about the position they had gotten themselves into. Jerry's deal signaled her graduation to warrior status. They were now a tactical unit, not teacher and student.

The gray sedan followed them all the way to the Lone Mountain turnoff.

Chapter 12

The Troll

The December meeting of the Militia of Wyoming featured a Christmas Eve lay service in the old church. After singing hymns and listening to Red Thorne preach, Jerry and Gabriele sat in the Mineral King bar, drinking. It was almost time to drive back to Lone Mountain when a stranger approached them and sat down on one of the barstools.

"Hi," said a short man with thick glasses and long curly hair. "My name is Rulon K. James... But you can call me Jesse." The smoke from his cigarette curled right into Gabriele's face. Bothered, she wondered how she had ever enjoyed smoking.

"Cute," replied Gabriele. "Very cute... My name is Gabriele, and this is my husband, Jerry. Pleased to meet you."

Jerry was still chuckling to himself about the nerdish middle-aged man. The guy was a wimp; he was obviously out of place in the militia crowd. "Jesse James, huh? Wish I had a name like that."

"If your name was Rulon," said the nerd, "you'd think of something else to be called. In my case, it was a hard nickname to avoid."

"Were you a train robber?" joked Gabriele.

"Draft dodger," responded James without expression.

Almost forgetting where he was, Jerry wanted to drag the little creep outside and beat the crap out of him. Gabriele intervened before he could do anything that stupid.

"Good for you, Jesse... There is nothing more immoral than serving a corrupt government. My husband spent a lot of years in the Navy before he figured that out. The government has no right to turn its citizens into killers." She cast a disapproving glance at Jerry.

"Tell us more," continued Gabriele.

"I beat feet for Canada when my number came up for Vietnam."

Gabriele went on with her lecture. "The Vietnam draft was one of the most unfair in the history of conscription. I'll bet your father was not a prominent member of the community."

"He was a bricklayer," replied James.

"That's typical," said Gabriele, not slowing down. "If he had been a senator or a judge, you would have received a deferment. You refused to become a government killer and opted for life as a lesser criminal. For that, you deserve praise." She took a quick breath. "Meanwhile, our wonderful democratic government tried to wage war with a two-bit thug from Asia who didn't pose the slightest threat to America."

"And got fifty-eight thousand Americans killed in the process," added Jerry. He was impressed again with Gabriele's rhetoric, thinking that, had his wife been a few years older in 1968, she'd have made a great campus radical. Having grown up in a nonpartisan military system, Jerry did not feel comfortable arguing politics. Gabriele would have to walk point for this part of their play.

Rulon K. James, it seemed, was also impressed. He ran a dirty hand through black hair, flecked with gray from his long exile. Crushing out his cigarette, James reached over and shook Gabriele's hand. "You're a true patriot… We would have made a great team back then."

Gabriele pretended not to be revolted. Jerry—to his great surprise—felt a pang of jealousy.

"No, *you* are the patriot," said Gabriele with an admiring smile. "How long did you have to live up north?"

"Twenty-six years." James screwed up his face and lit another cigarette. "I almost didn't come back, but Red convinced me it was best."

Jerry had the sudden realization that this was a more important conversation than they had thought. "Red Thorne? Did you know each other?"

"Not until he came up to Moose Jaw, looking for courageous protesters like me." He shot a smile at Gabriele.

"He recruited you," pressed Jerry.

"Yeah, I guess that's the right word. He told me there were better ways to protest government tyranny."

Jerry sat forward on his barstool. "Do you live in Mineral King?"

James leaned closer to Jerry and lowered his voice. His breath was so bad Jerry almost gagged.

"My wife and I live with Red and Jane at the ranch."

Yes!

"Lucky you," said Gabriele. "We live in Lone Mountain." She looked at her watch. "And we need to get back on the road, or we'll never make it home tonight."

"See you folks at the next meeting, then… Enjoyed talking with you." James got up and ordered another beer.

Jerry and Gabriele drove back to Lone Mountain, arriving at the Jumping Frog after midnight. Gabriele was still energized from their successful reconnaissance. She was sure that James had been the man in the gray sedan behind them on the snowy interstate. She passed the lonely morning hours worrying about it. Jerry was energized about something else. Susan was due at the ranch for a Christmas update. He looked at his watch just before turning out the light (he still slept with a Navy-issue Rolex on his wrist). It was almost two o'clock.

Susan would be in his house before the end of the day.

***

Jerry and Gabriele spent the late morning hours cleaning house. There had been times when he liked living alone, but cleaning up had not been one of those times. It felt good to have a woman around, even a woman who was just a friend. He hoped the lifestyle he and Gabriele had fabricated for the bureau was a preview of his new life. Jerry's dream was to replace his undercover wife with a real one. In a town as small as Lone Mountain, that would be difficult. But he didn't care. He would think of some way to explain that he was divorcing Gabriele and marrying her best friend. *Her maid of honor, for Christ's sake!*

After lunch, they took a long walk in the snow. Winter, it seemed, had stopped to catch its breath, leaving a blue sky that hurt their eyes. They needed a workout, and Gabriele did not have weight lifting at the top of her Christmas list. Jerry had agreed to a walk—as long as it was strenuous enough to count as part of their training. They kept a brutal pace, straight into the rocky folds of Lone Mountain itself. The spectacular display of winter beauty made Gabriele homesick for the forests around Waldenbuch, where, two lifetimes ago, she had always wished for snow.

More Lone Mountain magic.

Jerry led her to a draw they had not visited before, and Gabriele again found herself in awe. They stood at the intersection of the plain and the mountain, gazing up at the trees above the canyon rim. Below them spread the rising pasture, and she could see Jerry's ranch house in the distance. She caught movement in her peripheral vision and turned to see a snowy owl, perched on the rock ledge facing them. She thought of how Carl would have thrilled to the sight. The place where they stood was worth the considerable effort Jerry had put them through to get there.

"This is really special, Jerry." Gabriele spoke to his silhouette, cast against the sky. "I did not know that one could find such beauty in windy Wyoming!"

"The wind doesn't blow all the time," he beamed. "Even when it does, this canyon is protected."

"Do you come here often?" She was conscious of a serenity in him she had not seen before. The warrior had somehow become less warlike. Less intense. He wore an aura she could not quite visualize. His movements were slower, less deliberate. When he looked at her, she could sense deep thoughts lurking behind his softened blue eyes.

"This is my special place, *Schatz*. I come here to think…to connect with the God I know." He drew a deep breath and held it. She had the impression that he was trying to slow down the eruption of intimacy.

"My life has been like a long race, Gaby. I was winning when I stopped being a warrior, but I never saw the finish line. I found the finish line right here where I started life. When I stand in this spot, the race is over, and I feel like I won."

Gabriele was suddenly short of breath, but it had nothing to do with the altitude. She reached for more of his soul. "You really are a spiritual person, are you not?"

"As opposed to a religious person, Gaby…yes. The church has taken God indoors and locked him up. It's here that I see where life leads."

Gabriele watched him survey the rock face surrounding them on three sides. She could hear the sound of her preconceptions crashing down around her.

"This place reminds me of a poem," said Jerry thoughtfully.

"Can you recite it?"

"I'll give you part of it."

"I would like that."

"*My teacher calls,*
from lofty canyon walls.
He bends to lend a hand,
but never falls."

She was emotional. He wondered why she was so moved. Certainly, someone as sophisticated as Gabriele had heard better poems. He had gone this far in revealing his soft side to her; he couldn't stop now.

"Ya know who wrote that?"

"I would guess one of the Romanticists, possibly Blake."

"You would be wrong, Gaby… It was me."

"You wrote that?" She tried not to sound shocked. "It's beautiful!"

"You flatter me," replied the former warrior, beaming again. "It's from a poem I entered in last year's cowboy poetry slam. I didn't win. They didn't have any idea what I was talking about."

"Then they did not listen at all," replied Gabriele quickly. "I know *exactly* what you meant."

"You do?"

"Yes," she answered firmly. "You said that *your* God—as opposed to someone else's—guides you by means of natural creations rather than scripture…and that he does it without having to become human."

"That would be my philosophy," said Jerry, almost embarrassed. "Is that your concept of God too?"

Gabriele looked at him as an intellectual equal for the first time.

"Yes, Jerry… Yes, it is!" She wanted to take him in her arms and hold him against her racing heart. She wasn't sure why. It might have been that she had shared the same philosophy with Carl. It might have been loneliness. It might have been that Jerry was suddenly a soul mate. But she sensed that Jerry felt he had gone too far, that he regretted revealing so much of himself to her.

"Then I'm glad I shared it with you," said Jerry seriously. "Let's go home."

And just as quickly as it had appeared, Jerry's soft side was buried in the pursuit of violent exercise. Gabriele's confusing emotions were buried along with Jerry's.

***

They made it back to the ranch house in half the time it had taken them to reach the canyon. The sun was setting just behind the mountain by the time Gabriele got her Cornish game hens in the oven. Jerry was still getting dressed when the doorbell rang. Gabriele opened the door to find a very excited Susan Mackenzie waiting to come in. She gave Susan a long hug.

"You're just in time for dinner," announced Gabriele, holding her friend at arm's length. "We have a lot to tell you, dear… Do you want a drink?"

"Sure…that whiskey went down well last time." Susan followed Gabriele into the kitchen. "Smells great… Where's that gorilla husband of yours?"

Jerry came through the door and picked Susan up off her feet all the way to his shoulders. "Have you ever ridden a gorilla?" She straddled his neck with her muscled thighs as Jerry carried her around the room like a ten-year-old.

"I do tricks, ya know… Just feed me!"

"The hens will be another half hour or so," said Gabriele. "Let's see if we can get some business out of the way before then."

Jerry poured whiskey, and the three of them got comfortable in front of the fire. First Gabriele, and then Jerry, related to Susan everything that had happened after the meeting at Warren. Their reports covered the exact same material—the sedan tailing them, the militia meeting, and their encounter with Rulon James. But Susan noticed the accounts were complementary. It was as though Jerry and Gabriele had rehearsed for hours, but Susan knew they had not. They were simply a very good team. She could see that Jerry and his wife had completed the bonding process. She was, in fact, proud of them. She was also afraid. Except for her monthly visits, Susan was out of the loop.

Gabriele went into the kitchen to start dishing up. Jerry went to Susan and bear-hugged her. Just enough to reassure the woman he loved. Then he kissed her softly on the forehead. "I love you, Susan… I wish I could be with you all the time."

"I love you too, Jerry." Then she said, perhaps too straightforwardly, "I hope I get the chance to show you how much."

They left the hearth as unproven lovers and entered the kitchen as colleagues and friends. After another of Gabriele's gourmet meals, they drank hot, mulled wine and laughed until it hurt. Until all the stress was purged from their bodies.

It was time for bed. Jerry went first, leaving Susan and Gabriele to work out a new set of rules. If there was a way for him to pursue a sexual relationship with Susan, it would have to be with Gabriele's blessing. The mission would always come first; they all knew that. He lay in his bed, waiting for Susan to come to him. He heard footsteps on the stairs, and his heart raced. Then there was no sound at all.

Gabriele had gone to bed. Susan never came.

Jerry woke to the cheerful aroma of frying bacon and dark coffee. The sensation softened his disappointment and gave him the strength to get out of bed. Looking at his watch, he saw that he had overslept. Jerry Tompkins had not let the sun beat him to the punch in a long time. In the shower, he decided that it was frustration he felt rather than depression. Depression was reserved for only two contingencies: one, the mission would somehow fail or, two, Susan would not want him anymore. Failure was never an option. He knew Susan wanted him, but anything more would have to wait.

For now.

Jerry lumbered down the stairs and strode into the kitchen. Susan was pouring pancakes onto the griddle. He stopped just inside the door and looked around.

"Where's Gaby?"

Susan set the blender down and looked him right in the eye. She wore an apron over a pair of very tight jeans and a loose cowboy shirt. Jerry imagined her as his wife, with children at her feet. His children.

"She went to the library in Laramie."

The big man started laughing. "Yeah, right... Tell me another one. She's not a morning person. I've never gotten her out of here before nine, except for something mission-related."

"This *was* mission-related."

"How's that?"

"She told me it was time for you and me to spend more time together."

Jerry's frustration was swept away like snow in the Wyoming wind. "You mean, she wants us to be alone all day?"

"She insisted on it." Susan turned around to flip the pancakes. Jerry moved quickly. She dropped the spatula on the floor as they kissed long and hard. The smell of burned batter startled her. Pulling away from him, she rescued two large pancakes with a spare spatula. Loading them on a plate, she piled on the bacon and poured him a cup of coffee. Susan felt like a housewife, Jerry's housewife. At least for one day.

Jerry smiled his biggest cowboy smile. "You set me up!"

"*Gaby* and I set you up, big guy… Now eat! If I have anything to say about it, you'll need all the energy you can get!"

***

Gabriele sat in the library rereading Hannah Arendt's *The Banality of Evil*. She had never really understood the author's point. Now she did. Thorne and his gang were evil but normal. Not psychopathic. Not crazy. Amoral. Nothing special. They were banal. Looking up to consider her new perspective on the subject, she was startled to see the face of Rulon James at the far end of the reading room. He was watching her, ready to close the distance between them. Bracing for the ambush, Gabriele reached for her composure. It was *out* of reach. He had obviously followed her.

"Gabriele Tompkins, is that you?" Rulon James was as sloppy as she remembered him to be from their encounter in Mineral King. With his thick glasses and longish hair, he looked right at home in the university library. A rumpled professor, perhaps.

Gabriele peered over the top of her book as though she hadn't noticed him. She sat up abruptly, feigning surprise. "Jesse! What are *you* doing here?"

James sat down in the easy chair next to her. There was no one else in the room. Gabriele fought for control. This was the first time she had been alone with the enemy. No backup and no script. James looked at her more seriously than a surprised friend would have. She could feel his shifty eyes penetrating her facade of calm, searching for something.

She knew what he was looking for.

"I come down here a lot, Gaby. It's one of the only places in Wyoming where I feel completely comfortable." He raised his eyebrows as if he knew what she would say. "And what are *you* doing here?"

"Getting comfortable, Jesse. You probably understand that better than my husband."

"Don't you like the ranch?"

"I love the ranch… But I am an educated woman. I need the solace of a library from time to time." Gabriele had shaken off her shock; she began to improvise. "You came a lot farther than I did… just to get comfortable."

"Yeah, I did," replied James. "But, you know, Wyoming is like that. You have to be willing to drive a long way for just about anything."

"Did you drive all night?" Gabriele looked at her watch for effect. "It's only nine thirty."

"I got up early," said James with a grin. "Sometimes I just need to get away. It doesn't matter what time of day it is."

Gabriele wondered if James had been sitting under the trees, watching Jerry's ranch all night. That was certainly the only way he could have followed her to Laramie. Then she felt a jolt of recognition rend her brain.

Susan!

"I don't know how you do it, Jesse… I mean, Mineral King is about as far from civilization as one can get. Have you ever been to Lone Mountain?"

"Yes, I have… Nice little town."

"I must admit that I like living there. Jerry is just a dear about letting me come down here when I need a scholarly fix." She paused to make sure he was following her line of reasoning. "I left my best friend at the ranch to keep him company."

James canted his head and frowned. "You're a very trusting soul, Gaby… When are you going back?"

"I usually head back around noon. Would you like to come over on your way home?" Her frantic mind was a kaleidoscope of possible outcomes.

"No, thanks… I'm staying the night here. I have some business in the area."

James got up and stood in front of her. Before turning to leave, he smiled through the dirtiest teeth Gabriele had ever seen. "See you next meeting, Gaby. Tell that hunky husband of yours he shouldn't let a woman who looks like you go runnin' all over the state by herself. This here's still the Wild West. You sure I can't talk you into a cup of coffee?"

"No, thanks, Jesse. I have a lot to read before I go back. Please give my best to Jane and Red, okay?"

"I'll tell them I saw you." James turned and disappeared behind a rack of French political journals.

Gabriele had to get to a phone…fast! At a distance, she followed James to the door of the library and watched him get into a gray sedan. The she went to the pay phone in the basement.

Jerry's phone was off the hook. *Scheisse!*

Gabriele thought about following James. Then she thought about calling Gerhard. She didn't know what to do. She had no experience in tailing another car; James would see her. Even though Gerhard had given her an emergency number to call, Gabriele resisted the urge. The big question was whether James had seen Susan come into Jerry's driveway the evening before. The operation—and Susan's life—hung in the balance.

Gabriele tried to remember the draft dodger's eyes.

Analyze!

Were they the eyes of a man who had merely gotten up early and driven halfway across the state? Or the eyes of someone who'd spent all night watching the ranch with a spotting scope? James had certainly followed her to Laramie. He had the eyes of a man on a mission.

A man on his way back to Lone Mountain!

She decided to call Jack Ellis.

"Jumping Frog Ranch… Ellis here."

"Jack, this is Gaby." She expelled the air from her lungs, the way Jerry had taught her to manage stress. "I would like you to do me a favor." This, she thought, is the tricky part.

"Sure, ma'am, what d'ya need?"

"I need you to go over and knock hard on Jerry's front door."

Jack Ellis hesitated just long enough to let Gabriele know what an unusual request she had made. "I don't normally do that, ma'am… Otherwise, the boss would have no privacy at all. Know what I mean?"

"Yes, I do, Jack." Gabriele put two more quarters in the pay phone. "This is really important. Don't go in the house... Just bang on the door. He's not feeling well. I left Susan there to care for him, and I think she took the phone off the hook to let him sleep."

"Where are you?"

"At the university."

"Okay," said Jack. "You don't want me to leave a message at the door?"

"No!" she said too abruptly.

"I can just tell her that you're trying to call."

"Just bang on the door, Jack. No need to say anything. I'll call her in a few minutes."

Gabriele hoped the story sounded as good to Jack as it did to her. She also hoped that Susan and Jerry would figure out what was going on without going to the door. She could only imagine what they looked like at the moment.

"Got it... You coming home soon?"

"As soon as I talk to Susan... And thanks."

Gabriele got some more quarters from the reference desk. Five minutes later, Jerry answered the phone in his bedroom.

"Tompkins."

"Jerry, this is Gaby... I just ran into Rulon James at the library. He must have followed me here. That means he's watching the ranch!"

The afterglow in Susan's eyes turned to fear—and then to terror—as she watched and listened. Noticing her reaction, Jerry wrapped Susan in his free arm and tried to moderate his tone. "You did well, Gaby... Sorry about the phone."

"It is I who should be sorry... This is all my fault. If Susan has been identified, then we're all in trouble!"

"Did you tell James when you'd be leaving the library?"

"I told him I normally go home around noon."

"Stay there until then... And don't worry, Gaby. From what you said, I think James is coming back here to see what he missed. Susan will be long gone by then." Jerry hung up the phone.

Susan's terror turned to disappointment. "You're right, dear... I can't stay a minute longer. They might have additional surveillance out there." She kissed him with all the passion she had stored up for the rest of the day. Then she jumped out of bed to dress.

"That was a close one. I'm going to take the back way out, just in case."

Jerry admired her as she peeled off his knee-length cowboy shirt and put on a blouse. She stuffed her bra in a tote bag along with his shirt. He pulled the comforter up to their pillows as if to capture her scent for later.

"I can't say when we'll be able to see each other again, honey—let alone make love."

She fell into his enormous arms and felt safe again. "I understand, Jerry... Listen, this morning will last me a good long while. I love you even more than I thought."

"We'll just have to pick up where we left off," said Jerry. "Whenever that will be." His smile was gentle...unhurried...reassuring. "I love you. I'll think about you every day until then."

He kissed her again, and she was out the door.

***

Gabriele hung around the library until noon, trying to act normally in case James had left someone to watch her. During the wait, she falsely identified half the people in the building as James's accomplices. *This is paranoia*, she thought. Jerry had told her that only the deliberately paranoid survive. Now she knew what he meant. At the stroke of twelve, she was in Jerry's truck, driving as fast as she could back to Lone Mountain. She had lost her patience and her confidence. Jerry, she was certain, would give them back to her.

Chapter 13

The Invitation

The next three months went even slower than Gabriele had anticipated. The awful weather made things worse. She and Jerry had to assume that whenever they left the ranch, they would be followed. There was ample evidence that someone had assumed that duty from Rulon James or that James had used a series of different vehicles. The January meeting of the Militia of Wyoming had been uneventful, but "uneventful" (as reported to Susan) was not the worst-case scenario. The ghost of Seth Goldman stalked them.

At the end of January, a small curly-haired man had approached Ernie Sylvester in Lone Mountain, asking questions about the newlyweds, explaining that he was gathering information for a university study of rural Wyoming demographics. Ernie had gone to Jerry afterward, admitting without the slightest embarrassment that he didn't know what demographics were. The store manager had added that he was glad to help the school in some way other than rooting for its football team. Sylvester's loyalty had renewed Jerry's faith in his neighbors.

The February meeting of the militia had to be canceled due to heavy snow. Jerry and Gabriele were becoming impatient. The walls were closing in. They wanted to get the operation over with and return to normal life…whatever that was. Jerry had a vision; Gabriele had no idea. They were also slaves to the routines of countersurveillance. Rulon James had not severed their relationship with Susan completely, but hasty meetings at Warren during grocery runs were not the same as whiskey in front of the fireplace. Jerry and Susan held on to the memory of their morning alone; that was all they would get, at least for now. Gabriele clung to her memories of Carl. That was all she had. Perhaps all she ever *would* have.

In late March, they were again in Mineral King. Jerry had volunteered to give lessons in small unit tactics, survival, and guerrilla warfare to the men. With his vast experience, he was quickly replacing Roy Murdock as the principal trainer in the organization. Gabriele had begun a newsletter, announcing the militia's activities. The paper also served as a platform for strengthening her extremist credentials. By the time the second issue was in the mail, Gabriele was sharing the role of militia philosopher with Red Thorne. Thorne didn't seem to mind. There was renewed optimism in the ranks of the militia, and much of it could be traced to the arrival of Jerry and Gabriele. Thorne was smart enough to realize that the better Mr. and Mrs. Tompkins looked, the better *he* looked. Roy Murdock was not that smart.

Back home, Jerry was outside helping Jack Ellis mend the south fence when the phone rang. Gabriele, relaxing by the fire, was in the middle of writing another anti-government editorial for the newsletter. She was startled by the shrill sound of the telephone, running into the kitchen to pick it up.

"Tompkins ranch... Gabriele speaking."

The voice that spoke to her was friendly and menacing at the same time.

"Gabriele...*meine Liebe*...this is Red Thorne. I was hoping you and Jerry could come over tomorrow night for a special meeting."

She caught her astonishment in the back of her throat. "Of course, Red... You mean at the old theater?"

"No," replied Throne emphatically. "I mean at the ranch."

This was it, she thought with a mixture of fear and excitement. The long wait was over. "Very good, Red... I'll tell Jerry when he finishes outside. What time do you want us there?"

"How 'bout six o'clock." Thorne gave her the odometer reading for the junction of the dirt road to his compound.

"Do you want us to bring anything?" Gabriele almost made it sound like they were going over to a friend's house for dinner. Red Thorne had almost made her feel that way.

"Just your appetites and right-wing views, Gaby... See you then."

Reality hit her in the solar plexus as soon as she hung up. The pivotal scene in the play was finally upon them. Five minutes later, Jerry came in the back door and kicked off his muddy boots. Gabriele buried her terror under a shallow breath and a wide grin.

"It's showtime, cowboy."

***

"They're coming," said Red Thorne, putting down the phone. Three male heads nodded up and down then at each other. They had agreed only to host the prospects for a closer look. To go beyond that, Thorne knew he would need much more from his followers. He would need approval from each of the men for Jerry and Gabriele to become members of DEFCON One.

"Okay, men, let's review the bidding." He turned to Rulon James, sitting to his left at the round wooden table. "Shoot, Jesse."

James took off his glasses and began polishing the lenses with a handkerchief. "I've been following those two around for the last four months, Red. I have no reason to suspect they are aware of that." He coughed into the handkerchief and then resumed. "I couldn't get to the phone line, and I couldn't watch them all the time, but they look pretty clean. Shit...I even hacked into the defense personnel files. Tompkins actually did all of those brave things he told us about. I couldn't get into the CIA stuff, but I'm still trying."

"Then you're not opposed to bringing them in." It was a statement.

"I have a feeling, Red... No evidence yet, but a feeling."

Red Thorne smiled at his jack-of-all-trades. "You'll have to do better than that, my friend. We need the extra help around here, and I haven't seen a more promising couple since we got you and Linda."

"That's just it, Red... They're *too* clean." James looked at Roy Murdock, who was trying unsuccessfully to appear disinterested. "Jerry is right out of a Christmas catalog...well trained, disciplined, committed, and tougher than any of us." Looking back at Thorne, he continued, "And his wife is just perfect. She's a great spokesman for us. She can even shoot."

"She also improves the scenery around here!" interrupted Thorne.

"Yeah," admitted James. "But there's something about them that just doesn't wash with me. I see them go to the base every month. They go in, and two hours later, they come out with food stacked in the back of the truck. I don't know what they do in there. It bugs me."

"Sounds like they buy groceries," said Thorne. The other men sat silently, preparing their own thoughts.

"But I can't watch them after they go in, and they know it."

"I thought you said they don't know you're tailing them."

"I said that, but I'm not completely sure. I never told you this, but Gabriele had a 'best friend' who used to visit them at the ranch... probably the maid of honor Ernie Sylvester told me about. I don't know anything else about the woman except that Gabriele trusted her completely with Jerry. She admitted to me—almost too readily— that she left them alone while she went off to the university library in Laramie."

Red Thorne sat forward in his chair.

James sat back in his chair. "I went back to Lone Mountain to look for the woman, and she was gone. I've never seen her."

"Maybe her friend took advantage of the situation, Jess. Maybe Gabriele caught her in the sack with Jerry." Thorne laughed. No one else even smiled.

Thorne turned his attention to Roy Murdock. "So, what do you think, Roy?"

"I think I'd like to watch Jerry and his Nazi chick in the sack, Red... They could probably generate enough electricity to light up this whole town!"

Everyone laughed except Will Jeffers.

"That's if they actually sleep together," James put in. "I'd feel more comfortable knowing they fuck like rabbits."

Thorne got serious. "Jane and I listened to them in the motel room... Pretty exciting stuff... Plenty of electricity there."

"That helps," said James.

"So...Jesse and Roy are okay with bringing them over to take the next step." Red turned his attention to the fourth man in the room. "What do *you* say, Will?"

The woodstove in the corner was throwing out a lot of heat, but Will Jeffers still had his leather jacket on. He had removed his cowboy hat, but the others knew he'd rather have kept it on. His calloused and wrinkled hands remained folded on the table as he cleared his throat.

"I have nothing to say."

Thorne was used to this. Will was his right-hand man. A true patriot. Fully committed to the cause. Braver than anyone in the room.

But he could be a real prick.

"Come on, Will... This is important. At the very least, I need to know where you stand and why."

"I'll tell you after dinner tomorrow."

Thorne relented. All he needed was a thumbs-up or a thumbs-down.

Like the Romans.

***

Jerry finished his shower and bounded down the stairs for a cup of Gabriele's expresso. They had a lot to talk about. Tactics, techniques, and procedures. They also needed to call Susan at the untraceable number she had given them. By the time they finished their planning and reporting, it was late enough to turn in.

But Gabriele needed more from him.

"Tell me again what you said to Jose."

"I told him we got married."

Jerry's tone was so matter-of-fact it startled her. She narrowed her gaze and lowered her voice. "What else did you tell him?"

"That I was putting you in deep shit, Gaby."

"You are."

"Not exactly against your will."

"That is true… And I am still *grateful* for the opportunity to avenge what they did to Carl." She looked away from him and into the dying fire.

"Now all I have to do is get you out of it…alive," said Jerry evenly.

Looking back at Jerry's boyish face, reddened by the glow of the hardwood embers, Gabriele was overwhelmed by a feeling of camaraderie.

"I trust you completely, Butkus." She paused to savor the feeling. "What was Jose's field name?"

"Bosco."

"You say he'll have us covered from close range?"

"Yes. I have no doubt that he can monitor what we're doing better than the FBI can." Jerry drew a deep breath and shot her a sincere look. "I trust our friends, Gaby. Gerhard and Susan are every bit as professional as I am, but the situation could go way offtrack."

"I agree," she interrupted.

"I'm still a military man," Jerry went on. "I always err on the side of caution—until the decisive moment."

"And when is that?" asked Gabriele, now the student.

"When I have the chance to take them out."

Gabriele covered her mouth and gasped. "You plan to *kill* them?"

"If it comes to that, I will not hesitate."

"What about recording their conversations and dead-dropping the tapes for Susan?"

"That's the mission."

"But you don't think it will work that way."

"I don't know *how* it will work," said the big man. "I just want insurance against the unknown…what a German philosopher of war once called friction."

"Clausewitz," said the humanist.

"How did you know that?"

"I read," she replied. "I read a *lot*."

Jerry could not hide his admiration for Gabriele's academic journey. "Then you understand why we need a second communications channel."

"Completely...I feel better knowing you have one." Her eyes narrowed again in the near darkness. "But I do not know if I am capable of killing—even these people."

"You won't have to, Gaby. If it comes to that, I'll take care of it."

"And where will Jose be while we're inside Thorne's compound—assuming they admit us?"

"Here," said Jerry. "I want him to live at the Jumping Frog, but I expect he'll float back and forth between this place and Mineral King."

Jerry walked back to the kitchen and got Jose on the phone. Gabriele wasn't sure she even wanted to hear the conversation. She stayed at the hearth until Jerry got back. It couldn't have been more than a minute.

"Jose will be here when we get back from our meeting tomorrow night...not to stay... I just need to brief him."

Gabriele changed the subject. "Are you ready for bed?"

Jerry closed the fireplace screen. "Yup, see you in the morning, Gaby. Sleep as long as you want."

"I was considering that." She unfolded her legs, stood up, and headed for the stairs. "Good night, Jerry."

She got to the third step and turned around. "Did you and Bosco decide what to call *me* in the field?"

"He thinks you look like Claudia Schiffer... We'd like to call you Claudia."

She could not suppress a smile. "He's blind as a bat, but I'll take it."

Gabriele's confidence was back, but she searched for her patience in the darkness of the bedroom. Mind racing, she didn't find it until dawn.

Then she slept in.

***

At precisely six o'clock, Jerry turned onto the long dirt road leading to Thorne's ranch. He had driven south from Mineral King for exactly 9.6 miles. The road led to a notch in the hills separating semiarid grazing land from the desolation of the Red Desert basin. The ranch was hidden just beyond the notch. No signs. No sounds. Nothing but dust.

The wrought iron gate had been opened for them. There was no sign. As they approached the compound, Gabriele took in as much information as she could. Jerry had instructed her that the more they knew about the surroundings, the better their chances if they had to run. Jerry halted the truck at a hitching post. They surreptitiously inspected the buildings and trailers, arranged in a large square. It reminded Jerry of a military training camp. It looked to Gabriele like a prison camp.

Red and Jane Thorne stood at the front door as Jerry led his wife along the walkway. Gabriele was so nervous she tripped and almost went sprawling. Jerry caught her with his right arm.

"Don't fall down on us now!" shouted Red. "Those boots sure look nice, Gaby, but they ain't worth a damn to walk in."

"That's why I married this gorilla," she quipped through her fear. "He bends to lend a hand but never falls."

Jerry squeezed her arm. She squeezed back, feeling her strength return.

Inside, the house looked a lot like Jerry's. As soon as they had been relieved of their coats, Jerry and Gabriele were ushered into the dining room. Seated at the table were all the members of Thorne's extended family. To Gabriele, it looked like a doomsday cult, gathered for a mass suicide. The men—all of them armed with large pistols—stood up, and everyone was introduced. Jerry pulled out a chair, and Gabriele sat down to break bread with the strangest group of people she had ever seen.

Directly across from her sat Roy Murdock. She was still amazed at how closely he resembled her husband. She had often caught Murdock looking at her as if he *were* her husband. Jerry had given her a running account of his dealings with the guy at militia meetings. Murdock was a man with a grudge. Jerry made him look weak and ineffective just by showing up. The man gave her the creeps, but she understood that Jerry was the one who needed to fear him. Gabriele thought that if anyone blocked their path to Thorne's inner circle, it would be Roy.

To Murdock's left sat his wife, Sadie. The woman was as shy as her husband was loud. It was obvious to Gabriele that Sadie's face had once been pretty. Gabriele wondered how someone starting out pretty could end up looking so bad in just a short time. Like Roy, she seemed to be in her midthirties, noticeably younger than the rest of the women. And heavier. Sadie didn't say much, giving Gabriele the impression she had been abused, perhaps physically. Resigned to her fate. Two young children did not leave her many options. It was not a surprise to Gabriele that the woman had taken refuge in religion.

To Roy's right sat a man Gabriele had seen regularly at meetings but never once heard. Jerry had briefed her on Will Jeffers, saying that he was a good shot who seemed comfortable with all the weapons. No one they had met ever claimed to actually *know* Jeffers, but they all seemed to respect him. Taking off his leather jacket, he folded his hands on the table. Gabriele looked into the cold eyes and saw nothing behind them. There was piety on the man's face. Piety mixed with evil.

Then she noticed the tattoos! A flashback to the Air and Space Museum plunged her mind back into hell.

It's him! This is the man who killed my husband!

This was not a time to panic. Gabriele swallowed hard. She felt the rage boiling up from within her core. She wanted to throw up. Just before body language gave her away, she remembered Jerry's most important lesson.

Focus!

Jeffers was the only man at the table she had not met. Gabriele addressed him directly. "I'm pleased to finally make your acquaintance, Will. I was also hoping to meet your wife."

Jeffers looked at her with contempt Gabriele could *feel*.

"She died."

Gabriele reeled. "I am very sorry to hear that," she responded with what sounded like heartfelt sympathy.

Her husband's killer simply nodded.

Gabriele broke eye contact with Jeffers and glanced to her right. Rulon James seemed to be conducting surveillance on her even now. Gabriele wondered if James realized that she and Jerry were aware that he had been following them. Part of her *wanted* him to know. She knew they would have to watch James more than the others. He was the smartest. If she did not watch out for Murdock, Gabriele thought, she might be raped. If she did not watch out for James, she would be dead.

"We meet again," said James solemnly.

Linda Watkins-James sat on Gabriele's left, where she could easily be ignored. Gabriele decided she would rather look at Murdock than at the graying fiftyish bitch. The perfect partner for Jesse, she thought. Smart, sloppy, and secretive, Linda evoked fear as well as anger. She fit the profile of a terrorist much better than her nerdy husband. Gabriele knew from their previous encounters that Linda was an extreme feminist, opposed to everything and everybody. Adding to her lack of appeal, the woman reeked of tobacco. James had met his wife in Saskatchewan, and Gabriele wished they had both stayed there.

Gabriele said nothing more.

Jane Thorne had taken the end of the table to Jerry's right. Gabriele looked past her husband's bulky shoulder and found Jane smiling at her. Jane was always smiling at her. Gabriele had mixed emotions about that. On one hand, Jane's attention could get her and Jerry into the inner circle. Gabriele didn't want to think about the other hand. When Jane wasn't smiling, the woman was as homely as anyone Gabriele had ever seen. Six inches shorter than statuesque, with cropped brown hair, she was pale and rather skinny. Not shy…

even brash. When Jane spoke, people listened. And they heard the voice of Red Thorne.

Gabriele smiled cautiously at Mrs. Thorne.

Thorne sat at the other end of the table. The man really was bigger than Jerry, she thought, but it was obvious that he carried a lot of extra weight. Thorne had an aura of authority that challenged all of Gabriele's notions about leadership. Carl and Jerry were leaders; Red Thorne was a thug. She had always thought that leaders needed to have credentials. Thorne had none. He made up for it, though, with seductive, emotional oratory. Hate speech wrapped in patriotism. Germany had been ruined for generations by just such a man. Sensing his admiration for all things German, Gabriele planned to get closer to him. That would protect Jerry…and keep Jane on her toes.

They both nodded at the host, girding for whatever was coming.

"Welcome to Jerry and Gabriele," began Thorne. "This is a special night for us… We don't often have guests in our home." He looked around the table. "I want you all to join hands."

Gabriele took Jerry's hand in her right and Linda's in her left. Bowing her head for the prayer, she peeked at Rulon James. He was staring at her. So was Roy. Jerry squeezed her hand to signal his support.

And Thorne spoke.

"*Yahweh*, your providence sustains us. Thank you for bringing Jerry and Gabriele into our lives. Together let us serve you in our quest for freedom from tyranny on earth. We are white and free, armed and ready. With your divine assistance, we will forge a more perfect union—based upon your holy laws. Bless our family as we act out your will, O Lord. Bless the other patriots in this land who have sacrificed themselves to serve you. Randy Weaver and his family. David Koresh and his congregation. The martyr Timothy McVeigh. We are all humbled and inspired by their heroism. In your name, *Yahweh*, we pray for a just peace on earth… Amen."

The prayer sounded a lot like the newspaper item that had reported Carl's death. Incredibly, the realization took Gabriele off guard. *This is DEFCON One!* She could almost hear herself and Jerry being sucked into the deep end of the funnel. Exactly according to plan...but much faster than she had expected. Or wanted. What scared Gabriele the most was the recognition that she and Jerry were already at the point of no return. Everyone raised their heads and looked at Thorne. He raised his wineglass in a toast.

"To the revolution!"

Jerry and Gabriele Tompkins added their voices to the group's response.

"To the revolution!"

Chapter 14

The Test

Jerry and Gabriele spent the entire meal answering questions about themselves. Their cover stories were solid, but they were still cover stories. Susan had grilled them in practice sessions, anticipating just this situation. The most difficult thing about lying, Gabriele had remembered, was to be consistent. Fortunately, both she and Jerry had been blessed with excellent memories. The hostile intent behind the interrogation (there was no other word) had been partially masked by the folksiness of the Thornes. None of the others even attempted to be friendly, but in deference to Thorne, they remained civil. Characteristically, Will Jeffers did not speak at all. He sat waiting for the Tompkins couple to trip themselves.

They didn't.

When the coffee came, Gabriele savored it. She didn't know what would come next—and she almost didn't want to know. Before she got to the bottom of her cup, she found out.

"Jerry," began Thorne, "why don't we men go in the other room and let the ladies do whatever they do…shall we?" Red got an icy look from Linda Watson-James but didn't notice. As the men got up, the women moved into a seated cluster around Jane.

Jerry felt like he was standing on the tailgate of a cargo plane at twenty thousand feet, poised to jump into the night sky. The difference was that his heart had never beaten as fast as it did now. Not even in combat. He knew how to do combat; he didn't know how to do whatever was coming next.

He would have to work without a net.

Thorne and the other men led Jerry into a small room down the hall. While he stood, the rest of them sat down around a large wooden table. There was nothing on the table, and the walls were empty. A single bare light bulb hung over the scene. The room was too small for Jerry to fight his way out. The others were still armed. He had never interrogated anyone inside a building before, but this looked like the ideal place to do it.

"Take off your clothes," commanded Thorne.

Jerry was so taken aback that he hesitated, wanting to make sure he had heard the man correctly. "My *clothes*, Red?"

"Yes, Jerry… It's a precaution we've all been through." Thorne gestured to the table. "Right here."

Starting with his boots, Jerry laid every stitch methodically on the table. Jesse extracted the big man's wallet from the jeans and rifled through it. Jerry knew there was nothing incriminating to be found, but James's action made him feel even more exposed than he already was, standing naked in front of the men.

"He's clean," said James to the room. "Nothing in the boots either."

"Congratulations, Jerry," said Thorne in a softer tone. "You seem to be what you say you are."

"I am," replied Jerry without emotion. "Can I get dressed now?"

"Please do," said Thorne. "You do understand that we have to be sure, don't you?"

Jerry tried to respond with a mix of understanding and impatience. "Listen, Red… I spent a lot of years doing secret squirrel shit. I understand it better than anybody."

"Good… That's good."

Jerry got dressed quickly and sat down.

Red Thorne looked at every man individually before proceeding. Then he locked eyes with Jerry. "Now for business… I think you'll be interested to know that we've recently had a vacancy open up." Thorne paused and refocused. "We had to evict the previous occupants." He let a sense of dread hang in the stale air.

Jerry did not miss the veiled threat. He adjusted his tone to fall somewhere between deadly serious and sarcastic. "Sounds like you're running a hotel, Red."

"In a way, yes, we are," replied Thorne, back to his folksy delivery. "Jane and I provide a number of families with room and board in exchange for certain…services."

"What services?"

"We'll get to that in a minute. First we'd like to know if you and your beautiful bride would like to live here. The vacancy I mentioned is a trailer out back."

"That depends on what services you need from us."

Thorne thought for a few seconds. *He wants it blunt, he gets it blunt.*

"We have a revolution to start, and we're running out of time. We are looking to add to our…family." Thorne surveyed the room—the men of DEFCON One—then threw his attention back to Jerry. "We would like you to join us, but you'll need to do something first."

"What's that?"

"We want you to demonstrate that you're willing to kill."

"I've demonstrated that many times."

"Not to us."

"When do you want me to do this?"

"The clock starts right now."

"Who's the target?" Jerry was doing everything he could to sound as if this was a normal after-dinner conversation.

It was his worst nightmare!

"My only stipulation is that it be a nonwhite lowlife," instructed Thorne.

"Do you want me to use a weapon?"

"You can choose not to… Oh, that's right," said Thorne theatrically. "Your *hands* are lethal weapons, aren't they?"

"I usually don't use them unless I'm out of ammo." Jerry smiled menacingly, getting into the role completely. "I've only done that once."

"A pistol would be fine."

"Where?"

"Somewhere in Wyoming...but nowhere near Mineral King."

"You said you wanted a demonstration, Red... You want me to take a picture?"

"No. Jesse will accompany you. He'll take the picture."

"Are Gaby and I free to live here after that?"

"Yes. We need you." Thorne stroked his beard. "But you have to kill to get into this organization." The fat man doubled down. "I don't have to tell you there's only one way out."

"Blood in, blood out," said Jerry soberly. He understood too well that it was also Gabriele's blood on the line. "I need to go home and get my SIG... Gaby and I can pack in one day."

"You'll have to pack *for* her, big guy." It was Roy Murdock. "She's staying here."

Jerry fought to keep the panic in his throat. "Okay, no problem. I'll just go home and get our stuff right now."

"I'm following you home," James put in with a toothy grin. "I'll help you pack."

Jerry was unable to explain anything to Gabriele. All he had time for was a demonstration kiss.

"I'll be back soon with your gear, *Schatz*. Be good."

***

Jerry had three hours to think about what he was going to do. Barreling along the interstate, with Rulon James trailing openly in the gray sedan, he racked his brains for a way out of the developing situation.

Jose would be at the ranch when they got there!

Jerry needed to warn him they were coming. Approaching Rawlins, he reached for the cell phone in the glove compartment. Making sure he was not silhouetted by the sedan's headlights, Jerry made a quick call to Jack Ellis.

"Jack...sorry it's so late, but I need a big favor."

It was almost midnight. The exhausted rancher had been in bed for three hours. "That's okay, boss... What can I do for ya?"

Jerry glanced behind him and saw the sedan creeping closer. He speeded up as he talked. "Listen… This is very important… Go check my place to see if Jose is there yet. I left the door unlocked, so he's most likely inside the house right now."

Jerry raised his voice above the roar of the Dodge's engine. "I want you to take Jose—with all his things—to *your* house right now! Got that?"

"Yeah," said Jack, now fully awake. "You want me to hide your Mexican friend at my place. Sorry to ask this, Jerry, but is he an illegal alien or something?"

If Jerry had not been in the middle of a high-speed chase, Jack would have received a long lesson in manners. Instead, he got a short one.

"Jose lived in this country long before you were born, Jack, and he's from Colombia, not Mexico!"

Jack was nodding up and down vigorously at the other end of the line.

"Park his car in the back garage—and make sure the door is closed. Then tell him to wait for me just inside *your front door*. I'll be there in exactly two hours."

"Got it, boss. Ya want me to stay up?"

"No…as soon as Jose is in your living room, you can go back to bed… And, Jack, Gaby and I are going away for a while. Jose will be living in the main house while we're gone. If anybody wants to know where we are, tell them we're in the mountains. If they want to know why Jose is there, tell them he's helping you manage the ranch. Got that?"

"Okay, Jerry. I'm used to this, with you livin' in Virginia all these years… I guess I won't be able to contact you."

"That's right."

Jerry put the phone back in the glove compartment and slowed down. Now he worried that he'd lost James completely. As the plan came together in his head, he looked desperately for the gray sedan.

Now that I need that little prick, I can't find him!

Sorting through the headlights, he wished Gabriele was with him to spot cars. He wished Gabriele was with him, period. She was on her own with the likes of Murdock.

Gabriele is a hostage!

He found James's headlights and carefully kept station in front of the sedan. *That was close!* One hour later, Jerry put on his blinker and started to move into the exit lane. After a brief hesitation, the sedan did the same. Jerry slowed the truck and turned right, onto a fairly smooth gravel road.

Eat my dust, shithead.

Jerry wished he could hear the gnome's cursing as the sedan bounced along behind him, dust clouding its headlights.

Now in control, Jerry led his unwanted companion around the back side of Lone Mountain. About halfway to the Jumping Frog, where the road surrendered to the rugged terrain, he raced away from the sedan and made for the ranch as fast as he could drive. A four-wheel-drive truck versus a passenger car on a bad dirt road in the dark.

It was no contest. He would have at least ten minutes with Jose before a very pissed-off Rulon James finally made it to his front door.

Bosco was right where he was supposed to be. It was not a surprise to Jerry. Bosco was *always* right where he was supposed to be.

"Don't talk, just listen. We have ten minutes." Jerry closed the door. "You got the car stashed in the back?"

"Yes, but why?" Jose responded.

Jerry had been rehearsing what he would say for the last three hours. "Gaby and I have been asked to join the group." He glanced at the stairs to Ellis's bedroom and lowered his voice. "But they still don't trust us. One of them followed me home. I pulled ahead of him on the back road, but he's only a few minutes out." Obviously, we can't let him see you…or your car."

"No problem, man… What do you want me to do?"

Jerry paused for a few seconds. Seconds he didn't have! "They're testing me, Bosco." He looked straight into his friend's eager eyes. "I'm going to have to kill someone in order to prove my dedication to their cause."

"And you want to stage something with me." It was a statement.

"Exactly." Jerry did not have time to think about how he and Jose had become one mind in two bodies. An extension of their intuitive actions in the field. He pulled a road map out of his jacket pocket and thrust it in front of his teammate.

"Now look at this. Tomorrow night I need you to be in Kemmerer by twenty-two hundred. There's a small square in the middle of town. You'll know you're in the right place when you see the old JC Penney store. You can't miss it."

"I won't."

"Wait for me to drive into the square… I'll be there between ten and eleven…hunting for you. I'll have one of *them* in the truck with me. An observer."

"How do you want me to play it after that, man?"

"You let me see you…then get back in the car and drive north on 189." Jerry traced the road with his finger. They were still standing in Ellis's living room. "Turn again on 233, toward the reservoir. Find a turnout in the road, get out, and take a piss. A *long* piss."

"I can do that," said Jose cheerily.

"You can use my body armor." The big man looked nervously at his watch.

"I brought my own Kevlar…with a ceramic chest plate."

"Perfect," said Jerry with the smile he had forgotten to give his friend of twenty years. He pressed the map into Jose's dark-brown hands.

"This guy's gonna take a picture of the body… You'll need to look dead." Jerry shook Jose's hand and gave him a bear hug. "I wish we had more time to brief this thing."

"It's okay, man… I know what you need." Jose looked around the room. "You want me to stay here with Jack tonight?"

"Just until this creep and I are gone. Sleep at my house. I'm packing our gear for Mineral King. Should take less than an hour."

"Where's Claudia?"

"They have her, Bosco… If I pass the test, I'll get her back." Neither of them had to guess what would happen if Jerry failed the test.

Jose walked Jerry to the door. "I'll be there, man. Just wait till I turn around... Then hit me square in the chest. I hope you're using subsonic rounds."

"I got a whole box in my war bag."

"Good to go, man... I'll be driving a blue Neon... See you tomorrow night."

Jerry ran to the front door of his house, arriving just in time to see Rulon James's headlights bouncing along his driveway. By the time the knock came, he was drinking a cup of coffee. The troll was just as pissed off as Jerry hoped he'd be.

"Welcome to my home, you little prick."

James stormed into the house and threw his wool hat on the sofa. "Don't you ever do that to me again, dickhead!" He looked up at Jerry to see the big man smiling. James struggled for the upper hand.

"Let's get the rules straight, shall we? Unless or until you're officially working for Thorne, you're working for *me*. I'm the one who certifies you, asshole!"

"Is that why you've been following me and Gaby for the last four months?"

"You figured that out, huh?"

"Look, Jesse... I've been followed by the Mena Cartel and the CIA. I know when some amateur like you is on my tail."

James changed the subject. "Just take your time upstairs, Jerry. I'll be down here looking for surprises."

"You won't find any."

"It's my job to look, so let's just pack up and get out of here."

In ten minutes the big man was back with two duffel bags and a suitcase. He was wearing the SIG Sauer nine millimeter under his ski jacket in a shoulder holster. The gnome was still rooting around the living room, searching for some clue to the mystery woman who'd disappeared from the couple's lives so suddenly.

Jerry was glad he and Gabriele had sanitized the downstairs. Every trace of their former lives had been stored in the attic. He thought how lucky they were that James, now in a hurry, had not insisted on going upstairs.

"Good to go," said Jerry. He was speaking to James, but he was also reassuring himself.

"Let's go, rookie… This time I'm riding with you."

"What about the famous gray sedan?"

"I'll come back and get it later," said James with a smirk. "I know the way."

***

Jane Thorne had invited all the women to the dining-room table in the ranch house. It was after dinner on the day following Jerry's sudden departure. After helping Jane clear the table, Gabriele took her place as Linda and Sadie joined them. It was difficult for her to believe the two wives had anything at all in common—other than being married to white supremacist thugs. They were a study in opposites. Linda was skinny, pointedly outspoken, and palpably toxic; Sadie was overweight, virtually silent, and superficially pleasant. She hoped Linda would not try to talk to her directly; Sadie, she thought, would rather talk to God. Gabriele understood that the success of her mission required the removal of all doubt…about her. She regarded the evening as an opportunity to bolster her position in the organization.

"Thank you all for coming over… We don't do this enough." Jane cast her eyes around the table, exuding a convincing charm. There were bottles and glasses on the table, with napkins at each place mat. "I have wine and whiskey… What would each of you prefer?"

Gabriele was the first to respond. "Whiskey for me, Jane."

"Why, I thought a German girl would rather drink wine," said Jane playfully.

"I'm no longer German," said Gabriele, making serial eye contact with all three of her drinking companions. "Wine is for wimps."

"Then I guess it's whiskey for everyone," announced Jane, filling Gabriele's glass to the brim.

Linda and Sadie both nodded. Jane poured each of them just two fingers of rye. Neither woman said anything. Gabriele thought that perhaps Linda and Sadie had been summoned by Jane to act as props for an assault on her cover story.

"To the revolution!" toasted Jane.

"To the revolution!" came the response. Gabriele drained her glass and absorbed its punch.

Jane poured another round of drinks. Gabriele got another full glass. Jane turned to her, poised to speak. Gabriele felt like she was sitting once again for her master's comprehensive exam...only drunk!

"You sure can drink, Gaby... I like that in a woman."

"Good old American whiskey," replied Gabriele without choking.

The women talked about cooking, the weather, the Lord, and the Militia of Wyoming. One thing they did not talk about was the bloody deeds of their men. Gabriele believed they all knew full well what Thorne's henchmen were doing (Jane certainly did). Indeed, Jesse and Jerry were engaged in something sinister as the women made small talk!

But violence was not on Jane's agenda.

"Gaby, I understand your maiden name was Barnes. That's not a German name at all." Jane, now buzzed herself, looked at her with benign curiosity. "Were you married before?"

In her moderate state of inebriation, Gabriele rattled off the answer she and Jerry had rehearsed. "I was born Gabriele Bach... No relation to the composer. I kept that name until last year when I moved to Florida. It just seemed like the right time to let go of everything that reminded me of Germany. Since I was no longer German, I did not need a German surname. I chose Barnes because it is one of the most common American names." She exhaled slowly. "Now I'm Gabriele Tompkins...and very proud of it."

"I asked if you were married before Jerry," persisted Jane. The other women sat forward and listened more intently.

Gabriele acted more drunk than she was. Having grown up with wine and schnapps, she was well prepared for *George Dickel*.

"Oh, so you did! Sorry, but the drink is making me a bit slow." She winked at Jane. "Yes, I was married to a German man. He was a worthless alcoholic. He beat me and left me pregnant. I miscarried. Then I ran like hell for Washington and buried myself in my work."

"So how did you and Jerry meet? I mean, he lives way out here."

Gabriele took another gulp of whiskey, mentally forming the sentences she needed…so they sounded unrehearsed. "Yes, it was just plain, dumb luck. Jerry took a vacation to Captiva—you know, he really loves the water—and we met on the beach. I had never seen a body like that in my life!"

At that point, the questioning was discontinued while Gabriele's companions (even Sadie) lost themselves in thought about what had obviously happened next. The rest of the evening was a blur, as Gabriele finally succumbed to the medicinal properties of *George Dickel*.

She did not remember going to bed.

***

After spending the rest of the night on the road, Jerry pulled into a fleabag motel in Green River. Not surprisingly, James insisted on one room with two beds. By sunrise, the chaperone was asleep. Jerry's eyes were closed, but he was wide-awake, formulating his plan for the staged killing of Jose. Luck had been with him so far; he could not afford to make a mistake now. He finally slept when the plan was perfect. He was thinking of Susan as he drifted off.

At noon, they checked out of the motel and drove to Kemmerer, with James chain-smoking the whole way. Jerry was the first to speak.

"Here's the deal, Jesse. First we'll do an area recon, looking for ingress and egress routes. I also want to get a look at the *human* terrain—population density and demographics. Wyoming is not exactly a target-rich environment for nonwhite scumbags." Jerry flashed his companion a maniacal grin. "I think you guys had something to do with keeping those numbers down."

Jerry wondered which of the unsolved Wyoming murders Beck had mentioned could be attributed to the draft dodger sitting next to him. He masked his contempt for the man with grim humor.

"I know Kemmerer pretty well, though, and I'm sure I can find us a stray Mexican... Do I get extra credit for two?"

"Cut the crap, rookie. It's bad enough that I have to babysit you. Just don't get caught doing your duty, okay?"

It was time to execute the plan. Jerry drove all over Kemmerer without seeing a single representative of any recognizable minority group. He worked his way to the outskirts of town and came up dry again.

So far, so good.

James sat silently for the rest of the afternoon while Jerry pretended to hunt human beings. Still without quarry, they made a quick grocery run and drove to a remote parking lot. As soon as he finished his sandwich, James spoke again.

"Why the hell did you choose this little shithole of a town to find someone to shoot? Why not Cheyenne...or Laramie?" The troll took a long gulp of beer, giving Jerry time to think. "Just what the fuck are we doing *here*?"

"Trying to commit murder without getting caught," responded Jerry matter-of-factly. "You told me to be careful."

"So...what now?"

"We go back to town and see if we can find a target."

"I hope we find one soon," whined James. "I don't think I can stand another full day of babysitting."

"Whatever it takes, Jess... Red didn't give me a time limit, ya know."

Jerry drove around some more, hunting superficially. James's impatience grew as darkness fell. Jerry ignored the man's body language. After a while, James went to sleep.

They passed in front of the JC Penney at five minutes after ten. Jose was standing on the corner. Even though April had broken winter's back, the evening was cold enough to explain the bulky coat he wore.

Showtime.

"There's one," said Jerry without pointing. James woke up with a start and put on his glasses.

"It's about time, cowboy... Now can we get on with this?"

"That's up to the spic over there, Jess. Be cool. We got all night to hunt this fucker down."

Jose waited until Jerry parked on the other side of the square. Then he stood in the cold for another ten minutes. Suddenly, he looked at his watch, swore in Spanish, and walked quickly down the street.

"Looks like his drug deal didn't go down," observed Jerry. "He's getting into a car."

"What's the plan?"

"I'm gonna follow this guy until the decisive moment," said Jerry without taking his eyes off the target.

"And when is that?" asked James.

"I'll know it when I see it."

Jose drove out of the square and headed for the reservoir. He had driven the route earlier in the day and found what he needed. He knew how to play his part—up until photo time. He and Jerry had not had time to talk about that. They would have to improvise. He wasn't too worried. They had done a lot of their business that way.

Jerry kept the truck a normal distance from the Neon as he followed the quarry onto State Road 233 toward the lake. After making the turn, they were the only cars on the road. Everything was playing out according to the script. Jerry relaxed a bit. James even managed a smile. Without a word, they each thought about the stakes. For Jerry, it was one step closer to retribution. For James, a successful kill would bring a new couple into Thorne's inner circle. Four more hands to help with the important work ahead.

As the reservoir came out of the night on the left, both men focused on the taillights in front of them.

Suddenly the Neon swung left and stopped between the road and the lake.

James broke the silence as Jerry slowed the truck. "Now show me your stuff."

"With pleasure, Jess... Stay in the truck until after I shoot him."

James nodded in the pale light of the dashboard.

Jerry parked behind the car, turned off the headlights, and withdrew his pistol. He got out of the truck, leaving the door open behind him. The cabin light would be enough to ruin James's night vision.

Jerry's boots crunched gravel. Twenty yards ahead of him, Jose was taking a long piss. He had left the door of the Neon open in case Jerry needed the light. The big man quickly closed the distance by half and sank into a combat stance.

He shouted at the victim. "Hey, Mexican scum, get your ass over here! What are you doing in my country?" Loud enough for James to hear.

Jose turned toward him and, feigning protest, spread his arms. Like Christ on the cross.

Jerry fired once.

The underpowered bullet tore through Jose's jacket and flattened against the breastplate. Jerry watched painfully as his friend went down hard. He walked to the body and knelt.

Jose smelled of death.

Jerry rolled the body over and found a sticky pool of liquid. Blood. Real blood! For a long moment, he thought his bullet had missed the body armor. He was close to panic by the time he discovered a pulse in the neck. He bent to Jose's ear and whispered, "You okay?"

Jerry's heart started beating again with a squeeze from Jose's left hand. It was a strong squeeze. Still whispering, Jerry explained the plan.

"My babysitter is back in the truck… I'm throwing you in the lake… The anchor will not be attached."

Another strong squeeze.

"When we're gone, walk north to get the car. It'll be on the other side of the road in the weeds."

"You owe me big-time," whispered the corpse.

Jerry ran back to the truck and opened the tailgate. He had donned work gloves and fished a climbing rope out of his war bag by the time his accomplice joined him.

"I'm gonna get rid of the body in the lake, Jess. It's too bloody to carry away."

"Your call," said the gnome. "I'm gonna take a picture."

"No!" commanded Jerry. "I need some help with this." He dragged a heavy toolbox to the edge of the tailgate and started looping the rope through the box's handles. James watched him with fascination.

"You improvise well for a rookie," Jesse blurted out with barely disguised admiration.

Who's the rookie?

Without abandoning his knot tying, Jerry glanced at his new colleague. "Now help me carry this thing to the water."

Without speaking, James grabbed the other end of the toolbox. Together, they lugged the box to the shore of the lake, a few yards from Jose's body. James ran back to the truck to get his camera.

Jerry moved quickly to drag Jose into the water. He wrapped the rope loosely around his friend's waist. The big man was standing chest-deep in the freezing water—with an apparently dead Mexican floating beside him, blood dripping from his mouth—when James returned.

"Hold the body up so I can show it to Red!"

Jerry lifted Jose's torso out of the water and waited for the flash. Done. As James moved up the bank to get a picture of the bloodstained gravel, Jerry reached for the toolbox, lifted it over his head, and shot-putted it into deeper water.

Weighted down by his heavy vest, Jose followed the toolbox. The water was only about ten feet deep. Wriggling out of his coat and body armor, Jose clung momentarily to the rocky bottom. Slowly rising toward the surface of the lake, he counted for more than a minute.

"Cover up that mess!" shouted Jerry, running out of the water.

James had produced a flashlight!

Terrified Jesse would find the flattened slug, Jerry arrived kicking dirt and rocks on the spot where Jose had fallen. A few seconds later, he was pushing James back to the truck.

Jerry had one more command for his partner. "You drive the truck... I'll stash the car."

Jerry drove Jose's car a hundred yards north and parked it in the tall grass next to the road. He left the keys in the switch and ran back to the truck. He figured James would be watching *him* instead of scanning the lake.

Jose broke the surface without a sound and surveyed the commotion. Just like nearshore reconnaissance in Colombia. Only much colder!

James drove behind the killer to the hide site, stopping at the edge of the grass. Jerry opened the door and jumped into the passenger side of his truck.

"They'll never trace the hit to us… Sorry for making you work."

The word *us* had just slipped out, but both men understood they were now on the same team.

Armed with proof of the murder, James drove Jerry back to Mineral King…and Gabriele. Jose came out of the water and drove back to Lone Mountain. By dawn, everyone was in place for the next act.

Whatever that turned out to be.

Chapter 15

The Compound

Susan listened to the voice mail from Gabriele with mounting anxiety. She had to remind herself that the disappearance of her colleagues was actually good news. But her colleagues were also her friends. That was the bad news. A mental picture of the Thorne compound crystallized inside her brain. That image—which she expected would be rerun every night—featured dark, ghoulish figures, torturing her friends and laughing at the government's feeble attempt to stop them. Now she would just have to wait for a dead drop to find out what had happened to Jerry and Gabriele.

"Beck."

"Gerhard, you know I hate to call you on the cell phone, but I couldn't wait for the office to contact you."

"It's okay, Susan… Go ahead."

"Our friends have been invited to join the club. I got a rapidly delivered voice mail saying they'll contact us when they can."

Susan let out the deep breath that had parked itself in her lungs as she spoke.

"That's great news, Susan!" Gerhard was almost shouting. "I'll be on the next plane to Cheyenne."

"Come to the apartment first. Did you get the key I mailed you?"

"Yes, I have it," replied Beck. "Will you be there tonight when I get in?"

"Probably not… I have a lot of driving to do."

"Be careful, Susan. I'll see you when you're done."

"I'm worried, Gerhard... I need to talk to someone."

"I'll be there for you, honey. Just relax... They'll be fine." Beck did not let on that he was more worried than Susan. Gabriele was now living with the most ruthless people in his files.

Susan pulled on some jeans, put a variety of groceries in a paper bag, and went back to the bedroom to finish dressing. She looked at herself in the mirror and saw an old woman. Completely different from the mirror in Jerry's bedroom. She ran her hand over his flannel shirt, hanging all the way down to her knees. Grasping a chunk of material in her fist, she raised it to her face.

She could still smell him.

But she couldn't talk to him! Except, she hoped, by servicing the dead-drop site five hours down the road. Indirect contact, Susan decided, was better than no contact at all. She replaced Jerry's shirt with something she could tuck into her jeans and took the grocery bag to the car. It was just after eight in the morning on what promised to be a very long day.

***

Gabriele was still in Jane's bed—hungover and fearing the worst—when a truck pulled up just outside the window. Jane's room doubled as a guest room, but Gabriele could see from the wealth of personal items adorning the walls and dressers that it was not used that way very often.

It was Jerry's truck! She knew it by sound, the way a cat does. Gabriele threw off the comforter and ran to the window. She tore back the curtains and looked for him. It was still dark, but she could see her husband in the dim light of the courtyard. He got out of the truck and stood for a long moment, surveilling the buildings. Like a prisoner must do on his first day of confinement.

Jerry is already working on a plan to get us out of here!

Gabriele suddenly felt safer than she had a right to feel. Then she took a closer look at Jerry.

He was still wet up to his waist. Obviously tired. There was a dark stain at chest level on his coveralls. *Blood?* She frantically searched for some evidence of a wound. Then he relieved her panic by walking to the back of the truck without obvious pain.

The test—whatever they had made him do—was over. He was alive. She didn't know whether to congratulate him or pray for him. As Gabriele sifted through her emotions, Jerry gathered their bags as Rulon James got out on the driver's side. A ghoul in the shadows. Using Jerry's pistol, he pointed to Jane's bedroom.

Gabriele fumbled for her clothes in the darkness. By the time she had them on, there was a soft knock at the door. Before she could say anything, Jerry was in her room. *Their* room. She ran into his arms and buried her head in his shoulder. Too scared to speak, she waited for him to take over. She felt his strength flowing into her and just held him. A minute later, he was whispering orders.

"Don't talk, Gaby… Just listen. You have to assume they're recording everything we say out loud. Let me lead… Just take my cues." He paused slightly. "Nod if you understand."

Gabriele nodded vigorously.

"I know you're worried about what I did last night… Don't be. Jose played his part perfectly. I passed the test… I think we're in." As she touched the stain on his chest, he added, "The chicken blood is for show."

Jerry held her with outstretched arms and spoke loudly in his best redneck voice. "It's done, Gaby… I got me a Mexican scumbag." He smiled at her and waited for the response he needed.

"Well done! I didn't know there were any spics left in this state." She had rehearsed the tone, but she was improvising the script. "What now?"

"Don't know, *Schatz*… I guess we just enjoy the guest room until someone calls."

"Let me undress you, big guy." Jerry nodded approval as Gabriele continued talking to the assumed microphone. "After you get clean, I'll show you just how much I appreciate being married to a real man."

Jerry moved quickly to the shower and stripped off his coveralls. The hot water revived his body the way Gabriele had revived his spirit. Wrapping himself in a towel, he stood in the doorway to the bedroom. Feigning lust, he called to her.

"I'm clean and ready… Take me in here, *Schatz*."

"With pleasure, *Junge*… This is how I say congratulations."

Once they were safely in the bathroom, Jerry closed the door and turned the shower back on. "There are no electronic bugs in here. I think by now these people are convinced I have a fetish for hot water. I *want* them to think that. We can use the bathroom to talk normally—and give *them* something to talk about."

He sat on the edge of the tub and motioned her to the toilet seat. As steam billowed between them, Jerry reported on everything he had done since leaving her in the hands of Red and Jane Thorne. Gabriele relaxed as he talked, finally letting fatigue embrace her. She felt comfortable enough when he was finished to sleep the rest of the night.

Jerry got dressed and lay down on the floor. He slept fitfully.

The loud knock came at seven. "Hey, lovebirds, time for breakfast!" They recognized the booming voice of Red Thorne. "You got ten minutes… Then you're late!"

"Okay, Red… Thanks!" Jerry shouted at the door. He turned to Gabriele and spoke in a normal voice. "I guess we don't have time for another round."

"Later, cowboy… I want you to think about it all day."

Jerry and Gabriele joined their hosts at the dining-room table. None of the others came. Jerry guessed that Red and Jane ate most of their meals alone. He knew Roy and Jesse lived with their wives in the back of the compound. He had yet to learn where Will Jeffers hung his cowboy hat.

***

Susan made Split Rock a little after one. Having driven nonstop, she had a legitimate need to go to the bathroom. Even though Wyoming had finally thrown off winter, there were no other cars at the historic site. This road, she thought, is just as lonely as the Oregon Trail must have been. She stood in front of the mirror looking for the load signal.

Nothing.

Sitting down, Susan tried to focus her imagination on Jerry's situation. In all likelihood, he was only twenty miles away. The only thing she could visualize was Jerry making love to her.

Still alone, she checked the site anyway. She hoped that maybe they had their load signals crossed. Though she knew it was unrealistic to expect a message so soon after Jerry and Gabriele's disappearance, there was no reason *not* to check.

She walked to the sign, talking to him—and to herself.

I am so sorry I got you into this!

But at least Jerry was trained for dealing with danger; Gabriele, she now admitted, was in over her head. As Susan reached for the concealment device, she felt sorry for herself as well. Sorrow with more than a tinge of guilt.

There was nothing inside the plastic rock. She put it back exactly as it had lain before and walked back to the car. It was time to check the secondary site. She was not looking forward to driving an hour farther from Cheyenne, but that was the procedure. Without much hope for success, Susan sped down the road.

She was thinking about Jerry but also about Gerhard. Two men so different and yet so similar. Big, strong, passionate, and tolerably volatile. Exciting men, she thought. Men to be proud of. She smiled at the absurdity of her situation. Gerhard would sleep in the spare bedroom of her apartment this night while Jerry played husband to Gabriele. Her father had told her about life being unfair. Susan now realized that he had been understating the case.

Susan spread the grass apart until she found it. Glancing behind her again, she picked up the plastic dog turd and cracked it open.

Nothing.

Exhaling audibly, she put the device back and returned to the empty parking lot. She was tempted to leave Jerry and Gabriele a note, just to check in, but they had agreed that Susan would only respond to the couple's drops. Although the messages were in code, the team could not take a chance that someone would find them.

Susan reached for her binoculars and took a long look at the canyon sprawling in front of her. Herds of enormous elk dotted the far slope. The scene only reminded her how much she missed Jerry. She stretched her legs and got back in the car. It was three o'clock. Gerhard would be in her living room when she got back.

***

He was there. Always on time, at least for business. As she opened the door, Susan silently added another adjective to her long list: *reliable*.

"Gerhard, dear, how *are* you?"

The bloodshot eyes looked up at her. "You look tired, Susan."

She gave him a friendly hug. "I've been on the road for twelve hours… What's *your* excuse?"

"I've been working late a lot."

"What else is new?" she cracked. "Want a drink?" Susan took off her coat and laid it on the couch. She didn't have much to tell him, but she was glad to have someone to talk to.

"Whiskey…if you have it."

"I have it." She dropped a thin sheaf of papers in his lap. "Read this… I'll be right back. I want to tell you a story."

Gerhard stared at the front page of the newsletter, not quite believing what he read. At the top was the name of the publication, centered on the image of a pit bull. The title read *The Watchdog*. Under the dog was a line that made his head hurt: "*The Newsletter of the Militia of Wyoming*." He moved his eyes down the page and started to devour the lead article.

Taxation or Tribute?
By Gabriele Tompkins

In 1774 the citizens of Marlborough, Massachusetts, faced a situation similar to that which Wyoming citizens face today. They adopted the slogan "A freeborn people are not required to submit to tyranny." Like the men and women of Marlborough, we are a freeborn people, facing taxation without representation. Unlike them, we have chosen tyranny over revolution. At least for now.

In the first millennium of civilization, chiefdoms, states, and empires—formed through conquest—demanded tribute in return for peace. The federal government of the United States demands tribute from us for the same reason. They call it taxes. Political scientists through modern history have expounded the theory that a state must balance its requirement for security with the need for its citizens to enjoy liberty. Taxation, they tell us, is the only way to ensure that we have both. The truth is that—at the end of the twentieth century—we have neither security nor liberty.

Innocently, we have let ourselves be subjected to unjust taxation at all levels of government. In theory, the politicians we elect are the voices of the people, using tax money for the benefit of all. In practice, the strength of those voices varies inversely with distance away from Hometown, Wyoming. By the time they get to Washington, our elected leaders forget who we are and what we need. Tribute is no longer for the benefit of real Americans. Here are some of the things we get for our money:

* Gun control that is gradually and insidiously depriving us of our constitutional right to keep and bear arms
* Financial and diplomatic support for a global economy where developing

nations are free to put our citizens out of work (this is the ultimate form of affirmative action)
* Public schools that teach our children that America is *not* the best country in the world
* Gay rights
* Environmental policy that places the interests of owls above the interests of hardworking Americans
* Foreign policy contracted to the United Nations (for which we pay extra)
* The military industrial complex (we start wars—and keep them going—so that evil corporations can make money)
* Abortion rights
* Welfare for American wannabes who do not want to work and cannot even speak English

What can the average citizen of Wyoming do about tribute? Within the current system, not much. But a groundswell of opposition is building. Like the citizens of Marlborough on the eve of the American Revolution, we are on the verge of a major change in the way we allow ourselves to be governed. Through *Watchdog*, the Militia of Wyoming will keep you posted on the developing situation. We're ahead of the colonists in one respect: they did not have the internet.

If you have it, use it.

Stay tuned and on guard.

gtompkins@aol.com

Susan came into the room to find that Gerhard had removed his jacket and his shoes. His feet were propped up on the arm of the sofa.

Just like old times. He took the glass of whiskey with a silent nod as his ex-wife moved to a chair opposite the couch. She had changed into her pajamas and wore a bathrobe, a glass in her hand.

"I hope you don't mind, Gerhard. I just had to get out of my road clothes." She grinned. "It's not as though we have any secrets."

Gerhard sat up and waved a hand at her. "Not at all, not at all."

He drained the glass and smiled. "If we don't get Gaby out of there soon, she'll start a revolution all by herself!"

"That was the inaugural issue...*before* they disappeared." Susan was not smiling. "It came to the post office box last week. I wanted to show it to you in person."

"I'm very proud of her," said Gerhard wistfully.

He caught himself at once, returning to a professional tone. "So...what else can you tell me?"

Susan didn't have any additional information on the operation, but there was a lot she wanted to say. The whiskey gnawed at her inhibitions.

It was time.

She proceeded to tell him about her love for Jerry. She left out the sexual details but knew how easily Gerhard could fill them in. She didn't care what he thought. His ear was the catharsis she needed.

The more Susan talked, the more Gerhard found himself liking Jerry. He realized he'd been too hard on the man. In addition to his genuine misgivings about placing a self-avowed gun nut in the militia, he had been (unconsciously) protecting Susan. Her confessions relieved the last of his lingering guilt over their failed marriage. His newfound confidence in Jerry made up, to some degree, for the FBI man's remorse for putting Gabriele in great danger.

Gerhard was ready for his own confession.

"You accused me of having the hots for Gabriele, Susan," he began. "You're right... I do, but it's more than just a physical attraction. Her courage blows me away." Gerhard sighed again. "I just don't think she'll ever be able to love me."

"Have you told her how you feel?"

He winced. "Not yet... I don't want to make her situation even more complicated. I'll wait until this is all over." He produced a wan smile.

"Maybe then."

They went to separate beds, dreaming of lovers out of touch and out of reach.

***

Red Thorne stood up, signaling that breakfast was over. "Jane will take you folks to the honeymoon suite... I have some business to discuss with Will." He smiled at his wife and walked away. Jerry was astonished at how normal everything seemed. Good food, friendly chatter, a rancher on the run, his wife clearing the table. No talk of Jerry's exploits the night before. No anti-government tirades. Not a negative word about anything or anybody. Normality in the wake of cold-blooded murder made Gabriele shudder. They had confiscated his weapon; Jerry suspected their vetting had just begun. He felt the voice-activated tape recorder, back in place against his ankle. It would not be picking up anything useful here.

Jane took off her apron and stood at the kitchen door. "As soon as you get your bags, I'll walk you out."

Jerry and Gabriele went back to the guest room. Silently, they acknowledged to each other that someone had searched through their bags. It had been a sloppy job...possibly a greeting: "Dear Mr. and Mrs. Tompkins, welcome to the Thorne ranch. Don't try anything foolish." Five minutes later, they followed Jane across the compound to a row of three travel trailers that had not seen the open road in a long time. Carrying two of the three bags, Jerry paced the distance between Thorne's house and the middle trailer. Thirty-six inches times twenty-one paces. Sixty-three feet. He estimated the breadth of the compound to be about twice the distance. Until he could pace it off, that would have to do.

The dirt under their feet was hard, but deep tire tracks indicated it would not stay that way all year. He felt the sun on his back and noted that they were walking west. Turning around, he saw two oversize garages and a long shed lining the north side of the square. On the south end, he noticed cattle pens and a hay storage area. Driveways at each corner led vehicles into and out of the compound. Tractors stood poised for action. The enclosure was fenced by head-high wooden posts, with wire mesh between them.

Beyond the fences, spread pasture even drier than Jerry's. The landscape rose gently uphill to a barren ridge. The only trees on the property were in front of the house. Gabriele had recently observed to Jerry that, on the vast Wyoming plain, trees acted as markers, pointing toward human settlements. Planted trees, rising from the sage, were like seabirds leading mariners to distant islands. They were now on one of those islands—with no easy way off.

Alcatraz on the high plains.

Jane opened the door and ushered them into the trailer. The tour took all of two minutes. Compressed into a length of thirty-five feet were a small galley, a dinette, closet space, a queen-size bed, and a bathroom. Jerry leaned into the bathroom and found a shower. Perhaps a safe space to talk to Gabriele. The trailer had no television, no radio, no computer, and no telephone.

Nothing in, nothing out.

"If you need anything, I'll be in the house," said Jane. She gave Jerry a starstruck look and continued in the same hostess tone. "I bet you're tired, buckaroo. We have nothing on the schedule for you folks today, so just relax and enjoy."

"What about meals?" asked Gabriele.

"You'll eat with me and Red today," replied Jane, focusing on Gabriele. "Tomorrow morning you'll go with Linda to the grocery store in Lander."

"Just me?"

"Just you, Gaby. I'm afraid Red's rules are pretty strict. At least for a while, we have to insist that one of you is always here at the ranch."

Jane delivered the chilling news as if she were a flight attendant asking them to buckle up.

Chapter 16

The Ceremony

After Jane left them, Jerry and Gabriele met in the bathroom of the trailer with the shower on full blast. They reviewed their situation and agreed it would be impossible to get a message to Susan via dead drop. Gabriele couldn't see a way to ditch Linda during the grocery run long enough to visit either of the sites. As long as the hostage system persisted, they would *never* be able to contact Susan. Jerry was kicking himself for not anticipating such a predictable roadblock.

Clausewitz strikes again!

Jerry's principal concern at the moment, though, was over James's car, still sitting at the Jumping Frog. Jose would certainly be there when they went back for it. There was no way to warn him—at least not from the trailer.

Jerry and Gabriele came out of the shower, faking afterglow. Then they moved in. Looking out the trailer window, Jerry found his truck at the north end of the compound. James had kept the keys in his pocket, along with Jerry's P226. The big man now realized that shooting their way out was off the table. He and Gabriele would have to run.

It would be a long and perilous run.

Jerry needed to get into the truck. He had managed to throw the cell phone out the window during the drive back from Kemmerer. He was almost completely sure there was nothing in the truck that could expose them. But he had left a wad of cash in the glove compartment. Cash they could use during their escape. There was a chance the truck wasn't locked, and Jerry thought getting the cash would be worth the risk.

He quietly approached the truck. Sixteen paces. Forty-eight feet. He stood at the side of the vehicle and looked casually at the door locks. *Open.* He reached for the handle and yanked open the passenger door. Leaning inside, he looked over his shoulder to see if he was being observed. The compound was empty. He couldn't see Jane Thorne at the kitchen window.

Armed with a plausible cover for action (it was, after all, his truck), Jerry checked the glove compartment. *Gone.*

James had simply taken the cash. The fact that Jerry had hidden money in the glove compartment would not compromise his cover for status, but without cash, he and Gabriele would have fewer options as they ran. Perhaps even scarier was the message Rulon James had just sent him.

Welcome to the family. We don't trust you.

On the way back to the trailer, he decided what to do. Jane rapped on the window and waved. She was smiling, but that gave him no reassurance at all. He felt like a zoo animal.

Inside the trailer, he told Gabriele in a loud voice he was going to jump in the shower again (this time by himself, in order to actually get clean). Turning on the water, he took the tape recorder out of his boot and composed a short message to Jose. Ten minutes later, Rulon James knocked once on the flimsy trailer door and burst in without asking permission.

Another message.

Ignoring Gabriele, who stood in the galley arranging cookware, the gnome leaned to his right and found Jerry sitting at the dinette. The big man was reading his wife's latest editorial, still in draft form.

"Time to go, rookie."

"Where to?" asked Jerry, looking up from his reading.

"We're going back to get my car."

Jerry looked over his shoulder and winked at Gabriele. "I can think of better ways to spend the afternoon, Jesse."

James evidently didn't catch the humor. His eyes were darting around the trailer, still searching for evidence. There were only two things in the trailer that could get them killed: the device still in Jerry's boot and the mini cassette tape in his pocket. He was reasonably sure they wouldn't strip-search him again, and no man (especially not Jesse) would put a hand in Jerry's jeans pocket.

"Let's go," ordered James. He sounded to Gabriele like a prison warden leading a condemned man to the gallows.

Gabriele had confidence that Jerry could take care of himself, but the prospect of being left alone again was frightening.

Jerry brushed past James and kissed his wife. "Be good... I'll finish reading your stuff when I get back."

Gabriele looked at James, now standing outside the open door. "That's tonight, right?"

"That depends," said the gnome.

And Jerry followed the man through the door. Gabriele wanted to cry. She waved instead.

***

It was after four by the time they exited the interstate at Lone Mountain. Jerry was driving; James was smoking his seventh cigarette. Luckily, it was warm enough to ride with the windows open. Country music blared at them. Jerry knew the draft dodger hated it.

The long driveway to the Jumping Frog appeared, and Jerry closed the windows to keep out the dust. He turned to James as they bounced toward his ranch house.

"I'm gonna have to talk to my caretaker, Jess... Gotta at least ask him how he's gettin' along." Otherwise, he'll suspect there's something wrong. Jerry looked back at the driveway. "Just a handshake and a few words."

"Make it quick," barked James. "I'll be right behind you."

Jerry could see Jack Ellis standing by the fence beyond the barn. There was no sign of Jose.

"No problem, Jess... I just wanna look natural. I don't even need to go into the main house."

Without warning, Jerry leaned on the truck's horn.

"What the hell are you doing?" snapped a surprised James.

"Lookin' natural, Jess." The big man laughed heartily as he skidded to a halt and jumped out of the truck.

Jack Ellis started walking toward the truck. Jerry casually put both hands in his pockets. Walking slowly now, he met Ellis halfway to the cattle pens. James got out and followed Jerry like a bodyguard.

"Howdy, Jack," said the boss, extending his huge right hand. Without looking back, Jerry sensed he wasn't far enough ahead of James to have a private word with his foreman.

Worst-case scenario.

Jerry pumped the handshake three times, pressing a tiny cassette tape into Ellis's palm.

"I want you to let all my friends know that Gaby and I are having a great time upstate." As he spoke, Jerry cast his eyes to the main house. Rulon James could only see Jack's eyes, responding in the affirmative.

"Sure, Jerry… I'll make sure they all know. Nothin' ta worry about here. Diane and I got this place under control. When ya comin' back?"

"No way of knowin'," said Jerry truthfully. "Gaby and I love the Tetons. We're lookin' at buyin' a place." He gestured toward his bodyguard. "Jess here wants to sell."

Rulon James managed an awkward smile, tinged with impatience.

Jerry continued reading the script in his head. "We'll come back when we get tired of being alone with each other in the wilderness."

"That might take a while," quipped Ellis. "If I had a place in the Tetons—and a cowgirl like Gaby—I might *never* come home!"

"You get the picture, then."

Jack laughed. "I think I do, boss!"

James motioned to the gray sedan, still parked on the gravel where they'd left it two nights before.

"Let's move."

Without any further conversation, the two men were gone. Jack Ellis did not need any more cryptic instructions. He waited until the two vehicles got to the end of the driveway. Then he entered the main house and gave Jerry's tape to Jose.

***

Gabriele and Linda left before nine the next morning. Jerry was sitting at the dinette when he heard a soft knock on the trailer door. Surprised, he scanned the table and counter for evidence before answering. Satisfied, he opened the door to find Jane Thorne standing on the middle step.

"Jane! Mornin'," was all he could manage to say.

"Good morning, Jerry." She was beaming. "I wanted to give you my personal welcome to the Thorne ranch." She moved to the top step, bracing against the open door behind her.

Jerry did not want to invite her inside. He tried to stall. "Thank you, Jane… Gaby and I really appreciate your hospitality."

"I was talking to just you."

The door closed with a thud as she stepped into the trailer. The woman clasped her hands in front of the black dress that seemed to simply hang from her bony shoulders. Jerry noticed something about her hands. The prominent knuckles did not match her rounded face. *Maybe arthritis*, he thought. She wore clip-on earrings and a red splash of lipstick, hastily applied. Jane Thorne looked like a housewife with not enough to do. At first glance, harmless. Her body language spoke the opposite.

"What can I do for you?" said Jerry carefully.

"Give me what I want." She took another step forward.

Jerry froze. Before he could decide what to do, Jane reached for his belt buckle with both hands and began loosening the flap. The big man was now pinned against the kitchen cabinet by a woman half his size. Under ordinary circumstances, it would have been easy to deal with such a clumsy advance. But these were not at all ordinary circumstances! Jerry's mind raced for something to say. Anything.

"Is this part of my initiation?" He managed a shallow grin.

Jane fumbled for his zipper and smiled up at him. She was now on her knees.

"Sort of."

Jerry could feel his skin crawling. He had considered every conceivable event that might befall them. But not this! His first thought was of Susan. Then he began to calculate how much time it would take Gabriele to return with the groceries (evidently Jane had already done the math). He tried to relax and play the part. That was becoming more and more difficult to do.

"Jane, look, I'm trying to be a good husband."

"Very noble, Jerry, and I'm sure you are." Her attention shifted back to his face, directly overhead. "According to Jesse, you're also a very efficient killer… I like that in a man."

"But, Jane, *all* the men here are killers."

"Yes, but you are the most beautiful man I've seen in a long time." She lowered her head. "I've wanted to do this to you ever since you walked into that first meeting."

"With Gaby."

Without looking up at him, Jane ended the conversation. "Gabriele is the most beautiful *woman* I've seen in a long time."

With images of Susan in his head, it was over quickly. Jerry just stood there as Jane got up and left without another word. The silent implication was that she would be back—whenever she chose to take advantage of Jerry's prisoner status. For all he knew, Red Thorne had sanctioned his wife's behavior or perhaps even encouraged it. Although she hadn't said so, Jerry knew that if he refused to submit, Jane would tell Gabriele about what had just happened. Sexual blackmail. There was nothing he could do.

Jerry sat alone again at the dinette. He briefly considered running across the compound and bursting into the house. He would steal a gun, shoot all of them, and then just drive out. Analyzing this course of action revealed two problems: one, he didn't know where every one of the armed men was located; two, he didn't know where Gabriele was. Jerry thought he could wax most of the men.

But he wouldn't be able to kill *all* of them…at least not at the same time.

Working alone, Jerry would be killed by one of the stragglers. Gabriele would die soon after that.

***

Red Thorne's extended family had assembled again, this time in the living room of the main house. It was after dinner—the first meal Jerry and Gabriele had shared in the trailer. The chairs and couches had been moved to the walls. A white bedsheet lay over the carpet in front of the fireplace. Something was about to happen, but Gabriele had no idea what it was. She was so frightened that she thought the rest of the gang would surely notice. *Gang.* That was a good word to describe them. Jerry had called it a terrorist cell. *Too romantic*, she thought.

They're just a bunch of thugs.

"I suppose you folks are wondering why we're all here tonight," said Thorne. Gabriele glanced quickly at Jerry and found him smiling pleasantly. Sensing her anxiety, he took his wife's hand. Gabriele immediately felt better. She could not have known that her touch made *Jerry* feel better. Gabriele searched each face in the room for a clue to what was going on. Finding nothing, she braced for Thorne's explanation.

"The role of ceremony in history goes all the way back to the Stone Age." Gabriele hung on to Jerry's iron grip. A psychological anchor. Ceremonies, she knew, had a mixed reputation through history.

"The aboriginal world consisted of bands and tribes, bound together by kinship and common purpose. We are a modern-day band, growing slowly into a tribe. We will unite with other like-minded tribes. Those tribes will develop into a chiefdom, which will then grow into a new nation." Thorne paused and looked right at them.

"You have been selected to become founding members of this nation. The United States has been in decline for some time. We aim to start over, using the principles of the original Constitution. We will form a more perfect union, based on European identity, Christian beliefs, and frontier spirit. Our nation will be separate from the rest of America. We will be an island of sanity between the America that is failing and the Canada that has already failed. White people from both countries will flock to our sanctuary to live as they wish. Others will leave our land to live as *they* wish."

Thorne motioned Gabriele to the middle of the room. Releasing Jerry's hand, she stood up, heart pounding. A few steps later, she was facing Thorne. Jerry's size had always made her feel strong. Thorne's size made her feel weak. More than physical bulk, it was an aura of total control.

"Take off your pants."

Gabriele's weakness exploded into exhaustion. She was too tired to panic, too feeble even to cast a glance at Jerry. She had only enough strength to accomplish the simple task Thorne had ordered. She sat down on the sheet and began removing her boots. The sluggishness of her movements prolonged the horror taking shape in her mind. Jerry sat forward in his chair and watched his wife pull the tight jeans down over her knees then her feet. Smooth white skin glowed in the firelight.

Jerry watched with growing alarm. He could no longer play along. He had to break the spell! His facade of calm masked a surge of rage he would have to bury deep in his guts.

"And just where are you going with this, Red?" He knew where Thorne was going, but he could do nothing about it.

Unless it was a bluff.

"I'm going to do your wife while you watch." He smiled gleefully as Jerry's face tightened. "And then Jane will do *you*...while Gabriele watches."

They were about to pay a very high price for the sake of the mission.

Jerry's face tightened further. He looked around to see if there was a course of action available to him. Under any other circumstances, Thorne would already be dying in Jerry's well-trained hands. But all the men were armed and he was not.

He would just have to watch.

"On your knees," commanded Thorne.

Gabriele, like a robot, assumed the position.

"Bend over."

Gabriele placed her elbows on the floor and lay forward like an Egyptian sphinx. She was petrified, but she did not have the energy to cry or scream. She waited in terror for the monster to have his way with her.

Thorne moved behind a trembling Gabriele and slowly pulled the white panties down to her knees. It was then that Jerry noticed a metal bucket lying next to Gabriele's foot. Withdrawing a ball of cotton from the bucket, Thorne touched it to the curve of her left hip. She jumped, letting out a short gasp.

After a few seconds of swabbing, Thorne discarded the cotton and reached back into the bucket with both hands. This time, he withdrew what looked to Jerry like a piece of carbon paper and pressed it against the same spot on Gabriele's hip. Peeling off the paper, Thorne reached for something behind Jane's chair. As he extracted it, Jerry breathed an audible sigh of relief. Gabriele was shaking so violently she could not hear it. Neither could she see that Red Thorne held a tattoo gun. He turned it on and lowered the instrument to her skin.

"Don't move, Gaby... This will hurt a little bit."

Gabriele had never heard the sound that now filled the room. It reminded her of a swarm of bees, gentle but powerful. Soft...almost soothing. All of a sudden, she realized she would not be raped in front of the others. Her euphoria was quickly interrupted by the sharp pain of needles penetrating her skin. And Thorne's hand grasping her flesh to keep the ink flowing into the line of the template. The burning took her attention away from the horror of Thorne's touch. She thought her skin would be ripped apart. She began to hyperventilate.

"Relax," said Thorne in a soft voice, completely out of character. "Control your breathing and don't move. This will take about twenty minutes... I can't have you passing out on me."

Gabriele began taking short breaths, exhaling forcefully to expel the oxygen that was making her dizzy. She did not relax. The pain was agonizing. She bit into her lip and managed to avoid crying out. Thorne took the gun away for a few seconds, and she could feel the cotton again. Jerry was glad she couldn't see what the rest of them saw. Thorne was wiping blood and ink from the silver-dollar-sized design now taking shape. Gabriele heard the sound of bees again and braced for more pain.

Jerry strained to see what Thorne was drawing. As the minutes passed, he could make out a circle with lines running back and forth. A star. A star within a circle. The brand of the Thorne ranch! Jerry looked at the others, one by one. Each must have gone through the same ritual, or they would not be sitting here. Even fat Sadie.

Kinship and common purpose.

Thorne had chosen Gabriele to go first. Jerry would have given anything to spare her the terror. But he understood that *watching* her being terrorized was part of his initiation. All at once, it was clear to him why Thorne took couples rather than individuals into his inner circle. Jerry had not gone berserk. Perhaps this would be his final test.

God, let this be over!

The needle gun stopped. Gabriele took several more deep breaths but did not dare move. Thorne was smearing some kind of ointment over the tattoo. She stiffened again as the man pulled her panties back in place.

"Get dressed, Gaby… It's Jane's turn to do Jerry."

Gabriele pulled on her jeans as quickly as she could. In her pain, that wasn't very quickly. She was now sorry she had not worn sweatpants. Her hip felt like she'd fallen asleep naked in the hot sun. She couldn't wait to get back to the trailer and undress again. But she would *have* to wait. Jerry, she was sure, would take it better than she had.

Gabriele sat down gingerly on the sofa as her husband stood up and started unloosening his belt. She almost let out a scream when she remembered the tape recorder in Jerry's boot.

We're dead!

"Just the shirt," said Thorne.

Relieved, Gabriele willed herself to remain stoic.

Jerry unbuttoned his flannel shirt and wrestled it from his shoulders. He pulled the undershirt over his head and stood in front of Jane Thorne. Jane, clad in white, stared into the biggest male chest she had ever seen. Everyone stared. Gabriele felt a surge of pride. Roy Murdock felt a surge of hate. They all watched with fascination as Jane reached up and laid a cold hand on Jerry's shoulder.

"Sit down and cross your legs like an Indian."

Jerry sank to the floor as she guided him down.

Kneeling behind him, Jane repeated the procedure her husband had performed on Gabriele. She took more time to complete the tattoo than Red had. Gabriele couldn't determine whether the extra time was due to Jane's lack of expertise or to the obvious fact that she was having a great deal of fun. Red didn't seem to mind. Gabriele minded quite a bit.

Thirty minutes later, Jerry's left shoulder blade was done. Jane was the first to speak. "Show your wife what she now wears on her hip, Jerry."

Jerry stepped to the sofa, squatted in front of Gabriele, and twisted his torso to the right. The brand—raw and swollen—came alive for her on Jerry's back. It rose and fell with his breathing as the ointment glistened in the firelight. She was glad the threatening symbol had been burned into her in a spot where she couldn't see it herself. She hoped that, if they survived, she could get it removed. Nodding to Jane, Gabriele signaled she had finished examining the tattoo.

"A special honor in my life, Jane."

Gabriele and Jerry stood to face Red Thorne. In a bizarre way, the scene reminded Gabriele of their Lone Mountain wedding.

"Congratulations to both of you!"

Thorne clasped his hands and continued. "You are now among the anointed. You are Christian soldiers in the holy quest upon which we have embarked. From this moment on, everything you do is for the cause."

No one moved.

Inspecting his newest acolytes, Thorne wore a somber expression. He seemed to be looking inside them. "Jerry and Gabriele, do you swear to uphold and defend the organic Constitution of the United States against all enemies, foreign and domestic, under all circumstances, including the sacrifice of your own lives?"

"We do," the Tompkins's responded together. Jerry tightened his hold on Gabriele's hand to soften the blow of Thorne's words. The worst part was not being able to talk to her, not being able to tell her that she would live, that *Thorne* would be the one to sacrifice his life for the cause so that she would not have to.

But he couldn't.

Then Thorne broke into a smile and spoke to them informally. "You know...this is a cattle ranch. We brand our livestock to ensure they don't get rustled. We don't want the citizens of our new society to be rustled either. You now wear a circle with a five-pointed star inside. The circle stands for unity. The star is for lasting strength. We'll need both of those advantages in order to prevail against the forces of evil. Onward and upward!" Thorne paused for effect. "We have a lot of work to do."

Thorne's laugh reminded Jerry of his MP5 submachine gun firing three-round bursts. He fantasized about firing back. Thorne stopped firing, but Jerry did not stop fantasizing.

"Get ready for a wild ride to freedom!"

Chapter 17

The Statue

The days after their induction were spent mostly inside the trailer...waiting. The drama of the ceremony had made them feel like part of the group. A good thing as well as a bad thing. But now they felt once again like laboratory mice. Perhaps it was a measure of the skill with which they were playing the game, but Jerry and Gabriele were becoming bored. Boredom—as Jerry knew full well—was not the warrior's friend.

Gabriele focused on her writing. She was preparing another issue of *The Watchdog*, as well as a speech for the May meeting of the militia. She knew the e-mail was piling up on the AOL account in the main house, but Gabriele had not been assigned the task of answering it. Perhaps that would come later, when they were totally trusted. Writing was helping her cope. The Thornes could not record what she wrote. To a limited degree, she and Jerry could even communicate through writing, burning their notes surreptitiously. Of all the things Gabriele had given up, freedom of speech was by far the most difficult. Writing had given her some of it back, even if she didn't believe the hateful opinions she was churning out.

Jerry focused on surveillance. From one side of the bedroom, he could observe Thorne's house and the road; from the other, he could watch the back pasture and the ridge. Surveillance was to Jerry what writing had become to Gabriele. It passed the time and did not require talking. It was absolutely vital to the success of the mission and to their prospects for escape. With only occasional walks around the compound, Jerry spent three days drawing mental diagrams of the ranch and visualizing all possible action scenarios—what members of the gang might do and, more difficult, keeping track of them (almost never clustered in one place). He worked out his own courses of action for each situation and how to protect Gabriele when things went south.

Jerry was good at visualization, a benefit but also a curse. Susan was prominent in his mind. He was frantic to talk with her. Neither Susan nor Gerhard had fully appreciated Thorne's obsession with security. There was still no way to talk to Susan. Jerry and Gabriele were trapped.

Gabriele had never suspected that acting could be such hard work. Outside the trailer, she could react to events and comments thrown at her (she had found that she was very good at thinking on her feet). But inside their tiny home, it was necessary to invent dialogue without any external stimulus. She and Jerry were constantly having to make their private conversations sound real. Gabriele started teaching him existentialism. When she had gone through her master's thesis, she began teaching him to speak German. That, they had agreed, would eat up a lot of time.

Acting, she had discovered, was a creative and dynamic process. Deception became more difficult with time. Lying the first time was not challenging for Gabriele (she had been surprised by that). *Remembering* the lies—and making sure they fit together in a consistent narrative—was the growing problem she now faced. Time alone with Jerry, both inside and outside the bathroom, allowed Gabriele to memorize the pattern of lies that kept them alive.

Jerry began to notice another pattern. Each morning before dawn, Will Jeffers and Rulon James got in an old pickup truck and drove into the vast open spaces south of the ranch. Jerry had conducted an extensive map study of the area. He knew that the dirt road leading away from Thorne's ranch led through a narrow pass before separating into a confusing network of tracks across some of the most forbidding landscape in the country.

The Red Desert.

The tactical advantages of this geography were obvious: secrecy, ingress/egress, and the space for testing weapons. Jeffers and James were out there somewhere in the thousands of square miles of desolation, working on a project about which Jerry knew nothing. Had he still been in the Navy, steeped in operational security, such information stinginess would not have bothered him. Sitting on the only bed in the trailer, it bothered him a lot.

Gabriele looked up from her writing and called to him. "*Junge*, come in here and tell me if this sounds right."

The big man lumbered into the dinette and sat down next to her. The whole trailer shook when he walked. "Shoot, *Schatz*."

"Sam Adams was precisely the man America needed at a decisive moment in history," she read. "Long before he organized the Sons of Liberty and threw tea into Boston Harbor, Adams was a powerful revolutionary voice. He accused the British of having 'totally lost all sense of morality.' He went on to tell his fellow colonists that their enslavement was motivated by 'passion, cruelty, and revenge' on the part of the British. We in contemporary America are in the same position—and we have a lot to learn from Mr. Adams. He was at first branded by his own contemporaries as a fanatic, but he persevered to become the soul of the greatest revolution this planet has ever seen."

Jerry looked at the ceiling and then at her. "I love the way you write, Gaby… Read on."

"Sam Adams stood at Boston Harbor under a newly created flag—emblazoned with a green tree and the words 'Liberty Tree' and 'Appeal to God.' Later, he became the first to call for a 'Continental Congress,' in which he then served. Adams's constant demand in that body was simple: 'A state is never free but when each citizen is bound by no law that he has not approved of.' By that measure, we, the citizens of Wyoming, are not at all free. We are permitted to elect representatives to federal and state governments—but those officials do not pass the laws *we* want. Only the government closest to the people can conform to Sam Adams's litmus test for freedom. That is why we all feel so comfortable with our county sheriffs. That is why we find all other politicians so easy to hate."

"You got that right," interrupted Jerry. "I hope Red gives us something to do soon. I'd sure like to turn some of that hate into action!"

Gabriele continued her reading. "We do, however, have a savior in our midst. Red Thorne is a modern-day Sam Adams. He is precisely the man at *this* decisive moment in history to reveal the tyranny of the federal government and sound the trumpet of freedom. We in the Militia of Wyoming are blessed to have the prophet of the coming revolution—and it is our solemn duty to help Red Thorne spread the word. A groundswell of support is building steadily. The federal government is already afraid of our movement. In the coming months, they will step up their campaign to discredit private militias. Be on the lookout for unexplained bombings across the land. They will blame the violence on *us*. They want to create a police state!" She took a quick breath. "But *we* stand in their way—united against tyranny!"

"That's a great speech, *Schatz*. You missed your calling."

"I would love to have written speeches for the *Führer*," replied Gabriele animatedly. "Given that I did not come of age in the thirties, though, this will do just fine." She pointed at the hidden microphone then nodded at the bed.

"But all this excitement is making me *horny*... Take me *now*, you big lug."

Jerry and Gabriele faked their way through a demonstration of marital bliss. Half an hour later, there was a knock on the door. Quickly stripping off his shirt, Jerry moved three steps, yanked it open, and greeted Roy Murdock, standing on the outside step. The smirk on Roy's face told Jerry that the Tompkins show had been a great success. But he could tell that Murdock was about to tell him something else. Something ominous.

"Time to go to work, pal. I just met with Red."

Jerry put his shirt back on and followed Roy to the trailer next door. It was the first time he had been in one of the other trailers. It was bigger than his, with two bedrooms and a larger dinette area. Jerry wondered how in the world two young children could be raised properly under such conditions. The answer, pretty obviously, was that they couldn't. Murdock sat at the table and motioned for Jerry to do the same. Sadie and the kids were at a Christian Identity workshop on the other side of town.

"We have a mission tonight," said Roy. He was professional, almost military.

Jerry looked at his Rolex. It was just after two in the afternoon. "I'm ready, Roy... It gets boring just sittin' around in the trailer."

"*Riiight!*" answered Murdock sarcastically. "Listen up, man... This'll be a quick one."

"What's the plan?"

"You'll be the trigger man, hotshot." Murdock spread a Wyoming road map on the table. "This is the target." He was pointing to Exit 323 of the interstate, just east of Laramie.

"The Lincoln statue?"

"Exactly," replied Murdock. "We've wanted to get that bastard for a long time."

"Me too," said Jerry hastily. Then he thought some more and added, "Why not go to Washington and destroy the *real* monument?"

"Too much security," said Murdock.

With the tape recorder in his boot, Jerry thought he might actually get some hard evidence this time. Hiding that evidence and then passing it to Susan would be another matter altogether. But this conversation was a huge leap forward.

"Why do you say *that*, Roy? Someone had no trouble planting a bomb in the Air and Space Museum last year."

"And just who do you think that was, asshole?"

"I figured you guys probably had something to do with it."

"Let's just say," added Murdock carefully, "that Washington is off-limits for a while. After that fiasco, no saboteur in his right mind would get near the place."

It was true. Security on the mall and in most federal buildings in the capital had been increased significantly since the attempted bombing. Jerry kept probing.

"Overwhelming odds never stopped me and my guys in combat... We *specialized* in being outnumbered... We always fought more effectively when we were surrounded."

Roy did not take the bait. "We go with the statue here. In at midnight…make the hit…out by this route." He pointed to the road leading into Colorado. "Then home the long way." Roy traced an arc to the south and west, coming under the interstate and north over the Red Desert.

"And what are we going to hit Mr. Lincoln *with*, Roy?"

Murdock smiled, and Jerry thought he detected a hint of pride on the Californian's face.

"Your very own AT-4."

Jerry was both surprised and impressed.

"That's cool," he replied calmly. It was the safest answer he could think of. Then he added, "Now *there's* a weapon I left the Navy without stealing… Where'd you get it?"

"It wasn't easy," said Murdock, giving in to the urge to boast. "The black market ain't what it used to be… I had to steal a bunch o' them from an armory in California."

"I can't wait to hear *that* story!"

"You'll have to," said Roy firmly. "We got work to do."

The two men went over the plan again before Sadie and her kids returned to Murdock's trailer. Get the weapon, go to the target, fire the weapon, then leave. Simple… But Jerry worried about the leaving part. Anti-tank rockets were not the quietest thing he had ever fired. He felt better when Murdock showed him a pair of night vision goggles. They would be able to make the getaway without headlights.

Jerry went back to his trailer and briefed Gabriele in the bathroom. He spent the rest of the afternoon, mostly through sign language and scribbling, trying to steady her nerves. Just before sundown, Roy rapped on the trailer door again. Jerry opened it immediately and stepped outside. He followed Murdock to the Jeep, threw his rucksack in the back, and got in on the passenger side.

"Let's go," said Murdock.

Jerry gave Roy a fist bump. At least they didn't expect him to kill somebody this time.

***

Less than an hour after the men had gone, Gabriele sat at the dinette table with a book on Martin Luther. She admired Luther for his courage to challenge the pervasive and ruthless authority of the Roman church; the man had done more to change the world than almost anyone. This evening, she was looking for references to a darker side of Luther; he had vilified the Jews. Gabriele was fascinated by the tendency of religious thinkers to assert that everyone else's ideas were just plain wrong. That intolerance had led to Carl's death; now it would likely lead to her own. For the moment, Luther had replaced Carl and Jerry in her thoughts.

She was startled by a knock on the trailer door. Assuming it was Jerry, she dropped the book and struggled out from behind the table. She moved to the door and swung it back confidently.

"That was fast!"

Standing on the step was Jane Thorne.

Gabriele composed herself quickly. "Jane... I thought it was Jerry."

"He'll be gone all night. I thought I'd come over and keep you company for a while."

"How thoughtful," replied Gabriele cautiously. "Won't you come in?"

Jane stepped into Gabriele's cage and closed the door behind her. Gabriele wore a loose shirt and a pair of jogging pants (it was still painful to slide a pair of jeans over the tattoo). She noticed that Jane had changed her habitual baggy dress for cowboy clothes. Without a discernable figure, the smaller woman looked to Gabriele like a callow teenage boy.

"Thank you, Gaby." Jane looked around the trailer. "Sorry about the quarters... I hope you and Jerry are comfortable enough."

"We're fine," said Gabriele graciously, "even though the bed is too small for my gorilla husband to sleep in... Would you like some coffee?"

"That would be wonderful." Without any further small talk, Jane leaned against the counter as Gabriele prepared two cups of dark European coffee. Gabriele worked as fast as she could, conscious that Jane was watching her from behind. There was a tension in the air she could not explain. Gabriele had the impression that Jane knew something she did not. That was certainly true; Jane knew many things Gabriele did not.

"Here," said Gaby as Jane took the steaming cup. "Please sit down... I must use the bathroom."

Gabriele closed the bathroom door and took a few deep breaths. There was no evidence of her covert meetings with Jerry. The tape recorder was inside Jerry's boot. The tapes were stashed in the ceiling panel, along with a coded message, for delivery to Susan (Gabriele wondered if they would ever get the opportunity). If Jane came in to use the toilet, Gabriele figured it would be difficult for the woman to find anything incriminating. Relieved, she flushed for effect and joined Jane at the dinette.

"Well," she began. "To what do I owe the pleasure of having you in my home?"

Jane took a sip of coffee and smiled warmly. "I thought you might be lonely... Good coffee, by the way."

"That is one thing Europeans still do better than Americans."

Jane didn't miss a beat. "Are you European or American, Gaby?" It was the same question Carl had asked her on their first date. Understanding that this time it was not an innocent question, she gave Jane a different answer.

"Definitely American. Only here do I have the chance to make a difference. The German radicalism of the 1980s failed miserably. I was tempted to go home and join them, but neither the left nor the right had answers to anything I cared about. And German men are such wimps... Most of them were raised by their mothers after the war. I decided that America was the only place where it is possible to change the world one more time. It just took me a while to find the right man with whom to share my dream."

"Jerry."

"Absolutely... He's the best."

Jane nodded approval. "You're a lucky woman, Gaby."

"I know... He's just as smart as he is tough. He's completely devoted to the cause—and to me."

"You must be very proud of him."

"I am not worthy to be his wife… But he loves me dearly."

Jane looked Gabriele right in the eye. "He must be terrific in bed."

"He's incredible, Jane," said Gabriele with growing discomfort. "I can't begin to tell you…"

"Try, sweetheart." The soft tone barely concealed a demand. Jane sat waiting for Gabriele to describe the intimate details of her sex life. It was as if she had just asked about the weather. Gabriele drew a deep breath. She was stalling, thinking, improvising.

"He loves the water. He was a frogman, you know."

"Ah, yes," said Jane, grinning. "Is there enough room for both of you in that tiny little shower?"

"Yes, there is… But we have to get very close!"

"I bet you do, girl… I bet you do." Jane looked at her more seriously. "But what do you do when he's gone?"

"I miss him."

"You must get awfully horny."

"Let's just say that I miss him a *lot*," said Gabriele, thinking about how accurate a statement that was. At the moment, she wasn't sure that Jerry would come back at all. Then she might have to fight her way out of this place.

With what?

Gabriele fought instead for control of her emotions. A creeping sensation fought back. Then, before she realized what was happening, there was a bony hand resting on her shoulder. Jane was studying her in a way that made Gabriele instantly aware of why the woman was sitting in her trailer.

"Have you ever made love to a woman, Gaby?"

Horrified, Gabriele fumbled for a response. "I…I can't say that I have, Jane. I'm not sure I am capable of doing it."

"That's what Linda said the first time."

Gabriele fumbled again. "You and Linda are lovers?"

"Sometimes…yes. It depends on how I feel." Jane paused then flashed a mischievous grin. "It also depends on how Linda feels… Jesse takes a lot of trips." Jane let the implication sink into Gabriele's fertile imagination.

"And so will Jerry," she added.

"I don't feel like it right now, Jane."

"I understand… And, Gaby, this is just between us, okay?"

"Sure, Jane." Gabriele would never tell Jerry about what had just happened. She would only think about Jane Thorne in her nightmares. "I appreciate your being patient with me," was all she managed to say.

Jane left the trailer. Gabriele went in the bathroom and cried.

***

Roy Murdock drove out of the desert with a new toy lying in the cargo space of his Cherokee. Jerry reached around to make sure the rocket was still inside the army blanket. It looked like a dead body. That image reminded him that he and Roy would be dead if the cops happened to stop them. Then he recalled driving halfway across the state with blood on his coveralls. He had not been stopped then. In fact, Jerry could not remember ever being stopped by the cops in Wyoming. Not many people; not much crime.

Until now.

The Cherokee put mile after mile under its wheels as Murdock sat stone-faced. There was nothing to say. They had gone over "actions at the objective" twice more since picking up the rocket from Thorne's desert magazine. Jerry could feel that Murdock was testing him again and refused to initiate a conversation. Just because he knew the former surfer hated country music, Jerry tuned into the loudest, whiniest brand he could find. Murdock suffered for two minutes then reached out and turned off the radio. The silent stand-off continued for the three hours it took them to reach the Lone Mountain turnoff.

"You wanna go home, cowboy?"

Jerry cleared his throat and continued to stare at the road ahead.

"Nothing to go home to."

Murdock laughed. "Whaddaya need besides cows, anyway?"

"Gabriele, but she's back in Mineral King."

Roy whistled. "It's enough to drive a freedom fighter crazy, ain't it?"

"She's a hostage, Roy."

"You think we still don't trust you?" challenged Murdock. "You're right... At least as far as I'm concerned. You'll have to *earn* that trust—just the way I did." Then Murdock taunted him.

"But if you do well tonight, lover boy, you'll be back in bed with your Nazi chick before breakfast."

Against his better judgment, Jerry took the bait.

"And you'll be in bed with Sadie."

"Fuck you, Jerry."

That was the last sentence either of them uttered between Lone Mountain and Laramie. It was nearing midnight when the Jeep crested the highest point along the interstate. Abraham Lincoln seemed to watch them go by. Roy drove a few miles toward Cheyenne, scouting the escape route and judging the traffic. Occasional heavy trucks. Now and then, perhaps a bleary-eyed motorist. Jerry timed the interval between passing vehicles and found the average to be about two minutes. Plenty of time to do what he needed to do.

Roy got off at the next exit and stopped at the far end of the ramp. He grabbed the night vision goggles from behind Jerry's seat and hung them around his neck. Jerry climbed into the back and began unwrapping the AT-4.

"Ready, hotshot?"

"Good to go," Jerry responded. "I always loved the M136." He reached into his rucksack and withdrew a pair of earplugs.

Roy got back on the interstate, headed west. Nothing more was said until they sped up the exit ramp. The benevolent face of Lincoln gazed upon them in the dim light of the parking lot. Jerry could almost feel the courage and leadership emanating from the stone. Roy felt only contempt.

"The first diversity president," said Murdock. "How does it feel to play John Wilkes Booth?"

"Great!" said Jerry, cradling the weapon. "Booth is probably watching me right now, wishing he'd had one of *these* babies!"

The big man squatted in the back of the Cherokee, feeling like a warrior again. He was focused. Adrenaline poured into his veins. His whole body quivered with energy. He was back in the jungle with Carl, Jose, and Billy Joe. He wasn't thinking about his first act of terrorism; he was thinking about hitting Mr. Lincoln right between the shoulder blades.

Murdock circled the parking lot then halted the Cherokee under a tree. Like a parachutist, Jerry scrambled out the back. He ran laterally, measuring distance in his head, and dropped to one knee. Fifty meters from the target. Sufficient range for the warhead to arm; far enough away to duck the flying debris.

He rested the weapon on his right shoulder, aimed, and fired.

The high explosive round slammed into the stone and disappeared in a brilliant flash of yellow. Even before Jerry could stand up, Lincoln had been reduced to a pile of smoking rubble. The flame tongue of the rocket's backblast had torched the woods behind him, and he could feel intense heat. He sprang to his feet then fell forward immediately to avoid a piece of granite tumbling toward his head.

Deliberately dropping the launcher, he ran under the open hatchback of the Cherokee and pulled it down behind him.

"Go!"

Roy Murdock was laughing like he had just won the lottery. "Great job, Jerry… We're outa here!"

Jerry climbed into the front seat and hung on for what he knew would be a death-defying drive back to Mineral King. Back to Gabriele. Then—somehow—back to Susan.

The Cherokee was barreling along in the dark without headlights. Murdock was still laughing like a maniac. Jerry monitored their progress on the map in his head, waiting for the next waypoint. The ride reminded him of low-level flights in Air Force special operations helicopters. Bucking and banking, the vehicle tossed him all over the place. They flew under the interstate and headed for Colorado. Only then did Roy turn the headlights back on.

"Just like old times, eh, Jerry?"

"It ain't over till it's over… Just keep us on the road."

"Relax, big guy… We'll be home for breakfast."

And they were.

Gabriele came to the door and greeted Jerry with a bear hug worthy of the name. She was emotional.

"Thank God!" she mouthed, tears in her eyes.

Jerry held her close, as if to share his courage. Then he looked up and spoke to the microphone.

"Mission accomplished, *Schatz*. You know how I love it when a plan comes together. Roy and I make a great team." He paused to make sure that part of the script sank in. "Now I need a toilet and a shower."

She closed the door behind them. He briefed her on the attack... and the long ride home. "I'm beat," he said as he finished. "You'll have to let me sleep for a while."

Gabriele gave him a pained look. "I don't know how long I can do this, Jerry, and you could have been killed!" Jane Thorne's face flashed into her mind. "Don't we have enough evidence to just take the tapes and run?"

"They're planning something big, Gaby. I've watched Jeffers and James disappear into the desert every morning for a week. Red doesn't want us to know about it, but I think things are coming to a head. We can't leave just yet... not if we're in a position to stop them."

Gabriele didn't have to think about that one for too long. "You're right, of course. The mission is to stop them—one way or another."

"I also have a plan to contact Susan," said Jerry excitedly. "You ever been rock climbing?"

"No, I cannot say that I have. But I'll try anything just to get out of here for a while."

Jerry went into the bedroom to crash. Gabriele went back to the dinette to read. She would continue to follow Jerry's lead, but the prospect of her own death loomed ever larger.

***

Jerry slept until midafternoon and then went looking for Red Thorne. As he walked across the compound, he could see Jane at the window. He forced himself to wave like an old friend. She hurried to meet him at the back door.

"Well, Jerry, congratulations! I hear you're a crack shot with an AT-4."

"It was practically point-blank range, Jane… Where's Red?"

Jane looked at Jerry a little too confidently. "Red's in the outbuilding with Will… You want to see him?"

"Yeah, if it's not too much trouble. I think he owes me something for last night."

"And I think you're right," agreed Jane. She took a step forward. "Do you want anything that *I* can give you?"

"No," said Jerry firmly. "I want to get out of here for a little climbing practice over at *Vedauwoo*, do some battle damage assessment on the Lincoln statue at the same time." He paused. "I'd also like to take Gaby."

"That sounds like a lot more fun than helping me answer a ton of mail."

Jerry nodded. "Just tell Red what I said. I know he doesn't want me in on whatever it is that he and Will are planning." Then he smiled broadly. "You got any idea what that might be?"

"Not a clue, cowboy." Jane was trying hard, but allure was just beyond her reach. Jerry swallowed hard and looked at her like she was the most beautiful woman he'd ever seen. He was sure that Jane knew everything Red knew.

"Too bad, Jane. I can't work for the revolution if I don't know what's going on. If you find out what's happening, I'll be in the trailer."

"Well…now that you put it that way, big guy." She looked Jerry up and down like she was picking out a horse.

An hour later, there came a knock on the trailer door. It was Red Thorne. Jerry ushered him inside and found the man was too fat to sit at the dinette. Both men stood, facing each other in the small space. Gabriele retreated to the bedroom and slid the door shut.

"First of all, Jerry, I appreciate what you did for us last night. You and Gaby are already making a big difference around here."

Thorne glanced at the bedroom door, understanding that Gabriele was listening to every word.

Jerry spoke to Red enthusiastically, trying not to make it sound like the interrogation it was. "Are we taking credit for the Lincoln statue attack... And if so, how?"

Red stroked his beard and lowered his voice. "No credit. I tried that with the Air and Space Museum attack, and it had no real effect. This time, we're going to rely on the power of rumor."

"What's the rumor?"

"That this attack was made by the tyrannical federal government." Thorne continued. "We'll use militia members to spread that conspiracy theory and let it ripple through the American population. Your wife has already prepared our folks to expect a series of unexplained bombings. We just need to reinforce that idea."

"That's brilliant!" responded Jerry, thinking that it really was. "The government will blame DEFCON One—whoever *they* are—but nobody out here trusts the feds anyway."

"The bombings will continue until morale improves!" quipped Thorne. "A popular uprising can't be far behind."

Jerry shifted gears. "Red... I also wanted to ask you about the rock climbing exercise I mentioned to Jane."

Thorne cut him off. "Yes, you can go, but no, you can't take Gaby. Jane needs her all day tomorrow." Red locked eyes with his rising star. "You know the rules, Jerry. One goes, the other stays—at least for a while."

"I don't mind going alone."

"You're not," replied Thorne. "You're going with me."

Jerry's heart sank. He would not be able to leave Susan a dead drop at Split Rock—without first killing Thorne. As tempting as that was, it would be tantamount to murdering Gabriele.

"*Shit!*"

Chapter 18

The Building

The pile of rocks on the left side of the interstate was a testimony to shaped-charge technology as well as to Jerry's aim. A massive earthquake would have left Mr. Lincoln in better condition. *So much for battle damage assessment!* As much as Thorne enjoyed seeing the destruction of such an important symbol, he was more concerned with the level of law enforcement present. The area around the rubble was roped off, but most of the cops were already back on the road. Jerry was confident that someone had discovered the AT-4 launcher he'd left at the scene.

Jerry took the next exit and entered another world. "The Devil's Playground," better known as *Vedauwoo*. Out of habit, he slowed the truck to a crawl and gaped at the towering stone formations looming above them. Huge boulders, piled on top of each other, soared upward as he and Red descended to the floor of the bowl. If the devil had a playground, thought Jerry, this would be it. He followed the signs to "Box Canyon" and parked at the end of the small lot. He switched off the engine and turned to Thorne.

"Look at those rocks, Red! This is one of my favorite training areas."

"Tailor-made," said Thorne without enthusiasm. "What's the plan?"

"I'm gonna do some free climbing with a rucksack and a long rope. I'll be rappelling down from the top… You wanna come with me?"

Jerry knew damn well the fat man wouldn't come. He was lucky to have Thorne as a babysitter rather than Murdock. Roy might've been crazy enough to make the climb.

"Nooo!" laughed Thorne. "I want to watch you go up, though. We might need you to do some climbing for us sometime."

"That's why I'm here, boss."

Jerry went back to the truck and started putting on his backpack. It was full of field gear that included a coil of rope and one rolled-up pair of extra socks. But still no weapon. He had gambled that Thorne would not insist on inspecting the contents of the pack. Evidently, Jerry had at least the beginnings of the man's trust. He realized what a milestone that was. Adjusting the load, Jerry led his minder down an asphalt path among the devil's toys.

Exactly two hundred and thirteen paces.

He stopped walking when he came to a picnic table on the right. "You can sit here and watch me," said Jerry as Thorne nodded.

Jerry swapped his cowboy boots for soft rubber friction shoes as Thorne stretched out on top of the table, looking like a beached whale. The sun was almost directly overhead, flooding the canyon floor with May warmth. When Jerry was ready, Thorne pointed a stubby finger at him.

"Do your stuff."

Jerry strode quickly to the first boulder and stood studying the granite. He placed a foot, then a hand, and then another foot. Looking up, he found a second handhold and extended until he was high enough to reach it. He fought the weight of the pack with a combination of strength and leverage. Because of his size, Jerry had never been the lead climber, content to follow Billy Joe up whatever the team needed to scale. Often it had been an offshore oil rig. Sometimes a backshore cliff at night, high above the surf. Billy Joe had been a human fly; Jerry was a bear. Four solid purchases, lean away, boost, reach, and hold. Three more sequences and Jerry was on top of the boulder, staring at a wall of rock.

He worked his way diagonally upward, moving slowly and methodically. The crack in the rock carried him another fifty feet higher before opening onto a narrow ledge. Glancing down at

Thorne, Jerry shook the lactic acid out of his arms. The chaperone was shielding his eyes from the sun. *Perfect!* Jerry chalked his hands and moved higher, along another crack. Straight up. After sixty minutes of climbing, he was more than two hundred feet above the picnic table. Nearing exhaustion, he lifted his head above the top of the wall and found the wide ledge he knew was there.

"It's about time, man." Jose Rios grinned at his struggling friend.

Jerry shifted his weight one more time and hoisted his 220-pound body onto the ledge. Jose watched him from the shadow of the upper wall. Ignoring Jose, Jerry turned and looked back into the air below him. He could not see Thorne. Better, Thorne could not see him. Jerry took three steps into the cliff face and gave his friend a crushing bear hug.

"You're a sight for sore eyes, Bosco."

"I've been getting a lot of climbing practice for the last week, man... I thought you'd never show."

"I had a little trouble getting away."

"I believe it... But I knew you'd find a way to get here." Jose beheld his sweating teammate. "Even though you were never much of a climber," he added sarcastically.

Jerry finally got his breathing under control. "My new boss is at the bottom of the cliff... I have only a few minutes."

Jose bent down and pulled a cell phone from his rucksack. Jerry took it reverently and punched in a number. It was Sunday. There was a good chance she'd be home. Voice mail would get the job done... But Jerry wanted to talk. He *needed* to talk...just for a minute.

"Mackenzie." Susan's voice was the sweetest sound he had heard in his entire life.

"Susan! This is Jerry."

"Jerry! My god! Where *are* you?"

"On a rock ledge near Laramie... Listen... I don't have much time."

"What are you doing *there*?"

"It was the only way to contact you... They have us under such tight control there's no way to drop you a message." Aware they were on an open line, he left out a lot of details.

"I know... I've been checking every other day."

"Keep checking... But understand we're on the buddy system all the time. If I'm away from the ranch, the wife has to stay. And vice versa. We're living in the trailer on the right side of the compound, looking out the back of the ranch house. The ranch is 2.1 miles west of the dirt road that runs south from town. The right turn onto the access road is exactly 9.6 miles from town." Jerry stopped talking to let Susan catch up.

"You getting all this?"

"Yes," said Susan, copying furiously. "Go ahead."

"This is just in case you have to come in and get us...repeat... *just in case*! I do not want you to come *near* that place right now! Got that?"

"Got it... Did you have anything to do with Lincoln?"

"Yes."

"We've already traced the lot number on the launcher we found to a reserve army base in California. We're trying to connect the stolen rocket to the murder of an army sergeant in the same area."

"Good," replied Jerry quickly. "They have more of those... Not sure how many."

Jerry was running out of time!

"Whatever you do, honey, don't let them crash the party just yet. Something big is in the works. We might be in a position to stop it... You and your 'ex' sit tight. I'll call you again if I get the chance."

"I love you, Jerry!"

His heart stopped. Choking with emotion, he gave her the only answer he had time for. "I love you too, baby."

Jerry folded the phone and unzipped the pack. He extracted a cloth bag and opened the drawstring. Taking the battery charger from Jose, he wrapped the phone and the charger in a green T-shirt and stuffed it in the bag. He took out the rolled-up pair of socks and handed it to his friend.

"Take these, Bosco. Inside are three audiotapes. In the event of my death, the tapes need to get to the FBI...Susan Mackenzie or Gerhard Beck, now working out of Cheyenne. Here's the number."

Jose took the number and the socks.

"I heard you tell Susan you don't have enough information yet."

"Not quite... But what's on those tapes will get these thugs locked up for good." Then he added, "That is, if I don't take them out myself before the FBI gets to us."

Jose begged his former teammate. "*Amigo*...can't I just go back with you and finish this thing right now? We could start by taking out the fat guy down there." He pointed to the edge of the cliff with his chin.

Jerry had a ready answer. "The fat guy would be the easy part. The challenge is that they're all spread out and everyone has a gun... Any one of them can kill Gaby. We'd have to wax them all at the same time, and there's no way to do that—at least not yet."

Jose gave him a knowing look. "Or else you'd have already done it, right?"

"That's affirm," said Jerry, now visibly anxious about the time. "Just stay as close to us as you can get...and wait for me to call you in. Got that?"

"Got it, man." Jose held out his own SIG Sauer. "Don't you want this?"

"No, thanks, brother... If they find it, Gaby and I are dead. There's so many guns in that place... If I need one, I can always steal it. Dispersion of the enemy is still the problem... Then there's the women and kids. I'm afraid the only way to make sure Gaby gets out of there alive is to just drop everything and *run*."

"I'll be there to pick you up, man...wherever."

Jerry got the nylon coil out of his rucksack and began tying a large bowline on one end. "Help me find a place to anchor this thing."

Jose pointed to a pile of rocks on Jerry's left. "This is the place, man." Taking the bowline, he secured it around the base of the top rock and tested it. Jerry tossed the coil over the cliff. Then he took a short piece of manila rope and tied a tight harness around his hips. He snapped a carabiner into the harness and threaded the descending rope.

Jerry leaned against the rock anchor and bounced gently. He shook Jose's steady hand and crawled to the edge of the cliff. Then he was gone, jumping three times to the ledge below.

Right into the outstretched hands of Red Thorne!

"Good show, Jerry... Very impressive!"

"How did *you* get here, Red?" Jerry was flabbergasted but also worried that Thorne might have overheard him. He masked his anxiety by throwing a knuckle into the nylon. Right at Jose. The rope came pouring down from the high ledge like a long snake.

"I used to be a guide in the Tetons," explained the fat man as Jerry coiled the rope and placed it in his rucksack.

Jerry followed Thorne back down the steep trail leading to the parking lot. Jose waited twenty minutes then rappelled and scrambled down to the bottom. He was quick enough to catch a glimpse of Jerry's vehicle leaving the scene.

Jose followed the truck all the way to Mineral King.

***

Jerry still did not know what was going on. He hadn't gotten anything out of Red during the return trip to Mineral King. He and Gabriele had watched Will and Jesse disappear into the desert again the morning after he got back from *Vedauwoo*. Gaby had seen Roy Murdock leave the compound during Jerry's climbing trip; she had not seen him come back. An air of increased tension had settled over the Thorne ranch. Jerry called it anticipation; Gabriele used a more accurate term.

Dread.

The May meeting of the militia, two days later, did not reveal the answers to any of their questions. Murdock was not there, Jeffers and James only for the opening remarks and Gabriele's speech. Red Thorne was preoccupied...with something.

But what?

Gabriele received a standing ovation. It was clear by the time everyone sat down that the farmers and ranchers of the militia were ready to believe absolutely everything Gabriele Tompkins had to say about anything. She was convinced they even believed her warning that the federal government was about to initiate a campaign of violence, blaming it on patriotic, gun-toting Americans. Them.

The power of her words, fashioned into moving rhetoric, was scary. Standing behind the podium, listening to the deafening applause of misguided ordinary citizens, Gabriele understood the Germans of her parents' generation better than ever.

Back at the ranch, Jerry and Gabriele obsessed over what might be on Thorne's mind. Except for daily conditioning runs—permitted for each of them, but not together—they sat day after day in the confinement of the trailer, reading, writing, and acting out terrorist boredom. Most depressing was Jerry's inability to receive a cell phone signal from the trailer bathroom.

So they just sat.

Until the Monday following the militia meeting. Gabriele was invited to join Sadie on a shopping trip to Lander. Carrying Jose's cell phone in her purse, she hoped to slip away long enough to call Susan or Gerhard. If they were adhering to the schedule, Gabriele knew that both of them would be in the federal building all day. She was pretty sure about that.

After watching Gabriele leave, Jerry remained at his observation post by the window of the trailer bedroom. Drinking water from a plastic bottle, he waited for Jane Thorne. It took an hour, but she came bounding out of the house in a pink blouse and white shorts. Jerry could see her grinning halfway across the compound. She looked like a wannabe high school cheerleader cutting class. Jerry hoped she had something to tell him. If he was going to sacrifice his body for the cause, it would have to be for perfect information. He opened the door just as she was getting ready to knock.

"Mornin', Jane… Guess you came out here to tell me what's goin' on with Red and Will."

"No…actually not, Jerry." She looked worried. "Listen… I really do not know what they're doing, and I'm just as pissed about it as you are." She began to shout, revealing a frustration that convinced Jerry she was telling the truth. "That bastard, Red… I hate it when he's so secretive. He doesn't trust me any more than he trusts *you!*"

"I doubt that." Jerry slid past her and stood on the dirt in front of his trailer, dressed for a run.

"Where are *you* going?" asked a shaken Jane.

Jerry smiled as he ran his eyes over her anorexic frame. She had the palest legs he'd ever seen. Even in the heat, he thought he could see her kneecaps hammering bone. When he got to her face, the grin was gone. She looked back at the house. She was obviously out on a limb. Jerry was about to saw it off.

"I'm going for a nice long run… Wanna come?" The big man adjusted his Broncos ball cap and fitted a pair of Oakleys over his eyes. He bent from the waist, stretching.

"Are you crazy?" Jane was still flustered. "I'll be right here when you get back. If I can't find out what my own husband is up to, then I can at least have a little fun behind his back."

Gabriele was due back in two hours. Jerry decided that, even in the hot sun, he could run for that long. He was off in the next breath, leaving Jane to figure out what to do next.

***

Gabriele and Sadie had finished getting groceries at the Safeway in Lander, the nearest legitimate city. It was almost four o'clock in the afternoon. Gabriele was nervously clutching her purse the way she had when passing through the worst neighborhoods of Washington, DC. There had been no opportunity to make a cell phone call, and prospects were not good. Gabriele was still a prisoner. She considered overpowering Sadie and calling the local cops. Bad idea, she realized. The cops might well be members of the militia; Jerry could be killed before he even knew what she had done. He was a prisoner too.

Sadie inadvertently rescued her. "I have to make an Amway delivery up here, Gaby… You'll have to wait in the car for me."

Yes! "And how long do you think that will be?"

"Maybe five minutes."

"Take your time, dear."

As soon as Sadie left the car, Gabriele extracted her cell phone, slid down behind the dashboard, and punched in a number.

"Mackenzie."

"Susan!" Just saying the name lifted Gabriele's spirits. "This is Gaby… I have just two minutes to fill you in." She was whispering.

"Thank God," came the reply. "I'll have Gerhard pick up the other receiver."

"Don't talk, just listen." Gabriele spoke rapidly for one full minute.

"What's the plan *now*?" asked Susan, more concerned than ever.

"We're going to take a long walk one night and call you from the main road."

"What do you want us to do in the meantime?" asked Susan anxiously.

"Get closer to the target… Perhaps Rawlins. Keep your engines running… It will not be long now."

"You're just going to *run*?"

"Something big is in the wind, Susan. Jerry says you'll need to blast in there right after you pick us up…and sort out the legal details later. They have to be stopped…from doing whatever it is they're planning. We'll be ready to brief your shooters right before they go in. Jerry wants to be the lead door kicker. You can round me up like an escaped cow after you make the hit…"

Sadie came out of the house just as Gabriele closed her handbag.

"Let's go home," said the fat woman.

"My thoughts exactly."

***

Jeffers and James descended into the desolation that separated the Thorne ranch from the interstate. Sixty miles from north to south; one hundred miles from east to west. Thirty miles south and ten miles west, they stopped at a shallow depression in the red earth. A large, run-down pickup truck was parked beneath the only rock overhang they had ever found in the basin. There was no need to inspect it. A canvas cover, stretched tight, protected the precious cargo from view. Will Jeffers got out of James's truck and into the loaded vehicle. He started the engine and promptly circled around behind his companion.

Ready.

They drove in tandem over the flat terrain toward the interstate. There were many possible routes, but they took the most direct. James kept one eye on the rearview mirror so he wouldn't pull too far ahead. He set a slow pace to keep the dust down. For now, they were safe. The bleak landscape always reminded Jeffers that the moon landings had been staged by the government. Money laundering at the highest level. You couldn't trust the government to tell the truth. You couldn't trust the government at all.

That was why they had to take it down.

Going under the interstate at Wamsutter, the two vehicles separated enough to avoid giving the impression they were together. Jeffers remained in the rear position, protected by the lead vehicle. An evil version of *Smokey and the Bandit*. James scanned for threats ahead. Anything could happen. Some jerk from the coast might fall asleep at the wheel in the wrong place. A big rig could jackknife in front of James. A police checkpoint could pop unexpectedly. A cow could wander onto the road.

Red Thorne had warned them they could not fail. Still fearing the man who sustained them, the team took that warning very seriously. No more debacles like the Air and Space Museum. Straight in; straight out. Rawlins came and went. At two o'clock, they passed Lone Mountain. Rulon James began to taste his revenge. For Vietnam. For ruining his life. For selling the American dream to the highest bidder. Will Jeffers was not motivated by revenge. Mankind had ruined God's plan; Jeffers just wanted to start civilization all over again. They were committed. As Thorne had put it, "hurtling into history."

The same thing Thorne had said to them before the Washington operation.

They passed Laramie a little after three. On schedule. At precisely four o'clock, the Capitol dome glittered in front of them. It was the only evidence that the city of Cheyenne held any importance whatsoever. Jeffers and his cargo overtook James and got off the interstate. He sailed past the Union Pacific control tower like a pilot on final approach. James hung back until he spotted his accomplice on the bridge. It would not be long now.

Jeffers drove directly for the dome. Past the police station on the left. No activity, he noticed, but that would soon change. He almost wished he could stick around and watch. He turned left on Twenty-Second Street and parked the truck in front of a schoolyard. Will Jeffers did not think about the children; he was too busy looking up at the federal building's seven brick stories on the other side of the narrow street. He could see government agents moving back and forth in their offices.

Doing their evil deeds.

Jeffers reached under the dashboard and activated the timer. Then he casually got out of the stolen truck and locked the door. He looked at his watch. Everything was falling into place. There was even time left on the parking meter. He glanced up and down the street. No tourists lurking around this time to screw things up. He walked slowly to the corner and turned right. James was waiting at the intersection. Jeffers quickened his pace but did not break into a run. He got in next to James and closed the door.

"Message delivered."

James smiled at the road in front of him. Seconds later, as they drove by the Liberty Bell next to the Capitol building, he couldn't help himself.

"Give me liberty or give me death!"

"Amen," said Will Jeffers softly.

The blast came just as they merged onto the interstate going west. Smoke mushroomed thousands of feet into the air as a shock wave rocked the high plains for miles around. Within a few seconds, two thousand pounds of fertilizer mixed with diesel fuel had obliterated the school and reduced the north wall of the federal building to rubble.

Susan and Gerhard never had a chance.

Chapter 19

The Destroyers

Gabriele felt better now that Susan had the information she needed. Jerry was preparing for their escape and evasion. Susan and Gerhard would be planning the takedown of the compound by now. Speeding toward Mineral King, with Sadie lost in thought, Gabriele was struck with a sense of tempered optimism. She held to the belief that she and Jerry could sneak away, FBI agents would replace them at Thorne's ranch, arrests would be made without bloodshed, and Carl's murder would be atoned for. Then she would get on with her life.

What was left of it.

She was thinking about life when she reached for the car radio. "Mind if I get some music?"

Sadie did not respond. Gabriele guessed her driver was in the middle of a silent prayer marathon. Nothing that wouldn't benefit from a little Shania Twain.

What came out of the radio took several seconds to sink in. As it did, Gabriele felt the devil reach into her throat and rip out her stomach.

"There is no information yet on the number of casualties, but—looking at the building from the steps of the Capitol—it is obvious that the number will be high."

Gabriele managed to roll down the window. A mechanical act. Sweat leapt from her brow, a body reacting slightly ahead of cognition. The rushing air threatened to drown out the rest of the report!

She leaned forward to listen. Her pounding heart almost drowned it out again.

"*...Since the Oklahoma City bombing. Cheyenne is in chaos. For those of you who've just tuned in, the O'Mahoney Federal Center and the elementary school across the street have been largely destroyed by a tremendous explosion...almost certainly a bomb. People are running in and out of the rubble of the north wall, apparently trying to organize the rescue of survivors. I don't know how else to say this, but it doesn't look like there will be a lot of them. There is no way to describe the scene without using the word carnage. Dozens of children and a great many government people have died here today, but as authorities attempt to gain control of the situation, there is no way to determine exactly how many.*"

Gabriele vomited out the window. She managed to turn off the radio at the same time. Sadie was slow to react.

"What's wrong with *you* all of a sudden?"

Leaning into the rushing air, Gabriele could not hear. Her conscious mind fought for control as Sadie slowed to a stop on the side of the road.

"Carsick," was all Gabriele could will herself to say. Tears of fear ran down her cheeks. Sadie—and all the others—would unmask her. Then they would unmask Jerry. In the slow motion of realization, she thought about how quickly death comes. Carl had been taken from her without warning. Instantly, Susan and Gerhard had almost certainly been killed. She and Jerry would be next.

"I need to get you home, Gaby." Sadie was wiping puke from the seat where it had blown back inside the car. Gabriele was trying to get her breath back. Sadie actually sounded sympathetic. "What about the dirt road to the ranch?"

"I can make it," said Gabriele in the bravest voice she could muster.

She had to warn Jerry! They had to run...and *keep* running.

If there was still time.

It was rage that saved her again. Gabriele passed the next thirty minutes visualizing the arrest, trial, and execution of the men who had murdered her husband. The women would not walk, but Gabriele could not imagine them on death row. Not even Jane. Sadie drove into the Thorne compound still unaware of what had happened.

Gabriele knew that, with no radio in the trailer, Jerry was also unaware.

"I have to go to the trailer and clean up," she announced to Sadie. "I'll be back in a few minutes for my groceries."

She went straight to the trailer and pulled Jerry into the bathroom. This time, her tears came from anger rather than fear. Explaining that she had talked to Susan just moments before the blast, Gabriele's broken sentences tore him open. She had not seen Jerry cry since Carl's funeral. She held him like a son and rocked him. Gabriele gave him strength the way Jerry had given it to her so many times before. Together they grieved for what they were certain had happened to their friends.

A knock on the trailer door shocked them back to reality. Gabriele looked at Jerry's face and then her own. She would have to answer the door. Jerry jumped in the shower and stood under the hot water.

Gabriele opened the door to find Red Thorne standing on the step.

"You okay, Gaby? Sadie said you were pretty sick in the car. Tell that killing machine inside we got a meeting in the dining room at nine. After that, I need to see your husband alone."

Gabriele looked at her watch and nodded. It was five-thirty. She marched across the compound and started ferrying bags from Sadie's car. After three trips, she went back into the trailer bathroom.

"This is it," said Jerry, drying off. "We move tonight." He looked at her with his tactical face. "You ready for a long run/walk?"

Gabriele was amazed at how fast Jerry had composed himself. The warrior switch Carl had told her about. She found her own switch.

"Ready."

It was an enormous effort for Jerry to propose running away. Every instinct told him to kill them all. One by one. Even the women. He could do it any number of ways. But he wasn't sure he could do it *and* get Gabriele out alive. He had already chosen to get her out. He owed that to Carl.

Then he remembered Susan and Gerhard.

Now *who we gonna call?*

***

"So…the bottom line is that we got a lot of dead feds out there. It's a great day for real Americans."

"Where do we go from here, Red?" It was Jerry. The rest of the family stared at him. Gabriele thought for a brief moment that they all knew the truth. She visualized her own death, silently apologizing to Carl for failing in her mission. Her spirit was gone.

Then she heard the plan.

"Gabriele will write the press release." Thorne pointed at her. "You'll stay here with Jane and Linda… Jerry will come with us."

The men followed Thorne down the hallway to the small room where they had stripped Jerry naked the first night. Everyone called it the Tank. Jerry knew that the nation's highest military officers met in a room of the same name when planning to go to war. He walked into the tank, grieving for Susan and planning his own war.

Gabriele sat down to write a long accusation that the US government had bombed its own employees in order to break the militia movement. Her hands were shaking as she tapped out the sickening words. Each letter seemed to explode on the screen in front of her.

Jerry listened to Thorne with mounting fear. "Last year, we overextended. I never should have taken responsibility for that failure." Seated around him were Jeffers, James, and Murdock.

"But now," Thorne continued, "we can make the people believe that DEFCON One is actually the US government." All the men nodded, including Jerry. "A popular uprising in this country is not as difficult to orchestrate as the federals think."

Jeffers, just back from Cheyenne, was the first follower to speak. "I think *Yahweh* was telling us to back off for a while." Jerry felt the hair on the back of his neck stand up. He imagined himself tied to a railroad track. This was it… The train was coming!

"We *have* backed off," replied Thorne. "Most of the last year, we've concentrated on smaller actions, building up the confidence needed to make the bigger things happen." He turned to Jerry. "We've also added some new blood, and that blood has worked out very well."

Jerry locked eyes with Thorne. Iron discipline, honed through years of living on the edge, kept the sorrow from bursting onto his face. He buried his fear and played his part. A hand grenade, he thought, could stop this. But he didn't have a hand grenade. He didn't even have a pistol!

"Thanks, Red, and where's this wild ride to freedom gonna take us now?"

"We will blame the feds for Cheyenne…then go for the big prize."

"Washington?" asked Jerry. He looked around the table. The others seemed to already know.

"Silicon Valley," said Thorne firmly. "That place has everything that's wrong with this country. Kikes, queers, spics, niggers, and chinks…you name it. That valley's a cesspool of nonwhite blood and sin."

"It's also the lifeblood of the national economy," added James.

"And San Francisco is at the north end," Murdock put in.

"Too bad you can't go after the whole valley," said Jerry, probing for the concept of operations.

"But we can…and we will," announced Thorne with a maniacal gleam in his eye.

"How?" Jerry rubbed his face with both hands to hide the act of swallowing hard. "That would take a nuke."

"We have the next best thing." As Thorne continued, Jerry caught Jeffers in a smile. James merely nodded. Murdock beamed.

"What's that?"

"Anthrax," said Thorne.

Jerry almost choked. He tried to keep his voice under control. The word itself was terrifying.

"Are you sure you can handle that?" *Holy shit!*

"I'm not going to handle it at all," said Thorne coldly. "You and Roy will handle it for me."

"How are we going to deliver the stuff? We'd need a bunch of Scud missiles to take out the whole valley."

"We have the next best thing," said Thorne again.

"And what would that be?"

"A plane that can spray anthrax over a wide area."

"A Cessna 172," interrupted Murdock. "And I know how to fly it! You and I are going for a ride, cowboy."

"Why do you need *me*?" Jerry was trying to desperately to stay in character, but panic was fighting its way into his lungs.

"I need a parachutist," replied Murdock. "We don't do one-way missions here. We just don't have enough troops."

"So you want me to get in a plane with you and jump out before it starts spewing anthrax into the air?"

"Exactly."

"Do you have the parachutes?"

"Yeah… I bought two 'Stratoclouds' in Laramie last year. The guy told me they're older but perfectly functional."

"I used to jump that model—a long time ago," replied Jerry, just to keep breathing. "I'll need to repack those chutes before we go." Then he added, "Why not just use a model airplane and drive it remotely?" Jerry's mind was racing with possible ways and means.

"No way to disperse the spores…and not enough range." It was Jesse's turn to brag. "We looked at it hard… I couldn't find a jury rig."

"Why not just use a crop duster?" asked Jerry. "California is full of crops to dust."

Roy looked around the room and then at Jerry. "I cut my teeth on crop dusters around San Luis Obispo. They work great for pesticides, but it would be a hard way to deliver anthrax." Heads nodded on all sides. The group had obviously discussed this option before bringing Jerry into the loop. "Also," continued Murdock, "we're trying to pin the blame on the government… It's better to use stealth."

"And the crop duster would be a one-way mission for the pilot," said Jerry. It was a statement.

"Yes, that's right," replied Roy. "If he wasn't shot out of the sky first."

"And what are you gonna do for us, Jess?"

"I'll be working ground support. You and Roy will need me to hook up the automatic pilot, as well as a timing device for the sprayer. What we have here is a missile with a guidance system." James was trying to remain stoic, but the pride leaked through. "My own invention…you think I can get a patent from the government?"

James laughed. Jerry kept stalling.

"What's the range of this thing?"

"It's a 'P' model, explained Roy. With a full gas tank, it gets about 400 nautical miles, but I've only filled the tank halfway. That will compensate for the weight of the sprayer…and your oversize body. The plane only needs to get as far as San Francisco Bay. It doesn't need to come back."

"What happens after we bail out of the plane?" Jerry needed to know the full-mission profile in order to devise a plan to defeat it.

"You guys will dump your chutes and walk to the freeway. I'll come by in the Cherokee and give you a ride home…going south and then east," promised James. "After that, we'll just sit at the ranch and wait for the revolution." He looked at Thorne.

"That's the plan," said Red. "We're lucky to have exactly the combination of skill sets we need to execute this thing. Will here provides the jug full o' bugs and fits it into a box for the trailer. Jesse turns our California airplane into a crop duster. Jerry and Roy deliver the stuff. Everybody makes it back. We'll have other battles to fight."

"So how did we get the anthrax in the first place?" asked Jerry, stalling again.

"Jesse has Arab friends in Canada. They donated weaponized anthrax to the cause, and we just drove it over the border. The feds are so focused on the *southern* border it's easy to get stuff in from the north."

"And when are we going to launch?"

"Right away," said Thorne. "You guys will leave in the morning, big guy. Get ready… This is your chance to help us make a more perfect union."

Adding to the horror of what had just been said, Jerry realized that his own mission was doomed to failure. Knowing what he knew now, there was no way he and Gabriele could leave tonight.

They would have to find a way to stop this from happening.

He thought of Susan. Grief.

Then he thought of Gabriele. Hope.

Finally, he thought of Carl. Strength.

Only then did he think about his own fate. Death.

He tried to stall one more time.

"You just destroyed the federal building in Cheyenne, Red… Why can't we just stop there and rest for a while?"

"Because Cheyenne was a setup for Silicon Valley," responded Thorne. "We have to strike again while the feds are runnin' around, tryin' to figure out what happened. Cheyenne was the appetizer. The Valley is the main course."

Will Jeffers spoke for the first time. "*Yahweh* gives medals too, Jerry. You and Roy will be rewarded for beginning the great moral reversal."

"Look…*all* of you," said Thorne in a louder voice. "Pizzaro conquered the Incas with just 168 soldiers. We have the right strategy here."

"It was the Lord's victory," asserted Jeffers.

"That may be, Will, but smallpox had something to do with it."

"Disease was *Yahweh's* instrument then, and disease is his instrument now."

"But the Incas were completely centralized," Jerry broke in, trying to keep his tone under control. "Once the king was dead, they just fell apart. America is just the opposite. You can't count on the whole country collapsing just because we infect a bunch of despicable assholes in California."

"Sounds like you're not committed to this, Jerry!" said Thorne in a louder—almost threatening—tone of voice.

"Naw… I'm with you guys all the way," said Jerry convincingly. "Just sayin' that we might be sacrificing strategy for tactics… It's an easy thing to do."

Thorne replied to the group, but he was looking straight at Jerry. "You're wrong... Once Americans believe their government killed large numbers of its own citizens in order to justify declaring martial law, they will rise up!"

Jerry nodded in defeat masquerading as agreement.

Thorne had just one more thing to say.

"And Gabriele is going to write all the propaganda we'll need to convince Americans to do that."

***

Jose Rios watched as the Cherokee dragged a small trailer over the creek bridge. Having noticed other campsites in flat, dry riverbeds, he had not tried to conceal his own. He had fortified his observation post little by little over two days. A dome tent. A laundry line with underwear hanging in the sun. A stone fireplace with pots and pans strewn around. Plastic bottles placed next to a trickle of good water coming off the ridge. A Wyoming homeless person with nowhere to go and nothing to do, sitting under the only road leading to Thorne's ranch.

Not a threat to DEFCON One.

It was eight o'clock in the morning. Aiming his binoculars through the view hole, Jose could see three men in the car. Jerry sat in the passenger seat, staring straight ahead. The driver, who looked a lot like Jerry, coaxed the Cherokee gently over the bridge. Too gently. Jose guessed there was precious cargo in the trailer. In the back seat was a smaller man. A dark, scrooge-like figure who projected an air of filth, even from Jose's poor vantage. The Latino could almost *smell* the troll as he looked right at the tent. Jose looked at the back of Jerry's head as the vehicle moved away. There was nothing he could do for his friend—that is, without getting Gabriele killed. The Yamaha dirt bike in the bushes would do him no good. Thorne had separated the Tompkins family once again. Jose thought about Jerry's extraordinary field skills and felt a little better.

You're on your own, man!

However unwittingly, Thorne had forced Jose to choose. Bosco had watched Gabriele come back with the other woman the day before. Having scouted the surrounding terrain, he did not expect Gabriele to leave the house by any other route. He would have two choices: wait for her to run, or break her out.

He was tempted to go in and get her. Three of the men were gone; he wasn't sure for how long. That would leave two men in the compound, plus three women and two kids. Jose had listened to Jerry telling Susan which trailer they were in. He had to assume Gabriele would be in the trailer by herself. He could sneak her out, but he would have to first kill everyone in the compound (except for the children). If he did not, Jerry—wherever he was—would be toast.

He decided to wait. Carl had taught him the value of patience in the field. The decisive moment would present itself soon; he had to be ready. He would let Gabriele walk out on her own and simply pick her up. With the dirt bike, they would be in Lander within an hour. Jose would deposit Gabriele in a motel room and be back to his observation post an hour after that. If Jerry came back in time, he would help his friend take them all down. If not, Jose would assault the ranch by himself. With Gabriele safe, he would have no other option.

***

After Jerry had gone, Gabriele worked on the press release. She swallowed her emotions again and read the first draft.

US Government Bombs Its Own Citizens!
By Gabriele Tompkins

The tragic bombing of the O'Mahoney Federal Center in Cheyenne reveals to the people of this country just how terrifying a tyrannical government can be. The federals will try to blame their own citizens for this bombing.

After that, we citizens can expect a declaration of martial law. The sacrifice of thirty-eight government agents and innocent children was an act of terrorism—by the state. Henceforth, the word *Cheyenne* should be a rallying cry for all Americans standing against the government attempting to enslave them.

That enslavement has been going on for some time. Dissatisfied with the pace of totalitarian progress, the government of the United States has now resorted to large-scale violence. Fixing the blame for the Cheyenne bombing on ordinary citizens places the government in a position to justify tightening its grip on every one of us. Last summer, federal agents tried to bomb the Air and Space Museum in Washington, DC, blaming it on a mythical terrorist organization. That act was foiled by a lone American, on the scene by the grace of the Lord. Innocent people in Cheyenne were not so blessed.

The Watchdog of the Militia of Wyoming has been reporting to the people just how tenuous our freedom has become. Over the last year, we have laid out an agenda for what this country should be. Now the government has initiated a war against the people—for which this militia has been preparing. The Cheyenne bombing will not be the last attack on American citizens. Afraid of their own people, the federals will continue to blame *us* for the violence. Be prepared to defend yourselves and your families.

And stay tuned!

gtompkins@aol.com

Gabriele passed the paper to Jane Thorne and buried her nose in a well-used copy of *Atlas Shrugged*. She had never understood why a book about the sources of human genius had found such resonance in the militia movement. The revolution Thorne planned was far different from John Galt's willingness to simply let the world fall apart. Thorne and his followers were not willing to merely pick up the pieces. They were the destroyers. They had already destroyed everything she held dear.

Except Jerry.

His decisive moment was at hand. Hers was coming.

"This is good, Gaby. I'll take it to Red." Jane got up from the kitchen table and started to walk away. She turned to Gabriele, now sitting by herself. "And, Gaby, dear, Jerry will be gone for a few days. I know you'll want someone to comfort you tonight."

The only comfort Gabriele needed at the moment was a long run and a phone call. Then she was crushed by the reality that Susan and Gerhard were dead. *Oh my god!* On the verge of tears again, she forced herself to focus.

Jose, she remembered, would be at the Jumping Frog, waiting for a call. From someone. In the time it took him to pick her up, she'd just have to evade the posse Thorne would send to round her up.

She looked into Jane's eyes. "I'm still feeling pretty sick, dear… I wouldn't want to disappoint you on our first night together." Gabriele sighed. "Give me another day to recover… Then I will show you just how loving I can be."

Jane looked at her the way men had always done when Gabriele kept them at arm's length. A mixture of sadness and hope. She hesitated just long enough to give Gabriele the feeling she might not be *capable* of waiting. Then she spoke the words Gabriele needed to hear. "Okay, dear, I understand. Tomorrow, then."

"It will be more exciting if you have another day to think about it."

"I've thought about it ever since the first time I saw you, Gaby. I can wait one more day."

Gabriele had no intention of waiting that long. Thorne had insisted she sleep in Jane's room during Jerry's absence. Two of the men were gone—for a few days. Jane was going to leave her alone—

for one day. Gabriele was in great shape. Perhaps she could make it to the main road before they noticed she was gone. She would have to walk or run until she could get a cell phone signal. With or without Jose, she would then have to get to Medicine Bow.

Gabriele was actually *glad* that she and Jerry had been separated. If she didn't make it to the rendezvous, then perhaps he would. The mission would not be complete until one of them could contact the federal government. But the only FBI people who knew about Jerry and Gabriele were now dead. That would be a problem for later.

She would run tonight.

***

Somewhere in Nevada, Jerry was still waiting for a chance to subdue the other two men without spreading anthrax all over the highway. Murdock had driven all day, stopping only for burgers and gas. Jerry's accomplices did not let him out of their sight. They all used the side of the road as a bathroom. Jerry would have had no trouble killing the others with his hands, but he couldn't lure both of them both into his fighting circle at the same time. Back in the car, he was also hamstrung. Murdock and James—still sitting behind him—had each taken the precaution of arming themselves.

In the trailer, behind the deadly vessel, was the rest of the gear they would need. Jerry had been allowed to pack his own war bag, and to his relief, the others had not insisted on inspecting it. In the bag was everything he thought he might need—except a gun. The parachutes lay next to his war bag. Jerry would go through the motions of preparing the operation. Then he would, somehow, prevent the plane from taking off. Sitting in the front seat, with loaded weapons to his left and behind, Jerry was running out of options. He would have to kill the others…and soon.

One way or another.

Chapter 20

The Valley

Driving straight through, the three men entered California in the middle of the night. Jerry had taken a couple of hours to sleep. That was all he needed. As a sailor, he had developed the ability to sleep anywhere. Even here. Rest was one of the two weapons he had. His minders were not going to kill him. At least not yet. They needed Jerry for the attack.

He had both militia cell phones. They needed the devices for emergency communications with the Thorne ranch. Murdock and James had taken Jerry up on his offer to carry the phones. The men did not expect to be making any calls; they certainly hoped not to receive any. An incoming call would mean only one thing: mission abort. Jerry had understood right away that control of their communications was the second weapon available to him. Gabriele would be on the run by now. Thorne would be frantically trying to warn Murdock and James. Jerry had both phones in his pocket. He wasn't worried about Thorne's calls. He had turned the phones off.

The citizens of San Jose were asleep as they rolled by on Highway 101. Unknowing victims. Forty-five minutes later, they turned into a small airport adjacent to the highway. Jerry could see the outlines of dozens of private planes. Murdock pulled up to a hangar at the far end of the field.

"Okay, gentlemen… This is where it starts." Roy's tone had a military ring to it, a ring with which Jerry normally felt comfortable. They had a mission.

But this time, he had to stop it.

"I've waited a long time for this," said James, savoring his revenge, now taking shape. Jerry suspected that, at this moment, the man felt pride in his work, a rush of pleasure overriding all other feelings. Jerry had been there before. Operations were, to him, an art form. A creation to be appreciated for its own sake. Fighting in the jungle, Jerry had used tactical artistry to soften the reality of killing other men. James just wanted to kill as many people as possible.

Perhaps hundreds of thousands. Even millions. Jerry fought off the horror in his head.

Think!

Murdock unlocked the hangar and turned on the lights. Jerry carried his war bag toward the Cessna 172P and dropped it with a thud. There were no other aircraft in the building.

"Where did we ever get the money for this thing?" asked Jerry, staring at the plane.

"Jesse has *lots* of friends in Canada," said Murdock, reaching into his duffel bag for a flashlight.

James emerged from a storage locker carrying a heavy toolbox. "You talkin' about my Iraqi brothers, Roy?"

"I was just starting to explain to Jerry where we got this airplane."

"We're about to turn it into a Scud," replied James with a broad grin. "Saddam should like that… The US invaded his country and has been destroying his missile launchers for years. Now he gets to watch us drop anthrax on Silicon Valley. That's better than gassing the Kurds or rocketing the Israelis."

Roy laughed out loud. "Yeah, and all he had to do was buy us this little airplane!"

Jerry looked away and swallowed hard. *The Iraqis!*

He had missed Desert Storm, and he'd been upset about it (though he'd been plenty busy in Latin America). Now Jerry confronted the revenge of a defeated dictator…just like the Noriega operation six years before. But *this* dictator was acting through American traitors. Jerry had the power to stop it—if he could just draw Murdock and James close enough to him, and close enough to each other. Still without a sidearm, he looked frantically for an angle.

Any angle.

Jerry leaned toward the hangar door…and the Cherokee just beyond. "How 'bout a picture of you two in front of our Scud… I'll get the camera!"

"Get real!" shouted Murdock. "You're strong and brave, Jerry, but not very smart. Now go get the fucking sprayer!"

Perhaps sensing something, James followed him to the trailer. The man was still wearing his Beretta M9. Jerry understood that he was being guarded. James kept his distance, confirming what Jerry had known all along. Jerry Tompkins had the DEFCON One tattoo—but not the confidence of everyone in the group.

Murdock stayed with the plane. He also wore a Beretta on his hip. If discovered, they had agreed to shoot their way out. When Jerry had objected to not having a weapon, both men had promised to cover him. They had explained to Jerry (not very convincingly, to be sure) that he would be handling the deadly germs and could not be distracted by such things as personal weapons.

If he spilled the stuff, they would all be dead.

He hadn't had a good answer to that one.

Lugging the empty sprayer to the right wheel of the plane, Jerry set it down gently. He needed to stall some more. The others were in a hurry. They were tired. He had to throw them off-balance, and he had to do it soon.

"How come you guys don't do one-way missions?" he asked Murdock, now sitting in the cockpit, tinkering with the controls.

Through the empty doorframe came the answer. "We don't have enough soldiers yet. If we get ourselves killed now, the revolution stops."

Jerry watched James come back into the hangar. The gnome stopped just outside his kicking radius. Jerry replied to both of them.

"Too bad we're all Christians, guys. We can't get to heaven after a suicide—even if we kill ourselves in the Lord's name." He glanced at James. "It's not fair, Jesse. Your Islamic friends kill for Allah and go straight to the head of the line!"

Jesse looked at him with contempt. "They're not my friends, shithead… They just have the same goals."

Jerry burned a combat stare into James's eyes and taunted him. "No balls... You guys have *no balls!*"

Murdock climbed out of the plane before James could respond to Jerry's challenge. "You got the balls to sacrifice yourself for the cause, big man?"

Jerry spun around to face Murdock. The pilot was too far away for a spin-kick. He pointed at the Cessna. "Teach me to get that thing off the ground and I'll fly it right into the Castro...take out every queer in the district."

Murdock and James laughed together. "Pretty hard-core for a rookie," said James. "Now shut up and get those parachutes ready to go."

Jerry went back to the trailer...by himself! He rapidly thought through his options. He could make a last-ditch effort to kill both of them; he could try to get off a quick 911 call, or he could take his chances in the sky. What he really wanted to do was drive the Cherokee—and the cargo—away from the others, directly to a police station.

But he didn't have the car keys. And he didn't have time to hotwire the ignition.

Trying to kill them together at this moment was too much of a risk. If he lost the struggle, Roy would fly the mission himself. Even without a parachute, he would be able to coat San Jose with enough anthrax to kill many thousands. Then he would just land the plane back where he started. Jesse and Roy would drive away. They might get caught, but all those people would still be dead.

Before Jerry could boot up a cell phone, James was running out to join him by the trailer. "What's taking you so long, asshole?"

With James watching, Jerry reached for the chutes and carried them, one at a time, into the hangar. As he laid them out on the floor, James began fitting brackets for the sprayer under the rear fuselage of the airplane. As Jerry began packing the parachutes, Murdock watched him from the cockpit.

Not too close...and not too closely.

Jerry had packed the emergency chutes at the ranch before they left. Unobserved, he had tied Murdock's reserve in knots. Now he quickly knotted the suspension lines of Murdock's main canopy and stuffed all the nylon into the Stratocloud container. If he ever jumped from the airplane, Roy Murdock would go to hell ahead of schedule.

Twenty minutes later, just as Jerry was closing up his own rig, James came over and tapped him on the shoulder.

"Time for the bugs."

***

Gabriele sat on the bed, waiting for her moment. The sun was down; she could feel Jane's bony hands all over her. Skin crawling, she shook off the premonition. The window was locked from the outside. Gabriele stared at the door, the door through which she would have to run.

Suddenly, the door opened!

Anticipating a wrestling match with Jane, Gabriele was astonished to see the agitated figure of Will Jeffers standing before her. He held a piece of newspaper in his hand. His eyes were flashing like lightning. Without a word, he thrust the clipping into Gabriele's hand and watched her face as she tried to read it.

Gabriele held the paper in both hands, staring past it to the bare arms of the cowboy. A flashback to a hot day in Washington. The beginning of the end of her life. She knew what was in the paper without reading it.

"Come with me, Mrs. Barnes." The tone was seething, but the volume was low enough to convince Gabriele that Jeffers was trying to avoid detection. He was acting on his own.

Gabriele had no choice but to comply. She posted in her mind a picture of Carl's panic-stricken face. She wanted to remember his smile but could not pull up that image. Her fondest memories were blocked by the vision of her own death. Clutching the newspaper, she walked defiantly past Jeffers and out the door. Immediately, she felt cold steel in the small of her back.

She considered screaming. Perhaps Jane would be her savoir. Then she buried the thought. Gabriele would fight Jeffers to the end.

She willed herself to overlook the fact that she had nothing with which to fight.

Jeffers opened the driver's side door of his pickup and used the barrel of the pistol to shove Gabriele all the way across the bench seat. She stared straight ahead as he started the truck. A wave of disappointment washed over her, temporarily displacing the fear. *I am so sorry, Carl!*

The pistol was now aimed at her head.

"Where are you taking me?"

"For a ride, Mrs. Barnes. I'm taking you to hell. That is where you belong."

"You killed my husband." An almost conversational tone.

"And now I'm going to kill you!"

There was nothing she could do. All her work—all the training Jerry had drilled into her—had led to a simple end game: he had a gun, and she did not. The truck threw dust high into the air as Jeffers sped over the creek bridge toward the main road.

Jose watched them go by.

***

Jerry popped the sprayer from its new brackets underneath the Cessna and carried it to the trailer. Murdock continued to tinker in the cockpit. Jerry set the sprayer on the ground. With James watching, he donned a military gas mask and checked himself for leaks. Then he donned a plastic HAZMAT suit. The thick neoprene gloves came last. Staring at his outstretched hand, he practiced breathing through the mask to lower his pulse. *Steady, Butkus!* A minute later, the tremor was gone. As James backed away, Jerry reached far into the bed of the trailer and pulled the container toward him.

Slowly.

"If you spill that stuff, I'm outa here!" shouted the gnome. He was standing ten meters from Jerry. There was only a hint of breeze—perfect weather for spreading death—but James remained upwind.

Jerry flipped on a battery-powered lamp and set it on the end of the bed, illuminating both the container and the sprayer. Then he unsnapped the container hinges, opened the lid, and lifted a jar the size of a small trash can from its protective insulation. The ceramic vessel was lighter than he expected, noticeably lighter than ten gallons of water would have been. But it was still heavy, even for Jerry. He could feel the intense cold in his hands. A cloud of water vapor fogged his mask. Gently, he set the vessel on the ground next to the sprayer and unscrewed the top.

If he had been about to pour liquid explosive instead of weaponized biological agent, Jerry's decisive moment would be upon him. Subdue James, possibly taking a bullet. Grab Jesse's gun, run in, and shoot Murdock. Two men dead…maybe three. Countless lives saved. And Jerry briefly considered making it happen that way. Then he thought about the consequences of failure. About the millions of ordinary citizens from San Jose to San Francisco, now sleeping. Unaware. With a choke of emotion, he thought of Susan's sacrifice. And Gabriele. In the jungle, he had killed a lot of bad men and saved many good ones. During this operation, he had waited patiently—like a sniper—to sort out the bad from the good. Not trading tactics for strategy, Jerry Tompkins, jungle warrior, could wait just a bit longer.

He began pouring anthrax into the sprayer.

***

Jose mounted his dirt bike and took off in pursuit of the truck. He wore a medium-size green backpack. His P226 waited in a shoulder holster; he carried a second SIG in the pack. Also extra magazines and assorted field gear. After the confinement of his observation post, Jose felt the euphoria of freedom coursing through him. That, plus a good, stiff dose of adrenaline.

He pulled to within four hundred meters of the quarry and took station. The bike's headlight kept him on the road but did not penetrate the dust ahead. Jeffers couldn't have known he was there. Jose had no problem staying with the truck in the dirt. The hard part would begin when Jeffers hit the pavement.

Think, man!

Less than five minutes later, Red and Jane Thorne raced out of the compound in an old Suburban. They had both heard Jeffers leave. Jane had run to her room to find Gabriele gone. Disappointed and frightened, she had grabbed as many guns as she could from the living-room cabinet. Shouting over her shoulder, she had loaded the pistols on the run. Carrying an AK-47 in one hand and a banana clip in the other, Red had rushed past her. Falling in behind him, Jane had felt love again. She was back in the fray, no longer an appendage. Calamity Jane.

Jeffers spun onto the state road without lowering his pistol. He centered the wheel with his left hand and floored the accelerator. Gabriele continued to stare straight ahead, frozen. They were headed east, toward Split Rock.

"You and your muscle-bound friend never had me fooled!" Jeffers shouted above the whine of the engine. "Don't bother to say your prayers, woman… *Yahweh* doesn't listen to people like you."

Gabriele said nothing. She waited for the bullet and prayed it would come quickly. Silently, she would die a warrior's death. Carl was waiting for her. So were Susan and Gerhard. Jerry was probably with them by now.

The truck veered sharply to the left, slamming her against the door. Gabriele glanced quickly at her executioner and again felt the barrel of the gun at her side. Just above her DEFCON One tattoo. Jeffers braked abruptly, throwing her into the dashboard.

"Last stop, *bitch*!"

***

Jerry held his breath under the gas mask as he continued to pour a slurry of powdered death. The vessel became lighter as the sprayer filled to capacity. As the last of the mixture drained down, he let some air escape from his lungs and looked up. James was watching him warily, still out of reach. Jerry put down the vessel.

"Come over here and give me a hand with this," commanded Jerry.

"No way!" came the response from upwind. "Put the jar away and bring the sprayer to the plane. Roy ought to be ready by now."

Jerry fitted the cap on the vessel—with residual spores still inside—and carried it to the bed of the trailer. They had planned to simply leave it there, hoping to expose first responders and perhaps others around the airport.

The sprayer sat on the ground like a coiled snake. Jerry walked over, lifted it waist-high, and turned toward the hangar. He was starting to hyperventilate. Panic rose in his throat. He had to do something!

Take control of the situation!

He ripped the gas mask off his head and started screaming at James. "Listen, you little prick… I'm tired of being your butt boy. As of now, we're gonna do this my way!"

Carrying the sprayer, Jerry hustled into the hangar with James behind him, shouting.

"What are you… nuts?"

Jerry stopped several meters in front of the airplane. Murdock jumped out of the cockpit and stood facing him. Jerry saw confusion sweep across his face, then shock.

"What the fuck, over?" Roy tried to maintain his cool. He and James both drew their pistols and faced Jerry from opposite directions. Jerry turned slightly and backed up until he could see both of them.

"I got a new plan!" He brandished the sprayer at them. "You got the guns, but I have the germs."

"You'll get us all killed, you bastard!" James couldn't figure out what to do. He didn't want to die for the cause, and Jerry knew it. It was Murdock he wasn't too sure about. It was time to find out.

"Listen up, guys… This is what we're gonna do." Jerry finally had the upper hand. He paused for effect, lifting the sprayer overhead like a quarterback raising a trophy. James cowered. Murdock stiffened. Jerry went on improvising.

"This is now a one-way mission." Jerry managed to smile. "I've made my peace with the Lord. I suggest you do the same." He drew a deep breath. "It feels great to be free!"

"Fuck you!" shouted James. "I'm outa here!" The gnome turned and started to run away. Murdock raised his weapon and fired twice into James's back.

Rulon James went down in a heap, the Beretta at his side.

"I never liked that guy," added Murdock.

"He was a coward," said Jerry. "I *hate* cowards."

Realizing Jerry wouldn't be able to stop him, Murdock walked over and retrieved James's pistol and put it in the back of the airplane. He kept his own pistol in hand—not aiming but ready to shoot Jerry. Just in case.

Murdock took one step back. "You're the man, Jerry… What's the plan?"

"Same as before…except now we need a ride home. I guess we'll have to hijack a Ferrari."

Murdock starting laughing. "You mean that suicide business was just a test?"

Jerry stared at the pilot. "You passed."

"And how do you know we're not already dead?" Murdock looked like he didn't care, one way or the other.

"You haven't been exposed yet, Roy… And I couldn't get this disease even if I wanted to. Uncle Sam took care of that for me with a vaccination."

"Like I said, Jerry, you're the man!"

The two men were locked in a standoff. One of them would have to fix the now-full sprayer back into the brackets under the airplane. It wasn't going to be Murdock.

"Just get the sprayer into those brackets, Jerry, while I finish up in the cockpit." Murdock watched him as he worked.

Five minutes later, the sprayer was in place. Jerry gave Murdock a thumbs-up and took a step toward him. Murdock jumped out of the cockpit on the opposite side, maintaining his distance.

"All set," announced Murdock.

"Not yet," responded Jerry, trying to slow things down. "You need to show me how to fly this thing."

Roy rolled his eyes. "Why the fuck do you need to know that?"

"A habit of mine…redundancy. A best practice from my SEAL days."

"Really?" Roy drew his pistol again but kept it pointed at the floor.

"Look, Roy, if you don't at least tell me how to turn the engine on and off—and to fly straight and level—I won't be able to continue the mission if something goes wrong." Jerry took a shallow breath. "What if we get ambushed on the way out of here…and you get killed? At that point, I would just fly this sucker right into the big city."

Murdock thought for a long minute. "Okay… Here's all you need to know." Standing his ground, Roy gave Jerry a two-minute lecture on completing the mission.

Satisfied, Jerry gave him a thumbs-up, shouting and looking around. "Okay… Now we need to sanitize this place. We don't want the cops to trace this attack to us. Hey, lots more battles ahead, right?"

Roy shouted back, "You bet! Now put Jesse's body in the Cherokee while I tidy up in here. Then find a rag to stick in the gas tank. You can light the car on fire just before I take off."

"How about a thermite grenade?"

Still holding the pistol in his left hand, Roy's face lit up.

"Where in the hell do you get all this cool gear?"

"Government work has some advantages." Jerry pulled the thermite grenade out of his war bag. Roy stood a few meters from the rear of the airplane. A frag grenade was what he needed right now. Or a gun.

Having lost control of the anthrax spores, Jerry had nothing.

Roy watched Jerry pick the body up and turn toward the door. "And make sure you pile all our excess gear in the car too." Roy pointed with the gun to Jerry's war bag. "No evidence for the feds. Only a lethal trailer attached to an exploding SUV… Now *that's* cool!"

Jerry loaded the car and came back wearing a heavy canvas jumpsuit and flight gloves. He held the thermite grenade in his left hand. "I'll hold your weapon while you suit up."

Roy laughed at him. "No problem, cowboy. Put your rig on and go place the grenade in the car. "I'll be ready to go when you get back."

Jerry put on his parachute and moved quickly to the car. Roy donned his own rig, ran to the cockpit, and started the engine. The plane was rolling out of the hangar by the time Jerry got back. Roy had removed the starboard door to prepare for their midair exit. Jerry jumped into the passenger seat, ready to kill the pilot.

Murdock had one hand on the wheel and the other on the throttle. Jerry eyed the pocket behind Murdock's seat. In order to grab the weapon, he would have to twist to his left. Using the pistol still in his left leg holster, Roy would shoot him. Bad geometry. The Cessna gathered speed as Jerry accepted his fate.

There would be no easy way to end this.

Murdock lifted off the runway just as the Cherokee exploded in a yellow fireball behind them. Running just ahead of the shock wave, he pointed the nose of the aircraft toward San Jose. Climbing to eight hundred feet, he leveled off and flew for five minutes at ninety-five miles per hour. Beneath them stretched the 101 Corridor, leading north into Silicon Valley.

The heart of the American economy would start beating in less than an hour.

Chapter 21

The Atonement

"Get out!" commanded Jeffers.

Gabriele complied, resisting the urge to run. A bullet in the back would end it quickly and cleanly. But that would not be a warrior's death. If she was going to die, she wanted to look her killer in the eye. She would tell him he could take her life, but not her dignity. That's what Carl would have done.

Jeffers moved quickly around the front of the truck, gun leveled at her face. Gabriele opened the door carefully.

"I said move out!"

Raising her hands, Gabriele backed her way across the parking lot to the edge of the sagebrush.

"Hold it right there, *bitch*!"

Gabriele planted her feet and visualized the coming execution. She did not flinch. Jeffers took a shooting stance in the dim light, just beyond point-blank range.

Without warning, she lunged at him!

Jeffers dropped the gun and grabbed Gabriele in a bear hug. The killer's eyes were now in her face. Hardened fists dug into the small of her back as Jeffers wrestled Gabriele to the ground. She struggled underneath him like a roped calf.

Now in a rage, he tore open her shirt. "Now you'll die like the whore you are!"

Gabriele could not stop him from unbuckling her belt. Flailing away, she managed to get her hands around his throat. Other than her dignity, squeezing the breath out of Will Jeffers was the only thing she had left.

Jeffers headbutted her back to the ground and pulled a long knife from the sheath at his waist. Kneeling upright, he held the blade over her with both hands. Gabriele lay on the dry earth in a daze. Blood ran from her forehead. She saw the knife poised to end her life but could only watch it hang there. A deadly eclipse in the darkening sky.

Jeffers brought the knife down slowly and placed it on Gabriele's naked chest. It was still pointing at her throat, rising and falling with each gulp of air. He sat down between her legs and kicked off his boots. He struggled out of his jeans and knelt before the supine body he had wanted for months.

"This is for Carl, you dirty whore!" He spit into her face. "No one to protect you now!"

Gabriele felt her pants come down but could do nothing about it. She was going to lose everything.

Suddenly, there was blood all over her chest! A split second later, her brain processed the sound of the shots. Two shots in rapid succession. Jeffers fell forward, next to her on the ground, as Jose came running across the parking lot.

"Gaby! I'm here. It's okay."

She managed to sit up. The knife slid into her lap. Jose knelt beside her and checked for wounds. Other than the gash on her head, there was nothing to treat. A quick glance at Gabriele's legs told Jose he'd been just in time—the jeans were still around her knees. She was shaken but ambulatory.

Jose dragged the corpse away from Gabriele and quickly helped her dress. He did not have time to wipe the blood from her body. He picked up Jeffers's pistol and put it in his pack. Also the knife. Out of the pack came a battle dressing and a plastic poncho. Seconds later, Gabriele was wearing both. Looking nervously over his shoulder, Jose saw a pair of headlights turn off the highway into the parking lot.

Shit!

"We got to move, Gaby... Can you run?"

"I think so."

Jose took her hand and started picking his way through the brush. Away from the headlights. *To where?*

"They're coming, Gaby, whoever followed me from the ranch." Jose stumbled down a shallow slope, dragging Gabriele. Breathlessly, she spoke to him in the starlight.

"It's Red and Jane. Jerry and the other men left together... No one told me where they went."

Without slowing down, Jose interrogated her about the Thornes. He learned they were relentless but no match for him in stamina. They would have at least one rifle to make up for that. Probably no food or water. No car could go where he and Gabriele now went. Jose glanced over his shoulder again and saw a searchlight scanning the sage behind them. He was not ready to turn and fight. He had to find a place to hide.

An ambush site.

"Where are we going?" stammered Gabriele.

"Into the bush," said the warrior. "Until I figure out how to kill them."

"I can fight."

Jose stopped, turned, and grasped her by the shoulders. He could feel her muscles quivering with energy. "You might be *forced* to fight, Gaby... But now is not the time. Thorne has the advantage for the moment... But he won't have it for long."

"You're leading them away from their base of support."

Jose smiled to himself. "Jerry *has* taught you well, lady... Let's move!"

Gabriele tugged at his sleeve, restraining him. "If we keep going straight, we'll run into the Sweetwater River." Jose stopped again. The searchlight was closing on them. Relentlessly.

"You mean there's a river out here with water in it?"

"Yes!" said Gabriele excitedly. "That's what got the pioneers across Wyoming."

"And that's what's going to get us out," announced Jose. *¡Ten prisa!*

They ran faster through the darkness.

***

Murdock reached forward and switched on the autopilot. He was cackling with glee in anticipation of what they were about to do. Jerry needed to take him out of the problem…somehow. Both pistols were beyond his reach—at least not without a struggle. He couldn't risk a wrestling match with Murdock, even with the plane flying itself. Roy would shoot him first.

Fuck!

Having done a thorough map study while riding west, Jerry was aware that the hills on both sides of the valley were all higher than one thousand feet. They were in a long trench, headed north. At eight hundred feet.

"Ready!" he shouted into Murdock's ear. "Activating the timer." Jerry put his gloved fingers on the dial and turned it to the fifteen-minute setting.

Roy nodded vigorously without taking his eyes off the instrument panel. Jerry inched over to the right side of his seat and squeezed Roy on the upper arm. He reached into the slipstream for the wing strut. A blast of cold air sharpened all his senses. He needed those senses more than ever. He had lied to Murdock about the anthrax vaccination. Jerry Tompkins knew he would die soon, and he was okay with that. He just needed to live long enough to stop the attack.

At least Gabriele will get out of this alive.

Sensing Murdock moving toward him, Jerry leaned into the wind and climbed hand over hand along the wing strut. He looked back and motioned with his head.

"Come on, Roy!"

Murdock squatted in the doorway, looking straight at Jerry, finally trusting him.

"Showtime!" Jerry would not remember which one of them said it.

Jerry's body flew like a flag beneath the Cessna's wing. He tightened his grip and looked back into Roy's eyes. There was only one more thing to say.

"Ready…set…go!" *So long, sucker.*

Roy Murdock dived into the night. Jerry didn't even watch. He was too busy climbing back into the plane.

He was—literally—on a timer. In a big hurry to do something he had never done before. Hundreds of thousands of people—not one of whom would ever know—depended for their very lives on Jerry's return to the cockpit.

Hand over hand along the strut…one foot on the step…one hand on the doorframe…left leg through the door…butt in the passenger's seat…exhale and take one deep breath…climb into the pilot's seat.

Jerry reached for the timer and turned it off. *Whew!* The hardest part was just beginning.

He would have to fly the plane.

He did not want to risk turning off the autopilot. Murdock had told him quickly how to fly level. But that wouldn't be enough. The hills on either side might as well have been the Himalayas. He would not even *try* to get over them. A crash anywhere meant failure and catastrophe. He stared at the instrument panel. Heading due north. Ninety-five miles per hour. Almost half a tank of fuel. He touched his hands gently to the wheel and looked ahead. The lights of San Jose loomed. Lines of red taillights, headed that way. Working people. Victims. Fish in a barrel.

Jerry felt like a wild horse being led into a box canyon.

He needed to turn around.

Murdock had told him something important about the autopilot. *Think!*

Jerry could see individual cars moving below him. The carpet of lights appeared closer than eight hundred feet. Then he remembered the altitude at the airport: 281 feet. The plane was only five hundred feet above the highway. He felt the speed that comes with proximity to the ground. In the dawn, just before the wind, a perfect altitude for spreading the spores. And his altitude seemed to be holding steady.

That was it! Altitude hold. The autopilot would hold his altitude independently of plane's heading. He had asked Murdock about it because he'd worried about jumping from so low. The pilot had explained that he would be able to adjust course without changing the altitude parameter. He gripped the wheel and took one more deep breath. It would be his last deep breath for a long time.

Jerry found the heading bug on the plane's directional gyro. Adjusting the knob with his thumb and forefinger, he felt the Cessna begin to respond in a left turn. He let go of the wheel. With one eye on the lights below and one eye on the instrument panel, he waited for the plane come around until he was flying due south.

It was only a minute or so. It felt like forever.

He realized coming out of the turn that he would not need to focus on the compass; the gridlocked headlights coming at him would be all he needed. The map was clear in his mind, a personal heads-up display. He followed the highway toward the widening end of the trough and the smaller population center of the Monterey Peninsula.

***

Gabriele fell to the ground behind Jose. He stopped immediately, reached back, and took her hand again. "This is no time for a nap, lady… They're gaining on us!"

Humor in the face of danger. Essential. Lifesaving.

As she got to her feet, Gabriele put one hand in the dirt to push off. Instead of dry earth, she felt mud.

Mud!

"This is it, Jose, the river! It isn't much, but it's wet."

The searchlight was dancing above them on the ridge. Jose and Gabriele still had a two-hundred-meter lead, but the gap was closing. Jose guided her to the right, along the south bank.

"Stay in the mud and follow the river… I'll be right behind you." Jose pressed a SIG Sauer into Gabriele's hand. "I assume you know how to use this."

"I do," she said grimly.

"Do not use it unless you have to… Got that?"

"Got it." And she was off.

Jose reached into his pack again and produced a pair of night vision goggles. Hastily, he slipped them over his head and let Gabriele get far enough ahead of him.

Gabriele raced over the muddy earth. She didn't know whether the absence of moonlight was a blessing or a curse. She stumbled. She got right up. She pressed on.

Jose needed to be within fifteen meters for a sure-kill shot. Ten would be better. As he fitted the goggles onto his eyes, he could see a fat man carrying a long rifle. A figure walking quickly next to him trained the searchlight back and forth. Jose could not tell if the figure was a man or a woman. Whoever it was had a pistol in the other hand.

Now he had the enemy order of battle. And a plan.

Gabriele jumped a foot as Jose grabbed her by the right forearm. She stopped and spun around to face him. "I didn't hear you!" She was hyperventilating.

She couldn't see him, but she could hear his soothing voice. Yes, it was soothing! "Listen to me, Gaby… Everything will be okay." His confidence cut through her fear. He pulled her into a thick clump of bushes. She swallowed hard and listened intently.

The briefing lasted all of ten seconds.

The searchlight stopped at the riverbank. Jose and Gabriele could see the searchlight hesitate, look around, and then draw toward them like a magnet. Gabriele watched in horror as the beam found their footprints in the mud. Jose patted Gabriele on the shoulder and darted in front of her. She gripped her pistol in both hands and jogged after him as fast as she could.

Without slowing down, Gabriele glanced behind her. Thorne was jogging faster than she was!

Still wearing night vision goggles, Jose ran ahead of everybody. Another hundred meters along the bank, he found what he needed. He cut sharply to his right, stepped over sagebrush for about ten meters, and stopped short.

Gabriele went by him in a green blur.

Jose squatted behind a rock the size of a Volkswagen and raised his weapon, waiting for Thorne and his accomplice.

The accomplice was the first to cross into his sight picture. The searchlight blinded his open eye as it went by. He opened the other eye and fired two rounds into the ghostly figure's back.

The searchlight dropped to the mud as the body went down. Red Thorne stopped in his tracks, wheeled, and sent a burst of automatic gunfire right at him. Some of the rounds ricocheted off the rock, sending splinters into Jose's face.

Thorne ran for cover but found none. Jose aimed again and cut him down with two more shots.

Gabriele stopped running. She sank to the mud as ordered and waited for Jose. The shots had come exactly as he had told her they would. She was almost certain it would be Jose following her footprints now.

But not *absolutely* certain.

Jose walked carefully over to the body of Red Thorne and kicked it. Nothing. He bent down and took the AK-47 rifle in his hands. It was full of mud but still usable. *The ultimate people's weapon.* He slung the AK over his shoulder, found the searchlight, and checked the other body.

Jane Thorne was lying facedown in the muck. The body was thin, with a head of short hair. It looked like the body of a boy. A boy with two large holes in his back. Jose could tell by the hips that it was a woman. He had never killed a woman before. He was glad she looked like a boy.

He trained the beam down the bank and flashed a signal.

Dit, dit, dit...dah.

Gabriele didn't know Morse code, but she knew what the signal meant. Red Thorne and his wife were dead, and Jose was following her footsteps. She got her breathing under control and tried to imagine what had happened to Jerry.

***

Jerry was still at eight hundred feet, flying south. Had he been just a little higher, he would have seen the sun coming up behind the hills to his left. He checked his gauges again. A third of a tank of fuel. Nothing in the red. The plane's single engine droned on. He did not want to think about the consequences of engine failure.

But he had to.

The farther south he went, the wider the valley became. The rangeland to his east reminded him of Wyoming, and the ranch he would never see again. He considered a controlled crash into the remote region. He could just fly the plane into one of the ridges. Not knowing enough about either anthrax or aviation, he rejected the crash scenario. The hills were not completely empty. He looked ahead again and saw that his options were not multiplying.

The highway was taking him out the open end of the trough, but there was still nowhere to go. The eastern hills marched unbroken to a vanishing point in front of him. He knew from his map study that the cities of Salinas and Monterey lay ahead. More than two hundred thousand people. Beyond that, the Salinas Valley farm belt. Farther south and west lay the rugged and unpopulated backcountry of Big Sur.

But he didn't think he could make it that far.

That left the ocean.

He tried to remember the details about the road to the coast. He saw it in his mind's eye, branching off the main highway just north of Salinas. The road was straight, pointing to the bay. That would be his final option. The sea had always been Jerry's refuge. For a frogman in combat, it was the light at the end of the tunnel. He was going home.

Just like Carl.

He calculated that he had fifteen minutes before the right turn. Fifteen minutes to think. Susan was in his head immediately. He would have gladly traded his life for hers. Too late for that. He hoped to be with her wherever he was going, but his faith was not strong enough to be sure of that. He did believe that he would not suffer after death. He had done the best he could, after all, to root out evil in the world.

But he hadn't done enough. Thorne and Jeffers were still alive. Susan and Gerhard were dead. There was no guarantee that justice would be served.

Jerry's thoughts turned to Gabriele, his unattainable wife. She would get the ranch and everything else he had. But she deserved so much more than that. Her happiness had ended at the beginning of all this. Jerry's death would be the final chapter in her nightmare. He would not be at the Virginian Hotel to link up with her. He trusted Jose to find her. At least she would live to see the sun come up each day. That thought comforted him.

The sun was now above the eastern ridge. Daylight revealed a ribbon of asphalt to his right connecting the highway to the shoreline. Monterey Bay beckoned in the distance. With a surge of confidence, Jerry began a slow turn and felt the plane come around. He knew for the first time since boarding the Cessna that he would not have to crash it into the ground.

He would ditch it in the sea.

Not just any piece of sea. His map study had not stopped at the beach. He had noticed the hundred-fathom curve just offshore of the Moss Landing jetty. And the thousand-fathom curve not too far beyond that. The Monterey Bay Canyon was deeper than the Grand Canyon. And it got deep very quickly.

He flew over the power plant. It was bigger than it had looked on the map, with twin chimneys rising halfway to the path of the plane. Light smoke drifted into the morning sky. A landmark for fishermen.

Jerry stared at the open doorframe to his right. The wind roared by…inviting him. He checked the gas gauge. Almost empty. The pilot and his load of anthrax would disappear into the deepest part of the canyon. Jerry's body would never be found.

He just sat there, waiting for the inevitable.

For about ten seconds.

Jerry abruptly slid his bulk across the console and into the passenger's seat. There was still some fuel left in his body; he didn't know how much. He reached behind the pilot's seat and grabbed Jesse's

Beretta. He checked the chamber and magazine out of habit and secured the weapon inside his jumpsuit.

He needed to live long enough to go back to Wyoming and kill Red Thorne. And Will Jeffers. And anyone who tried to protect them.

Extending his left hand, Jerry pulled out the red mixture knob. The engine sputtered and died. The propeller windmilled but no longer bit into the air. Moving quickly, he climbed back out along the wing strut and hung there for a few seconds.

He let go of the dying plane and took the last parachute jump of his life.

***

The searchlight came closer. Gabriele stood in the muck of the Sweetwater River and waited for the man who had just saved her life. The warm air was still, and the night echoed with the sound of a million frogs. The sounds of a summer evening in the Black Forest of her childhood. Soothing sounds to accompany the sudden release of extreme tension. Drained by adrenaline, all she wanted to do was lie down and go to sleep. Physical exertion had also left Gabriele bathed in sweat. She pulled off the poncho to let the night air cool her.

"*Vamenos*," called Jose from a few yards out. "Let's go!"

Gabriele watched the light swinging back and forth. The beam found her legs and moved to her chest. She squinted to see Jose. A quick glance at her own body revealed torn jeans and a tattered shirt completely covered with blood. Will Jeffers's blood! She wanted more than anything to wash.

Jose didn't even stop. She fell in behind him and followed the light for ten minutes. She found herself in waist-deep water before she could say anything. "What's the plan, Jose? Tell me what is going on."

Without turning around, Jose trained the searchlight on the opposite bank and began to explain. "Over there… We can rest over there."

Gabriele waded the across the river and joined Jose on a dry patch of ground. He was holding the flashlight against the soil, with a small amount of illumination to guide her.

"I don't think there's anyone else back there, but I didn't want to take that chance… Are you okay?"

"I think so…just dirty. And I'm worried sick about Jerry."

"You can clean up here," said Jose, reaching into his pack. "And don't worry about Jerry. He'll be okay…trust me."

"I trust you, Bosco."

"Put this on after you get rid of that shirt." He handed her a sweatshirt and restowed the poncho.

Gabriele waded back into the river. Stripping off her shirt and the remains of her bra, she rubbed herself as clean as she could. Pulling the sweatshirt over her head, she waded back to Jose.

"Ready." Gabriele stood in front of him, still knee-deep in the river. She didn't want to leave the refuge of the water.

"Gaby, I am very sorry it had to go down that way." He addressed her in a calm voice, almost relaxed. "I waited as long as I could to get you out of that place safely. It would have been bad for you if I'd come in with guns blazing."

She climbed out of the water and sat down next to him in the darkness. "You saved my life, Jose. I don't know what I'll do with it, but you have given it back to me."

"The first thing you're gonna do is follow me out of here." He stood up and pulled her to her feet. "Then we're gonna find Jerry."

"I'm supposed to meet him in Medicine Bow."

"He told me."

"Escape and evasion," said Gabriele. "Jerry has prepared me for this."

"That doesn't surprise me," replied Jose. "I'd love to just go back and give you a lift on my dirt bike." She couldn't see his face, but she could tell he was smiling.

"But we can't take that chance, can we?"

"No, I'm afraid we'll have to walk east."

They would have to move away from the crime scene where Jose had just killed three people and from where he had to assume Thorne had called for reinforcements to track them down.

"Along the river…like the pioneers," said Gabriele.

"Until we get to a road, yes. Then we can find something better than a covered wagon." Jose was smiling again. If he had been able to see Gabriele's face, he would have seen her first smile in a long time. Since before Jerry had been taken from her. That had been less than twenty-four hours ago. It seemed like a lifetime.

"Let's go," said Gabriele. "He'll be there waiting for us. I have great confidence in Jerry."

"*Yo tambien*," said Jose. "So do I."

Jose walked in front of her without the flashlight. She held onto a short length of rope tied to the back of his pack. He wore the night vision goggles again. The ground was flat, and they made good progress for the next two hours. Sometime after midnight, they stopped to take a break. Gabriele lay on her back and tried to relax without going to sleep. The next thing she knew, Jose was shaking her awake.

"Time to move."

Gabriele sat up quickly. "Jerry!"

"No, Gaby, it's me, Jose. You were dreaming."

She threw her arms around him and buried her face in his filthy shirt. "Carl is gone, Jose! And now Jerry! What are we going to do?"

"We're going to Medicine Bow," said Jose firmly. "Jerry will be there." He handed her a Power Bar. "Eat this."

Gabriele devoured the calories and took a long drink of river water from Jose's canteen. Energy surged back into her limbs. "Thank you. I'm ready to walk some more."

"You want to walk point?" Gabriele had often listened to Carl talk about walking at the front of the patrol. Taking most of the risk. That was Carl. She wanted to be like Carl. And Jerry. And Jose. She reached for the goggles hanging around Jose's neck.

"Show me how to wear these things."

Jose shined the flashlight in her face. "First I need to change that battle dressing." He reached up and gently pulled the gauze away from her bloody forehead and pulled another bandage out of his pack.

"You seem to have an unlimited supply of everything we need in that rather small pack."

"I wish I had room for a steak dinner and a car."

Gabriele managed to laugh. Jose was good at making people laugh, she thought. Even here.

Jose changed her bandage. Then, with his assistance, she put on the goggles, and they walked through the darkness for the rest of the night.

Still in full combat mode, Bosco walked the equally important position of rear security. He kept looking back for signs they were being followed. There were none. Now all they needed was a road. And a car. He was beyond his ability to plan, improvising all the way. He was good at improvising.

The road came with the dawn. A dirt track leading along the river, intersecting another dirt track. Jose got out his map and checked the alignment of the two roads. They had a choice. The short way… or the long way. The crossing road led back to the highway leading away from Split Rock. The crime scene. The road along the river intersected the main road to Casper. If they took the crossing road, they could be at the highway in a couple of hours. If they stayed on their present course, it might be all day until they found a place to rent a car.

Jose chose the long way.

Chapter 22

The Search

Jerry flew his parachute toward the horizon and watched the Cessna crash into the dark-blue void. He felt a sense of triumph. His own death would have meaning. He had saved more lives than he could count. He had rid the world of two men who would have tried again to kill large numbers of innocent people. He had every reason to believe that Gabriele had walked to her own freedom. Carlos would be proud of his old friend Butkus.

But there was one piece of unfinished business.

The descent from eight hundred feet did not give Jerry much time to think. He pulled down hard on the right steering toggle. The ancient Stratocloud lifted him in a long arc to the left then swept him into a short run toward the beach and a fast downwind landing. He released the chute and kicked to the surface.

Free, but not home-free. Dead, but still very much alive.

The power plant stood in front of him. The fisherman's landmark was now his. He guessed the chimneys were about two miles away, a long swim under any circumstances. A *very* long swim in fifty-six-degree water. Bending his body into a ball, still wearing flight gloves, Jerry reached to untie his shoelaces. He would need to jettison the jungle boots before his fingers became useless. He knew the odds favored the cold taking him before he got to the beach. Jerry Tompkins had never let the odds beat him before, and he was determined to beat them one more time. Reaching deep into his guts, he pulled strength into his mind where it would do him the most good. He was back in training. *Think past the pain!*

He swam sidestroke. *Kick, stroke, glide.* He grieved for Susan. He prayed for Gabriele. He wished he could talk to Jose. Then he pointed his mental laser at Red Thorne, working out all the ways he could kill the man. And Will Jeffers. He wanted them to suffer. Susan was gone, but Gabriele was safe. Jose would be with her by now.

Kick, stroke, glide. One eye on the power plant, the other eye submerged in ice water. The heavy jumpsuit slowed him down considerably, but it delayed the onset of hypothermia. Blood pooled in his core, leaving his limbs starved for oxygen. He knew that swimming was the quickest way to die in cold water.

Kick, stroke, glide—gut it out.

The eastern Pacific Ocean was even colder than he remembered. Jerry knew that—at some point—his ability to swim would be stopped short by his steadily declining core temperature. He had been swimming for about an hour. He stopped and treaded water. The twin chimneys appeared larger than before, but he reckoned they were still at least a mile away. He noticed that he had stopped shivering. A bad sign. He could not feel his hands or his feet. Another bad sign. Panic threatened. He swallowed the fear and recovered his focus.

Kick, stroke, glide.

The day wore on. The useless sun would not warm him or the water in which he swam. But with the warming of the land came rising wind from offshore...a stiff breeze pushing up big waves and moving them toward the beach. He swallowed a lot of water as the waves grew, tossing him forward. Tossing him toward the beach!

The chimneys were closer now. It was not just his imagination. During the second hour, Jerry became more and more certain he would make it to shore alive. Against the odds.

Forget the odds!

His body was screaming at him. He shut out the sound, kicking almost frantically toward the crashing waves right in front of him. They pounded the sand to the left of the rock jetty. Purely out of habit, Jerry stopped swimming and surveyed the beach for human presence. Two figures, heads down, looking for shells. Birds everywhere. A few boats navigating the inlet to his right...too far away to notice a swimmer in the froth. He proceeded carefully. His mind was in combat now, swimming ashore to recon the enemy. He was back with Carlos and Bosco. He wouldn't let them down. They were the reason he risked death. For them, he had gone far beyond the limits of human endurance. For them, he had killed other men.

Thorne...I'm still alive, and you're a dead man.

The wild surf dumped him onto the sand like a 220-pound piece of driftwood. He did not move for a long minute. Habit again...but also exhaustion. He could not stand up. Like a cripple without a wheelchair, he dragged himself up the berm, past the high-water line, and onto the backshore. Burrowing into the soft sand, he let all his systems crash and lay there soaking up the heat of the sun.

Like a Harbor Seal.

***

The long way was longer than Jose had thought. It took most of the day for him and Gabriele to walk the distance remaining between the river junction and the asphalt road. They had plenty of water, but Jose was out of Power Bars. They were getting close to the road, but his cell phone was out of battery and out of range. Survival, as always, would come down to human ingenuity, relentlessly applied.

Jose had been surprised by the stunning remoteness of the landscape. On one hand, he was grateful for the space to move without being seen; on the other, he didn't think it would ever end. He had done the right thing, he thought, by going long. After taking down three enemy, he'd been more concerned about explaining his actions to the police than confronting potential Thorne reinforcements. Gabriele had filled him in on the Cheyenne bombing, and that had given Jose an even greater fear of the police. They would be on a hair trigger, looking for revenge as well as suspects. He considered dumping the assault rifle to soften their profile. He and Gabriele were fugitives—from anyone who didn't know who they were or why they were there.

That included every living human being except Jerry Tompkins.

Gabriele stopped walking and looked up into the sun. Vultures circled them.

Jose pointed to the sky. "Whatever you do, Gaby, do *not* start limping. Those birds look hungry!"

She managed a laugh. "I'm afraid I must take off this sweatshirt, Jose. I'm getting soaked with sweat."

"Take this," he replied, hastily removing his shirt. "And when you see Jerry, tell him I gave you the shirt off my back!"

"But the *sun*... Won't you get burned?"

The dark Colombian face smiled ironically. "Sometimes it pays to be a spic."

Gabriele took Jose's shirt and went to the side of the road. She turned away from him and pulled the sweatshirt over her head. The vultures watched her wrap the faded garment around her bare torso and button it. She looked up again.

"Not today, boys."

And they walked some more, guided by the road map and thoughts of Jerry. With the AK over his brown shoulder, Jose felt like the bad guy in a B movie. Gabriele wore a third battle dressing like a headband. It soaked up the sweat as well as the blood. Jose thought she was the most beautiful woman he'd ever seen.

Gabriele looked back at him. "We are quite a pair, are we not?" she said through cracked lips.

"I wish I had a camera."

"You mean you forgot something besides a car and a steak?"

Jose grinned from ear to ear. "I forgot how much fun this is."

Gabriele returned the grin. "Jose, you save my life, and now you keep me laughing. How do you guys do it? I'm just a middle-aged weakling. You make me feel like a warrior...like I can do *anything*!"

"You can."

Gabriele found herself pumped full of energy again. "Then let's go get that steak and find Jerry."

Jose nodded, and they picked up the pace.

About a mile farther on, they saw a tractor-trailer rig in the shimmering heat. Jose stared at it. Not a mirage! The truck came from the south, drew closer to them, and then disappeared over the north horizon. The road to Casper!

***

Jerry's eyes were too blurry to see the time on his Rolex, but the angle of the sun told him it was late afternoon. It was the shivering that had awakened him. He convinced himself that his shivering was from the cold, that it was a good thing. He did not feel the flu-like symptoms he knew were coming. It was, as far as he knew, still too early for the disease to have taken hold. He stood up slowly, rubbed his eyes into focus, and surveyed his surroundings. Nobody on the beach. Fishermen on the jetty to his left. Surfers in the water to his right. A wooden path leading to steps over the dunes.

He followed the path.

Jerry needed three things, and he needed them fast. A change of clothes, a car, and enough cash to get him to Wyoming. He sat shivering in the dunes and patiently watched the parking lot until he found two of them.

One by one, the surfers came out of the water and followed the boardwalk through the dunes. Jerry sized them up as they walked by. Literally. One of the last young men was blond and almost as big as Jerry. In his exhaustion, he thought for an instant it was Roy Murdock. *Shit!*

Then he remembered that Murdock was dead. The authorities were no doubt, at this moment, trying to figure out how in the world a lone parachutist had fallen to his death in the dark somewhere between Morgan Hill and San Jose. Jerry savored the flashback. He then pulled up the image of James falling to the deck of the hangar.

Two down, two to go.

Since halfway through the swim, he'd begun talking to himself. Another sign he was losing control. *Just get it over with, frogman!* He watched the big surfer carry his board to a beaten-up Volkswagen van full of bumper stickers in a lonely corner of the parking lot. There were no other young men following him. No surfer girls waiting in the icy wind. *Okay, kid, you're my ticket out of here!*

It was time to move.

Jerry walked as quickly as he could out of the dunes. The victim's surfboard was already on the roof. He was taking off his wet suit, the long blond locks buried temporarily in neoprene, his powerful arms struggling to separate rubber from skin. Jerry knew the target would be absolutely helpless for the next ten seconds. He broke into a run.

There was no way to fight back, so the kid simply raised his hands. Jerry kicked him in the stomach, just to make sure. The young man fell to his knees. Jerry produced a length of parachute cord and tied the surfer's hands behind his back.

"Listen up, asshole. Do everything I say or I *will* kill you!"

The victim thought he was being robbed. He could now see Jerry's bulky figure, wearing a sandy jumpsuit and a crazed expression.

"Okay, man, okay. Waddaya want? I don't have much, man."

Jerry stood him up and shoved the kid into the van on the passenger's side. Mission success would now require a quick exit from the parking lot and a steady stream of traffic.

"I want your clothes, and then I need a ride to the nearest car rental." Jerry relaxed his tone. "Can you drive?"

"Yeah, man… I think so."

Jerry drew the pistol from his jumpsuit then cut the kid's wrist restraints with his hook knife. The young man responded by moving carefully into the driver's seat.

"All I got is a pair of really old jeans and a polo shirt. No shoes… just flip-flops." He glanced behind the seat. "Stuff's back there, along with a wet towel."

"Let's go, kid… I'll change once we get out of here. I'm not gonna shoot you unless you try something." The van moved past a few other surfers and their vans, all getting ready for the drive home. Jerry—with a young face, big shoulders, and blond hair—looked like a surfer *should* look as they drove out of the parking lot.

The tone was now almost conversational. Jerry was actually impressed with how quickly his victim had recovered. He thought the kid might be stoned.

"You're all *wet*, dude!"

"I had an accident," explained Jerry calmly. "I belong to the Monterey Parachute Club. We got a little off course, and I ended up in the bay."

"Cool."

"Cold," corrected Jerry, as they pulled onto the highway. "I'm *freezing*... Pull over up there." He pointed to a turnout on the side of the highway. The driver parked, and Jerry climbed into the back to change clothes. He would toss the jumpsuit in a dumpster later.

"Killer tattoo, man... Hey, do you work out with weights?"

Jerry pulled the polo shirt over his head. "I do."

"I guess you lost your wallet."

"I have a credit card," said Jerry, sliding two pieces of plastic out of the jumpsuit's sleeve pocket. He never went anywhere without a credit card and driver's license—this time, under a false name provided by the FBI. He found the flip-flops and put them on his bare feet.

"Let's go... To Watsonville, right?"

"Perfect, man... I *live* in Watsonville. Only gringo in the whole place, I think."

"Just get me to a rental office... Then you can go about your business. Sorry about roughing you up back there... But I really need to get back to my club." Jerry was pretty sure his cover story—especially the gun—would become the stuff of local surfing legend. He didn't care if the kid called the cops. In a couple of days, Butkus the warrior would be dead.

"No problem, man." The van chugged along Highway 1, headed north. "You think I could learn to jump out of a plane?"

"I'd stick to surfing if I were you," said Jerry without a trace of humor. "Airplanes can be dangerous."

***

Jose squatted by the road and put on his sweatshirt while Gabriele washed at the river. She had insisted that one of them be clean enough not to attract undue attention. Jose had resisted the temptation to tell Gabriele that, dirty or clean, she would attract *lots* of attention. Her ablutions also gave him time to break the assault rifle into its basic parts and stuff them in his backpack.

Gabriele came back from the river looking even better than he had imagined. Still wearing Jose's shirt, she had finger-combed her shoulder-length hair and gotten rid of the battle dressing. The wound was now covered with a red bandanna.

"Ready?" asked Jose, settling into a roadside ditch.

"Ready." Gabriele walked to the side of the road. She turned to face the traffic coming from the south, sticking out her left thumb and a long leg.

It happened quickly. The first truck slowed down long enough to check her out. The second truck, a large semi, actually screeched to a halt on the tarmac. The driver came out of the cab like a paramedic on a 911 call. From his concealed position, Jose admired the fat trucker's agility.

"You okay, ma'am?" The man was running across the highway, eyes fixed on the woman apparently in distress. Gabriele waved to him and winced as he was almost cut down by a speeding car.

"Yes... I'm okay," she answered, smiling broadly as the trucker approached. "But my husband and I need a ride to Casper."

The fat man stopped in midstride, walking the last few paces. "Oh...I thought you were alone and in trouble."

"We *are* in trouble, sir... Our car broke down about five miles back." She was still smiling as her companion emerged slowly from the ditch. Gabriele held the trucker's attention until Jose jogged to her side. He was not brandishing a weapon, but he could easily have taken down the driver. She didn't know if Jose knew how to drive a big rig, but it wouldn't have surprised her.

"This is my husband, Jose."

"*Muchas gracias, señor*," said Jose with a straight face. The speechless driver led them across the road to his truck.

They rolled into Casper a little after five. The first order of business was to find a car. Jose rented a silver Ford Taurus while Gabriele found a pharmacy down the street. When Jose picked her up, she was better groomed and ready for the second order of business.

Even Denny's steak had never tasted so good. Gabriele inhaled her meal with such concentration that she missed most of the stares. Jose—back to the wall and focused on the door—was acutely aware of the leering. Rough men were looking at Gabriele, trying to figure out what she was doing with *him*. He didn't care. He leaned across the table and spoke to her in a low tone.

"I want to hit Medicine Bow right at sunset. I know you're anxious to see Jerry, but we have to be careful down there."

Gabriele looked up at his rugged Latin face. "Ambushes happen on the way home."

"Did you learn that from Carl, or from Jerry?"

"Both."

"It's a good lesson to remember, Gaby, and we're almost home."

They walked to the car and drove ninety minutes south to the rendezvous point. It was just past eight o'clock when Jose pulled into the dusty parking lot of the Virginian Hotel. They sat in the car, watching the place for another hour. Gabriele did not have the field discipline Jose had. She fidgeted nervously as they waited.

Jose was the first to speak. "I think it's okay, Gaby." His eyes were still searching in all directions. He checked his cell phone purely out of habit; there would be no signal, even if the battery was charged. There was no movement on the street. Just a few pickup trucks lining the log curb where a hitching post used to be.

"You go in, Gaby… I'll watch the building for another thirty minutes. If neither of you comes out by then, I'll assume you and Jerry are hostages. I know how to rescue hostages." He looked into her eyes, now full of anticipation and confidence.

"Don't forget to mark the door if you're *not* a hostage."

Gabriele nodded and got out of the car. She walked to the hotel lobby and hurried to the front desk. Passing the bar, she heard harmless sounds of drinking and baseball. An older woman in a Victorian dress stood behind the vintage cash register. Gabriele almost asked her if she had actually witnessed The Virginian threaten his rival Trampas in this very room a hundred years before.

When you call me that, smile.

"I am Mrs. Meredith, ma'am. My husband was supposed to meet me here. I think he has already checked in."

"First name?" The skeptical look from the woman made Gabriele even more nervous than she already was.

"Jerry…with a *J*."

"I have nothing under that name."

Gabriele's nervousness escalated to shock. She harbored so much faith in Jerry she had just assumed he would be there. Her own escape from Thorne's ranch had taken a long time. What would Jerry be doing that could possibly have taken longer?

"Are you *sure*?" Panic attacked her. She hesitated, looking over her shoulder, trying to assess what might be happening.

The woman behind the desk interrupted Gabriele's security assessment. "I'm sure… Do you want a room or not?"

"Yes," said Gabriele, recovering her composure. I would like a king-size bed on the top floor." Then she added, "Do you have a honeymoon suite?"

The woman managed a wry smile. "Does this look like a honeymoon kind of town?"

Gabriele faked a matter-of-fact response. "Right… Please give me the quietest room you have. My husband will be along shortly."

***

Jerry sped along the interstate somewhere east of Reno. It was after midnight, and he was beyond exhaustion. But he had vowed not to rest until Red Thorne was dead, along with anyone else he happened to find at the Mineral King ranch whose name was not Gabriele. He was almost finished with his mission. He would have plenty of time to rest—wherever he was going next.

God would forgive him for what he was about to do. It wasn't murder, he assured himself; it was an eye for an eye.

He got off the road near Winnemucca to gas up the Explorer. He'd been lucky to find an SUV, but he cursed the fuel-hungry engine. *Too many stops!* He would need to be able to drive anywhere, on any surface, just in case he ended up in a chase. He did not have a cell phone, so he took the time to dial Jose's cell from an old pay phone in the truck stop (they had agreed not to call the hotel). No answer. He left Jose a long voice mail then went into the store. He bought a pair of work boots, socks, a can of all-purpose oil, and a rag. Back in the car, he broke the Beretta down and oiled every single part of the gun. Salt water and sand had not been kind to the weapon. Storing the Beretta in the glove compartment, he discarded the surfer's flip-flops and put on his new boots. Then he pulled into a Burger King drive-through to load up on hamburgers and coffee. Calories and caffeine—plus field discipline—would get him through the night.

Unless the germs inside him exploded first.

He had been monitoring his bodily functions closely since leaving Watsonville. There was no sign of the disease yet, but he knew it could be as long as forty-eight hours before he felt sick. He expected it. In one sense, he dreaded it. In another sense, he welcomed it.

What are clouds but an excuse for the sky?
What is life but an excuse for death?

Jerry had always admired—no, revered—the Japanese *samurai*, warrior-poets representing the apex of his profession. The death poem gave him strength and solace at the same time.

The Explorer barreled down the pavement at eighty miles per hour. He would have driven faster, but he didn't want to be stopped. His plight would be impossible to explain. He would go to jail. Thorne would outlive him.

Jerry was in a race against time. Actually, two races: one for Gabriele's life; the other for what was left of his own life. In order to win the first race, he would have to win the second. He set the cruise control and turned on the radio. Country music. Better than coffee. He tried to sing, thinking it might keep him awake. For all that had happened—and all that was *about* to happen—Jerry Tompkins was not in a singing mood. It seemed somehow inappropriate. So was music itself. He turned off the radio. Silence would give him more time to think.

Too much time.

He turned his thoughts to Gabriele again. He had been assuming (perhaps hoping) she'd simply walked out in the middle of the night. He continued to believe she had managed to escape, but he wasn't completely sure. He realized now that he would have to assume she was still in the Thorne compound. Still in the trailer. Given that assumption, there were two actions to be taken: one, to rescue Gabriele; the other, to kill her captors.

He decided to kill the others first. One by one.

He castigated himself for leaving Jose out of the loop in Lone Mountain. Jerry hoped that, somehow, Jose and Gabriele had linked up. Also that Jose had found a signal and listened to his voice mail. He hoped that Thorne would still be at the ranch. Thorne at the ranch *with* Jeffers would be better. Thorne, with Jane and all the others, would be best of all. But the enemy situation was unclear.

Hope is not a strategy!

Assuming Gabriele *had* succeeded in running, Thorne's women would now be frantically searching the landscape. Maybe they had already recaptured her. Aware by now the Silicon Valley mission had failed, the men—armed more heavily than Jerry—were probably holed up at the ranch.

Waiting for him.

He turned the radio back on and surfed the channels. He slammed the steering wheel with the heel of his hand. *God, what is going on out there?* After all he had been through, Jerry would not have been surprised to receive an immediate verbal response from the Almighty. Just after dawn, east of Salt Lake, he received a partial answer from Fox News.

"Authorities, rescue workers, and volunteers have recovered all the bodies that lie in the rubble of the federal building in Cheyenne, Wyoming. The FBI, which lost two agents in the blast, refuses to comment on who might be responsible for this act of terrorism. Fox News has learned that the FBI did not have a permanent field office in the O'Mahoney building. The two agents had been working out of an office borrowed from the Bureau of Alcohol, Tobacco, and Firearms, the ATF. Dead are Special Agent Gerhard Beck and Officer Susan MacKenzie, seconded from the Washington, DC, police force. In a touching side-

light, the two had been married, divorcing only last year. More on the Cheyenne story as it develops."

Jerry sat stunned. He thought he had accepted Susan's death, but the announcement returned him to a state of shock. Rage boiled to the surface. He turned off the radio and concentrated on all the ways he could exterminate the vermin who had taken the love of his life away from him.

All of them.

That was more than enough to keep him alive until he got to Mineral King.

Chapter 23

The Finish

Jose walked confidently through the lobby and up the stairs. Everyone was in the bar watching the Rockies clobber the Cubs. There wasn't much else to do in Medicine Bow on a summer night. Jose noted that the bar was loud. The noise would cover up whatever was about to happen—unless it involved gunfire. He made it to the top floor unnoticed. Gabriele's red bandanna hung from the doorknob on room 17. He knocked softly and opened the door.

She was alone, and she was in tears. Jose recognized the symptoms. Post-traumatic stress. Mind and body finally rejecting a long period of extreme tension. Gabriele's unconscious attempt to find some kind of balance. But there was no balance to be found. There was only Jose. Without making eye contact, he walked across the room and took her in his arms.

"Jose!" she cried. "I don't know what to do."

Jose hugged Gabriele tightly, looking past her into the parking lot. Then he buried his face in her shoulder. She smelled of death and sweat.

Jose backed away and held his nose. "The first thing you need to do is take a shower."

She started laughing. Mirth cut through the tears and took a big chunk out of her stress. "There you go again."

"Don't worry, Gaby… Jerry will be here soon."

"What if he doesn't come?"

"I'll stay here tonight. If he doesn't show by noon, I'll go out and track him down."

"But you have no idea where he went!" Gabriele the warrior was gone. She sounded like a scared little girl.

"That does make it harder," admitted Jose. "But I'm good at finding people, and Jerry's a big guy." He opened the door to the bathroom. "Now get under some hot water and relax. Then you need to sleep."

"You can't sugarcoat it, Jose. Jerry's in big trouble."

"He can handle it, Gaby…believe me. He's been in lots of tough spots before." Jose sat on the bed and fixed his eyes on the window again.

"Okay," said Gabriele tentatively. "I will stay in this room until Jerry arrives…or until you bring him back."

Jose nodded. "I think we're safe here. No need to go to the secondary rendezvous point."

Gabriele went into the bathroom and took a long shower. She came out wearing her dirty jeans and Jose's tattered shirt. That was all she had. Jose had been digging into his backpack again. The AK-47 had been reassembled and lay next to the pistol on the nightstand. She smelled gun oil. Jose reached up to examine her forehead.

"It looks like I won't need to give you stitches, Gaby… But I think you'll have to wear a scar."

She did not hesitate. "Then I will wear it with pride…just like the rest of the team." Jose was wearing the sweatshirt again, but she had seen his naked torso. "Where did you get your war wound?"

"This one is homegrown," he explained, grabbing his shoulder. "It came from the Colombian FARC…just like Jerry's." He lightened the mood again. "But I don't have a cool tattoo like you have."

"I was hoping you wouldn't notice."

"It's a wound of a different kind, Gaby…but still a symbol of your courage." He grinned. "I would keep it."

That seemed to help. Now she wanted nothing more than to see Jerry walk through the door.

Jose put his last battle dressing on Gabriele's forehead then walked to the window as she got into bed. He extracted a pair of binoculars from the backpack and hung them around his neck.

"Sleep well, Gaby… I've got the first watch."

***

It was midmorning as Jerry sped northeast toward Mineral King. He needed to test fire the Beretta. He could not carry the pistol into a gunfight without putting at least one round through the barrel. But not *more* than one round. He had to plan on shooting two men and perhaps two women. The M9's only magazine held just fifteen rounds of nine-millimeter ammunition. He would have to double-tap every target, leaving very little margin for error. Jerry had not fired the Beretta in a long time. It was his least favorite secondary weapon (the slide was apt to fly into the shooter's face). But there was no time to find a gun store to shop for what he *really* needed.

He would have to do the best he could with what he had.

He turned abruptly onto a dirt road intersecting the highway, following it for about a mile. The sound of a single round would not be noticed, but it was critical that he avoid observation by some bored trucker with a CB radio. He got out of the Explorer and immediately took a combat stance, facing east. Taking the weapon in both hands, he thrust it to arm's length, switched off the safety, and fired his one round. He wasn't completely sure the gun would fire a second round, but he had neither the time nor the ammo to find out. He jumped in the car and hurried back to the main road. Mineral King was just sixty minutes in front of him.

Jerry was dead tired, but not nearly dead. Images of Thorne and Jeffers dying in his sights kept him going. He thought of the Virginian, his personal hero, hanging a man at dawn on the Wyoming frontier for stealing cattle from Judge Henry. That single act had justified the kind of summary execution Jerry was about to administer. Thorne and his gang had killed hundreds of innocent people. They had almost killed hundreds of thousands. If anyone needed a dose of frontier justice, it was Red Thorne. The others—all of them—were just as guilty.

At precisely noon, Jerry turned into the gas station in Mineral King. He wanted to see Jose waiting there, armed and ready to clean house. But rural Wyoming in the year 2000, he knew, was not a good place to communicate by cell phone. Jose was not there. Jerry would be going in alone and completely blind. He left the gas station and drove to the junction of the long dirt road leading to Thorne's ranch.

He slowed the vehicle to dampen down the dust. He would approach the target as stealthily as he could in broad daylight. Glancing to his right, he noticed a campsite in the creek bed. He hadn't noticed it on the way out. He *should* have. Looking at it now, Jerry saw it for what it obviously was: an observation post. He stopped the car and scrambled into the draw. He threw back the tent flap, thinking, in his delirium, that Bosco might actually be there… ready to back him up.

His teammate wasn't there… But his absence, thought Jerry, could actually be a good thing; he might be with Gabriele somewhere safe. Unable to contact Jose, however, he would have to assume otherwise.

The Explorer rolled to a stop just outside the ranch house. Jerry got out, leaving the door open. With the Beretta at arm's length, he walked quickly to the front door. The big man took a few deep breaths, loaded his right foot, and kicked the door so hard it shattered the wood. Anyone in the house would be waiting for him—possibly holding Gaby as a hostage. Speed would be his tactical advantage.

Speed without haste. Anger without rage.

Scanning for targets, he moved like a cat through the living room and into the kitchen. Nothing.

Into the Tank. Nothing.

The bedrooms. Nothing.

Upstairs. Still nothing.

He blasted out the back door and ran across the compound. On the way, he decided not to shoot the women, unless they tried to shoot *him*. He visualized Jane Thorne holding a shotgun. That would be enough.

The flimsy door to the first trailer came down easily. The trailer was empty. Rulon James was on a permanent business trip. Linda wasn't there either, but he saw that she had taken everything she could carry. *Where did she go?*

Jerry moved to the middle trailer. Roy Murdock was out of the picture—way out. Sadie was no threat. She would be with her children. He hoped to God they weren't in the trailer. He took down the door with another kick of his work boot. Not a soul inside. That left Jerry's trailer. And Gabriele.

He went back into the heat of the compound and scanned the grounds again. Nothing. No vehicles, moving or stationary. The place was dead.

Acting on instinct, Jerry froze at his own front door. Standing on the step, he forced himself to breathe as he visualized the inside of the trailer. He wasn't sure Gabriele was there. If she was, then he had to assume she was being held with a gun to her head. He rammed his fullback's shoulder into the door. It came completely off its hinges and landed against the galley counter.

No time to look both ways!

Jerry flash-remembered that Thorne was too fat to sit at the dinette. He pivoted left toward the bedroom. Nothing!

Then to the dinette. Nothing again.

He was almost disappointed. Despite having planned her escape, he had secretly hoped to rescue Gabriele. Completely drained, he sat for a minute trying to recharge and refocus. He realized immediately that the trailer had been ransacked. It looked like the aftermath of a tornado. The bathroom door had been torn off. He stuck his head into the small space above the ceiling tiles. Someone had found the tape recorder. He could find no blood (that was good), but one of Thorne's men (or women) had gone through the place in a rage. Clothes were strewn everywhere, dishes lying broken on the floor, books thrown the length of the living area.

Books!

He found it under a pile of clothes. An innocent-looking paperback dictionary they had planned to use for writing coded messages. He put the book in his pocket, grabbed a pencil and paper off the floor, and left the trailer. Still scanning for targets, he patrolled back to the Explorer. He slammed the door and raced back to the state road.

Twenty minutes later, he was approaching Split Rock. Jerry had never seen more than one or two cars at a time visiting the site. Now he counted five police cars and one ambulance. Slowing down, he saw yellow tape around most of the parking lot. Inside the cordon, he could see a pickup truck and a small motorcycle. Still on his adrenaline high, Jerry forced himself to calm down. He needed to know more.

He parked on the other side of the highway and walked across. The cops were not stopping traffic because there was almost no traffic to stop. Jerry carefully approached one of the officers outside the cordon.

"Mind if I use the bathroom, Officer?"

The young policeman sized him up and took a long look down the road. There were no facilities for many miles in either direction. The bathroom was outside the perimeter of yellow tape. Nothing wrong with letting someone use the toilet rather than the side of the road.

"Okay," came the answer. "Just stay outside the yellow tape," added the highway patrolman.

Jerry pressed. "What's going on?"

The officer hesitated. Jerry tried to look like a typical tourist.

"Someone was killed here."

Jerry froze. *Shit!* He was no longer sure if he wanted more details. "Man or woman?"

"I've already told you more than I'm supposed to," said the cop, turning away.

"You might as well just tell me the gender of the victim," said Jerry sincerely. "My wife is missing, and I want to be sure she hasn't been hurt or killed… You can understand that, can't you?"

The officer turned back to Jerry and looked into his eyes. "It was a man… That's all I know."

"Thank you," said Jerry, trembling. He was already leaning toward the bathroom.

A few steps later, Jerry was on the "Ladies" side. He looked in the mirror, and his heart started pounding again. On the lower right corner was a smear of mud.

The load signal!

He walked quickly out of the bathroom and around the perimeter of the crime scene to the sign. With all the commotion, Jerry could see that he wasn't being observed. He bent down and retrieved the concealment device. Palming the fake rock, he walked back across the highway to the Explorer. The device lay in his lap for a full minute before he generated the courage to open it.

There was a piece of paper inside.

He drove down the highway until he could no longer see the crime scene. Sitting in the driver's seat with both windows open, Jerry began to decode the message. It was a time-consuming but simple procedure. Susan and Gabriele had carried the same dictionary as Jerry. With clever wording (and no punctuation), it was possible to say almost anything. Without the reference book, a message could not be decoded. Clumsy but very effective.

Jerry was in tears even before he finished. He wiped his eyes as he read it all the way through.

> *my love i know .we are not to use this method for personal communication but i had to i am afraid something bad will happen i am sorry i got you into this i will always love you please protect yourself and your wife come back to me at the end i love you*

Susan had signed her name. Jerry stared at the note and wept again. He wanted to die. Then he remembered he was *going* to die. His faith was not strong enough to convince him he would actually see Susan after death. He cried for Susan's innocence and for his own lack of faith.

Jerry composed himself and started driving again. He needed to find Gabriele. He wanted to say goodbye. He turned south at Muddy Gap, headed toward Rawlins.

Then he fell asleep at the wheel.

The rocky shoulder of the road shook him awake. He veered back into the middle of the pavement and fought the overwhelming fatigue. But it was more than fatigue, and he knew it. For a brief moment, he wished he could be taken quickly by an oncoming truck.

He pulled the Explorer to the side of the road, turned off the engine, and leaned back in the seat. For the first and only time in his extraordinary life, Jerry Tompkins gave up.

***

At precisely noon, Jose left for Mineral King. Gabriele had ventured into town before he left, buying groceries and a clean T-shirt. Jose had given her a pistol for self-defense. She had assured him that she could survive until he came back or…until he didn't come back. She was beginning to think she would never see Jose or Jerry again. *What then?*

Jose decided not to retrace the route north to Casper. Instead, he drove west, past the Hanna coal mine and on to Rawlins. He pulled over just outside the town and checked his recharged cell phone. There was a voice mail he had not been able to retrieve the night before.

"Bosco…Butkus. I'm on my way to Mineral King for unfinished business. I'll do it alone, but I would much rather have you there to help me clean house. If you get this in time, meet me at the gas station at 1200. All I have is a pistol and one mag. Bring a long gun and whatever else we need… Out here."

Jose looked at his watch. 1315. *Shit!* He got back on the highway and sped north. He did not have time to check out the blue Ford Explorer parked on the opposite side of the road, halfway to Muddy Gap. Jose could not have imagined what Jerry had been through. A lack of situational awareness forced him to assume that Murdock and James had been waiting at Thorne's ranch for the final shootout. That firefight would be over by now; he was pretty confident Jerry had taken them down. Even with just a pistol. But he and his friend urgently needed to share information. They might as well have been treading water in the middle of the ocean. Without cell phone connectivity, he would have to find Jerry and tell him in person that Jeffers and the Thornes were dead and that Gabriele was alive.

***

Jerry woke up with a jolt. At first, he didn't know where he was. He could see nothing on the late-afternoon landscape. There was no sound. Expecting death, he thought for an instant that he had actually died. He felt his carotid artery and found a strong pulse. Breathing deeply, he opened the car door and got out, bending over to touch the earth. It was still there. Groping for a mental anchor, he remembered that he hadn't found Thorne. As far as he knew, the threats were still out there. Somewhere. He needed to find them. And he needed to find Gabriele.

Halfway to Medicine Bow, Jerry began to think he wasn't sick after all. In fact, after his combat nap, he felt pretty good. Something he had read about anthrax crashed into his consciousness. *Inhalation anthrax is not one hundred percent fatal.* Perhaps, having descended from cattlemen, he had a natural immunity! Jerry delighted himself with the possibility that his ancestors had bequeathed to him more than just a cattle ranch.

The joyful prospect of his survival was overwhelmed by his anxiety about Gabriele. Jose had not linked up with him at Mineral King; he could only conclude that was good news. But he wasn't sure. Uncertainty was the enemy now. He continued east, as fast as the Explorer would go. He was no longer concerned about being stopped. All the cops were at Split Rock! He was sure the murder scene there was related to Gabriele's escape; he kicked himself for not interrogating further. The cop had identified the victim as a man. Which man? And where was Gabriele now? Was she lying dead in the sagebrush or sitting at the hotel?

There was only one way to find out.

Forty-five minutes later, he drove slowly into Medicine Bow. At seven o'clock, the town was dead. Medicine Bow had been dead since Owen Wister finished writing *The Virginian*. The only vestige of that era stood in front of Jerry now. A stone building of three stories.

Three possibilities confronted him: one, Gabriele was alone inside; two, Thorne and Jeffers held her hostage; or three, she was dead and they waited there to ambush Jerry. Could Thorne really have tracked Gaby to this site?

Anything was possible.

Taking one more look around, Jerry got out of the Explorer and walked into the hotel lobby. He strode quickly to the front desk.

"Evenin', ma'am... I'm Mr. Meredith."

The old woman looked down at her register. "I put her in room 17 yesterday... Haven't seen her since."

Jerry's spirits soared! He was halfway up the second set of stairs before he caught himself. *Careful, you dumb shit.*

He stopped at the top of the stairs and drew his pistol. He patrolled stealthily down the hallway to room 17. A red bandanna was hanging on the doorknob. Jerry took another look around. He stood to the left of the door and tested the knob.

The door was locked.

Jerry had noticed other doors on his way down the hall, and he knew he could not kick this one down. *They don't make hotels like they used to.* Knocking was also a problem; the door was heavy, but it would not stop a point-blank shotgun blast. He raised the Beretta and called to Gabriele from where he stood.

"Claudia!"

No response.

He repeated the name. "Claudia!"

Again, no response. He tried one more time. "Claudia!"

The door opened; Jerry lowered the pistol, and she was in his arms.

"Jerry... Thank God! Where have you been?"

He pushed her gently back into the room and sat her on the bed. He spoke rapidly. "It's a very long story... I thought you might be a hostage in here...especially when you didn't open the door right away."

"It took me a few seconds to remember my field name."

Jerry looked into her eyes with tears in his own. "I was afraid they'd killed you!"

"Jose made sure that would not happen. He took out Jeffers, Thorne…and even Jane." She took a deep breath. "I also have a long story to tell *you*."

"I took care of the other men," said Jerry solemnly. "There's no one left to threaten us."

"Does that mean we can go home?"

Jerry was so tired he missed out on the pleasure of hearing Gabriele refer to his ranch as *their* home. "Are you ready to check out?"

"Ready." She walked over and picked up her pistol, instinctively doing a press check to be sure a round waited in the chamber. "This is the only baggage I have." She untucked her T-shirt and concealed the weapon in the small of her back, ready for checkout.

"You look wonderful, *Schatz*."

"So do you, *Junge*… So do you."

The desk phone rang. Jerry reached over and grabbed it. "Butkus."

"Bosco here… Where the hell have you been, man?"

"It's a story even longer than yours, Jose. I'm with Gaby now. Just meet us at the Jumping Frog. We have a lot to talk about… Then we'll have to figure out how to explain all this to the FBI."

"Got it, man." Jose hesitated then spoke from the heart. "And thanks for getting me back in the field, Jerry."

"Just like old times, brother. My gratitude is beyond words. We'd be dead without you."

"*No te preocupes, hermano… Hasta pronto.*" No worries indeed.

Jerry put down the phone and stood next to the bed. "Let's go home."

They drove west into the sunset. Lone Mountain was less than an hour away. Jose was about three hours out. They sat in silence, trying to deal with the sadness of lost loves and attempting to digest the idea of freedom, mentally wandering through the chaos behind them.

Jerry was the first to speak. "Churchill was right."

"How is that, dear?"

"When the sun is at this angle, it's hard to know whether it's rising or setting."

Gabriele thrilled to the sound of Jerry's intellectual side. She drew her eyes away from the horizon and studied him with a new-found pride.

"Huxley was also right."

"What did *he* have to say about all this?" countered Jerry.

"Experience is not what happens to you. It's what you *do* with what happens to you."

Jerry nodded without looking at her. "In other words, it's up to us to describe the sun." The road was perfectly straight. No traffic in either direction. When he turned to her, he was wearing a broad smile.

"My head says it's going down… But my heart says it's coming up."

"Then it's coming up," said Gabriele firmly.

She watched the western sky as the road curved slowly south. As the last of the sun sank below the vastness of the plain, high clouds burned brightly in its wake. The cotton puffs sent vaporous flames rising to the edge of space. Before her eyes, the clouds darkened to the color of hot coals past their prime. A minute later, they were gray, used up, and cold.

"Definitely coming up," said Gabriele, reaching for Jerry's hand. She held it to her side, too emotional to speak.

Jerry felt a stab of electricity run through him. By the time it passed, everything in his life had changed. In that moment, he looked away from the tragedies behind him and glimpsed the future. He did not want to ever let go of Gabriele's hand.

Experience is what you do *with what happens to you.*

But he needed both hands to navigate the dirt road to their ranch. Keeping his eyes on the road, Jerry unloaded some pent-up spiritual baggage.

"I feel like God has given me a second life to live, Gaby. I've been close to death before… But I've never felt like I do just now."

"How do you feel just now?"

"I keep remembering what General Stewart told us at the funeral…that each of us has a preordained purpose."

"So do I." Gabriele shifted toward Jerry on the bench seat as he spoke.

"I thought my purpose," Jerry continued, "was to avenge Carl's death."

"So did I."

"But…now that I've done that, I realize there's more to it. There's another reason God let me live."

"I have the same feeling," said Gabriele nodding. All of a sudden, she knew the reason Jerry had been spared. In perfect iambic quadrameter, she said the first thing that came into her head.

"*Come live with me and be my love.*"

"Christopher Marlowe," responded Jerry without hesitation.

A warm wave of confidence washed over Gabriele. "It appears that I am married to a warrior-poet."

Jerry looked over at her in the dim light as they bounced into the driveway. The SIG Sauer was still in her lap. "And I am married to a poet-warrior, Gaby. You and I seem to have met halfway."

He stopped the car in front of the house and walked around to help her out. Gabriele took his hand as he led her to the door. They stood beneath the porch light and watched Lone Mountain disappear into the night. She turned to face him and held both his hands.

"Do you think we could live in Florida during the winter?"

Jerry's new life flashed into focus. This was his reward. A real marriage. *Gabriele Tompkins.* He almost said it out loud. Gabriele looked up at his brightening face and finally found solace. In that moment, both of them understood that they were bound to each other for good. Physical love, they knew, would come much later, to be blended carefully with memories of Susan and Carl.

Jerry heard a voice call to him. *Protect yourself and your wife.*

"We can live anywhere that makes you happy, Gaby."

He bent forward and lifted her until she lay comfortably in his arms. Then he gently kicked open the door and grinned down at her. "I never got the chance to do this."

And Jerry Tompkins carried Gabriele over the threshold of her new life.

About the Author

Paul Shemella lives in California with his wife, finally settled after more than forty years of traveling on behalf of the United States government. He was a Navy SEAL for over half that time. Becoming an academic, he taught counter terrorism to foreign governments around the world. He has written important textbooks on terrorism, maritime security, and African governance. Now in retirement, he writes fiction. *A More Perfect Union* is the sequel to *Jungle Rules*, published in 2018. The third book in a planned trilogy is due in 2021.

CPSIA information can be obtained
at www.ICGtesting.com
Printed in the USA
LVHW092335240420
654333LV00008B/512